BLUEBERRY MUFFIN MURDER

A glimmer of light caught Hannah's eye. The pantry door was open a few inches and someone had turned on the light. Hannah grabbed the first weapon she could find, the heavy pot she used to make boiled frostings. If the person who'd frightened Connie Mac away was hiding in her pantry, she'd get in a few good licks before she turned him over to the sheriff!

Once she had moved silently into position, Hannah inched the door open with her foot. She glanced inside, and what she saw caused the pot to slip from her nerveless fingers. Her earlier assumption was wrong. Connie Mac hadn't left last night.

The Cooking Sweetheart was facedown on the pantry floor. She had been struck down by a massive blow to the head in the act of sampling one of Hannah's Blue Blueberry Muffins.

Shock rendered Hannah immobile for a moment, but then she knelt down to feel for a pulse. The biggest celebrity ever to set foot in Lake Eden would never star in another episode of her television show or pose for pictures in her magazine. Connie Mac was dead . . .

Books by Joanne Fluke

Hannah Swensen Mysteries

CHOCOLATE CHIP COOKIE MURDER
STRAWBERRY SHORTCAKE MURDER
BLUEBERRY MUFFIN MURDER
LEMON MERINGUE PIE MURDER
FUDGE CUPCAKE MURDER
SUGAR COOKIE MURDER
PEACH COBBLER MURDER
CHERRY CHEESECAKE MURDER
KEY LIME PIE MURDER
CANDY CANE MURDER
CARROT CAKE MURDER
CREAM PUFF MURDER
PLUM PUDDING MURDER
APPLE TURNOVER MURDER
DEVIL'S FOOD CAKE MURDER
GINGERBREAD COOKIE MURDER
CINNAMON ROLL MURDER
RED VELVET CUPCAKE MURDER
BLACKBERRY PIE MURDER
DOUBLE FUDGE BROWNIE MURDER
WEDDING CAKE MURDER
CHRISTMAS CARAMEL MURDER
BANANA CREAM PIE MURDER
RASPBERRY DANISH MURDER
CHRISTMAS CAKE MURDER
CHOCOLATE CREAM PIE MURDER
CHRISTMAS SWEETS
COCONUT LAYER CAKE MURDER
CHRISTMAS CUPCAKE MURDER
TRIPLE CHOCOLATE CHEESECAKE MURDER
CARAMEL PECAN ROLL MURDER
JOANNE FLUKE'S LAKE EDEN COOKBOOK

Suspense Novels

VIDEO KILL
WINTER CHILL
DEAD GIVEAWAY
THE OTHER CHILD
COLD JUDGMENT
FATAL IDENTITY
FINAL APPEAL
VENGEANCE IS MINE
EYES
WICKED
DEADLY MEMORIES
THE STEPCHILD

Published by Kensington Publishing Corp.

A HANNAH SWENSEN MYSTERY
WITH RECIPES

BLUEBERRY MUFFIN MURDER

JOANNE FLUKE

KENSINGTON BOOKS
Kensington Publishing Corp.
http://www.kensingtonbooks.com

KENSINGTON BOOKS are published by

Kensington Publishing Corp.
119 West 40th Street
New York, NY 10018

All Kensington Titles, Imprints, and Distributed Lines are available at special quantity discounts for bulk purchases for sales promotions, premiums, fund-raising, and educational or institutional use. Special book excerpts or customized printings can also be created to fit specific needs. For details, write or phone the office of the Kensington special sales manager: Kensington Publishing Corp., 119 West 40th Street, New York, NY 10018, attn: Special Sales Department, Phone: 1-800-221-2647.

Kensington and the K logo Reg. U.S. Pat. & TM Off.

ISBN-13: 978-0-7582-7841-8
ISBN-10: 0-7582-7841-1

First Kensington hardcover printing: March 2002
First Kensington mass market printing: February 2003

30 29 28 27 26

Printed in the United States of America

This book is for our Billie,
Moishe's girlfriend

Acknowledgments

Thank you to my dedicated circle of taste-testers. It's a tough job, but somebody's got to do it. My special thanks to Ruel, whose skin was beginning to turn a little purple after sampling three dozen batches of Blue Blueberry Muffins, and to Lyn, for rhapsodizing over Lisa's White Chocolate Supremes.

Thanks to John S., my much-appreciated editor, who's always full of ideas and enthusiasm, and to all the other folks at Kensington who've supported and encouraged me. A big thank you to Terry Sommers, who gives my recipes a final test. (Your oven is preheating, isn't it, Terry?) Thanks to Jamie Wallace for perfecting www.MurderSheBaked.com— the official Hannah Swensen web site. And another big thank you to my new E-mail friends who wrote to say that they enjoy Hannah Swensen and her extended family almost as much as I do.

Chapter One

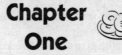

Hannah Swensen awoke to a curious sensation. Her body was warm, but her nose felt like an icicle. She sat up in bed, reached out to snap on the light, and stared at the little puffs of moisture her breath left in the air. No wonder her nose felt so cold! The furnace had gone out again and Lake Eden, Minnesota, was smack-dab in the middle of a February cold snap.

"Moishe? Where are you?" Hannah glanced around the bedroom, but her feline roommate wasn't in any of his usual places. There was no orange-and-white cat nestled in the cushioned depths of her laundry basket, the top of her dresser held only its usual collection of books, and the windowsill with its view of the bird feeder was bare. There was, however, a good-sized lump in the middle of her bed.

Hannah stared at the lump for a moment. It was too small to be one of her pillows and too large to belong to an errant sock. She lifted the covers to find her feline roommate curled up in the middle of her bed, soaking up the warmth from her electric blanket.

"What are *you* doing under there?" Hannah asked, eyeing her fiercely independent tomcat with surprise. Moishe seldom cuddled for more than a few moments, and he'd never crawled under the covers with her. The cold must have driven him under her quilt and blanket. And *he* came equipped with a fur coat!

As if on cue, the alarm clock began its infernal electronic beeping. It was time to get up in the predawn freeze, when all Hannah really wanted to do was crawl back under the covers. She sighed and reluctantly swung her feet over the edge of her bed, feeling around with her toes for her slippers.

One slipper was immediately accessible. Hannah wiggled her left foot inside and attempted to find its mate. This took a moment, for it was hiding out near the foot of her bed. By the time Hannah located it and shoved her foot inside, her teeth were chattering in a lengthy drum roll.

"Come on, Moishe. Today's a big day." Hannah slipped into her warmest robe, a quilted relic from Lake Eden's only thrift store, and belted it around her waist. Then she folded back the covers until Moishe was exposed with no place to go. "I know it's cold. We'll have breakfast in front of the fireplace."

Hunger must have won out over comfort in Moishe's mind, because he padded after her down the hallway and into the kitchen. Hannah flicked on the lights and gave a thankful sigh as she saw that the timer on her coffeemaker had worked. She poured a cup of the strong brew, cupped it in both hands, and took a scalding sip. There was nothing better than hot coffee on a very cold morning. Then she filled Moishe's bowl with kitty crunchies and carried her coffee and Moishe's breakfast out into the living room.

The fireplace sprang into life as Hannah flicked the switch on the wall, and Moishe settled down in front of the blaze to have his breakfast. Hannah pulled up a chair, rested her feet on the hearth that was home to the fireplace tools she didn't really need, and gave thanks for the wonders of a gas log. All things being equal, she preferred a real fireplace that could burn aromatic woods like cedar and pine, but a gas log was much more convenient. She never had to carry wood up the stairs to her second-floor condo, or sweep out the ashes and haul them down to the garage Dumpster in a metal pail. Her fireplace was hassle-free and the warmth was instantaneous. Flick, it was on. Flick, it was off.

As she sat there toasting her feet and waiting for the caffeine to jump-start her morning, Hannah heard a distant clanging from the nether regions of the basement. Someone was working on the furnace. Which early riser had notified the maintenance people?

Hannah considered it as she sipped her coffee. There was a separate furnace for each building, and her building contained four condo units, two on the ground floor and two on the second floor. It was doubtful that Mrs. Canfield, who owned one of the ground-level units, would have noticed the problem. She'd once told Hannah that she didn't stay up past ten, and the furnace had been working just fine then. Clara and Marguerite Hollenbeck, the two unmarried sisters who owned the unit above Mrs. Canfield, were out of town this week. They'd stopped by Hannah's cookie shop on Monday to tell her that they'd be attending a Bible teachers' conference at Bethany Lutheran College. The Plotniks lived directly below Hannah and they were the most likely candidates. Phil and Sue had a four-month-old baby, and he still demanded an occasional bottle in the middle of the night.

There was a grinding noise from the basement, and Moishe looked startled as he lifted his head from his food bowl. The grinding was followed by a series of clanks and clunks, and Hannah felt a surge of warm air emerge from the heater vents. The furnace was back on. At least she wouldn't have to worry about leaving the gas log on for Moishe, or putting her stash of Diet Coke in the refrigerator to keep the cans from freezing and popping their tops.

"I've got to get ready for work, Moishe." Hannah gave him a pat, drained the last of her coffee, and flicked off the fireplace. Once she'd carried his bowl back to the kitchen and given him fresh water, she headed off to the shower. Today would be a busy day and she had tons of cookies to bake. As the proprietor of The Cookie Jar, Lake Eden's coffee shop and bakery, she'd contracted to provide all the cookies for the Lake Eden Winter Carnival.

As Hannah turned on the water, adjusted the temperature, and stepped into her steamy shower enclosure, she thought about the plans that Mayor Bascomb and his Winter Carnival committee had made. If they were successful, the carnival would bring new life to Lake Eden at a time of year when everyone needed a boost. There wasn't much winter business in their small Minnesota town, and the promise of crowds with cash to spend had everyone filled with enthusiasm.

Lake Eden was a popular tourist spot in the summer months, when the town was flooded with visitors. Every year, on the day that fishing season opened, a lengthy parade of fishermen towing boats drove through Lake Eden to try their luck at the lake that was just within the town limits. The sky blue water was peppered with boats from dawn to dusk in the summer, and a record number of walleyes were pulled from its depths.

Good fishing wasn't all Eden Lake had to offer. With its picturesque shores and sandy beaches, it was also a popular family vacation spot. Summer cabin rentals were in high demand, and the lucky locals who owned them used the profits to pay their mortgages and fatten their savings accounts for the lean winter months.

When the summer season was over, right after Labor Day, the tourists and vacationers left town. The fine restaurants that overlooked the lake shut down their grills, the Lake Eden Bait and Tackle Shop boarded up its windows, and the boat launch was chained off for the winter. By the time the leaves on the trees had begun to display their fall colors, only the year-round residents were left.

Hannah liked the fall season. The nights were brisk with a hint of snow to come, and hoarfrost lined the edges of the road when she drove to work. Winter wasn't bad either, at first. Then the snow was white and pristine, the crisp, cold air made the inside of her nose tingle, and her regular customers at The Cookie Jar were full of holiday plans and good cheer.

When Christmas and New Year's were over, it was another story. Heating bills soared and seemed to approach the magnitude of the national debt, and business slowed down to a trickle. There was a brief flurry of activity for Valentine's Day, but after the heart-shaped boxes of chocolates were only a pleasant memory, winter seemed to stretch out endlessly with no spring flowers in sight.

Late February was the dreariest time of year in Lake Eden. The weak, anemic sun barely peeked out of overcast skies, and tree branches were black and stark against a horizon that was sometimes indistinguishable from the colorless banks of snow. It was difficult to maintain a sunny disposition when every day looked exactly like the one before it, and depression became the epidemic de jour. To combat this yearly malady, Mayor Bascomb had scheduled Lake Eden's very first Winter Carnival in the third week of February.

Not to be confused with the Winter Carnival in St. Paul, with its gigantic Ice Palace and hundreds of thousands of visitors, Lake Eden's event was set on a much smaller scale. Hannah regarded it as a cross between a county fair and a mini Winter Olympics. There would be Nordic skiing, snowmobile competitions, speed-skating exhibitions, dogsled races, and ice fishing on Eden Lake. There would also be contests in Lake Eden Park for the kids, including the best family-made snowman, the best "snow angel," and a host of others that even the little ones could enjoy.

The Jordan High auditorium had been designated as the hospitality hub, and all the Lake Eden clubs and societies were busily setting up displays and booths. Winter Carnival visitors would park their cars in the school lot, and shuttle sleighs were scheduled to leave Jordan High every thirty minutes to transport people to the event sites.

Hannah gave her hair a final rinse and stepped out of the shower to towel it dry. The air outside her steamy bathroom was frigid, and she shivered as she quickly dressed in jeans and her official Lake Eden Winter Carnival sweatshirt. It was bright blue with a flurry of white snowflakes that formed block letters on the front. The legend read "LAKE EDEN," because "LAKE EDEN WINTER CARNIVAL" had exceeded the manufacturer's ten-letter maximum.

Moishe had joined her in the bedroom, and he watched as she pulled on warm socks and slipped her feet into a pair of high-top moose-hide moccasin boots with rubber soles. Then he followed her down the hall to the kitchen, attempting to snag the laces on her boots.

Hannah refilled Moishe's food before he had time to yowl for more, poured herself another cup of coffee, and sat down to organize her day at the old Formica table she'd rescued from the Helping Hands Thrift Shop. But before she could flip to a blank page in the steno pad she kept propped up next to her salt and pepper shakers, the phone rang.

"Mother," Hannah said with a sigh, and Moishe halted in mid-crunch to give the phone a baleful look. He wasn't fond of Delores Swensen, and Hannah's mother had six pairs of shredded pantyhose to prove it. Hannah stood up to grab the wall phone and sat back down again. Her mother wasn't known for brevity. "Good morning, Mother."

"You really shouldn't answer that way, Hannah. What if I'd been someone else?"

Hannah gave a fleeting thought to the logic class she'd taken in college. It was impossible for someone to be someone else. She decided not to argue the point—it would only prolong their conversation—and she settled for her standard reply. "I knew it was you, Mother. It's never anyone else at five-thirty in the morning. How are the shuttle sleighs coming along?"

"They're all ready to go, and that includes the one that Al Percy's uncle donated." Delores gave a rueful laugh. "You should have seen it, Hannah. It was such a wreck that all they could keep were the runners and the hardware. The shop class had to build a whole new body and it looks fabulous."

"Great," Hannah commented, and took another sip of her coffee. Delores had been instrumental in helping Mayor Bascomb round up sleighs for the Jordan High shop class to rejuvenate. She had a real knack for ferreting out antiques, and old sleighs in decent condition weren't easy to locate.

"I found a picture on a Christmas card and they modeled

it after that. The boys are lining it with white fur throws to-day, and we're going to use it for the Prince and Princess of Winter."

Hannah pictured it in her mind. It sounded perfect for the Winter Carnival royalty. "How many sleighs do you have?"

"Twelve." There was a note of pride in Delores's voice. "And before I got involved last month, they only had two."

"You did a great job. I'll bet you could get a fleet rate on the insurance with a dozen."

There was a silence, and Hannah heard her mother draw in her breath sharply. "Insurance? I hope the Winter Carnival Committee thought of that! Why, someone could fall off and sue the town, and—"

"Relax, Mother," Hannah interrupted her. "Howie Levine's on the committee and he's a lawyer. I'm sure he thought of it."

"I hope so! I'll call the mayor this morning, just to make sure. I promised to call anyway, to tell him when the Ezekiel Jordan House was finished."

"It's all finished?"

"It will be this morning. All I have to do is hang the drapes and put up some pictures in the parlor."

"Good work, Mother," Hannah complimented her. She knew that Delores hadn't been given much time to whip the project into shape. At their January meeting, the Lake Eden Historical Society had decided to create a full-scale replica of the first mayor's house for the Winter Carnival crowd to tour, and they'd rented the two-story building next to Hannah's cookie shop for the purpose. Since Delores was Lake Eden's foremost antique expert and a founding member of the historical society, she had taken on the project. Carrie Rhodes had volunteered to help her, and when the two mothers weren't actively working on the re-creation, they were busy making plans to marry Hannah off to Carrie's son, Norman.

Replicating the Ezekiel Jordan House was a difficult task. Since there were no existing pictures, Delores and Carrie had contacted the first mayor's descendants to request any information they might have about the five-room dwelling.

One of Mrs. Jordan's great-great-grandnieces had responded by sending a box of her ancestor's effects and a stack of letters that the first mayor's wife had written to her family back east. In several of the letters, Abigail Jordan had described her home and furniture in detail, and Delores had used her knowledge of antiques to fill in the blanks.

"Will you have time to stop by this morning, Hannah?" Delores sounded a bit tentative, and that was unusual for her. "I'd like your input before anyone else sees it."

"Sure. Just bang on my back door when you're ready and I'll dash over. But you're the antique expert. Why do you need *my* input?"

"For the kitchen," Delores explained. "It's the only room Abigail Jordan didn't describe. She talks about baking in every one of her letters, and I'm not sure I have all the utensils in the proper places."

"I'll check it out," Hannah promised, knowing full well that her mother had never used a flour sifter or rolling pin in her life. Delores didn't bake and she made no bones about it. The desserts of Hannah's childhood had always come straight from the Red Owl grocery store shelves.

"Thank you, dear. I'm sorry to cut this short, but I have to get off the line. Carrie's picking me up and she said she'd call when she left her house."

"Okay. Bye, Mother." Hannah hung up the phone and made a mental note to tell her sister, Andrea, never to mention the option of call-waiting to their mother. This morning's call had been the shortest in history. After a glance at her apple-shaped kitchen clock, Hannah rinsed out her coffee cup, refilled Moishe's food bowl for the final time, and scratched him near the base of his tail, an action that always made him arch his back and purr. "I've got to run, Moishe. See you tonight."

Hannah had a routine to perform before she left her condo in the winter. She shrugged into her parka, zipped it up, and pulled her navy blue stocking cap down over her unmanageable red curls. Then she went into the living room to turn the thermostat down to an energy-saving sixty-five degrees, flicked on the television to keep Moishe company, picked up her purse, and slipped on her fur-lined gloves. She gave Moishe one more pat, checked to make sure she had her keys, and stepped out into the dark, frigid morning that still looked like the middle of the night.

The security lights on the side of the building went on as Hannah descended the outside staircase. Because of the Northern latitude, they got a real workout during the winter, when the days were short and the sun shone for less than eight hours. Most Lake Eden residents drove to work in the dark and came home in the dark, and if they worked in a place without windows, there were days at a stretch when they never caught a glimpse of the sun.

Hannah blinked in the glare of the high-wattage bulbs, designed to ensure a crime-free environment, and held onto the railing as she went down the steps. Once she arrived at ground level, another set of stairs led to the underground garage. Hannah was about to descend them when a tough-sounding male voice rang out behind her.

"Put up your hands and face the wall, lady. Do exactly what I say, or I'll blow you away!"

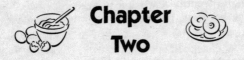

Chapter
Two

Hannah wasn't sure whether to be frightened or angry as she raised her hands in the air. There'd never been any sort of crime in her condo complex before, and it was the last thing she'd expected. Mike Kingston, head of the Winnetka County Sheriff's Detective Division, had promised to teach her some self-defense moves, but he hadn't gotten around to it yet. Hannah dated him occasionally, and after two separate occasions when she'd found herself in imminent danger of occupying one of Doc Knight's steel tables at the morgue, Mike had suggested she learn what to do if someone threatened bodily harm.

Even though she didn't appreciate being waylaid only a few feet from her door in a condo complex that had been gated to keep out intruders, Hannah knew she shouldn't take foolish risks. She took a deep breath and dutifully recited the phrase that her father had drummed into her head when she'd gone off to college. "Take anything you want, but please don't hurt me."

"Hug the wall and don't move a muscle. Keep your hands up where I can see them."

Hannah frowned as she followed his orders. His voice sounded familiar, but she couldn't quite place it. She was still trying to identify it when a snowball splattered harm-lessly over her head, raining snow down on the top of her stocking cap.

"Gotcha!"

The moment the man laughed, his voice was paired with a freckled face in Hannah's mind and she whirled around an-grily. "Greg Canfield! Of all the idiotic, senseless . . ."

"Sorry, Hannah," Greg interrupted her tirade. "I saw you walking to your truck and I couldn't resist. Are you mad at me?"

"I *should* be. You scared me half to death!" Hannah gave him a reluctant smile. When they'd been in third grade, Greg Canfield had made a practice of lying in wait and pelting her with snowballs on her way home from school. Not one to take things lying down, Hannah had fought back. She'd landed her share of cold missiles that had dripped icy snow down Greg's neck, and their snowball battles had lasted all winter, despite dire warnings from both mothers. When fourth grade had begun, Greg and Hannah had called a truce and they'd become friends. Hannah had been very disappointed when Greg's parents had moved to Colorado, pulling Greg out of school before they entered the ninth grade.

All through high school, Hannah had thought about Greg and how much easier her social life would have been if she'd had a friend of the opposite sex. She'd even imagined that they might have been a lot more than just friends until she'd heard that Greg had married his high school girlfriend right after graduation.

"It's good to see you again, Hannah."

"Same here . . . I think," Hannah responded, wondering why Greg was here. His grandmother, Mrs. Canfield, was one of her downstairs neighbors, but it was too early for a visit. "You're not going to wake up your grandmother, are you?"

"Of course not." Greg stepped forward to brush the snow from her cap. "Grandma always sleeps until nine."

Hannah was even more confused. "Then what are you doing out here so early?"

"I woke up when the furnace went out and I went down to the basement to fix it. It was simple, just a loose connection. I didn't want Grandma to wake up to a cold house."

"You're living with your grandmother now?"

"It's just temporary. I had to stick around to tie up some loose ends and the house sold a lot faster than I expected. You never got out to my store at the mall, did you?"

Hannah felt a twinge of guilt. Her former classmate had moved back to the area a little over a year ago. He'd bought a house in a neighboring town and opened an import store at the Tri-County Mall. "I'm sorry, Greg. I really meant to drive out to see it, but the time was never right."

"You should have come for my closeout sale. I had some incredible bargains."

"I heard. Andrea was there and she said she practically bought you out. I'm sorry your store closed, Greg."

"Water under the bridge," Greg said with a shrug. "Retail really wasn't my thing anyway. The hours were too long, and dealing with my suppliers was a nightmare."

Hannah felt a bit uncomfortable. She really didn't know what to say to someone who'd lost his business. "How about your wife? Is she living with your grandmother, too?"

"No. Annette flew to Denver right after the house sold. That's where her parents live."

Hannah nodded, wondering if Greg's wife had bailed out on him. She'd met Annette only once, and she'd been left with the impression that Greg's wife spent money as fast or faster than he could make it. It hadn't taken Annette more than three minutes to inform Hannah that she'd been a classmate of Greg's at one of Colorado's most prestigious private schools, and that her parents lived on an estate in an exclusive suburb of Denver.

With a start, Hannah realized that Greg was gazing at her expectantly, and she responded with the first thing that popped into her mind. "Will you be staying in town for the Winter Carnival?"

"I wouldn't miss it." Greg started to grin, the same friendly grin Hannah recalled from her childhood, and the one she'd hoped would be smiling down at her in her senior prom picture. "It's a great chance to see some of the kids I used to know. Maybe we can all get together for dinner at the Lake Eden Inn."

"That would be great," Hannah agreed. The inn's owners, Dick and Sally Laughlin, had agreed to stay open for the Winter Carnival crowd. Between the Hartland Flour Bakeoff last November and the party crowds at Christmas, the inn had generated good winter business. Sally had told Hannah that if the Winter Carnival turned into an annual event, they might be able to stay open year-round.

Greg glanced at his watch and frowned slightly. "Let's try to get together later, Hannah. I'd love to stand here and chew the fat, but it's almost time for me to go to work."

"You're working in Lake Eden?" Hannah was surprised that Greg had taken a temporary job. Perhaps his closeout sale hadn't gone very well.

"I'm working out of Grandma's condo and it's going just great. I've made more money in the past three weeks than I ever made in retail."

"Really?" Hannah was pleased for him. "What are you doing?"

"On-line stock trading. All I need is a computer and a modem and I can work anywhere."

Though Hannah was certainly no expert, she knew something about on-line stock trading. Dick Laughlin, a former stockbroker in Minneapolis, had written a series of articles about it for the *Lake Eden Journal*. "But isn't day-trading risky?"

"Only if you don't know what you're doing. You ought to try it. I could give you some tips."

"Not me. I don't have any money to spare. Everything I have is tied up in The Cookie Jar."

"But you don't need a lot of venture capital to get started. And you can always borrow the money and pay it back when your stock hits."

"Is that what you did?"

"No. I took the proceeds from my closeout sale and put

every cent in Redlines. They're the hottest new Internet provider. When it peaked yesterday morning, I sold."

"And you made money?"

"I tripled my original investment, and it was more than enough to pay off my creditors. I put the rest of my profits in some other hot stocks, and they were way up at closing yesterday. I've got a system, Hannah. I figure that by the time I leave for Denver, I'll be worth close to a million."

The doubts in Hannah's mind grew by leaps and bounds. Dick Laughlin had called day-trading the newest form of gambling, and he'd warned of the consequences of investing borrowed money. Greg thought he had a system, and he'd been lucky once, but what if that system failed? Hannah was reminded of the spots on late-night television that advertised a sure-fire system for winning at blackjack. She figured that if a gambler really had a winning system, he wouldn't need to peddle books he'd written about it.

"I've got to run, Hannah. I want to be on-line when the market opens in New York. Sorry about that snowball."

Greg waved as he headed around the side of the building, and Hannah waved back. Then she walked down the stairs to the underground parking structure, feeling very uneasy. It was just as Dick had written in his articles. Some day-traders did make money playing the market, but there were others who guessed wrong and lost. At least Greg had paid off his creditors and he was only gambling with his profits.

Hannah went to the strip of outlets that ran along the garage wall and unplugged the cord that fed electricity to her head-bolt heater. She wound the cord around her front bumper, unlocked the door to her candy-apple red Suburban with "THE COOKIE JAR" lettered in gold on both sides, and climbed in behind the wheel.

The interior of her truck was frigid. Hannah was careful to breathe through her nose so she wouldn't fog up the inside of the windshield as she started the engine and backed out of her parking space. She drove up the ramp to ground level, flicked on her headlights, and took the winding street that led out of the complex. Her tires swished through the snow that had fallen during the night, as she broke trail for the other residents who would follow her tracks in an hour or two. Her truck was the only vehicle moving, and everything was dark and quiet. It was always like this on winter mornings, and Hannah often felt as if she were the sole survivor in a frozen wasteland.

As she approached Old Lake Road, she spotted headlights and flashing blue lights in the distance. Her sense of isolation vanished with a roar as a county snowplow lumbered by. Hannah drove forward over the bank of packed snow and chunks of ice that the huge blade had left in its wake, and eased out onto Old Lake Road to follow the snowplow to town.

It was slow going, but Hannah didn't mind. As she drove, she thought about the great job of snow removal the state of Minnesota accomplished. Snowplow drivers were on call during the winter months, and at the first sign of a heavy snowfall, they were dispatched. Most other states didn't begin plowing until the snowstorm was over. By then, the snow had accumulated in deep drifts and it was more difficult to clear.

When she reached the town limits, Hannah turned off and let the snowplow carry on alone. She stepped on the gas, traveled another few blocks at well over the twenty-five-mile-per-hour limit, and detoured past the Lake Eden Community Center to see if the Winter Carnival committee had hung their advertising banner last night.

"Nice," Hannah commented as her headlights illuminated the blue banner. It had been ordered from the same company that manufactured the sweatshirts, and Mayor Bascomb had kicked in the extra money to exceed the ten-word maximum. The bright blue banner, strung up between two lampposts on opposite sides of the street, sported brilliant white snowflake letters proclaiming, "LAKE EDEN WELCOMES YOU TO THE WINTER CARNIVAL."

Wondering just how much extra money the mayor had paid from his own pocket, Hannah turned down Fourth Street, the block that housed her cookie shop and bakery. Though none of the neighboring businesses opened until nine, it seemed that everyone was out early. Yellow light spilled from the plate glass window of the Cut 'n Curl, Lake Eden's beauty shop, and Hannah spotted Bertie Straub bending over the shampoo chair, her hands suds-deep in a customer's hair. Bertie always charged double to come in early, and someone had paid dearly for a shampoo and set.

The New York Barbershop, next to the Cut 'n Curl, was also busy. A man Hannah couldn't recognize behind a face full of lather was getting an early morning shave. Hannah waved at the barber, Gus York, who had taken over his father's barbershop and added "New" to the name. The summer tourists who came in for haircuts assumed that Gus had been a barber in New York City, and they flocked to fill the row of chairs that lined the wall.

A surprised look crossed Hannah's face as she turned her attention to the shop just south of The Cookie Jar, the site of the Ezekiel Jordan House. The plate glass windows were covered with brown paper to discourage curious eyes, but there was a light on inside. Carrie must have collected Delores shortly after their early-morning conversation and they were already working.

Her shop was next, and Hannah's eyebrows shot up even further as she drove past. Her partner, Lisa Herman, had also come in early, and she was decorating the windows with a border of white snowflakes.

"Hi, Lisa," Hannah called out as she breezed in the back door a few moments later. "The windows look great."

"Thanks, Hannah." Lisa came through the swinging restaurant-style door with a smile on her face. Her petite form was swaddled in a baker's apron that had been hiked up in the middle and knotted in place with the apron strings.

"What are you doing here so early?" Hannah asked, hanging her parka on a hook by the back door. "Now that you're a partner, you can't earn overtime."

Lisa laughed. "I know, but I like to come in early. It's easy to get the baking done when there aren't any customers."

"You *finished* the baking?" Hannah's eyes widened in surprise as Lisa nodded. She'd mixed up twenty batches of cookie dough before they left for the night. If Lisa had baked them all, she must have come in at four in the morning!

"I love to bake. You know that, Hannah. And it was a good thing I came in early, because your sister called a couple of minutes ago. She said she tried your place, but she must have just missed you."

"Oh?" Hannah headed for the sink to wash her hands. "What did Andrea want?"

"She said to tell you that Janie Burkholtz is in town."

"I haven't seen Janie since Andrea's wedding." Hannah smiled as she lathered her hands. It would be good to see Janie again. Andrea and Janie had been best friends in high school, and then Janie had gone off to college. She'd come home a few times during her freshman year, but after her parents sold their Lake Eden house, Janie had spent the rest of her college vacations at their new condo in Florida. "Is Janie back for the Winter Carnival?"

"Yes, but it's not a pleasure trip. Andrea said she's working for Connie Mac as her personal assistant."

"Really!" Hannah was impressed. Connie MacIntyre was the star of a popular cable television cooking show, *Cooking With Connie Mac.* Almost everyone in Lake Eden stayed home from three to three-thirty on Saturday afternoons to watch Connie Mac banter with her guests, give advice on how to improve your marriage, and cook a complete dinner, all in thirty minutes. An attractive woman in her early fifties, everything she touched had turned to gold. Her cookbooks were bestsellers, her chain of kitchen boutique stores was thriving, her television show had a number one rating, and copies of her monthly magazine, *Home Sweet Home,* were flying from the shelves of the newsstands. The Connie Mac empire, run by her husband, Paul MacIntyre, was a multimillion-dollar industry.

"Janie's staying out at the inn with all the other Connie Mac people. Andrea and Bill are meeting her there for dinner tonight, and you're invited, too. Andrea said to tell you that Janie would love to see you again."

"I'd love to see her, too." Hannah said, wondering if she'd

be up for a fancy dinner out after what promised to be a hectic day.

"There's one other thing. Mayor Bascomb dropped by to see you. He's at the barbershop now, but he's coming back after Gus finishes up with him."

"Did he tell you what he wanted?"

Lisa shook her head. "Not exactly. He just said he needed to talk to you about something really serious."

"I hope it's not a snag in the Winter Carnival plans." Hannah turned toward the door that led to the coffee and cookie shop. "He'll probably want coffee. I'll put it on."

"It's all made. I put it up right after he left."

"Bless you, Lisa," Hannah said gratefully. "Have I told you lately what a gem you are?"

Lisa gave a girlish giggle, and Hannah was reminded of just how young she was. Howie Levine, Lake Eden's only lawyer, had broached that subject when Hannah asked him to draft their partnership agreement. Hannah had cut off his objection at the pass by insisting that Lisa was a better worker and manager than most people twice her age. Steady, reliable, and capable of handling any emergency that came their way, Hannah was certain that she'd never regret signing over a third of her enterprise to Lisa.

"Sit down and I'll bring you a cup," Lisa offered, motioning to a stool at the work island. "I have a feeling you're going to need it."

"Because of Mayor Bascomb?"

"Yes. He was really upset, Hannah. I offered him a warm Peanut Butter Melt and he said he couldn't eat a thing."

"Oh-oh. That's not a good sign." Hannah gave a deep sigh as she sat down on the stool. Mayor Bascomb had an active sweet tooth and he was wild about her Peanut Butter Melts. For him to refuse to even taste his favorite cookie meant that there was definitely trouble in the making.

Peanut Butter Melts

Preheat oven to 375ºF,
rack in the middle position

1 cup melted butter *(2 sticks)*
2 cups white sugar***
2 teaspoons vanilla
⅛ cup molasses *(2 tablespoons)*
1 ½ teaspoons baking soda
1 teaspoon baking powder
½ teaspoon salt
1 cup peanut butter *(either smooth or crunchy, your
    choice)*
2 beaten eggs *(just whip them up with a fork)*
2 ½ cups flour *(no need to sift)*

Microwave the butter in a microwave-safe mixing
bowl to melt it. Add the sugar, vanilla, and molasses.
Stir until it's blended, then add the baking soda, baking
powder, and salt. Mix well.

***If you like a sweeter cookie, add ½ cup more of
sugar or roll the dough balls in sugar before baking.

Measure out the peanut butter. *(I spray the inside of
my measuring cup with Pam so it won't stick.)* Add it
to the bowl and mix it in. Pour in the beaten eggs and
stir. Then add the flour, and mix until all the ingredients are thoroughly blended.

Form the dough into walnut-sized balls and arrange them on a greased cookie sheet, 12 to a standard sheet. *(If the dough is too sticky to form into balls, chill it for a few minutes and try again.)*

Flatten the balls with a fork in a crisscross pattern. *(If the fork sticks, either spray it with Pam or dip it in flour.)*

Bake at 375°F for 8 to 10 minutes, or until the edges are just beginning to turn golden. Cool on the cookie sheet for 2 minutes, then remove to a wire rack to finish cooling.

My niece Tracey's Favorite PBJ snack: Spread jam on one cookie and stack another on top. Mother likes PBFs better (that's fudge frosting between the cookie layers).

Chapter Three

"That's *all* you want?" Hannah was surprised when the handsome mayor of Lake Eden nodded. She'd expected a problem of gigantic proportions, but all he'd asked her to do was meet Connie MacIntyre at the Lake Eden Inn at noon today. "Of course I'll do it, no problem."

"Thanks, Hannah." The mayor brushed a nonexistent piece of lint from his jacket and reached out to take a Peanut Butter Melt from the plate Hannah had placed between them on the stainless steel surface of the work island. "You know how these celebrities are. If someone doesn't meet her and take her on a guided tour, she'll feel slighted."

Hannah supposed that he was right. Connie Mac was a star and she'd expect to be treated like visiting royalty. It had been an incredible coup for Mayor Bascomb when a member of Connie Mac's staff had called to say that she'd be honored to attend their Winter Carnival and bake the official Winter Carnival cake for tomorrow evening's banquet. Hannah, who seldom took things at face value, suspected that the "Cooking Sweetheart" hadn't agreed to attend this small-town event purely out of the goodness of her heart. One of Connie Mac's kitchen boutiques was opening at the

Tri-County Mall three days from now, and promoting it at the Winter Carnival was a smart business move.

"Make sure you drive past the venues on your way to town," Mayor Bascomb instructed between bites of his cookie. "Then take her to Jordan High so she can visit the hospitality hub and see the shuttle sleighs."

"Will do."

"Then drive her to the community center and show her the library. Marge is looking forward to meeting her."

Hannah grinned at that obvious understatement. Marge Beeseman, their volunteer librarian, had been positively ecstatic when Connie Mac had agreed to sign copies of her new cookbook as a fund-raiser for the library. According to Delores, Marge had paid Bertie Straub a small fortune to cover up the gray and give her a new, sophisticated hairstyle.

"When you're through with Marge, take her down to the banquet room. She wants to go over the menu with Edna."

"Got it," Hannah responded, wondering how Edna Ferguson, Jordan High's head cook, would react if Connie Mac suggested changes in the menu. The food for the banquet had already been ordered, and Edna had done most of the preparation in advance. "Where shall I take her after that?"

"The Ezekiel Jordan House. Your mother promised she'd have it ready by noon. I called her yesterday to see if I could drop in for a quick peek, but she won't allow anyone in until it's completely finished. You know how your mother is, Hannah. She's treating this whole thing like a state secret and there's no reason she should . . ." Mayor Bascomb stopped speaking as the back door opened and Delores stuck her head in.

"Speak of the devil," Hannah murmured, and then she put on a bright smile for her mother's benefit. "Hi, Mother. Is the house finished?"

"Not yet, dear. I just came over to ask you about a very peculiar rolling pin I found with Mrs. Jordan's kitchen utensils. Hello, Ricky-Ticky. I didn't expect to find you here."

Hannah covered her gasp of startled laughter with a

cough. Her mother was the only person in town who dared call the mayor by his childhood nickname. Hannah's grand-parents had lived next door to the Bascombs, and Delores had been his babysitter one summer.

"Morning, Delores." Mayor Bascomb gave her a smile that didn't quite reach his eyes, and Hannah could tell that he didn't appreciate being reminded of those early childhood years. According to Delores, he'd been a spoiled brat. "I've got to run, ladies. My meeting with the steering committee starts in fifteen minutes. The cookies are delicious, Hannah. I'm going to pick up a bag from Lisa on the way out and treat the committee."

Hannah watched as the mayor clamped his hat on his head and headed toward the swinging door that led into the coffee shop. The moment he was out of earshot, she turned to her mother with a frown. "I think you embarrassed him when you called him Ricky-Ticky."

"Of course I did. That's exactly what I intended." Delores walked over to take the mayor's stool and reached out for a cookie. "He's been acting like a big shot lately and it's time someone reminded him that he had his diapers changed like every other child in Lake Eden. Now, about that rolling pin, Hannah . . . it's carved on the outside with little panels of de-signs."

Hannah nodded. "It's probably a Springerle rolling pin. They're used to make a type of rolled German cookie."

"Oh, yes. One of your great-grandmother Elsa's friends used to bake them every Christmas. I always had to eat one to be polite, but I never liked them. They were flavored with licorice."

"Close enough," Hannah said, not wanting to get into a discussion about the subtle differences between anise and licorice. "Most women who had Springerle rolling pins liked to show them off by hanging them on the kitchen wall. They were handed down from generation to generation, and some-times the carvings were personalized."

"I'll put it on the wall above the kitchen table," Delores

said, finishing her cookie and rising to her feet. "I've got to get back, Hannah. We're almost ready to hang the parlor curtains."

"Hold on a second." Hannah carried the plate over to the counter and transferred the cookies to one of her distinctive carrier bags. It was a miniature shopping bag, white with red handles, and the words, "THE COOKIE JAR," were stamped in red block letters on the front. "Take these with you. Carrie loves my Peanut Butter Melts."

"I know she does. So does Norman." Delores frowned slightly as she took the bag. "You've been neglecting him lately, Hannah. Carrie tells me that Ronni Ward has been in twice this month to have her teeth cleaned, and you know what *that* means!"

"Her teeth are dirty?" Hannah teased, knowing full well what her mother had meant.

"Don't be flippant, Hannah. Norman's single and he's got eyes in his head. Just in case you've forgotten, Ronni won the Eden Lake Bikini Contest three years in a row."

Hannah sobered as her mother went out the door. She found it difficult to picture Norman with a beauty queen, but thinking about it gave her an unpleasant sensation in the pit of her stomach. She told herself that it couldn't be jealousy. Just because she dated Norman occasionally and their mothers continually tried to push them together didn't mean that she was serious about him. All the same, it certainly couldn't hurt to give Norman a call to let him know that she was still alive and kicking.

Hannah felt a real sense of accomplishment as she glanced around her kitchen. Trays of cookies filled the slots on the baker's racks and covered every inch of the counter. It had been a productive morning. While Lisa had waited on their customers, Hannah had baked more cookies. Even if the Winter Carnival visitors were as ravenous as a pack of starving wolves, they'd have enough cookies to last through tomorrow morning's events. By then there would be fresh cookies, and Hannah planned to drop them off at the warm-up tents by noon at the latest.

Unable to resist tasting her work, Hannah plucked an Old-Fashioned Sugar Cookie from a nearby rack and nibbled at the edge. The taste of butter and sugar blossomed on her tongue and she smiled in satisfaction. Her cookies were perfectly baked, crisp on the outside and sweet and flaky inside.

There was a knock at the back door, and Hannah ditched the cookie in her apron pocket. She'd gone to her mother's house on Tuesday for their weekly mother-daughter dinner and saved herself from store-bought pound cake with canned whipped cream, pre-chopped nuts, and jarred caramel syrup by claiming that she was on a diet.

"Hannah? You're here, aren't you?"

It was her sister's voice. Hannah retrieved the cookie from her pocket and opened the door.

Andrea blew in on a gust of wind, balancing a stack of real estate flyers in her arms. "Did Lisa give you my message?"

"Of course. It'll be great to see Janie again."

"I know. I'm really excited about it." Andrea set her flyers down on the only available space, the top of a stool at the work island. "Good heavens! How many cookies did you bake?"

"Enough to last until noon tomorrow. The girls from Mrs. Baxter's home ec class are setting up food stands in the warm-up tents."

"If the weather stays this cold, they're bound to have lots of customers."

Hannah noticed that Andrea was shivering, and she poured her a mug of coffee. "Here. You look half-frozen."

"I am. Is that decaffeinated?"

"No. Do you want me to put on a pot?"

"Absolutely not. I need all the caffeine I can get this morning. Al wants me to drop off flyers all over town. I even have to drive some out to the Lake Eden Inn."

Hannah placed a plate of Chocolate Chip Crunch Cookies

in front her sister. They were Andrea's favorite. "You'd better have some chocolate for energy."

"That's a great excuse; I'll take it." Andrea grabbed a cookie and took a huge bite. "Mbsoluphly muov mmm-meese."

"I know you do." Hannah interpreted her sister's mumbled comment, "Absolutely love these," correctly. "I'll take the flyers to the inn for you. I have to go out there at noon to meet Connie Mac."

Andrea swallowed her bite of cookie in a rush. "*You're* meeting Connie Mac?"

"That's right. Mayor Bascomb's tied up with a meeting and he asked me to give her a tour of Lake Eden."

"You have all the luck!" Andrea sounded envious. "Let me go with you. Please, Hannah?"

Hannah remembered Tom Sawyer and the whitewashed fence. Andrea would be a big help on the tour, but she didn't want to seem too eager. "I don't know. I'm supposed to do it alone. Are you hoping to run into Janie?"

"Janie won't be there. She told me she'd be out at the mall most of the day, helping Mr. MacIntyre with the boutique. But I'd just love to meet Connie Mac. I'm her biggest fan, and I can help you give the tour. You know how good I am with people."

"True," Hannah conceded. Andrea had the knack for turning a stranger into a friend in five minutes flat. It was one of the reasons that she was so successful as a real estate agent.

"Can I, Hannah? I'll do something for you, I promise. Anything you want."

Hannah began to smile. The expression on Andrea's face was the very same one she'd worn in sixth grade when she'd begged to wear Hannah's pearl confirmation earrings to school. "Well . . . I guess so."

"Oh, thank you, Hannah!" Andrea glanced down at her red plaid jacket and tailored slacks. "I wonder if I should dash home and change clothes."

"You look fine," Hannah said, averting what would surely

turn out to be an hour of primping. "We have to leave in thirty minutes, and we don't want to be late."

Andrea glanced at the clock that hung over the sink. "You're right. We certainly wouldn't want to make Connie Mac wait for us. Maybe we should leave now."

"Half an hour," Hannah insisted, amused at her sister's eagerness. "It only takes twenty-five minutes to drive out to the inn."

"All right, if you think so. Maybe I should drive."

"Good idea," Hannah agreed quickly. She'd been meaning to clean out her truck for weeks, but she hadn't gotten around to it yet. Andrea's car was always pristine because she used it to transport her potential buyers.

There was a knock on the back door, but before Hannah could get up from her stool, Delores opened it herself. "Oh, good. I'm glad you're here, Andrea. Now both of you can see the Ezekiel Jordan House. Put on your coats and come right over. And use the front door so you can get the full effect."

The door closed again and Andrea looked amused as she turned to Hannah. "Nothing's changed. Mother still orders us around like she did when we were kids."

"I know," Hannah said, getting up to grab her parka. "But it's not just us. Mother orders *everyone* around."

"I can't believe Mother put the whole thing together in less than a month," Andrea commented as they emerged from the back door of the Ezekiel Jordan House and walked across the snow to her Volvo.

Hannah waited until her sister had unlocked the doors and then she slid into the passenger seat. "I'm just as impressed as you are."

"It's bound to be the highlight of the Winter Carnival." Andrea started her engine and pulled out into the alley. "Especially since she's got Ezekiel Jordan's original rosewood desk. What I wouldn't give for a desk like that! The gold inlay is just spectacular."

Hannah thought about the re-creation they'd just seen as they drove down the alley. Delores had a real knack for arranging period furniture for display, and despite her concern about Abigail Jordan's kitchen utensils, Hannah had found only two out of place. "I liked the parlor the best. It looked so authentic, I could just see Ezekiel and Abigail sitting on their horsehide sofa watching television."

"Television?" Andrea turned to give her a sharp look, but then she noticed the grin on Hannah's face. "Stop teasing me, Hannah. You know they didn't have television a hundred years ago!"

"That must be the reason they had so many children. No electricity. No television. There was nothing else to do at night."

Andrea did her best to appear disapproving, but she blew it by laughing. "You're incorrigible."

Hannah leaned back in her seat and enjoyed the ride through town. The streets were bustling with activity today. Everyone was getting ready for the Winter Carnival.

"You should have told me that Norman was going to take period portraits in Ezekiel's parlor," Andrea said, pulling out on Old Lake Road and picking up speed. "I could have signed up early."

"I didn't know. I haven't talked to Norman for a week or so. It's a great idea, though. I love those old sepia-toned pictures."

"Mother told me that Norman's going all out for the Winter Carnival. He hired another dentist to fill in for him at the clinic, he's taking all those portraits to raise money for the historical society, and he's even judging a couple of the contests. Norman's really a wonderful man."

"It sounds like Mother converted you."

"What do you mean?"

"She's been singing Norman's praises to me all week. I think she sees a potential son-in-law slipping away."

Andrea took her eyes off the road for a moment. "Why? Is Norman dating someone else?"

"Not yet. Watch the road, Andrea. There's an icy patch up

ahead." Hannah waited until her sister had turned her attention back to the road. "Carrie told Mother that Ronni Ward's been having her teeth cleaned too often."

"Ronni Ward and Norman?" Andrea thought about it for a moment. "That's not quite as crazy as it sounds. Norman makes good money, and Ronni always said she wanted to marry a doctor."

"Norman's a dentist," Hannah pointed out.

"But people still call him Dr. Rhodes. That's all that matters to Ronni. She always wanted to be Mrs. Dr. Somebody-or-other."

"Maybe she should concentrate on Reverend Knudson. He's a doctor of divinity."

Andrea laughed, and Hannah knew she was imagining their dour Lutheran minister with Lake Eden's three-time bikini queen. "Maybe you should call him to remind him that you're still available."

"Reverend Knudson?"

"No, Norman."

"I will. But I thought you were rooting for Mike as a brother-in-law."

"I adore Mike; you know that, and so does Bill. Bill says that he's the best partner he's ever had. But it's like Mother always says: *Don't put all your eggs in one basket.*"

"So you think that I should keep dating both of them?"

"It couldn't hurt. You've got to play the odds, Hannah. Think of how you'd feel if you ditched Norman and Mike didn't propose. Or vice versa."

"Disaster," Hannah said, nodding solemnly. And then she turned away to hide a grin. Andrea was just like their mother. They were both trying to marry her off, and the event seemed to matter much more than the identity of the groom.

Connie Mac's limo driver seemed intent on his driving, and that suited Hannah just fine. She'd never been any good at uttering polite banalities in the name of social grace.

Connie Mac had arrived at the inn an hour behind schedule, and she'd offered the services of her personal limo and driver for the tour. Hannah had climbed in front to direct the driver to the venues, and Andrea, who was sitting in the back with Connie Mac, had explained which events would be held there. After a brief stop at Jordan High, where they'd viewed the displays, examined the shuttle sleighs, and spoken to the principal, Mr. Purvis, they were on their way to the Lake Eden Community Center to meet Marge Beeseman at the library and to check in with Edna Ferguson.

Everyone who was walking down Main Street stopped to stare as Connie Mac's limo passed by. That didn't surprise Hannah. Connie Mac was the first big celebrity to come to Lake Eden, and her limo was definitely an eye-catcher. It was painted peach, Connie Mac's favorite color, and her name was lettered in flowing gold script on the doors. Even though the windows were tinted so that no one could see in, anyone who could read knew exactly who was riding inside.

The intercom chimed as they neared the community center, and Connie Mac's voice came over the speaker. "Pull up in front of the door, Spencer."

"Yes, ma'am." The driver pulled up next to the curb in a no-parking zone and hopped out of the limo to open the door. As Hannah watched him usher Connie Mac out, she wondered if Spencer ever felt silly in his uniform. It was black, the type that chauffeurs always wore in the movies, but his shirt and tie were peach to match the color of the limo.

Andrea and Hannah scrambled out of the limo with no assistance from Spencer. He obviously knew his priorities. They followed Connie Mac up the front steps that led to the community center and into the lobby.

"This won't take more than a few minutes," Connie Mac told Spencer. "Park in the lot and watch the door. When I come out, pull up in front."

"Yes, ma'am," Spencer said, tipping his cap and turning to go.

"Spencer?"

Spencer halted and turned to face her. "Yes, ma'am?"

"I've warned you before to wait until I dismiss you. I won't remind you again."

Spencer shifted from foot to foot and dropped his gaze to the brown indoor-outdoor carpeting that covered the floor of the lobby. The color crept up the back of his neck, and Hannah knew he was embarrassed at being reprimanded in front of them.

"Your notepad, Spencer?"

Spencer responded, pulling a small leather-bound notebook and pen from his pocket. "Yes, ma'am?"

"Call the chef at the inn and tell him I want free-range capon tonight, no substitutes."

"Yes, ma'am. Would you care for a salad?"

"Endive, radicchio, and butter lettuce with a vinaigrette of extra virgin olive oil and balsamic vinegar mixed at tableside. No potatoes. In a small town like this, they'll probably be french fries."

Hannah bit her tongue to keep silent. Her friend, Sally Laughlin, was the chef at the inn and her french fries were legendary.

"Rolls with the salad course, but make sure they're not commercial," Connie Mac continued, "and fresh raspberries drizzled with Grand Marnier for dessert."

Spencer jotted that down and then he looked up from his notepad. "Will there be anything else, ma'am?"

"Contact the desk and have them send up a maid to unpack for me. She should hang everything on padded hangers and press anything that's wrinkled." Connie Mac stopped and frowned slightly. "Make sure someone from my staff is there to keep an eye on her. I brought some of my good jewelry for the banquet tomorrow evening. Do you know if the inn has a safe?"

"No, ma'am."

"Call the desk and ask. And tell them to send a bottle of properly chilled Pouilly Fuisse to my suite." Connie Mac paused and a tiny frown appeared on her forehead. "I know there's something else, but I can't think of it right now. That's all, Spencer. You may go."

"Thank you, ma'am."

Spencer tipped his hat again and this time he made it out the door. Hannah tried to catch her sister's eye, but Andrea seemed starstruck and completely oblivious to the fact that the Cooking Sweetheart had just embarrassed her chauffeur, insulted Sally's culinary skills, and questioned the honesty of the maids at the inn.

Chapter Four

"I'm just so thrilled to meet you, Mrs. MacIntyre." Marge Beeseman's voice shook slightly as she reached out to take Connie Mac's hand. Her brown hair was clipped short and frosted with blond, but it was clear to Hannah that Marge's new "do" hadn't succeeded as a total confidence builder. "Your cookbooks arrived yesterday, all two hundred of them."

Connie Mac smiled the sweetest smile that Hannah had seen yet, the very same smile she used on her show. "You really must call me Connie Mac. 'Mrs. MacIntyre' is simply too formal. May I call you Marge?"

"Of course," Marge breathed, obviously impressed by Connie Mac's tailored suit of peach wool and her gracious manner. "Just follow me and I'll show you the table I set up for your book signing. It's going to be such a wonderful fund-raiser for the library! Everyone in town wants to meet you and buy an autographed copy."

Connie Mac frowned as they approached the table that Marge had set up at the back of the library. "*This* is where you want me to sign my books?"

"Yes, I set it up this way on purpose. When people come

in, they'll get to see the whole library on their way to your table."

"That's certainly important," Connie Mac said pleasantly, but Hannah could tell that she wasn't pleased. "I have an idea, Marge. I think we should move my book signing to the lobby of the community center."

"But we want people to see the library. If you're in the lobby, they won't come all the way back here."

Connie Mac linked arms with Marge and walked her back toward the entrance of the library. "Let's put our heads together, Marge. I'm sure that between the two of us, we can come up with a solution to our little problem. We have to decide which is more important, raising funds for the library, or giving people a tour."

"They're both important," Marge insisted, digging in her heels.

"Of course they are, but how about this? I'll sign copies of *Sweets For Your Sweetie* in the lobby and you'll sit right next to me at the table. Then, when people ask about the library, you can tell them about it and invite them to come back to visit when the Winter Carnival is over. With all the other activities going on, I doubt they'll do much reading this week anyway."

Hannah waited for Marge to explode. The Lake Eden Community Library was her baby. She was proud of what she'd done and it was only natural for her to want everyone to see it.

But the expected explosion didn't come. Marge just looked flattered as she asked, "You want *me* to sit with you?"

"Of course I do. The mayor told me how instrumental you've been in planning this library. He said it was all your idea and you should take credit for it." Connie Mac patted Marge's arm. "And I must admit that I have a selfish reason for wanting you to sit with me, Marge."

"Really?"

"Most people don't know this about me, but I'm really a very shy person and I just hate the idea of sitting in the lobby all alone. If you're with me, you can introduce me to all your friends."

Marge preened a bit. "I could certainly do that. I know everyone in Lake Eden. I was born and raised here."

"I'm sure we'll have a wonderful time together," Connie Mac said, stepping out of the library and into the hallway. "I'll see you tomorrow, Marge."

Hannah rolled her eyes as she followed Andrea and Connie Mac down the stairs to the banquet room. The Cooking Sweetheart was a steamroller when it came to getting her way, but she had charm and she knew when to dish it out. After only one dose, Marge Beeseman, one of the most obstinate women in Lake Eden, had caved in like an underbaked cake.

"Edna? We're here," Hannah called out as they entered the banquet room in the basement of the community center.

Edna, a thin woman with wiry gray hair that had been permed to death, bustled out of the kitchen. She was wearing a new, sparkling-white apron that Hannah knew was her version of "all dressed up."

"Hannah, Andrea." Edna smiled as she greeted them and then she turned to Connie Mac. "I'm real pleased to meet you, Mrs. MacIntyre. Where's the cake?"

Hannah choked back a laugh. Edna had always been blunt. But it didn't seem to faze Connie Mac, because she just smiled.

"It's in my supply van and my driver is bringing it," she told Edna. "It's six tiers high, the decorations are white on white, and I worked on it for simply hours last night. Where do you think we should display it?"

"We could set up a card table," Edna suggested.

Connie Mac considered it for a moment and then she sighed. "I'd rather not do that. Card tables are so unstable." She pointed to the pedestal in the center of the room. "How about that pedestal? It looks sturdy enough."

"We can't use that." Edna shook her head. "That's where the crowns for the Prince and Princess of Winter are going to be displayed."

"But we could put them on that card table you mentioned. The pedestal is just the right size for my cake."

Edna looked as if she wanted to object, but she didn't. That made Hannah suspect she'd been warned to be extra nice to their favored celebrity. "I'll have to ask Mayor Bascomb."

"I'm sure he'll agree. After all, my cake is the star of the show, so to speak. I'll have one of my people rig up a spotlight and it'll create a wonderful photo op right here in the center of the room. I think we should pose for a picture together, don't you?"

"Well . . . I don't know about that. I'm going to be pretty busy in the kitchen."

"It'll only take a few minutes. I'd really like to have a picture of us together, Edna." Connie Mac paused and looked a bit embarrassed. "You don't mind if I call you Edna, do you?"

Edna shook her head. "Edna's fine. That's what everybody calls me."

"Good. And I hope you'll call me Connie Mac. I'd like to be friends since we'll be working on the banquet together."

"*You* want to help me cook for the banquet?"

Connie Mac gave a sweet little laugh. "I wouldn't dream of interfering, especially since the mayor told me that you're the best cook in the county. Have you heard about my new kitchen boutique at the Tri-County Mall?"

"'Course I have. Your grand opening's on Monday. Rod Metcalf ran an article about it in the *Lake Eden Journal*."

"I do hope you'll come out to take a peek, Edna. It's going to be our largest store, and you have no idea how many new things I've ordered! As a matter of fact, I went down to our main warehouse in Minneapolis this morning to see what I could find for you."

Edna looked surprised. "You brought me something from your boutique?"

"It was the least I could do. After all, you're organizing the whole banquet. I chose a dinner setting for two hundred, including glassware, linens, silver, and some simply lovely decorations for the tables. It's a gift from the new Connie Mac's Kitchen Boutique."

Edna seemed stunned at this largesse. When she recovered, she gasped, "Well, my goodness! We could use those dishes, that's for sure. Whenever we throw a big supper like this, Rose over at the café lets us use her plates and silverware. Problem is, we have to schedule it after she closes. And since Rose doesn't use tablecloths, we have to make do with the paper kind."

"Those days are over now, Edna. You'll have your own things." Connie Mac reached out to give Edna's arm a friendly pat. "Could we go into the kitchen for a minute? I'd love take a peek at the banquet menu and see if there's anything else you need from my boutique."

Andrea waited until Connie Mac had gone into the kitchen with Edna and then she grabbed Hannah's arm. "Did you hear that? A complete dinner service for two hundred! Isn't Connie Mac the sweetest, most generous person you've ever met?"

Hannah grunted, settling for the most noncommittal reply she could make. She was no accountant, but she was willing to bet that everything Connie Mac had donated to the community center would qualify as a tax write-off.

"It's just wonderful to have this time with Connie Mac," Andrea gushed. "When we get back to the limo, I'm going to ask her about her recipes."

"Recipes? Who are you trying to kid, Andrea? You never cook."

"But Connie Mac doesn't know that. And if I *did* cook, I'd follow her recipes. There was one last week that Bill would adore, meatloaf with three different sauces."

"I saw that episode," Hannah said, and then she clamped her mouth shut. Connie Mac's recipe for a meatloaf dinner was totally ridiculous. There was no way any busy Minnesota housewife would have the time and energy to mix up a meatloaf, wrap it *en croûte,* prepare three different sauces, drizzle them artistically around the lip of an oversized china plate, and arrange slices of meatloaf in an overlapping design that was garnished with piping hot deep-fried parsley.

"Didn't it look just wonderful?" Andrea insisted.

"Yes," Hannah admitted truthfully. It had been a beautiful presentation, but she suspected that how food looked on television was a lot more important to Connie Mac than how it actually tasted.

"You seem stressed, Hannah," Andrea said, looking concerned. "Are you worried about getting back to The Cookie Jar?"

No, I'm worried that my tongue will start bleeding from biting it so many times, Hannah thought, but she didn't say it. Andrea had just presented her with an acceptable excuse for bowing out. "You're right, Andrea. I still have a lot of baking to do. Could you finish the rest of the tour without me? All you have to do is show Connie Mac the Ezekiel Jordan house and escort her back out to the inn."

"Of course. No problem." Andrea looked very pleased. "I'll stop by later to tell you how it went."

"Great. I'll dash back to The Cookie Jar then. Make my excuses, will you?" Hannah shrugged into her parka and practically flew up the stairs, leaving Andrea to cope with the biggest sweet-talker and manipulator ever to set foot in Lake Eden.

"Try this," Hannah said, handing Lisa one of the blueberry muffins she'd baked for the Winter Carnival judges.

"Gladly." Lisa took a bite and a rapturous expression spread over her face. "It's perfect. I *love* blueberry muffins."

"So do I. I just wish I had fresh blueberries."

"The frozen ones are almost as good." Lisa took another bite and chewed thoughtfully. "My blueberry muffins taste like vanilla, unless you happen to bite into a blueberry. Yours taste like blueberries all the way through. How did you do that?"

"Blueberry pie filling. I mixed some in before I added the

frozen blueberries. The dough turns a little purple, but I like the end result."

"So do I. They're absolutely delicious." Lisa finished the last bite and picked up the plastic boxes that Hannah had filled with muffins. "Do you want me to put these in the cooler?"

"They don't need to be refrigerated. Just stack them on a shelf in the pantry and I'll deliver them tomorrow morning."

Lisa opened the pantry door and stashed the muffins on a shelf. Then she came back and sat down again. "I still can't believe that Connie Mac asked your mother to repaint the kitchen walls."

"And I still can't believe that Mother actually agreed to do it." Hannah just shook her head. Andrea had reported in right after the final leg of Connie Mac's tour, and she'd described everything that had happened at the Ezekiel Jordan House. Not only had Connie Mac asked Delores to paint the kitchen walls peach so that she could have her picture taken in the first mayor's kitchen, she'd also managed to talk Norman into coming in late this afternoon for a special portrait sitting.

Lisa glanced up at the clock on the wall. "It's almost six. They must be through with the pictures by now."

"Maybe, but I have a feeling that Connie Mac was late. I think she likes to make people wait for her."

"She's on a power trip?"

"That's the impression I got. She sure knows how to make people do what she wants. You should have seen Mr. Purvis cave in when she asked him to reserve the special sleigh for her. He couldn't agree fast enough."

Lisa looked puzzled. "But I thought that sleigh was for the Prince and Princess of Winter."

"Not anymore. They're riding in one of the regular sleighs now. Connie Mac can get anything out of anybody."

"Not you."

"I'm a hard case." Hannah began to grin. "Actually, that's another reason I bailed out of the tour. I didn't want to find out what Connie Mac wanted from me."

The phone rang and Lisa got up to answer it. She listened for a moment and then she handed it to Hannah. "It's Janie Burkholtz. She's calling from Connie Mac's cell phone."

"Great," Hannah said with a smile. She hadn't spoken to Janie for years. "Hi, Janie. I'm sorry we missed you when Andrea and I came out to the inn. What's up?"

"Your mother said I should call you, Hannah." Janie sounded on the edge of panic. "We've got a real disaster on our hands. Mrs. MacIntyre's supply van went into the ditch on the way here and the Winter Carnival cake was ruined."

"That's terrible. Was anyone hurt?"

"No. The driver's fine and there were no passengers. All the other supplies came through just fine, but Mrs. MacIntyre is determined to bake a replacement cake and we have to find some commercial ovens to use."

"How about the school?" Hannah suggested.

"I already spoke to Mr. Purvis and they're replacing the kitchen floor this weekend. And I tried the inn, but Sally's serving hot appetizers tonight and she's using all of her ovens."

"The kitchen at the community center?"

"That won't work either. Edna's baking rolls and she'll be there until midnight or later."

"Really?" Hannah's surprise was reflected in her voice. "I thought Edna was buying breadsticks and setting them out in baskets."

"She was, but Mrs. MacIntyre thought crescent rolls would be a nice touch with the salad course."

"I see," Hannah said and sent sympathetic thoughts Edna's way. Baking crescent rolls for two hundred guests was a lot of work.

"Your mother suggested that I call you before you left for the night. She thought maybe we could use your ovens."

Hannah hesitated. She didn't like the idea of Connie Mac baking in her kitchen, but Janie was on the spot and the Winter Carnival cake was important. "Sure, Janie. We were just getting ready to lock up. Come on over when you're through with the pictures. We'll wait."

"We're all through. We finished a couple of minutes ago," Janie said, still sounding stressed. "Thank you, Hannah. You don't know how much this means to me."

"No problem."

"Can you hold on for just a second? Mrs. MacIntyre wants something."

"Sure. Take your time." Hannah covered the mouthpiece and turned to Lisa, who was staring at her curiously. "Connie Mac wants to use our ovens. Her supply van went into the ditch and the Winter Carnival cake is mush. I told Janie they could bake here."

"Then I'd better make sure everything's clean." Lisa jumped up and grabbed a bottle of cleaning solution and a sponge. She wiped down the door of the cooler and then she started to giggle.

"What?"

"Now you know what Connie Mac wants from you. And you gave it to her, just like everybody else in town."

"Hannah?" Janie came back on the line. "Mrs. MacIntyre is very grateful and she wants to do something for you in return."

"That's not necessary, Janie."

"But she insists. Norman is going to bring over his equipment and take Mrs. MacIntyre's picture in your kitchen. She thought you'd want to hang it over your counter in the coffee shop."

"That's . . . uh . . . very nice of her." Hannah hung up the phone and snorted. Hell would freeze over before she'd hang Connie Mac's picture over the counter in her shop!

Blue Blueberry Muffins

Preheat oven to 375°F,
rack in the middle position

¾ cup melted butter *(1 ½ sticks)*
1 cup sugar
2 beaten eggs *(just whip them up with a fork)*
2 teaspoons baking powder
½ teaspoon salt
1 cup fresh or frozen blueberries *(no need to thaw if
    they're frozen)*
½ cup blueberry pie filling
2 cups plus one tablespoon flour *(no need to sift)*
½ cup milk

Crumb Topping:
½ cup sugar
⅓ cup flour
¼ cup softened butter *(½ stick)*

Grease the *bottoms only* of a 12-cup muffin pan *(or
line the cups with cupcake papers)*. Melt the butter.
Mix in the sugar. Then add the beaten eggs, baking
powder, and salt, and mix thoroughly.

Put one tablespoon of the flour in a plastic bag with
your cup of fresh or frozen blueberries. Shake it gently
to coat the blueberries, and leave them in the bag for
now.

Add half the remaining two cups flour to your bowl and mix it in with half the milk. Then add the rest of the flour and milk and mix thoroughly.

Here comes the fun part: Add ½ cup blueberry pie filling to your bowl and mix it in. *(Your dough will turn a shade of blue, but don't let that stop you—once the muffins are baked, they'll look just fine.)* When your dough is thoroughly mixed, fold in the flour-coated fresh or frozen blueberries.

Fill the muffin tins three-quarters full and set them aside. If you have dough left over, grease the bottom of a small tea-bread loaf pan and fill it with your remaining dough.

The crumb topping: Mix the sugar and the flour in a small bowl. Add the softened butter and cut it in until it's crumbly. *(You can also do this in a food processor with hard butter using the steel blade.)*

Sprinkle the crumb topping over your muffins and bake them in a 375°F oven for 25 to 30 minutes. *(The tea-bread should bake about 10 minutes longer than the muffins.)*

While your muffins are baking, divide the rest of your blueberry pie filling into ½-cup portions and pop

it in the freezer. I use paper cups to hold it and freeze them inside a freezer bag. All you have to do is thaw a cup the next time you want to make a batch of Blue Blueberry Muffins.

When your muffins are baked, set the muffin pan on a wire rack to cool for at least 30 minutes. *(The muffins need to cool in the pan for easy removal.)* Then just tip them out of the cups and enjoy.

These are wonderful when they're slightly warm, but the blueberry flavor will intensify if you store them in a covered container overnight.

Grandma Ingrid's muffin pans were large enough to hold all the dough from this recipe. My muffin tins are smaller, and I always make a loaf of Blue Blueberry tea bread with the leftover dough. If I make it for Mother, I leave off the crumb topping. She loves to eat it sliced, toasted, and buttered for breakfast.

Chapter Five

Once Connie Mac, Janie, and Norman arrived at The Cookie Jar, there was a flurry of activity. While Lisa showed Janie how to operate the kitchen appliances and Norman took Connie Mac's picture, Hannah loaded Lisa's car with the cookies they'd baked so that she could drop them off at Jordan High on her way home.

"Okay. Janie's all set." Lisa came out the back door just as Hannah had finished stacking the last box of cookies in her trunk. "These cookies go to Mrs. Baxter's room?"

"Right. The girls will help you unload them. They're all working late, making sandwiches for tomorrow. They're going to have ham and cheese, and egg salad."

"At least they won't have to worry about the mayo going bad in weather like this," Lisa said with a shiver, opening her car door and sliding into the driver's seat. "See you tomorrow morning, Hannah."

"I don't think so."

"Oh? Are you taking the morning off?"

"No, *you* are," Hannah told her. "You did the lion's share of the work today, and I'll pick up the slack tomorrow morning. The earliest I want to see you here is a quarter to twelve."

A delighted grin spread over Lisa's face. "Dad's been wanting to go out to see the venues and I just didn't have time to take him. But are you sure you can spare me, Hannah?"

"Sure, I'm sure. We shouldn't have much business. Almost everybody in town will be out at the venues. I'll have plenty of time to bake, and when you come in I'll run the cookies out to the warm-up tents."

"Okay," Lisa agreed, smiling broadly. "Thanks, Hannah. Dad's going to be so excited when I tell him."

Once Lisa had left with her sugary cargo, Hannah went back inside. The sight that greeted her when she opened the door made her blood pressure go through the roof. Her whole kitchen was in the process of being rearranged, and Connie Mac hadn't even bothered to ask her for permission!

Norman walked over to her, carrying his bulky camera bag. "Come on, Hannah. Let's get out of here."

"Just a second," Hannah said, heading over to the counter to grab her purse before Connie Mac could rearrange that, too. Then she turned to Janie, who looked as if she could use a dose of blood-pressure medicine herself. "Do you have everything you need, Janie?"

"Yes. Thanks, Hannah." Janie moved closer and lowered her voice. "Don't worry. I'll put everything back and make sure your kitchen is spotless before we leave. And if there's ever anything I can do for you, just . . ."

"The mixer's in the wrong place, Janie." Connie Mac interrupted their conversation. "You know I like to stand in the center of the work space."

Janie dutifully moved the mixer, but there were no electrical outlets at the center of the work island. "The cord doesn't reach, Mrs. MacIntyre."

"Then get an extension. Honestly, Janie. It doesn't take a college degree to know that."

Hannah pulled open a drawer, got out an appliance extension cord, and handed it to Janie. "Good luck," she muttered under her breath.

"Thanks," Janie whispered back. "She's on a real tear tonight."

Connie Mac clapped her hands to get Janie's attention.

"Let's go, Janie. I know you're on overtime and you want to get in as many hours as you can, but I'm not going to pay you if you don't work."

Hannah followed Janie to the work island and stepped right up to the Cooking Sweetheart. "Excuse me, Connie Mac."

"Yes, Hannah?" Connie Mac put on a smile for Hannah's benefit.

"I need to give Janie some last-minute instructions and then I'm out of your hair." When Connie Mac nodded, Hannah gave Janie's arm a comforting squeeze and drew her away to the far end of the kitchen. She'd seen enough of Connie Mac to know that it couldn't be pleasant to work for her. "Okay, Janie. When you're all through, leave by the back door. Just push in the button to lock it behind you."

"Don't worry, Hannah. I'll test it to make sure it's locked."

"Thanks. Goodnight, Janie." Hannah shrugged into her parka and headed back to Norman, deliberately ignoring Connie Mac. When she got to the door she turned again, almost tripping Norman, who was close on her heels. "One more thing. I baked Blue Blueberry Muffins this afternoon and they're in the pantry."

"The same muffins you used to bake when I stayed overnight with Andrea?"

"That's right. Just help yourself if you get hungry."

"Janie can't eat sweets," Connie Mac warned, giving Janie a stern look. "She has to lose at least twenty pounds before we start taping for next season."

A dull flush rose in Janie's cheeks. Connie Mac had embarrassed her, and Hannah had the urge to throttle the Cooking Sweetheart. Janie had always been full-figured, even in high school. And while it was true that she was far from model-thin, she wore clothes that flattered her figure and she was extremely attractive. "Why does Janie need to lose weight? She looks great."

Connie Mac turned to Hannah with a frown. It was clear she wasn't used to being contradicted. "I realize that Janie is your friend, but facts are facts and she's just too heavy. If my assistant is overweight, my viewers will assume that my recipes are fattening. That could reduce sales of my videos and cookbooks."

Hannah was stunned speechless for a moment. She opened her mouth, prepared to give Connie Mac a well-deserved piece of her mind, when Norman grabbed her arm.

"Come on, Hannah," he whispered. "Anything you say will only make it worse for Janie."

Hannah didn't like it, but she realized that Norman was right and she let him open the door and pull her through. "Goodnight, Janie," she called out as Norman closed the door behind them.

"It's a good thing we left," Norman muttered, taking a deep breath of the freezing air. "I was ready to kill that woman!"

"You're second in line behind me," Hannah shot back.

"Because she made Janie rearrange your kitchen?"

"That's only half of it. She implied that Janie was fat! You don't think she is, do you?"

Norman shook his head. "Janie's big, but she's not fat. And she'd look great on camera. That excuse Connie Mac gave about how Janie could hurt her sales is a crock. Julia Child didn't look thin on any of her cooking shows, and her cookbooks were bestsellers."

"That's right," Hannah said, wishing she'd thought of that in time to tell Connie Mac. Then she remembered what Norman had said as they walked out the door, and she turned to him with a question. "You said *you* wanted to kill Connie Mac. What did she do to you?"

"What are you doing for the next eight hours? If I tell you everything, it'll take all night."

Hannah laughed. "Maybe you'd better give me the abbreviated version."

"Connie Mac was an hour late for her appointment with me. Janie apologized, but Connie Mac didn't say a word. And then Connie Mac ordered me to take her portrait in the dining room and I was all set up in the parlor."

"So you had to move all your equipment?"

"Oh, yes. Six times. She kept changing her mind. And then, when we were finally finished and I'd already packed up all my camera gear, she decided she needed one more series of shots sitting behind the first mayor's desk."

Hannah frowned. Ezekiel's desk was a valuable antique and Delores had secured the area around it with museum-style velvet ropes. "Mother didn't let her do it, did she?"

"Of course she did. Connie Mac sweet-talked her right into it."

"Really!" Hannah was surprised. She'd thought that Delores would be the one person in town that Connie Mac couldn't sway. "So how long did this photo session take?"

"An hour and a half, and it seemed like months. By the time we finished, I was ready to bash her head in with one of Mrs. Jordan's rolling pins."

"It's a good thing you didn't. It might have hurt the rolling pin." Hannah smiled up at him and reached out to take his arm. Norman covered her gloved hand with his and they crunched through the snow together on the way to their cars.

"I haven't seen you for a while," Norman said, escorting her to the driver's side of her truck. "I've missed you, Hannah."

"I've missed you, too."

"How about some dinner? We could drive out to the inn. At least we know *she* won't be there."

"True, but I'd probably fall asleep with my head in the soup," Hannah said, stifling a yawn. Today had been a full day, and the strain of being pleasant to Connie Mac and baking ten times as many cookies as usual had taken its toll.

"Do you have another date?"

"No way. I'd really like to have dinner with you, Norman, but I'm just too tired. Can I take a rain check?"

"Sure, but you still have to eat. Do you want to stop by the Corner Tavern? That would be quicker."

"Not tonight. I just want to go home and crawl into bed with a glass of wine and a toasted sardine sandwich."

Norman made a face. "That doesn't sound very nutritious."

"It's not as bad as you think. Sardines are protein, and I always use the ones in ketchup sauce. That takes care of the vegetable. And the buttered toast provides the fat and the carbohydrates. It's a very well-balanced sandwich, if you think about it."

"I'd rather not." Norman unplugged her electrical cord, wound it around Hannah's bumper, and opened the door of her truck for her. As she slid into the driver's seat, he said, "Hannah?"

"Yes, Norman."

"Let's try to get together more often, okay?"

"Sounds good to me," Hannah said, reaching for her seat belt and buckling it.

"I was thinking about it last night and I realized that I was cutting off my nose to spite my face."

"What do you mean?" Hannah asked.

"Whenever our mothers start trying to push us together, I rebel like a teenager."

"So do I," Hannah admitted. "Mother suggested that I call you today, and I didn't. It wasn't that I didn't want to call you, it was just that I didn't want to give in to her."

"That's exactly what I mean." Norman looked very serious. "I think we should stop letting our mothers influence our behavior. We'll do what we really want to do, even if they suggest it first."

Hannah nodded. "That's a great idea, but there's one drawback."

"What's that?"

"It requires that we act like adults."

Norman chuckled. "Do you think that we can handle it?"

"Of course. The next time Mother suggests I call you, I'll call you."

"Good for you," Norman said, looking pleased.

"And then, when Mother starts preening because I followed her advice, I'll just stick my tongue out at her."

* * *

"Why don't you order something different, Andrea?" Hannah suggested, closing her menu and handing it back to the waitress. "You always have baked chicken."

"I *like* baked chicken."

"Whatever," Hannah sighed. "At least try Sally's cream of radish soup. It's wonderful."

Andrea shook her head. "I'm sticking with the Caesar salad. It's perfect with baked chicken."

Hannah shrugged and gave up the fight. She'd come out to the inn for dinner after all, but it hadn't been her choice. The phone had been ringing as she unlocked the door to her condo, and it had been Andrea in an absolute panic. Could Hannah please have dinner with her? Janie had canceled, Bill had paged her to say he'd be late, and she'd been sitting at a table in the dining room all alone. After a few minutes of pleading, Hannah's sisterly compassion had won out.

"They have excellent wine by the glass, Hannah." Andrea interrupted her thoughts. "Would you like me to pick out a nice chardonnay for you?"

"No, thanks. I'm so tired, it would knock me right under the table."

Andrea had the grace to look slightly guilty. "I probably shouldn't have called you, but I just couldn't face sitting here all alone. You understand, don't you?"

"Yes, I do," Hannah said. As the most popular girl at Jordan High, Andrea had always been surrounded by admirers. She had grown accustomed to being at the center of attention, and the prospect of eating dinner in a restaurant alone was anathema to her.

"Oh, good! There's Bill!" A happy smile spread over Andrea's face and she stood up to wave. "I thought they'd be much later than this."

"They?" Hannah glanced over at the entrance and felt a delicious tingle when she spotted Bill's partner and boss, Mike Kingston. He towered over Bill, who was almost six

feet tall, and most of the women in Lake Eden said that Mike
was the best-looking man in town. With his dark blond hair
and rugged physique, he reminded Hannah of the capable,
fearless early settlers who had carved out a niche for themselves in the Midwest.

"Don't they look great in their uniforms?" Andrea asked.

"Yes, they do," Hannah responded, hoping she didn't sound
too breathless. Mike always had this effect on her. Then she
realized that Andrea hadn't been surprised to see Mike, and
her eyes narrowed. Andrea and Bill were always trying to set
her up with Mike. "Did you know that Mike was coming?"

"Bill said he was going to ask him, but I wasn't really
sure."

"Did you plan this dinner to throw the two of us together?"

"Of course not!" Andrea looked perfectly indignant. "I
invited you this morning, remember? And Janie was supposed to be here, too. I just thought we could all have a nice
time together."

Hannah still wasn't sure that Andrea hadn't played
matchmaker. After all, she'd learned from an expert, their
mother.

"Smile, Hannah," Andrea urged. "You want Mike to think
you're happy to see him, don't you?"

Hannah smiled. That part was easy. Seeing Mike always
made her smile.

Two hours later, Hannah unlocked the door to her condo
for the second time that night and headed straight for the
phone in the kitchen to exercise a little damage control.
Once Mike and Bill had joined them, one thing had led to
another with surprising rapidity. Sally had moved them to a
secluded table by the big rock fireplace, the ambience had
been romantic and intimate, and Mike had flirted with her
outrageously. Hannah had stayed much longer than she'd
planned, and that had turned out to be a big mistake.

Hannah wasn't sure when Delores and Carrie had come in, but they had been eating their main course when Mike had walked Hannah through the room on her way out. It was obvious that Norman had told them she'd refused a dinner date with him, because neither mother had spoken to her as she passed their table with Mike. If scathing looks could kill, Hannah knew she'd be toes-up on the floor of Sally's dining room right now, deader than the sardines she'd been planning to eat for dinner.

"Norman?" Hannah was pleased when he answered the phone on the first ring. "I wanted to catch you before your mother got home. I need to explain."

"Explain what?"

"I had to go out to the inn, after all. Andrea had a dinner date with Bill, but he called to say he'd be late and she talked me into driving out to keep her company. Then Bill showed up with Mike, and Andrea asked him to join us."

"Okay." Norman sounded perplexed. "Why did you call to tell me that?"

"Because our mothers showed up and saw us together. I knew they'd tell you, and I wanted to get to you first."

"It's okay, Hannah. I know you go out with Mike sometimes."

"I know you know, but I didn't want you to think that I refused to go to dinner with you and then turned around and went out with Mike. I figured that if I didn't explain it, you might be hurt . . . or maybe even jealous."

"I wouldn't be jealous. We don't have an exclusive relationship and you can go out with anyone you want to. Besides, I like Mike. He's a nice guy." Norman paused. "Hannah?"

"Yes, Norman."

"How about coffee tomorrow morning? I have to be at the Ezekiel Jordan House early, and I could stop by The Cookie Jar."

"That's fine. I'll treat you to a blueberry muffin."

"Great. I'll see you then. And thanks for calling, Hannah. It was very considerate of you."

Hannah was frowning as she hung up the phone. Norman hadn't been jealous—not even a little. Hannah guessed she should be glad that he wasn't, but it was real blow to her ego.

Chapter Six

Hannah's headlights cut two converging tunnels through the darkness to illuminate the stop sign at the corner of Main Street and First Avenue. She was early, an hour ahead of her normal schedule, but she felt good about giving Lisa the morning off.

Nothing was moving as Hannah drove through the silent business district of Lake Eden. Norman's dental clinic was locked up tight, Hal & Rose's Café was dark, and there was only a dim security light shining through the front window of the Lake Eden Neighborhood Pharmacy. The town was still slumbering, but Hannah was alert and ready to go to work. This was the opening day of the Winter Carnival, and the cookies they'd baked yesterday wouldn't last through the day. She had to bake more and deliver them to the warm-up tents.

Instead of driving down the front of her block, Hannah turned into the alley and passed the back of Claire Rodgers's dress shop, her neighbor to the north. Claire had mentioned that she planned to open Beau Monde Fashions early this morning, but early for Claire was a whole lot later than early for Hannah. No one would want to buy designer dresses or Winter Carnival wear at five-thirty in the morning.

Hannah frowned as she turned into The Cookie Jar parking lot, and her headlights flashed across the rear of the building. The back door of her shop was slightly ajar.

The fact that her door was unlocked didn't set off warning bells in Hannah's mind. Everyone in Lake Eden knew that she emptied the cash register before she went home, and there wasn't much else to steal. If some homeless person had jimmied the back door to secure a warm place to sleep, Hannah couldn't really blame him. It had been a bitterly cold night. She'd just give the unfortunate soul a hot cup of coffee and a bag of cookies and send him on his way.

Hannah parked in her usual spot, plugged her extension cord into the strip of outlets on the white stucco wall, and walked closer to examine her door from the outside. The lock was intact and the door showed no sign of pry marks. Janie had simply forgotten to lock it when she left with Connie Mac. Thanking her lucky stars that the gusty winds hadn't torn her door off its hinges and caused a massive jump in her heating bill, Hannah pushed it open and flicked on the lights.

At first glance, her startled mind refused to believe what was right in front of her eyes. Then her mouth opened in a soundless gasp of shock. A bag of cake flour was on the floor, its contents scattered over the tiles like super-fine snow. Stainless steel mixing bowls filled with dried cake batter covered every inch of the work island, and sticky spoons and spatulas stood up inside them like miniature flagpoles. Several cartons of eggshells and dirty utensils were piled on the counter near the sink, and next to them was Hannah's industrial mixer with cake batter glued to its beaters.

Hannah fumed as she surveyed her usually immaculate kitchen. Janie never would have left this incredible mess. She must have gone back to the inn early, and Connie Mac just hadn't bothered to clean up before she left.

Uttering a string of expletives that would have made her mother run for the soap, Hannah stepped inside. It would take her at least an hour to clean her kitchen, and she didn't have any time to waste. She had just started to wipe off the counters when she realized that there was a sickeningly sweet, charcoal-laden smell in the air. Something was burning!

Hannah raced to her oven, opened the door, and jumped back as a cloud of black smoke rolled out. Through the smoke, she could see several charred, smoldering lumps that had once been layers for the official Winter Carnival cake.

With lightning speed Hannah turned off the gas and hurried to her second oven. Smoke was beginning to leak out the door, and she didn't have to look to know that there were similar lumps inside. She turned it off, ran to the windows to yank them open, and flicked the exhaust fan on high. Coughing slightly from the smoke and the exertion, she ran out the back door and propped it wide open behind her.

Hannah was livid as she paced back and forth in the parking lot, kicking up snow with the toes of her boots and waiting for the smoke to clear. Connie Mac had waltzed out of The Cookie Jar with cakes in the ovens, and if Hannah hadn't come to work early, The Cookie Jar might have burned to the ground!

After ten minutes of pacing and fuming, Hannah approached the doorway and took a tentative sniff. There was still a trace of smoke in the air, but it no longer made her eyes water. She stomped into her kitchen with a scowl on her face and headed straight for the sink. There was no time to waste. She had to clean up the mess and begin mixing her cookie dough for the day.

Hannah swept the egg cartons and shells into the nearly overflowing trash can and turned on the hot water to fill the sink with soapy water. Once she'd set the dirty dishes to soak, she carried out the trash and lined the can with a new plastic bag. She was gathering up her cake-batter-encrusted mixing bowls from the work island, preparing to move them to the counter by the sink, when she noticed something that made her stop cold.

Connie Mac's leather handbag was sitting on top of a stool. She must have forgotten it, unless . . . Hannah swiveled around with a frown on her face. Connie Mac's sable coat was still hanging on a hook by the back door. It had dropped down below zero last night. Connie Mac must have been in a real rush to leave if she hadn't taken the time to grab her coat.

Suddenly, the pieces clicked into place, and Hannah glanced around her uneasily. Janie had left early. That much was obvious. Her car was gone, and so were her coat and purse. Connie Mac had been here alone, and someone or something had frightened her away.

A glimmer of light caught Hannah's eye. The pantry door was open a few inches and someone had turned on the light. Hannah grabbed the first weapon she could find, the heavy pot she used to make boiled frostings. If the person who'd frightened Connie Mac away was hiding in her pantry, she'd get in a few good licks before she turned him over to the sheriff!

Once she had moved silently into position, Hannah inched the door open with her foot. She glanced inside, and what she saw caused the pot to slip from her nerveless fingers. Her earlier assumption was wrong. Connie Mac hadn't left last night.

The Cooking Sweetheart was facedown on the pantry floor, her arms and legs sprawled out like a kid who'd hit the surface of Eden Lake in an ungainly belly dive. She had been struck down by a massive blow to the head in the act of sampling one of Hannah's Blue Blueberry Muffins.

Shock rendered Hannah immobile for a moment, but then she knelt down to feel for a pulse. The biggest celebrity ever to set foot in Lake Eden would never star in another episode of her television show or pose for pictures in her magazine. Connie Mac was dead.

Chapter
Seven

Hannah was pacing the parking lot, trying to banish the gruesome sight from her mind, when she spotted the headlights of an approaching car. As it passed under the streetlight in the middle of the alley, she realized that it was Norman's car and that they had an early-morning coffee date.

Norman stepped on the gas when he spotted the sheriff's department cruiser. One glimpse of his concerned face as he jumped out of his car was all it took for Hannah to forgive him for not being jealous of her dinner with Mike.

"Are you all right, Hannah?" Norman asked, pulling her into his arms before she even had time to answer.

Hannah nodded, almost hating to admit it because it was so good to be hugged. Norman was solid and dependable, and it felt a lot better than she'd remembered to be in his arms. Actually, it was quite habit-forming. Once there, she didn't want to leave.

"What happened?" Norman asked her.

"Connie Mac's dead and I found her in my pantry this morning and someone bashed in her head when she was eating one of my muffins and I called the sheriff's department and that's why they're here." Hannah's words came out in a rush, with no pause for punctuation. She reminded herself to slow down so that Norman could understand her, and went on. "Someone killed Connie Mac last night while she was baking the Winter Carnival cake."

"That's horrible. Do they know what time it happened?"

Hannah shook her head. "Not yet. Doc Knight's examining her now."

"Well, it must have been after nine."

"How do you know that?"

"I grabbed a quick sandwich and then I came back to test my fill lights. I saw Connie Mac and Janie through your window when I left to go home."

"You'd better tell Mike and Bill."

"I will. I'm sorry you were the one to find her, Hannah. It must have been awful."

"It was." Hannah nodded. Then she took a deep breath and managed a shaky laugh. "After all the others, you'd think I'd be used to it by now."

"I don't think you ever get used to something like that."

"Maybe not, but if I keep on finding dead bodies, I'd better put the sheriff's number on speed-dial."

Norman chuckled. "Your sense of humor is coming back. You're going to be fine, Hannah."

"Of course I am."

The back door of The Cookie Jar opened and Mike stepped out. He frowned when he spotted Norman, but then he put on a polite smile as he strode forward across the snow. "Hi, Norman. It's a good thing you're here. Hannah shouldn't be alone at a time like this. I would have stayed with her myself, but I've got a job to do inside."

"Go ahead," Norman responded. "I'll stay with Hannah."

That comment earned another frown from Mike, and Hannah's eyebrows shot up in surprise. Norman and Mike were facing off like two banty roosters, and she was no spring chicken.

"I've got some bad news for you, Hannah." Mike didn't look happy as he turned to her. "Your shop is a crime scene. We'll be securing it in a couple of minutes."

It took a moment for that to sink in. When it did, Hannah groaned. She'd seen enough cop shows and movies to know that only authorized personnel were allowed past the barrier of yellow crime scene tape. "You mean I can't go back inside?"

"I'm afraid not. I'll send Bill out with your purse. I really shouldn't do it, but since it wasn't here when the crime was committed, I'm willing to bend the rules a little."

"So what am I supposed to do?" Hannah asked him.

"Go home, get some rest, and try to forget about this. The forensics guys are on their way and we'll take care of everything."

Hannah's thoughts were so jumbled, it was difficult to think clearly. If she couldn't get into her kitchen, how could she bake the cookies she needed for the Winter Carnival? "I know I have to wait until the forensic team is through, but I can get back in soon, can't I? I've got to bake cookies for this afternoon."

"Sorry, Hannah." Mike looked glum as he shook his head. "I can't let anyone disturb the scene until the lab results are in."

"How long does that take?"

"It depends. Our lab's not set up for DNA testing and we have to send it out. And depending on the results, our guys may have to come back in to collect more samples. I know it's an inconvenience, but I can't let you contaminate possible evidence."

"Just a minute," Norman said, stepping up to face Mike squarely. "You didn't answer Hannah's question. How long could she be locked out?"

"It's not up to me, Norman. If I had my way, I'd let Hannah back in just as soon as we collect all the samples. Unfortunately, it's not up to me."

"How long could she be locked out?" Norman repeated his question. "At least give Hannah a ballpark figure. She's got to make plans."

Mike sighed and turned to Hannah. "Worst-case scenario, it could be as long as it takes us to catch the killer."

"What happens if you *don't* catch the killer?" Hannah frowned at the man who had recently been the subject of her romantic fantasies.

"We will. I just spoke to Sheriff Grant and he's putting every available man on this. You have to be patient. It could take a while."

Hannah's frown turned into a glare. "But I don't have a while! If my shop is locked up for long, I'll go bankrupt."

"Let's not borrow trouble." Mike reached out to take her arm, but Hannah snatched it back out of his reach. "I'm not the enemy here, Hannah. It's police procedure and there's nothing anyone can do about it."

Hannah glared at him. "Is it fair that I should lose my business because a killer committed murder in my pantry?"

"Of course it's not fair, but I have to follow procedure here."

Hannah knew that Mike was a by-the-book cop. When it came to procedure, nothing would budge him. "Could you bring out my muffins? They're on a shelf in the pantry in plastic containers, and I need to deliver them this morning."

"Sorry. There could be prints on some of the containers."

Hannah gave a resigned sigh. Her muffins would be history by the time the crime scene guys got around to lifting the prints. "How about the cookie dough I mixed up last night?"

"That depends. Where is it?"

"In the cooler, and that's completely separate from the pantry. Since Connie Mac brought her own ingredients, there was no reason for her to go in there."

"If we don't find any suspicious prints on the cooler door, I'll release your cookie dough. In the meantime, try to find an oven you can use temporarily."

Once Mike had left to go back inside, Norman pulled Hannah close again. "It's not the end of the world. All we have to do is find you another oven to use. Let's go to the clinic and I'll help you make some calls."

"It won't be that easy." Hannah was about to explain the difference between a home oven and a commercial oven when she saw another car pull into the alley. "Oh-oh! There's Mother. She's convinced I'm on a perpetual safari for dead bodies just so I can embarrass her."

Delores fishtailed to a stop when she noticed the sheriff's cruiser. She rolled down her window and called out to Hannah. "Are you all right?"

"I'm fine, but Connie Mac's dead."

With no regard for any other traffic that might come along, Delores left her car in the center of the alley and got out. When she arrived at Hannah's side, she was breathless. "Did you say *dead?*"

"That's right," Norman said, moving close to Hannah. "Someone killed her last night while she was baking the Winter Carnival cake."

"In *my* shop," Hannah added. "Now it's a crime scene and Bill and Mike are going to close it down."

"That's terrible!" Delores gasped.

"Yes," Hannah said, not sure if her mother was referring to Connie Mac's demise, or the fact that The Cookie Jar would be closed.

"A murder scene right next door," Delores moaned. "Now no one will come to tour the Ezekiel Jordan House."

Hannah glanced at Norman, who was having trouble keeping a straight face. Delores wasn't concerned that her daughter's business would be closed, or the fact that Connie Mac was dead. Her only worry was that people wouldn't come to see her historic re-creation. "Relax, Mother. Most people are fascinated by murder scenes. Since they can't get into The Cookie Jar, they'll take your tour and peek through the windows."

"Do you really think so?"

"Absolutely."

"Maybe you're right. I went to a lot of work, you know, and everything is absolutely authentic for the . . ." Delores stopped speaking and her eyes narrowed. "Who found her?"

Hannah winced. It would come out sooner or later, and it might as well be now. "I did."

"Hannah! You've simply got to stop finding bodies. I

swear you attract them like a magnet. If you're not careful, everyone's going to get the wrong impression of you."

"That's unfair," Norman objected. "Hannah just happened to be in the wrong place at the wrong time."

"That's exactly what I thought . . . the first few times. But *five?* That's enough to make people wonder. If she's not careful, no decent person will want to associate with her."

Norman gave Hannah's hand a squeeze and then he stepped up to Delores. "I'm not afraid to associate with Hannah, and I certainly don't have the wrong impression of her."

"Well . . . I'm glad to hear it." Delores backed off slightly. "You're a good man, Norman."

"I try to be."

Delores turned back to Hannah. "Where did you find her?"

"In my pantry."

"Don't tell anyone. If people hear that she died in your pantry, they won't want to eat your cookies. You'd better throw everything out and start fresh."

Hannah didn't follow that logic at all, but she nodded. "Yes, Mother. I'll do that just as soon as they let me back in."

"Good. If you're sure you're all right, Hannah, I have to run. You have no idea how many last-minute things I have to do before we open to the public."

"I'm fine, Mother. Go ahead."

"I'd stay to lend moral support, but—"

Norman held up his hand to interrupt her. "Don't worry, Delores. I promise I'll take care of Hannah."

"All right, then."

Hannah watched as Delores turned and walked back to her car. Then she looked over at Norman. "You'll *take care of me?*"

"Just a figure of speech. I figured she'd like that sort of thing." Norman glanced up as another car turned into the alley. "Is that Andrea?"

"Yes, and Tracey's with her. Bill must have called her to tell her what happened."

Andrea pulled up and got out of her Volvo. The passenger door remained closed, and Hannah assumed that she'd told Tracey to stay in the car until she assessed the situation.

"Hannah! You poor thing!" Andrea rushed up to her. "Bill told me all about it. Have they taken her away yet?"

"Not yet. Doc Knight's still in there."

Andrea waved and the passenger door opened. A moment later, a small blond-haired bundle in a bright pink parka hurtled across the snow toward Hannah.

"Hi, Aunt Hannah." Tracey gave her a hug. "Mommy said you found another one, and now Grandma's going to be so-o-o mad at you."

Hannah glanced down at Tracey's earnest face, and she had all she could do not to laugh. "Oh, well. That's nothing new."

"Grandma never gets mad at me. Why does she get mad at you, Aunt Hannah?"

"Because I'm all grown up and I'm supposed to be perfect. You're four years old and you're still allowed some mistakes."

Tracey thought about that for a moment and then she nodded solemnly. "We came to tell you that you can use our oven for your cookies. It's a really nice oven and Mommy's only used it once."

"From the mouths of babes," Hannah commented, glancing at Andrea who was having trouble keeping a straight face. Then she turned back to Tracey. "That's really nice of you, honey, but I can't use your oven. I need to find one that's a lot bigger."

Tracey looked very disappointed. "But I was going to help you and everything. I need to learn how. I heard Daddy ask Mommy why she never bakes cookies and she said it'll be a cold day in . . ."

"That's enough, Tracey," Andrea warned, but Hannah could tell that she was more amused than angry. "Give Aunt Hannah a kiss and then go back to the car. We need to talk about some grownup things."

"I never get to listen when you talk about the good stuff," Tracey said with a sigh. "Grownups get to have all the fun."

Norman turned to Tracey. "I know something you can do for fun. If your Mom says it's okay, I'll take you next door to see the house your grandma made."

"Can I, Mommy?" Tracey asked, starting to smile again.

Andrea nodded. "That's fine if Norman doesn't mind taking you."

"Oh, good." Tracey slipped her hand in Norman's. "Let's go, Uncle Norman."

"*Uncle* Norman?" Hannah asked when Tracey and Norman were out of earshot.

"Tracey wanted to know what she should call him, and I couldn't think of anything else." Andrea looked a bit embarrassed. "'Doctor Rhodes' was just too formal, you know? Tell me what happened, Hannah. You know how Bill is when he calls me from the field. He never tells me any details."

Hannah had just begun to tell the story again when the back door opened and Mike came out. He strode across the snow, greeted Andrea, and then he turned to Hannah. "More bad news, I'm afraid."

"What now?" Hannah snapped. She was in no mood to be charitable to the man who'd just closed down her business.

"You said that Janie Burkholtz was here with Connie Mac last night?"

"That's right. They were baking when Norman and I left."

"Well, she's disappeared. I just called the inn, and no one's seen her since she left with Connie Mac yesterday afternoon. I sent one of the maids up to check her room, and all her luggage is gone."

"Oh, no!" Andrea's face turned pale and she reached out to grab Hannah's arm. "Connie Mac's killer must have kidnapped Janie!"

"Calm down, Andrea. A killer wouldn't stop at the inn on his way out of town to let Janie collect her belongings."

Andrea thought about it for a second, and then she looked a bit sheepish. "You're right. I didn't think about that. But . . . what happened to Janie?"

"We'll find her," Mike promised. "Our CIO pulled her picture from the DMV file and we put out an APB."

Hannah swallowed hard. She'd been around Mike long enough to know that when he started to speak in initials, it was serious business. Connie Mac was dead, she'd been an impossibly nasty boss, and now Janie was missing. Hannah didn't think for a moment that Janie had killed Connie Mac and fled town, but she couldn't blame Mike for being suspicious. "Is Janie a suspect?"

"I'm afraid so."

Andrea's face was still pale, but her eyes were blazing. "Janie didn't kill Connie Mac. That's impossible."

"You could be right," Mike backed off when he saw how upset Andrea was. "Miss Burkholtz could have a perfectly innocent reason for leaving town, but we won't know what it is until we ask her."

Andrea didn't look entirely pacified, and Hannah decided to change the subject. "Come on, Andrea. I have to go out to the inn. You and Tracey can come along."

"Hold it." Mike reached out to grab her arm. "Why are you going out there?"

"I have to find another place to bake and Sally's got a whole bank of commercial ovens in her kitchen."

"You're not going out there for any other reason?"

"I have to bake somewhere," Hannah said, putting on the most innocent expression she could muster. "You're not going to tell me I can't use Sally's ovens, are you?"

"No. As much as I'd like to, I can't legally keep you away from the inn. Just stay away from Mrs. MacIntyre's employees and don't talk to anyone connected with the case. That's a direct order, Hannah. If you interfere with our ongoing investigation, I'll charge you with obstruction."

Several retorts occurred to Hannah, but she was wise enough to voice none of them. She simply turned to her sister and said, "Come on, Andrea. We've taken up enough of Mike's time."

Five minutes later, they were zipping through town in Hannah's cookie truck, heading for the house that Lisa shared with her father. It was a slight detour, but Hannah wanted to tell her partner what had happened before she heard it from someone else.

"Hannah?" Andrea asked, glancing in the back to make sure that Tracey was engrossed in one of the books she'd brought along for the ride.

"Hmm?"

"Are Sally's ovens the only reason we're going out to the inn?"

"That's what I said."

Andrea looked disappointed. "You mean you're just going to let Mike tell you what to do?"

"He's an officer of the law, Andrea. He has the right to tell me what to do."

"But you're not going to listen, are you?"

"Let's see . . . one of our oldest friends has been accused of murder, I'll have to scrub for hours to get the bloodstains out of my pantry floor, Mother's still mad at me for finding another body, and Mike just shut down my business. What do *you* think?"

Andrea gave a big smile of approval. "That's just what I thought. I'll help."

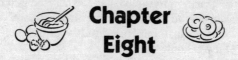

Lisa opened the door of her father's house, and she smiled as she saw Hannah, Andrea, and Tracey standing on the front step. "What a nice surprise! Come on in out of the cold. I've got coffee and cinnamon-apple coffee cake in the kitchen."

As they followed Lisa to the cheery yellow kitchen in the rear of the house, Hannah silently blessed her for not asking what they were doing at her front door at seven in the morning.

Lisa's father, Jack Herman, was seated at the table, finishing a slice of Lisa's coffee cake. When he spotted them, he held out his hand and gave a big welcoming smile. "Hello there, friends. Did you come for a piece of Lisa's cake?"

"Not exactly, but it looks delicious." Hannah walked over to Lisa's father and shook his hand. Jack Herman had Alzheimer's, and even though he'd known Hannah all his life, there were times when he didn't remember her. "I'm Hannah Swensen, Lisa's partner at The Cookie Jar."

"Of course you are," Jack said, giving her hand a squeeze. "I recognized you right off today. And that's your sister?"

Andrea reached out to take his hand. "Andrea. And this is my daughter . . ."

"Tracey." Tracey interrupted her mother and promptly took the chair next to Jack. "I'm four. How old are you?"

"I'm older than that, but I used to have a daughter just your age. Did you know that?"

"Lisa?" Tracey glanced over at Lisa and giggled.

"That's right. Would you like to have a piece of her cake?"

"Yes, please." Tracey nodded and Lisa served her a piece. Once Tracey had tasted it, she looked up at Lisa and smiled. "This is the best cinnabun apple coffee cake I ever had. When Daddy says it's okay for The Cookie Jar to open up again, you should bake this for breakfast."

Lisa looked confused and she turned to Hannah. "The Cookie Jar is closed?"

"Mrs. Mac got killed there," Tracey explained, before Hannah could even think about answering, "and Daddy and Uncle Mike put yellow tape over the doors."

Andrea shot Hannah and Lisa a warning glance and then she turned to her daughter. "Tracey, honey, I really think it would be better if—"

"It's okay, Mommy," Tracey interrupted, hopping down from her chair and retrieving her plate. "I'll just go into the other room to finish my cake." She started off toward the door to the living room, but then she turned back to Lisa's father to explain. "Mommy never lets me listen when they talk about the really good stuff."

Jack Herman's eyes twinkled, but he nodded seriously. "I know just what you mean. Hold on a second and I'll go with you."

"They don't want you to listen either?" Tracey looked surprised.

"I don't think so." Jack picked up Tracey's glass of milk and pushed back his chair. "I'll set up a tray for you in the living room. And when you're finished with Lisa's cake, I'll show you my animal collection."

"That would be nice," Tracey said, beginning to smile. "Are your animals real?"

"They look real, but they're carved from pieces of wood. And they're much smaller than real animals."

Tracey nodded, stepping aside so that Lisa's father could lead the way. "Do you have a hippopotamus? They're my favorites."

"I don't remember. Let's go look and see."

Hannah, Andrea, and Lisa kept their lips zipped until Jack had left the room with Tracey. Then Lisa leaned forward across the table. "Is it true?"

"I'm afraid so." Hannah sighed deeply. "Connie Mac was murdered last night while she was baking the Winter Carnival cake. I found her in our pantry when I came in this morning."

Lisa shivered. "Good heavens! I didn't like her much, but . . . murdered?"

"Somebody must have liked her even less than you did."

"I guess! What about Janie? Is she all right?"

"We think so. The only problem is, Janie's disappeared."

It took a moment for this news to sink in. When it did, Lisa looked worried. "You don't think she saw the murder and the killer . . . ?"

"No," Andrea said quickly. "Janie packed up all her things and left the inn last night. Bill and Mike are looking for her to find out if she saw anything. As of right now, Janie's a suspect."

Lisa was frowning as she turned to Hannah. "Are you going to prove that she didn't do it?"

"Yes."

"That's good. Did they say how long we'd be closed down?"

"Mike wouldn't give me a definite answer, but he admitted that it could be as long as it takes them to catch Connie Mac's killer."

"I don't like the sound of that." Lisa looked very worried. "I guess we'd better find another place to bake."

"We're working on that. Andrea and I are going to run out to the inn to ask Sally if we can use a couple of her commercial ovens."

"That's a good idea," Lisa said, and then she turned to Andrea. "I'll keep Tracey with me this morning. Dad loves kids, and we'll take her out to some of the Winter Carnival venues with us. That'll give you two a chance to set up your headquarters out at the inn."

"Headquarters?" Andrea looked puzzled.

"For sleuthing. If Sally lets us use her ovens, I'll handle all the baking. The sooner you catch Connie Mac's killer, the faster we can get back into The Cookie Jar."

"Something sure smells good!" Andrea exclaimed as they stepped into the rustic lobby of the Lake Eden Inn.

"And how!" Hannah began to smile. "It must be Sally's breakfast buffet."

Andrea sat down on the long wooden bench that was attached to the boot rack and pulled off her boots. She placed them on the rack and unzipped her tote bag, preparing to switch to her shoes. "Hurry up and I'll treat you to breakfast. I didn't get to eat this morning and I'm starving."

As Hannah joined her sister on the bench, she recalled that Andrea had eaten two large pieces of coffee cake at Lisa's. For someone who never did more than nibble at a slice of toast for breakfast, she was uncharacteristically hungry. Hannah had been off at college when her sister had been pregnant with Tracey, but Bill had mentioned that she'd gained ten pounds in the first month. Was the stork about to pay another visit to the Todd household?

"What?" Andrea asked, intercepting Hannah's searching look.

"I was just wondering why you're so hungry, that's all," Hannah explained, shedding her boots and pulling on the pair of suede slip-ons she carried in her purse.

"I'm not, you know."

"Not what?"

"Pregnant. I saw that look in your eye. You were wondering if you were going to be an aunt again, weren't you?"

Hannah laughed. She was caught dead to rights. Andrea

had always been able to read her expressions. "It did cross my mind."

"Well, forget it. It's just the cold weather. My body's telling me to put on an extra layer of fat for insulation."

"An *extra* layer?" Hannah glanced at her thin and fashionable sister. "You don't even have layer number one. There's not an ounce of fat on you."

"That's because I burn it all off. I have a very active metabolism. Remember how you used to make us oatmeal with brown sugar and chocolate chips when I was in high school?"

"Of course I do."

"You really sold me on breakfast, Hannah. It's my favorite meal."

"Then why don't you ever make it?"

"The last time I tried to cook oatmeal, it burned on the bottom and I had to throw away the pan. Toast and cold cereal is a lot safer. I can't mess that up."

Hannah tried to think of something kind to say, but absolutely nothing occurred to her. Andrea was a terrible cook.

"Let's find Sally and offer to help her. That'll give us a chance to ask her some questions."

"Good idea." Hannah stood up and followed Andrea past the old-fashioned reservations desk. She glanced at the wall of pigeonholes behind it and noted that there were no keys in the little cubicles. That wasn't a surprise. When she'd talked to Sally a few days ago, she'd mentioned that The Lake Eden Inn was fully booked with Winter Carnival guests, reporters, and the people in Connie Mac's entourage.

Andrea pushed open the door to the large dining room. It was deserted, and she turned to Hannah in surprise. "Where are all the people?"

"They're still in their rooms," Hannah told her. "It's Saturday and Sally doesn't open the buffet until nine."

"But it's . . ." Andrea stopped speaking and glanced at her watch. "It's only eight. I thought it was much later than that."

Hannah reached out to pat her sister's shoulder. Andrea liked to sleep in on Saturday mornings and she never lifted her head from her pillow until nine. The fact that she'd arrived at The Cookie Jar at six-thirty was tangible proof of her sisterly devotion.

The two sisters walked past the neatly set tables and headed straight for the inn's large industrial kitchen. As they pushed through the swinging door, Hannah started to smile. Sally's kitchen was her favorite place at the inn, combining modern stainless-steel restaurant equipment with homey touches that were Sally's alone.

The floor was tile, a must for a restaurant because the health code required that it be kept spotless. But instead of the solid-color ones that most restaurateurs used, Sally had installed designer tile that simulated an old-fashioned multi-colored braided rug. The areas that weren't covered by the oval-shaped rug design were formulated to look like wood, and if you didn't examine it closely, the floor looked like one you might find in an unusually large farmhouse kitchen.

The long wall that Sally's kitchen shared with the dining room had a window that ran from the stainless-steel counter all the way up to the ceiling. This meant that Sally's kitchen staff was always on display, and they were dressed to take full advantage of that. The women wore frilly caps that satisfied the health department's requirement for head covering and were patterned to match their bib aprons. The men were also on display in colored chef's coats and matching toques. The color scheme changed every day, and today's theme was green.

"There's Sally," Hannah said, directing her sister's attention to the far wall, where Sally was removing a tray of freshly baked popovers from the oven.

Andrea nodded and her face lit up in a smile. "Popovers! Sally makes the best popovers in the world!"

"I heard that." Sally looked pleased as she walked to a clear space at the long stainless-steel counter and tipped the popovers out in a napkin-lined basket. "Pull up a stool and have one while they're hot."

"Do you have time to join us?" Hannah asked.

"They can get along without me for a few minutes." Sally passed the basket of popovers to Andrea and set out a tub of butter and a jar of apricot jam. "What took you so long? I thought you two would be out here an hour ago."

"You *know?*" Hannah was surprised. The sheriff's department never released the news of a murder until after the family had been notified.

"Of course I know. I was listening to KCOW radio in the kitchen and it was the lead story at five-thirty."

"Five-thirty?" Hannah was astonished. She hadn't found Connie Mac's body until ten to six. "But . . . that's impossible!"

"You know that, and I know that, but you'd be surprised how many people actually believe in them."

"Time out." Andrea held up her hands. "It's obvious that you and Hannah are talking about two different things. You first, Sally."

"Okay. At five-thirty this morning, Jake and Kelly announced that Ezekiel Jordan's ghost was haunting the halls of the Lake Eden Inn, looking for revenge."

"Revenge for what?" Hannah asked the obvious question.

"For losing his prized rosewood desk in one of F. E. Laughlin's poker games. You see . . ."

"Wait a second, Sally," Andrea interrupted. "Is that the same desk Mother has in her re-creation?"

Sally nodded. "Ezekiel and Dick's great-great-grandfather were contemporaries a hundred years ago. When Dick and I found the desk up in the attic, we assumed that F. E. bought it after Ezekiel died, but Francine uncovered the story about the poker game."

"Your stepmother's still here?" Hannah asked. She'd met Francine at Sally and Dick's Christmas party. Francine had planned to stay for a couple of weeks to help out with the new baby, but little Danny was almost two months old.

"Everything worked out so well, Dick and I invited Francine to spend the winter with us. When she's not baby-sitting with Danny, she's researching Dick's family for him on the

Internet. That's how she found out about the poker game and
Ezekiel's desk. Do you want the long story or the short story?"

"The long story." Hannah jumped in before Andrea could
open her mouth. "Tell us about the poker game."

"It happened almost exactly a hundred years ago. F. E.
and his cronies came out here to do a little ice fishing and
hunting. They always played poker on Saturday nights and
they invited some of the notables in town to drive out and get
in the game. Ezekiel Jordan came out to play, but he wasn't a
very good poker player and he ran out of money early."

"So he bet his desk?" Andrea looked shocked.

"That's right. Francine found the slip of paper he tossed
in the pot with a bunch of F. E.'s other papers."

"Go on," Hannah urged her.

"F. E. won the pot, and the very next day, Ezekiel loaded
up his desk and hauled it out here. On his way home, a winter storm blew up and Ezekiel caught a bad chill. If you
know your Lake Eden history, you can guess what happened
next."

Hannah thought about it for a moment and then she nodded. "Ezekiel died of a lung ailment, didn't he?"

"That's right, three days after his trip out here. He blamed
F. E. because he got sick, and he told everyone in town that
the poker game was rigged."

"Was it?" Andrea wanted to know.

"I don't know," Sally shrugged, "but it's certainly possible, especially if F. E. wanted that desk bad enough. He
could be ruthless."

"So what happened next?" Hannah did her best to get
them back on track.

"Ezekiel swore on his deathbed that he'd come back for
his desk and take revenge on everyone who played in that
poker game."

"Okay." Hannah nodded. "But that all happened a hundred years ago. Why is KCOW saying that Ezekiel's ghost is
here now?"

Sally started to grin. "Francine mentioned it to one of the

reporters that's staying out here for the Winter Carnival. He must have called the radio station and told them about it."

"But why did Francine tell the reporter about it?"

Sally poured herself a cup of coffee and sat down next to Hannah and Andrea. "Do you want the long story on that? Or the short story?"

"The short story," Hannah said, even though she suspected it would be the same length as the long story.

"Yesterday morning Francine met the reporter in the hall. He said he woke up in the middle of the night, looked out his window, and saw somebody walking around outside. Francine told him he must have seen Ezekiel Jordan's ghost coming back for his desk. Francine was just kidding around with him, but he must have taken her seriously. And now everybody's going to think our inn has a ghost. In a way, I'm glad Dick's gone. He'd be worried about how it would affect our business."

"Dick's away?" Hannah was surprised. Sally hadn't said anything about it when Hannah had called her last week.

"He had to leave for Arizona on Sunday. His mother was going to wait until summer to have her hip fixed, but the doctors wanted to do it now. I told Dick that I could handle everything, but I didn't count on the ghost story. I just hope all our guests don't check out."

"They won't," Andrea said and she sounded very confident. "People who don't believe in ghosts will ignore it. And the believers will stay right here, hoping for a sighting. It's a win-win situation, Sally. Ghosts sell."

"They do?"

Andrea nodded. "Remember the old Walker place? It was on the market for a solid year with no offers. Then someone started a story about how it was haunted by Beulah Walker's ghost and it sold for over asking price."

Hannah turned to give her sister a searching look. "You didn't!"

"No. But I might have, if I'd thought of it."

Sally got the coffee pot and poured them all a second cup.

"I'll be right back. I just need to tell them to start setting out the buffet."

Hannah watched as Sally walked over to an attractive dark-haired woman in her late forties. They spoke for a moment and then the woman began to direct the rest of Sally's kitchen staff as they loaded dishes on rolling carts and prepared to wheel out the buffet.

As the feast on wheels started to move past them, Hannah saw Andrea reach out to snatch a glazed doughnut. "You had three of Sally's popovers and you're still hungry?"

"I'm starving. I just can't resist Sally's doughnuts."

"And I can't resist her bacon," Hannah commented, snagging several pieces as a second cart rolled by.

For several minutes the sisters chewed in silence, attempting to finish their pilfered bounty before Sally returned. Andrea had just swallowed the last of her doughnut when Sally headed back in their direction.

"Okay, that's done," Sally declared, sitting down on her stool and turning to Hannah. "Now tell me what dragged you out all the way out here when you must have tons of baking to do."

Hannah hesitated. Everyone told her that she was too outspoken, but she couldn't think of any tactful way to tell Sally what had happened to Connie Mac. "I'm glad you're sitting down, Sally, because your most important guest just got murdered."

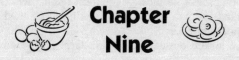

Chapter
Nine

Sally's coffee was cold by the time Hannah had finished telling her about finding Connie Mac. She took one sip, made a face, and set the cup back down again. "I'm sorry she's dead, but there's one good thing. When the news breaks, it'll knock our ghost story off the front page."

"Maybe not," Andrea mused. "It all depends on how much mileage that reporter wants to get out of it. He could always say that Ezekiel's ghost took his revenge by killing Connie Mac."

Sally looked puzzled. "But Connie Mac wasn't in that poker game. It happened a hundred years ago."

"I know she wasn't there personally, but while we were touring Mother's re-creation, Connie Mac mentioned that her family was one of the first to settle in Minnesota. With that kind of background, she could have been a shirttail relation to *someone* who was in F. E.'s poker game."

"Andrea's right," Hannah said. "If you go back far enough, a lot of Minnesotans are related."

Sally gave a resigned sigh. "I hate to admit it, but you girls have a point. I guess our ghost story is going to be around for a while, at least until the real killer is caught. You're working on the case, aren't you?"

"Yes, but that's confidential," Andrea told her. "After Mike locked Hannah out of The Cookie Jar, he made her promise not to interfere."

"You're locked out of The Cookie Jar?" Sally turned to Hannah.

"It's a crime scene and they roped it off. I know it's a lot to ask, but I've got all the Winter Carnival cookies to bake and . . ."

"Save your breath," Sally interrupted her. "You can bake here."

"Are you sure you don't mind?"

Sally shook her head. "That's what friends are for. Besides, it gives me the inside track on your investigation. You'll be out here and I can hear everything firsthand."

"Thanks, Sally." Hannah felt a giant weight slip off her shoulders. Her immediate problem was solved, but there was an even bigger one to tackle. "Do you have a minute to tell me about the people who worked for Connie Mac? We need to find out if any of them had a reason to kill her."

"If you ask me, they *all* had reasons. Connie Mac was a terror to work for."

Andrea's eyes widened and she stared at Sally. "Are you sure? She seemed so nice."

"That was just her public image. She was a lot different when somebody crossed her."

Hannah set down her coffee cup and pulled out her notebook. "Then everyone who worked for Connie Mac is a possible suspect?"

"That's about the size of it. And don't forget my staff. Connie Mac was only here for a couple of hours, but she managed to send four of my maids downstairs in tears."

"I just can't believe it!" Andrea still looked shocked. "She was really *that* bad?"

"She was worse. To tell the truth, I'm surprised someone didn't kill her long before this."

Hannah glanced at her sister. Andrea was wearing an expression that reminded her of the first fish she'd ever caught. "I think we should try to narrow the field," Hannah said, turning her attention back to Sally. "Is there anyone who had a particular grudge against Connie Mac?"

"There's the man who drove her supply van in the ditch. Earl Flensburg pulled him out and he let the guy use the phone in his tow truck. Connie Mac wouldn't even let him tell her what happened. She just fired him right over the phone."

Hannah jotted a note to check with Earl. "Anyone else?"

"There's Alan Carpenter. He's Connie Mac's lawyer and she threatened to fire him yesterday afternoon."

"How do you know that?"

"I was there. I was filling in for my bartender and Alan was sitting at the far end of the bar. When Connie Mac came in, right after your tour, she really lit into him."

"What did she say?" Hannah asked, her pen poised to take notes.

"Let me think." Sally paused for a moment. "I was heading over to take her order, and I heard her say, 'Half? But he can't do that!' And Alan said, 'He's already done it. It's signed and witnessed.'"

"Who's this *he*?" Hannah asked, silently apologizing to Miss Parry and her sixth-grade grammar class.

"I don't know, and I sure didn't ask. Connie Mac looked so mad, I backtracked to polish some glasses."

"But you could hear what they said?"

"Of course. I was only a few feet away and I could see them in the mirror behind the bar. Connie Mac glared daggers at Alan, and that's when she threatened him. She said, 'Get him to change it, or you're fired. Don't forget that you're my lawyer and I can have you disbarred for not protecting my interests.'"

Hannah added Alan Carpenter's name to her list of suspects, then glanced over at Andrea. Her sister still looked like a hooked fish. "Are you all right, Andrea?"

"I'm okay." Andrea straightened up and took a deep breath. "I just don't understand how I could be so gullible. I can usually read people better than that."

Sally reached over to pat Andrea's shoulder. "Connie Mac

pulled the wool over everyone's eyes. She had me fooled too, at first."

"That's what TV stars get paid to do," Hannah commented, and then she turned back to Sally. "Where is Alan Carpenter now?"

"He left with Connie Mac's husband right before you got here. I didn't know it at the time, but they must have been going to officially identify the body."

"You're probably right." Hannah shifted gears. She didn't want to think about how a husband must feel having to identify his wife's dead body. "What's your impression of Connie Mac's husband?"

"I like Paul. He's everything that Connie Mac just pretended to be." Sally hesitated, and faint worry lines appeared on her forehead. "Is he a suspect?"

"Not if he has an alibi," Hannah told her. "Was he here all night?"

"I don't know. Paul didn't come in while I was bartending, but he could have been up in their suite. One of my maids might know."

"I'll talk to them later," Hannah said, and jotted another note. "How about Spencer, her chauffeur?"

"He told me he was on call. Connie Mac was supposed to call him when she finished baking, and he had to go pick her up. He was in the bar until I closed at one."

Andrea looked shocked. "Spencer was drinking?"

"Only coffee. I think he went through about a gallon while he was waiting. When I closed the bar, he went out to the lobby. My night man said he sat there in a chair by the fireplace all night."

Hannah nodded and crossed Spencer off her list of suspects. If he'd been at the inn all night, he couldn't have killed Connie Mac. "Did you meet everyone on Connie Mac's staff?"

"Yes. When they checked in on Monday, Paul introduced them to me. Most of them spent a lot of time at the mall, arranging for the grand opening of the boutique, but they all came back here for dinner. They seemed like a nice bunch of people, Hannah. Connie Mac was the only exception."

"How about Paul and Connie Mac? Do you think it was a good marriage?"

"It wouldn't surprise me if it wasn't. He was nice and she was nasty. They must have mixed like oil and water."

"Was Paul here when Connie Mac checked in?"

"Yes, but they didn't see each other, if that's what you're asking. I worked the front desk from noon to two and Paul called down to leave a message for her. Connie Mac was supposed to come straight up to their suite when she arrived, because Paul needed to talk to her about something important."

"And you gave her the message?"

"Of course. She stood there and read it right in front of me. Then she slipped it in her purse and went straight back out to her limo."

"She didn't even bother to call him?" Andrea began to frown when Sally shook her head. "But she saw him when she got back from the tour, didn't she?"

"I don't know. My bartender called in sick and I had to work the bar for the rest of the day. Connie Mac came in at four to meet Alan, and she was hopping mad before she walked through the door."

"How could you tell she was mad before you saw her?" Hannah was confused.

"I heard her coming down the hall, and those boots she was wearing couldn't have hit the floor any harder."

"Boots?" Andrea gave Sally sharp look. "Are you sure they were boots?"

"I'm positive. I noticed because they were so unusual. I've never seen boots in peach-colored suede before. I bet she had them dyed to match the flowers on her sweater."

"Connie Mac was wearing a sweater?" Andrea sounded surprised.

"That's right. It was part of a three-piece outfit. Her slacks and top were chocolate brown, the same color as the background in the sweater."

"Was she carrying a purse?"

"Yes, a peach-colored suede shoulder bag with a strap made of gold links. She threw it on the top of the bar so hard, I thought the strap was going to wipe out a bowl of salted nuts."

Hannah frowned at her sister. Leave it to Andrea to side-track a murder investigation by getting into a discussion of fashion with Sally. "That's enough, Andrea. We don't need a blow-by-blow description of Connie Mac's wardrobe."

"Yes, we do," Andrea countered, giving Hannah a tri-umphant look. "If you'd paid attention, you'd know that Connie Mac was wearing a peach designer suit with black leather shoes when we went on the tour. And her purse was a black leather clutch with a diamond clasp. She must have gone up to her suite to change clothes, and that means she probably saw her husband. Don't you think *that's* impor-tant?"

"It's important, and I'm glad you noticed." Hannah felt a little guilty for jumping on her sister. Andrea always noticed what other women were wearing. Usually it bored Hannah to death, but this time it had come in handy. "I think it would help if we tried to reconstruct Connie Mac's afternoon. What time did you finish the tour, Andrea?"

"Three-thirty. I looked at my watch when Spencer dropped me off at my car. I wanted to see if I had time to stop at the cleaners before I picked Tracey up at preschool."

Hannah wrote the time in her notebook. "So Connie Mac got here at three-thirty and she had time to change clothes before Sally saw her at four?"

"She *barely* had time," Andrea corrected her. "I don't think Connie Mac was the type to go out in public unless she looked perfect. And don't forget that she had to switch purses. I figure she had about two minutes to spend with her hus-band, just long enough to give him his orders for the rest of the day."

Hannah chuckled at her sister's turn of phrase. Andrea's opinion of Connie Mac had obviously hit rock bottom. "So you think it wasn't an ideal marriage?"

"Not on your life! Any woman who doesn't spend more than two minutes with her husband, especially after they've been separated for five days, is a really lousy wife."

"I'll take your word for that," Hannah said, turning back to her notebook. "Was Connie Mac angry about anything when you left her, Andrea?"

"Not that I could see. She was all smiles and she even invited me to the grand opening of her boutique. Something must have happened after she went up to her suite."

"At least we know she didn't have a fight with her husband. There's no way he could make her that angry in two minutes." Hannah looked up from her notes as Sally and Andrea started to laugh. "What did I say?"

Sally tried for a straight face, but it didn't work. "You don't understand, Hannah. Dick can say something to make me mad in less time than that."

"And Bill can do it in thirty seconds flat," Andrea added. "You don't know much about marriage."

"And I'm not sure I want to. Then you two think she might have had a fight with Paul?"

"It's certainly possible," Andrea answered, "but it's also possible that something happened on her way down to the bar."

"That's true. How long did she stay in the bar, Sally?"

"Five minutes tops. She went out the same way she came in, as mad as a wet hen. She was really on the warpath, Hannah. My stepmother was carrying Danny down the hall and she heard Connie Mac yelling at Kurt Howe in his room. She was so loud, Francine could hear her right through the closed door."

"What time was that? And who's Kurt Howe?"

"A quarter after four. Kurt Howe works for Savory Press, the people that publish her cookbooks. He's a nice young guy and he's got a tough job. He told me that they sent him here to *handle* Connie Mac, and it wasn't easy."

"That's got to be the understatement of the year," Hannah said, venturing a grin, "especially when Connie Mac's the one who's used to doing the handling. Does Francine know why she was yelling at him?"

"Not really. She just caught the tail end of it. But she did hear Connie Mac say that she was going to call the publisher in the morning and have Kurt fired."

Hannah almost choked on a sip of coffee, and Andrea reached over to thump her on the back. "Are you all right, Hannah?"

"I'm fine, but we've discovered five suspects already and we just started. Sally's right. It looks like everyone had a reason to want Connie Mac dead."

"Five suspects?" Sally looked confused. "I thought you had only four."

"The van driver's number one. He must have been steaming about being fired. And Alan Carpenter is number two. Connie Mac threatened to fire him *and* have him disbarred."

"We have to include Paul," Andrea said, taking over the count, "at least until we find out if he has an alibi. If they had a fight, he was probably just as mad as she was. And Kurt Howe is suspect number four. He could have killed her so she couldn't call the publisher to get him fired."

Sally nodded. "Okay, but that's still only four. Who's the fifth, Hannah?"

"Remember that conversation you overheard between Connie Mac and Alan? The man who was getting half of something could have killed Connie Mac to keep her from changing their agreement."

"I didn't even think of that," Sally said, obviously impressed. "But how are you going to find out who he is?"

Hannah turned to her sister. "You can ask Alan. He'll probably try to fob you off with lawyer-client privilege, but it's worth a try."

"I'll get it out of him," Andrea promised.

Sally glanced at her watch and sighed. "This is getting interesting, but it's past time for me to go out there and play hostess. Come on and I'll treat you to the buffet."

"Just one more thing before you go." Hannah stopped

Sally before she could leave. "Do you have any idea where Janie Burkholtz is?"

"She's probably at the table with the rest of the Connie Mac people. They always sit together."

"She's not there," Andrea said. "Mike called her this morning, and when Janie didn't answer the phone in her room, he sent one of the maids up to check. There was no sign of Janie, her bed hadn't been slept in, and all of her things were gone. We need to find her before Bill and Mike do."

Sally nodded. "Why don't you ask Paul? Janie had dinner with him Thursday night, and she would have told him if she needed time off."

"We'll do that," Hannah promised, and then she started to frown as another, very unwelcome thought occurred to her. "Did you get the impression that Janie and Paul were close?"

"I guess you could say that. They seemed to have a great time together. As a matter of fact, one of my waitresses said. . . ."

Sally stopped speaking abruptly and Hannah leaned forward. "What?"

"It was probably nothing. You know how Dot Truman is. She just got engaged and she sees romance under every bush."

Under any other circumstances, Hannah would have laughed at Sally's description, but this was far too serious. "I still need to know what Dot said."

"All right. It's just that Paul and Janie sat there for quite a while, laughing and talking and whatever. And that was the night *before* Connie Mac got here."

"And Dot said . . . . ?" Andrea prompted.

"She told me it was pretty obvious to her that Paul had something going on the side."

Hannah glanced at her sister in time to see her wince. It wasn't the sort of news that either of them wanted to hear. "Is Dot Truman scheduled to work today?"

"I'm not sure. I'll have to check." Sally got to her feet.

"Come on, you two. I have to mingle with the guests and you have to eat. We can talk more later."

Sally and Andrea got up, but Hannah didn't. She was still considering what Dot Truman had said. Janie had a sensible head on her shoulders, and Hannah didn't think she'd be foolish enough to have an affair with her boss's husband. On the other hand, common sense could fly out the window when love walked in the door.

"Come on, Hannah," Andrea nudged her.

"Okay." Hannah slipped her notebook into her purse, and then another thought occurred to her. What if Janie and Paul were perfectly innocent and it only *looked* as if they were lovers? If Dot Truman had assumed that they were having an affair, Connie Mac could have come to the same conclusion. That would certainly explain why she'd been on the warpath yesterday afternoon.

"Hannah?" Andrea nudged her again. "Let's go get something to eat."

"Right." Hannah slid off her stool, intending to leave, when another piece of the puzzle clicked into place.

"Hannah?" Andrea sounded impatient.

"Hold your horses; I'm coming." Hannah grabbed her purse and followed Andrea into the dining room. On any other morning, the sight of Sally's buffet table would have made her as hungry as a bear, but she barely glanced at the tempting array. Her mind was still back at the crime scene, thinking about Janie and Connie Mac.

Once Bill and Mike had interviewed Dot Truman, they'd suspect Janie of being the "other woman." Jealousy was a powerful motive for murder, and even if Paul swore that he wasn't involved with Janie, it wouldn't hold much water. Mike and Bill would expect him to deny it.

"Get in line, Hannah."

Andrea gave her a none-too-gentle shove, and Hannah got in line at the sideboard, where Sally's staff had set out the plates and the silverware. She moved forward automatically, still thinking about the case that Mike and Bill could build against Janie. Money also was a powerful motive for murder, and Connie Mac had made millions over the years. They might even think that Janie had killed Connie Mac so that Paul could inherit her empire.

Hannah sighed as she reached the front of the line and picked up a plate. One thing was clear. They had to find Janie and get her side of the story before Bill and Mike had time to build an even stronger case against her.

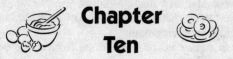

Chapter Ten

The two sisters split up when they arrived at the buffet table, and went down opposite sides. Sally always set out a mirror-image buffet to shorten the lines. Then, by unspoken agreement, they headed off toward the horseshoe-shaped mahogany bar. Sally and Dick didn't open the bar until lunchtime, and it was the only unpopulated spot in the room.

Once they'd hoisted themselves up on the comfortable padded-leather barstools, both Hannah and Andrea spent several minutes eating without exchanging a word. Sally put on the best breakfast buffet in three counties, and both sisters believed that it would be a crime to let her Eggs Benedict or Quiche Lorraine get cold.

"It's not true. Janie would have told me," Andrea insisted, finishing the last bite of her quiche.

"Are you sure? You haven't been in touch for a while."

"We're still just as close as we were in high school." Andrea speared one of Sally's famous breakfast sausages with her fork. "Besides, Janie doesn't have an aggressive bone in her body. There's no way she could have killed Connie Mac."

"Unless she did it in self-defense."

"What do you mean?" Andrea stopped in the act of lifting her fork to her mouth.

"I've got a possible scenario. Listen, and I'll run it past you."

"Okay. Go ahead."

"Let's assume that Connie Mac thought Janie was having an affair with . . ."

"Hold it right there!" Andrea set down her fork with a clatter. "Janie would never have an affair with another woman's husband!"

"I said *thought*. It doesn't really matter whether Janie was or wasn't, as long as Connie Mac thought she was. Once they were alone at The Cookie Jar last night, Connie Mac confronted Janie about it and it turned ugly. . . ."

"It wouldn't have happened that way," Andrea interrupted again. "Janie would have done everything she could to convince Connie Mac that she was wrong."

"You know how stubborn Connie Mac could be. What if Janie couldn't convince her?"

Andrea thought about that for a minute. "Then Janie would have left."

"What if Connie Mac blocked the back door? Do you think Janie would have pushed her out of the way?"

Hannah let Andrea think about it while she stared at the glasses that were hanging on a rack over the bar. They were absolutely spotless, and she wondered idly whether Sally's staff had to wash them every day.

"Janie wouldn't have pushed her," Andrea said at last. "I'm pretty sure of that. If she couldn't leave, she would have gone into another room until Connie Mac cooled down."

"Which other room?"

"The coffee shop, or . . ." Andrea hesitated, and then she sighed. "I see where you're going. You think Janie ducked into the pantry to get away and Connie Mac followed her."

Hannah nodded. "Knowing Janie, do you think it could have happened that way?"

"Maybe. It *does* make sense. But we won't know for sure until we find Janie and ask her."

"Exactly. Any ideas about where she is?"

"Not really. Janie told me her parents were on a cruise. I don't think she'd drive all the way down to Florida if they weren't home."

"Could she be hiding out with someone in town?"

"When she called me, she said she hadn't kept in touch with anyone in Lake Eden. Besides, I'm her best friend. She would have come to me."

"Are you sure?" Hannah didn't say anything else. She just kept silent and let Andrea work it out by herself.

Andrea sighed deeply and shook her head. "She might have wanted to call me, but she knows what Bill does for a living. Maybe she contacted one of the other girls we ran around with in high school."

"Do you have their numbers with you?"

"Of course. You never know when a hot property is going to hit the market, and I like to give my friends first crack." Andrea reached inside her purse and pulled out her cell phone. She punched in a number and then she looked up at Hannah. "I know it's crazy, but I'm still hungry. Will you get me a couple of Sally's biscuits?"

"Sure. I'll be right back."

"Bring some ham slices, too. And don't forget the butter and apricot jam."

"Coming right up."

Even though the situation with Janie was grim, Hannah was grinning as she left the bar and headed back to the buffet table. Andrea claimed she wasn't pregnant, but perhaps she just didn't know it yet. If her sister's breakfast this morning was any indication, Hannah would have a brand-new niece or nephew by Thanksgiving.

"Hannah?" Sally caught her on her way to the buffet table. "Dot Truman's not on the schedule for today. And I've been thinking about who might know where Janie's gone. I think you should talk to Alex Matthews."

"Is he one of the Connie Mac people?"

"No, and he's a she. Her first name is Alexandra, but she prefers Alex and she's my temporary assistant. I hired her the day after Dick left for Arizona, and she's fabulous. You must have seen her in the kitchen. She organized my staff when they wheeled out the buffet."

Hannah nodded, remembering the efficient dark-haired woman who'd directed Sally's kitchen help. "Janie and Alex are close?"

"Closer than most. It was one of those instant rapport things. They just clicked, you know?" Sally glanced at her watch. "Alex is upstairs right now, checking on the maids, but she'll be back in the kitchen in about ten minutes."

"We'll talk to her. Thanks, Sally."

After Sally had left on her rounds again, Hannah filled Andrea's plate and headed back to the bar. She got there just as Andrea was slipping her cell phone back into her purse. "Any luck?"

"No. I called everyone we hung around with in high school, and no one's seen Janie. They didn't even know she was in town. I think she must have left Lake Eden."

Hannah hoisted herself up on the bar stool and set the plate she'd filled in front of her sister. "Sally just gave me a possible lead."

Andrea sliced open a biscuit, spread it with butter and apricot jam, and slipped in a slice of ham. She took a bite and smiled. "Just let me finish eating and we'll go follow up on it."

Hannah bit her tongue to keep from voicing the comment that popped into her head. If they waited for Andrea to finish eating, Janie would have time to get halfway around the world in a rowboat.

They found Alex in the kitchen, taking her coffee break. After they had introduced themselves and told her that Sally had sent them, Hannah asked her about Janie.

"Yes, I know Janie." Alex looked a bit worried. "Is anything wrong?"

Hannah smiled to reassure her. She'd found that she

learned much more when she didn't alarm the people she questioned. "Janie's a good friend of ours. Andrea went to high school with her."

"Of course." Alex turned to Andrea with a smile. "I didn't connect the name at first. You're her best friend and you married the handsome quarterback. Janie flew back here for your wedding and she caught your bridal bouquet."

Andrea smiled back. "That's right. Bill helped me practice for a solid week and I pegged it straight at her."

"How did you meet Janie?" Hannah pressed on before Andrea could ask what else Janie had said about her wedding.

"One of the maids called in sick the day she checked in, and I took some fresh towels up to her room. She's a lovely girl."

"Then you didn't know her before she checked in at the inn?"

Alex shook her head. "We just got to talking and we discovered that we had a lot in common."

"Like what?" Hannah asked.

"Just a lot of little things. Janie's crazy about old musicals and so am I. Our favorite dessert is coffee ice cream with chocolate sauce, we do crossword puzzles to relax, and we both like to read biographies. Janie says we're birds of a feather."

"Do you happen to know where Janie went when she left the inn last night?" Hannah asked.

"I didn't see her at all last night. Why? Is there something wrong?"

Hannah started to shake her head, but then she reconsidered. If Alex was a friend, she deserved to know the situation. "We're not sure. Janie packed up all her things last night and left."

"She did?" Alex was clearly surprised. "Do you know why?"

"We think she might have had a fight with Connie Mac," Andrea answered the question.

"That's possible. I was at the desk when Mrs. MacIntyre

left, and she stomped out of here in a huff. Janie came down a minute or two later and I asked her why she wasn't riding in the limo. She said that Mrs. MacIntyre had told her to take her own car and that she was in a nasty mood."

"Do you think Janie quit?" Andrea asked.

"Oh, no. Janie needed her job and she's not a quitter. Mrs. MacIntyre probably fired her again."

Andrea's mouth opened, and Hannah sent her a warning glance. It snapped shut again and Hannah turned back to Alex. "You said *again*. Was Janie fired before?"

"Oh, yes. But she said it was never more than a few hours before Mrs. MacIntyre would call to rehire her."

"Why would she go back to a job like that?" Hannah was amazed.

"That's exactly what I asked her." Alex gave a little laugh. "And Janie said that Mrs. MacIntyre was the only fly in the ointment. She loved her job and she really liked all the people on the staff."

"How about Mr. MacIntyre?" Hannah glanced at her sister, but Andrea's mouth was glued shut.

"She absolutely adored him. She said he was a saint for putting up with his wife all these years, and that he deserved a lot better."

Hannah almost groaned aloud. She didn't think that Janie and Paul had been more than friends, but Bill and Mike would put a very different spin on Alex's answer.

"Janie never goes along to the book signings," Alex went on, "and we were going to get together this afternoon. I hope Mrs. MacIntyre called to rehire her this morning."

"She didn't," Hannah said, not relishing the task of telling someone else that Connie Mac was dead.

"But why? She needs Janie. No one else can put up with her. She went through twelve assistants the year before Janie came on board."

"I'm sure she *would* have called Janie," Andrea said, taking over, "but that was impossible. Connie Mac died last night.

Alex's eyes widened. "She's dead? Why didn't anyone tell

me? I thought her face was awfully red when she left yesterday afternoon, but I figured she was just angry. Was it her heart?"

Hannah clamped her lips shut to keep from saying, *Of course not. Connie Mac didn't have a heart.* Andrea had barged in and now *she* could deal with telling Alex how Connie Mac had died.

"Well . . . actually . . ." Andrea shot her sister a pleading glance, but Hannah pretended not to notice. "It was a little more serious than that. Connie Mac was . . . uh . . . killed."

"You mean *murdered?*" Alex gasped and her face turned pale.

Hannah looked over at Andrea. She still had that pleading look on her face. Andrea, the smooth talker who could handle any situation, needed to be bailed out.

"The police think it's murder, but it could be an accident," Hannah explained. "That's why we need to find Janie. She was with Connie Mac last night and we want to ask her what happened."

"Do the police think that Janie killed Connie Mac and ran away?" Alex looked sick at the thought.

Hannah took over. "They think it's possible. That's why we want to find her before they do. We want to help her."

Alex sat there quietly for a moment, and Hannah noticed that her hands were trembling. "I'd help you if I could, but I really don't know where Janie's gone."

"If she calls you, will you tell us?" Hannah asked.

"Yes, I will."

Andrea pulled out one of her cards and handed it to Alex. "Here's my cell phone number. Call me anytime, day or night."

"I will." Alex took the card and slipped it into her apron pocket. Then she blinked, and Hannah could see that she was fighting tears. "Just find her, please. And tell me the minute you do. Poor Janie must be so frightened, out there all alone."

There was nothing else to say, and Hannah motioned to Andrea. They had other people to see. It wasn't until they had left the kitchen that she asked the question that had been hovering in her mind ever since they'd concluded their interview. "Don't you think that Alex's reaction was a little strange?"

"What reaction?"

"When we told her that Janie was missing, her hands started to tremble. And when she asked us to hurry and find her, she was blinking back tears."

"That's not so strange," Andrea objected. "She was concerned."

"I realize that, but don't you think it was a little out of proportion?"

"Not really. I feel exactly the same way. Every time I think about how lonely and scared Janie must be, I get tears in my eyes."

"So do I, but we've known Janie all our lives. Alex only met her five days ago."

"Oh." Andrea was silent for a long moment. "You're right. What does it mean?"

"I'm not sure, but I think we'd better find out. Let's go to the lobby and plan our strategy."

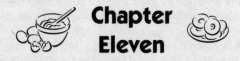

Chapter
Eleven

Hannah led Andrea into the lobby and they took two over-stuffed chairs next to the massive granite fireplace. It was as far from the desk as they could get, and they had the huge room all to themselves.

"Sally told me the granite slabs for the fireplace came from Cold Spring," Andrea informed her. "F. E. Laughlin used local granite and he had it carved with his own designs. Isn't it beautiful?"

"It's certainly impressive," Hannah said, deciding not to risk further comment. With murder foremost on her mind, the three-dimensional angels that appeared to be emerging from the gray-veined surface reminded her of headstones in a graveyard.

Andrea inched a little closer to the blaze that was burning in the grate and then unzipped her leather-bound organizer. "What do you want me to do first?"

"Go talk to Francine." Hannah found the page of notes she'd taken when they talked to Sally. "Find out what she knows about the fight that Connie Mac had with Kurt Howe. Then ask her opinion of the reporter who wrote the story about the ghost."

Andrea jotted it down with her gold Cross pen. "Do you

really think he might have murdered Connie Mac to add excitement to his ghost story?"

"Not really, but it's something we have to rule out. And don't forget to ask if Francine knows Janie."

"You want me to ask everyone about Janie, don't you?"

"Absolutely."

"I'm writing down a series of questions," Andrea said, her pen flying swiftly across the page. "I want to know the last time they saw her, any friends she talked about, and whether she ever mentioned a particular place she liked to go, like a hotel or a resort."

"That's a very good idea." Hannah was impressed. Andrea seemed to have the questions about Janie covered.

"Then I'll ask them to put themselves in Janie's place and tell me where they think she might . . ." Andrea stopped speaking and stood up. "My phone's ringing."

"I didn't hear anything."

"I switched it to vibrate so it wouldn't disturb us. Maybe it's Alex. We asked her to phone if Janie called."

Hannah thought that was a little too much to hope for, but she was on full alert as Andrea retrieved her cell phone and answered the call.

"Hello?" There was a pause and then Andrea smiled. "Hi, honey."

It had to be Bill, and Hannah settled back in her chair. Tracey was the only other person Andrea would call "honey."

"Of course Hannah's with me. We're out here at the inn. Sally said she could bake out here. Do you want to talk to her?"

Hannah reached out for the phone, but Andrea shook her head. She listened for another few moments and then she started to smile. "That's just great, honey. I'll see you in about half an hour."

"That was Bill," Andrea said, pressing a button and dropping the phone back into her coat pocket.

"I gathered that."

"They're on their way out here and they're bringing all your cookie dough."

Hannah gave a huge sigh of relief. Once she had her cookie dough, today's baking would be a snap. "Let's get our things together and go talk to Earl Flensburg about the man Connie Mac fired. I saw him drive in, and he should be finishing his first cup of coffee about now."

"Too bad Ray didn't wait a day to tell her what happened." Earl picked up the remainder of his glazed doughnut and stared at it thoughtfully. He was a bear of a man, and his quilted orange parka with the Winnetka County Towing Service insignia on the right front breast pocket made him look even larger than he was.

Hannah guessed what was on his mind. "Because then she wouldn't have had the chance to fire him?"

"Yeah. I should call him to tell him what happened, but I never got his number. Didn't get his last name either, come to think about it. We just need the owner's name for the form."

"Sally told us the accident wasn't his fault," Hannah prompted.

"That's right. A semi spun out in front of him and he took the ditch to avoid it. The van was fine, if you don't count the sissy color. Not a scratch on it."

"So the only thing damaged was Connie Mac's cake?" Andrea asked.

"That's about the size of it. Ray was fine, too, but he was shook up bad. I told him to sit in the rig while I hooked up. His face was as white as that snowbank he hit."

"Were you there when he called Connie Mac?" Hannah asked, even though Sally had already told her. It was always better to get things firsthand.

"You betcha. I let him make the call from my rig. He had the phone up to his ear real tight, but I could still hear her yelling at him."

"Connie Mac wasn't exactly known for her sweet disposition." Hannah ventured a small grin. "Didn't Ray tell her that he couldn't avoid the accident?"

" 'Course he did, but it didn't count for a hill of beans with her. Guess I should say I'm sorry she's dead, but I'm not. She was real nasty to Ray."

"From what we hear, she was nasty to a lot of people," Andrea commented.

"Doesn't surprise me. But chickens come home to roost, you know?"

"That's what they say," Hannah agreed. "Do you think those chickens had any help from Ray?"

"No way!" Earl shook his head emphatically. "All Ray wanted to do was crawl home with his tail between his legs. I seen enough people in my life to know he wasn't the killer type. Besides, he was nowhere near here last night."

"Are you sure?" Hannah asked, not willing to rule out Connie Mac's driver solely on Earl's assessment of his character.

"Sure, I'm sure. After she fired him, I dropped him out at the Quick Stop so's he could catch the bus home."

"Do you know where he lives?" Andrea asked the next question.

"Can't say as I do. He lives with his folks, though. He told me that. Hope they weren't too mad at him for losing his job. From my way of thinking, it was the best thing that ever happened to him. A clean-looking kid like Ray's gonna get another job real fast."

"Clean-looking?" Hannah prompted.

"Dark hair cut short, a real nice smile, and a polite way of talking. He called me 'sir,' and hardly nobody does that. Said he wanted to go to college, but he had to work for a year first."

"He does sound nice," Hannah commented. "What time did you drop him off at the Quick Stop?"

"I got my next call at four-thirty, and that was right after I dropped him off." Earl's eyes narrowed and he stared at Hannah suspiciously. "You gonna go check to make sure Ray got on that bus, even after I told you he couldn't have killed her?"

Hannah hesitated. She didn't want to hurt Earl's feelings, but she wasn't going to lie, either.

Andrea stepped in. "I think we should go out there and check. If Hannah and I can prove that Ray got on that bus, the police won't have to bring him back here to question him."

Earl thought it over for a minute. "That's a good idea. If the police drag Ray all the way back here, it would just about kill a sensitive kid like him. You girls go check. And tell Sean and Don I sent you."

Hannah stood in Sally's kitchen and watched as Bill and Mike carried in her cookie dough. There were thirty-five bowls, each covered with plastic wrap. The Winter Carnival guests wouldn't have to go hungry for cookies this afternoon.

Mike placed the bowl he was carrying on Sally's stainless-steel counter and turned to Bill. "Is that all?"

"I think so. I'll go back out and check."

"I really appreciate this, Bill," Hannah said, addressing her brother-in-law and pointedly ignoring Mike.

Mike's eyebrows shot up, but he didn't say anything until Bill had gone back out to the cruiser. Then he turned to Hannah with a frown. "Come on, Hannah. I know how hard it is for you to be locked out of your shop, but I was just doing my job."

"Some job!" Hannah muttered, but she had to admit he had a point. Perhaps it was time to lighten up a little and see what information she could weasel out of him.

"I don't like it when you're mad at me. How long am I going to be in the doghouse, anyway?"

The note in Mike's voice made Hannah fight back a grin. He sounded like a petulant little boy who'd just been told he couldn't have dessert until he finished his vegetables.

"Was that a smile?"

"It was the ghost of a smile," Hannah admitted. "And speaking of ghosts . . ."

"I heard all about it from Sheriff Grant. He said he got a call from someone who thought we should put Ezekiel's ghost on our suspect list."

"Sheriff Grant didn't take that seriously, did he?"

"No, not at first. Then I pointed out that the killer could have started the ghost story as a diversion to throw us off the track."

Hannah was impressed. She hadn't thought of that angle. "Then you're going to investigate the ghost?"

"It sounds a little crazy when you put it like that, but yes. If we find the person who started the ghost story, it could lead us to the killer."

Hannah bit back the urge to tell Mike who'd written the ghost story and why, but he'd told her not to interfere with his investigation, so he could figure it out by himself. "Any news about Janie?"

"No. You're not trying to find her, are you?"

"No," Hannah said, and it was the truth. They hadn't even started their search for Janie yet. "Did Doc Knight tell you when Connie Mac was killed?"

"Why do you want to know?"

Mike looked suspicious, and Hannah knew she had to give him a reason that had nothing to do with her investigation. "I have a vested interest. She was killed in my pantry, and something like that doesn't happen every day."

"I guess it can't hurt to tell you. Doc said the murder weapon was a heavy, rounded object, and she was killed between ten and midnight."

"From ten to midnight," Hannah repeated, and then she began to frown. "I just thought of something. Connie Mac must have been in the habit of staying out all night."

Mike looked surprised at her comment. "What makes you think that?"

"Because her husband didn't report her missing when she didn't come back to their room last night."

"You're barking up the wrong tree, Hannah. Mr. Mac-Intyre got in late, and they have a suite with connecting bedrooms. When he didn't hear any sounds coming from her room, he assumed that she'd already gone to sleep. He didn't know that she wasn't there until we called him this morning."

Hannah didn't say what was running through her mind. After the nasty mood Connie Mac had been in that afternoon, she couldn't blame Paul for not wanting to wake her. "Where was Paul MacIntyre last night?"

"Out at the Tri-County Mall, doing a walk-through of the kitchen boutique with the mall manager. After that, they went over all the paperwork to make sure everything was in order. Alan Carpenter was with him, and they both said they didn't get back here until after midnight."

"Then they're both in the clear, right?"

"They will be if their story checks out." Mike reached out and took Hannah's arm. "Did you know that Norman was at the Ezekiel Jordan House last night?"

"He told me. He also told me that he didn't notice anything wrong at The Cookie Jar when he left at nine."

"And you believed him?"

"Of course I did." Hannah pulled back slightly. She didn't like the turn their conversation was taking. "What are you getting at, Mike?"

"Something came up when we did interviews in the area this morning. We found out that Norman had a compelling reason to be angry with Mrs. MacIntyre."

Hannah took a giant step back and stared at Mike in shock. "You think *Norman* killed Connie Mac?"

"It's possible. I spoke to your mother and she said Mrs. MacIntyre was a royal pain when Norman photographed her. She didn't like any of the old-fashioned costumes, and it took all of your mother's tact to persuade her to wear one of them."

"My mother's tact? My mother doesn't *have* any tact! She's even worse than I am."

"Maybe, but she said Mrs. MacIntyre made Norman move all his equipment at least six times, and she was very condescending to him. Your mother thought Norman showed remarkable restraint, but she could tell that he was steaming. The way I see it, Norman's the type that suffers in silence.

And then, long after the situation is over, he dwells on how ineffectual he was. It preys on his mind, you know. He thinks, *I should have done this, I should have done that, but I just stood there and took it like a wimp*. He gets more and more frustrated at his own inability to act until . . . wham! The whole thing explodes in an act of violence."

Hannah's mouth dropped open. Mike was spouting pop psychology like a talk-show host. She wanted to tell him to stuff it, but that would do Norman more harm than good. "But it doesn't track, Mike. You said that Connie Mac was killed between ten and midnight, and Norman left the Ezekiel Jordan house at nine."

"That's what he says, but no one saw him leave. He could have left at ten. Or eleven."

"Norman was home at eleven. I called him after I got home last night."

"Why did you call *him*?"

"Just to talk," Hannah said, not wanting to get into the real reason she'd called Norman. "He sounded perfectly normal to me."

"That doesn't prove anything. If he killed her at ten, he had a whole hour to calm down. Look, Hannah . . . I know it's not something you want to believe about Norman, but you've got to admit it's possible it happened the way I just said."

Hannah closed her eyes. If she stared at Mike's earnest face looming over hers, she'd probably hit him right in the beak. And *that* would bear out his theory! She took a deep breath, collected her wits, and looked up at him again.

"Well, isn't it possible?" Mike prodded her for an answer.

Obviously, the man didn't know when to quit. Hannah sighed and gathered herself to speak in her calmest, most rational voice. "No, Mike. It isn't possible. Norman told me about all the trouble he had with Connie Mac right after we left The Cookie Jar last night. He was over being miffed with her. As a matter of fact, he was even joking about it."

"Of course he was. Norman wouldn't let you know how angry he was, not if he was planning to kill Mrs. MacIntyre later."

"He wasn't planning on killing her," Hannah argued, even though she knew it wouldn't do any good. She took a deep breath, calmed her jangled nerves, and addressed exactly what he had said about Norman's motivation. "Listen to me, Mike. The situation with Connie Mac didn't prey on Norman's mind, he didn't explode in an act of violence, and he didn't kill Connie Mac."

Mike didn't look at all convinced. "Why not?"

"Because Norman's not a killer. Besides, if every person Connie Mac ordered around had taken offense and clubbed her, she would have looked like a piece of Swiss steak!"

"How do you know that? Have you been running around out here asking questions?"

Hannah sighed. She'd already promised herself that she wouldn't lie to him. Mislead perhaps, but not lie.

"Have you?" Mike prodded her for an answer.

"You have my word, Mike." Hannah looked him straight in the eye. "I haven't seen or spoken to any of the Connie Mac people."

"Then how did you know that Mrs. MacIntyre ordered people around?"

"It's simple. You're forgetting that Andrea and I took her on a tour of Lake Eden. It was impossible not to notice something like that."

"Oh," Mike said, appearing to accept that at face value. "For a minute there, I thought you were playing detective again."

"There's no way I'll ever play detective again," Hannah declared, pushing down the little niggle of guilt that she felt. She wasn't going to *play* at being a detective. She was going to *be* a detective and solve Connie Mac's murder before he did.

Mike reached out to give her a hug. "I've got to get back to work. Just promise me that you'll be careful around Norman."

"Norman didn't kill Connie Mac."

"I know you don't believe that he could do it, but I understand Norman a lot better than you do."

"Really?" Hannah worked hard to keep the sarcasm out of her voice. As far as she knew, Mike hadn't spent more than a few casual moments with Norman.

"That's right. Men understand each other better than a woman ever could. I can appreciate your loyalty to Norman, and I'm not asking you to believe that he's the killer. I just want you to stay away from him until we find out, one way or the other."

Hannah stared after him as he walked out the door. In just one morning, Mike had managed to close down her business, tie her down with a promise not to interfere with his investigation, accuse a man she was dating of murder, and claim that a woman couldn't possibly understand a man's motives. This whole thing with Mike was enough to make her pick up the phone and make an appointment with the nearest shrink. For the life of her, she couldn't understand how such an obstinate, boneheaded chauvinist could make her pulse race and turn her insides to jelly.

Chapter
Twelve

Hannah had just finished stashing the last bowl of cookie dough in Sally's walk-in cooler when Andrea came into the kitchen. There was a smile on her face and she looked excited.

"Hi, Hannah. Sally said I'd find you in here. I got tons of information from Bill and I wrote it all down." Andrea patted her leather organizer. "And I've got something else, too."

Hannah watched as Andrea opened her large leather purse and pulled out a bulky packet. "My recipe file?"

"That's right. Bill snitched it when Mike's back was turned. He told me this kind of surface couldn't be dusted for fingerprints anyway, but you know what kind of a stickler Mike is when it comes to procedure. He wasn't even going to let you take your purse this morning until Bill got after him."

"Thank Bill for me. This saves me a whole lot of time." Hannah gave a big sigh of relief as she took the packet. She'd been planning to drive back to her condo to pick up copies of her recipes, and Bill had saved her the trip.

"Before I forget, I'm supposed to tell you that Lisa's on her way. Bill spotted them at one of the venues and he told her that you were all set up to bake out here." Andrea took the stool next to Hannah's and stared at her sister for a moment. "Okay. What's wrong? Did you have a fight with Mike?"

"Not exactly."

"But Mike did something, right?"

"You could say that."

"Just give me the highlights," Andrea coaxed. "I need to know what Mike said, so I can compare it to what Bill told me. That's the only way we'll know if they're holding out on us."

Hannah hesitated. She didn't really want to talk about her conversation with Mike, but she had learned some things about the official investigation. "Okay. Mike said they haven't found Janie, Doc Knight put Connie Mac's time of death between ten and midnight, the murder weapon was a heavy, rounded object, and Paul's alibi is Alan Carpenter. Both of them claimed they were together at the boutique last night and they didn't get back here until after midnight. Unless it's a conspiracy, they're both in the clear."

"Bill told me all that. What else?"

"What makes you think there's anything else?"

"I can read it on your face."

Hannah caved in. Andrea had always been able to tell when she was upset. "Mike told me that Norman's a suspect."

"*Our* Norman?" Andrea's mouth dropped open when Hannah nodded. "But . . . why?"

"Bill didn't tell you?" Hannah answered her sister's question with one of her own.

"Bill didn't say a word about Norman. Why does Mike think he's a suspect?"

"Mother."

"*Our* mother?"

"One and the same. She told Mike that Connie Mac was nasty to Norman and now Mike thinks that Norman went back to The Cookie Jar last night to get even with her."

"That's crazy! Bill was with Mike when they talked to Mother, and he didn't say anything about Norman being a suspect."

"Maybe he didn't want to tell you."

Andrea shook her head. "Bill would have told me. He tells me everything. And that means Bill doesn't think that Norman did it, but Mike must have some reason to . . ." Andrea stopped in mid-sentence, and a huge grin spread over her face. "Of course. I get it."

"What do you get? And why are you grinning like that?"

"Because it's so obvious. Mike's the only one who thinks Norman is a suspect. And that's because he *wants* Norman to be guilty. Don't you get it, Hannah?"

Hannah thought about it for a moment and then she shrugged. "Not really. It can't be personal. Mike's always said he liked Norman."

"Naturally. He can't admit that he's jealous. That would make him look bad. So what does Mike do? He accuses his rival of murder. I bet he even told you to stay away from Norman. He did, didn't he?"

Hannah nodded. "Yes, but . . ."

"I knew it. I'm right! And you didn't even see it!"

"See what?" Hannah was puzzled.

"Mike's in love with you, Hannah. That's the reason he suspects Norman."

"That sounds like something Doctor Love would say." Hannah referred to the psychologist who answered callers' questions on KCOW talk radio. "Have you been listening to her show?"

"Of course not. I don't have any reason to listen. I have a very happy marriage."

"I'm glad to hear it," Hannah said, and she was, especially since she suspected that her sister's family was about to increase by one.

"It's like this, Hannah. Men in love behave irrationally. Since Mike is behaving irrationally, he must be in love in you. That's simple logic."

"That's bad logic," Hannah corrected her. "You're affirming the consequent."

"I'm doing what?"

Hannah thought about explaining, but this wasn't the time to give her sister a lecture in Logic 101. "Never mind. But if Mike is in love with me, why didn't he just send me a valentine?"

"Because Valentine's Day is over and maybe he wasn't in love with you then. He might have just realized it this morning. I know I'm right, Hannah. Mike is definitely in love with you."

Hannah made a face. "If that's love, I don't need it. Telling me that Norman was a suspect was an awful thing for Mike to do. He lied to me."

"Mike didn't lie. Norman *is* a suspect, at least in Mike's mind. I'm sure he believes he has some kind of case against Norman."

"But Norman didn't kill Connie Mac."

"I know that, and you know that, but Mike doesn't."

Hannah frowned as the full implication of her sister's words sunk in. "But Mike's a good cop. I can't believe that he would make up a case against Norman."

"Of course he wouldn't, but he's going into this investigation with a bias. Innocent people have been convicted before, you know. And police work is so objective."

"Subjective."

"Okay, subjective. I always get those two mixed up. I tell you, Hannah, Mike doesn't even know he's biased against Norman. It's totally unconscious."

"Subconscious."

Andrea rolled her eyes at the ceiling. "Stop correcting me. I'm trying to make a point here. I'm sure Mike will come to his senses eventually, but Norman could find himself in a lot of hot water in the meantime."

Hannah thought about that for a moment and then she sighed. "I hate to admit it, but you could be right. We'd better find out if Norman has an alibi."

"Hi, you two." Lisa breezed into the kitchen. "I dropped Dad off at the seniors' center and Tracey's in the dining room with Bill and Mike. They're having breakfast and she's snitching their bacon."

"That's fine." Andrea nodded absently.

Lisa walked over to join them, but she stopped short as she noticed their serious expressions. "What's wrong?"

"Mike thinks Norman's a suspect," Hannah told her.

"Norman Rhodes?"

"That's right," Andrea confirmed it. "Did you happen to see him last night between ten and midnight?"

"Not me," Lisa replied, sitting down next to them, "but I'll ask Herb. He bowled last night and then he came over for night lunch."

"What's night lunch?" Andrea asked her.

"That's what Herb's mother calls the little snack you have before bedtime so you won't get hungry in the middle of the night. She told me to try it with Dad and it's working just great. He never wakes up and wanders around in the dark anymore."

Hannah tried to keep her mouth shut, but she just had to ask. "How is Marge getting along with your dad?"

"They're just great together," Lisa said with a smile. "Marge is always offering to come and sit with him when Herb and I want to go out. They used to date in high school, you know. Now that Mom's dead and Herb's father is gone, I keep thinking that Marge and Dad might have gotten together again, if only . . . you know."

Hannah understood what Lisa wasn't saying, and she reached out to give her arm a sympathetic pat. Marge Beeseman had never been credited with being a martyr, and it was unlikely that she'd choose to marry a man who'd been diagnosed with Alzheimer's. "A lot of times life isn't fair."

"I'd better let you two get to work," Andrea said, rising to her feet. "I'm going up to talk to Francine and I'll take Tracey along. She adores babies, and she hasn't seen little Danny yet. I'll check in with you right afterwards, Hannah."

Lisa waited until Andrea had left, and then she turned to

Hannah. "I didn't want to say anything in front of your sister, but Tracey might have gotten us into trouble."

"What happened?"

"We ran into Edna Ferguson when I dropped Dad off at the seniors' center, and she was in a panic about what to serve for dessert at the banquet."

Hannah groaned, guessing the rest. It wasn't the first time her precocious niece had volunteered her services. "Did Tracey promise Edna that we'd bake the Winter Carnival cake?"

"I'm afraid she did. She told Edna that her Aunt Hannah could do anything."

Hannah laughed. "I guess I should be flattered, but there's no way we can replace Connie Mac's cake. We could bake it, no problem, but cake decoration isn't my long suit."

"Mine, either. I can decorate cookies, but doing a cake is a huge project. Do you want me to call Edna and tell her that we can't do it?"

Hannah shook her head. "We'll just give her buckets of Little Snowballs for dessert."

"Snowballs?" Lisa looked shocked. "You're joking, aren't you?"

"I'm perfectly serious. The snowballs I'm talking about are cookies that my Grandma Ingrid used to bake. We'll present them in the crystal ice buckets Sally uses to chill champagne, and they'll fit right in with the Winter Carnival theme."

"They sound just perfect." Lisa glanced over at the swinging door as it opened. "Here comes Alex. Sally introduced us when I came in through the dining room."

Alex spotted them sitting at the counter and hurried over. "Sally said to tell you that you could use anything in the pantry, and she sent me in to help you bake."

"That's great," Hannah told her. "We can use all the help we can get. Just let me check my recipe file and I'll give you a list of what we need."

While Lisa and Alex retrieved the bowls of cookie dough from the cooler, Hannah found her grandmother's recipe and made a list of the ingredients. When she was through, she handed it to Alex. "Could you gather these up for us? We'll bake the cookies for the Winter Carnival first, and then we'll start in on the Little Snowballs."

"Go do what you have to do, Hannah," Lisa said after Alex had left them. "I'll handle the baking with Alex."

"Are you sure?" Hannah felt a little guilty. Every time she got involved in an investigation, Lisa ended up doing all the baking.

"I'm positive. The faster you solve Connie Mac's murder, the faster we can get back into our own kitchen." Lisa gestured toward the bowls of dough they'd set on the counter. "I should have these ready for you by noon."

"Great. I'll drop them off at the venues. You shouldn't have to do everything."

"Okay, but only if you want to."

"I do. I have to go out there anyway. Norman's a judge at the dogsled competition, and I need to warn him that he's a suspect."

"I hope he's got an alibi, and I won't forget to check with Herb. Is there anything else I can do?"

Hannah started to shake her head, but then she thought of something. "See if you can get Alex talking about her background. I need to know everything I can about her."

"I can do that," Lisa said, and then she began to frown. "Do you think Alex killed Connie Mac?"

"No, but everyone's a suspect until we can eliminate them. And there's something about Alex that puzzles me. She was really upset when she found out that Janie was missing, and they only met a couple of days ago. I thought she overreacted, and I'm wondering why."

"Okay. I'll find out everything I can for you," Lisa promised. "Working with you, I've learned how to get people to spill their guts."

Hannah went out the door with a smile on her face. Perhaps some people wouldn't regard what Lisa had said as a compliment, but she did.

* * *

"Look, Aunt Hannah. Isn't Danny wonderful?" Tracey looked up and smiled. "He's got all his toes. Francine took his booties off so I could count."

Hannah laughed. She'd been keeping Tracey occupied while Andrea spoke to Sally's stepmother, an attractive silver-haired lady whose smile seemed to be a permanent fixture on her face. "Does Danny have all of his fingers?"

"Oh, yes. He has eight and that's just right."

"Not ten?" Hannah couldn't resist teasing her niece a bit.

"Of course not, Aunt Hannah. You know that people have only eight fingers. The other two are thumbs."

"That's right. I was just testing you. Thumbs aren't fingers."

Tracey nodded. "But they're really important. They're opposable and we couldn't pick up things if we didn't have them. Watch and see how Danny does it." Tracey picked up a rattle and dangled it front of Danny. The baby reached up to grab it, and Tracey leaned down to kiss the top of his head. "Good boy, Danny. You did that just fine."

"Did Miss Cox teach you that in school?" Hannah asked, wondering how Janice Cox, Tracey's teacher at Kiddie Korner, was managing to cope with such a bright four-year-old.

"No, Mr. Herman told me about it when we looked at his animal collection. Monkeys and gorillas have opposable thumbs, and there was another animal, too. I think it had something to do with oranges."

"Orangutans?"

"That's it."

Hannah reached out to ruffle Tracey's blond hair. "You liked Mr. Herman?"

"Oh, yes. He knows lots of things, but he told me that sometimes his memory turns into a butterfly."

"A butterfly?"

Tracey nodded solemnly. "He has to sneak up on it if he wants to catch it and there's a trick he uses. If he can't remember something right away, he makes himself think of something else. Then it flutters straight into his mind."

"Ready, Tracey?" Andrea came over to take her daughter's hand. "Thank Francine for letting you play with Danny."

After Tracey had thanked Francine, Andrea herded her toward the door. Hannah lagged behind to take one last peek at Danny. He'd fallen asleep with his fist in his mouth, and as she stood there, she found herself wishing that her life had taken a different turn. If she'd married, she'd probably have children by now.

"He's a very good baby," Francine said softly, reaching out to straighten his blanket. "Sally and Dick are so lucky."

"Yes, they are. I'd better go. I'll see you later, Francine."

Hannah walked out and shut the door softly behind her. Danny was sweet and he'd definitely awakened her maternal instincts.

"What took you so long?" Andrea called out from the end of the hallway.

"I was just looking at Danny." Hannah hurried to catch up with her sister and her niece. They had a murder to solve, and she could think about her lack of progeny later.

Chapter Thirteen

It was only five miles to the Quick Stop, and Hannah negotiated the icy roads with a practiced ease. Once she'd reached a straight stretch of highway, she glanced at her sister. "Did you find out anything interesting?"

"A couple of things." Andrea swiveled in her seat to look back at her daughter. "We can talk about it. Tracey's got one of her books and she never listens to anyone when she's reading."

"That'll come in handy when she's sharing a dorm room in college," Hannah said, remembering the times she'd lost herself in her studies when her roommates were discussing the men they were dating.

"Francine feels awful about mentioning Ezekiel's ghost. She had no idea that reporter would take her seriously. His name is Larry Kruger, by the way. And I was right about Connie Mac's ancestors. Her great-great-uncle was F. E. Laughlin's secretary."

"But was he playing in that poker game?" Hannah stepped on the gas to pass a lumbering bus.

"Francine says he could have been. F. E. always took his secretary along when he came to Lake Eden. He liked to work in the daytime and relax at night. And we know his secretary was there, because Francine found a letter he'd written on that date."

"All right. You convinced me," Hannah conceded, turning off the highway to take the access road. The Quick Stop was impossible to miss, even in a near-blizzard. The old wooden building was painted bright red with yellow trim around the windows, and it loomed like a beacon against the banks of snow.

Andrea waited until Hannah had parked at the side of the building. "It's time to put your book away, Tracey. We're here."

"But I'm just getting to the best part." Tracey looked up from her book reluctantly. "Can't I stay here and read?"

"It's too cold, honey. You'd turn into an icicle in two seconds flat."

"But Aunt Hannah can leave the heater on. I won't touch anything, I promise."

Andrea shook her head. "That's not a good idea. Come on, Tracey. If you come inside with us, I'll buy you a snack."

Hannah had all she could do not to laugh. Andrea, the mother who'd vowed to do everything perfectly, was bribing her daughter with fast food.

"Okay, Mommy." Tracey shut her book and stashed it in her backpack. Then she looked up at her mother and grinned. "Can I have a hot dog?"

"*May* I have a hot dog," Hannah corrected her.

"You don't have to ask, Aunt Hannah. You're all grown up and you can eat anything you want to."

Andrea cracked up and so did Hannah. When they'd recovered, Andrea turned to her sister with a teasing smile. "See what you get for correcting people all the time? Now you'll have to eat one of Sean and Don's hot dogs."

"That's not exactly a punishment," Hannah informed her, "especially if it's smothered with mustard and pickles."

"That's exactly the way I like mine," Tracey commented, zipping up her parka and waiting for her mother to get out and open her door.

After Tracey had climbed out of her truck, Hannah retrieved a bag of the twins' favorite cookies. She never sold day-old cookies in her shop, but the twins wouldn't mind. Her cookies were a whole lot fresher than the cookies they sold in little plastic packages.

The snow crunched underfoot as they walked the few feet to the front door. The building itself was almost fifty years old, and the twins had spent one whole summer renovating it. They'd added living quarters in the rear, put on a new roof, and painted it inside and out. Their color choices more than made up for the black-and-white Minnesota winter landscape outside the windows. The front counter was bright blue, the shelves were bright yellow, and the inner walls were a brilliant green.

The first aroma that hit Hannah's nose when they pushed open the door was of freshly brewed coffee. Quick Stop coffee was a source of controversy in Lake Eden. Some people said it was so thick, your spoon would stand straight up in the cup. Others argued that you'd lose your spoon if you stirred it for more than a second, because the acid would melt it away. Hannah wasn't sure which opinion was accurate, since she'd never had occasion to put it to the test. She drank her coffee black.

"Hi, Hannah. Tell me that bag is what I think it is." Sean, or perhaps it was Don, looked up from the newspaper he was reading at the counter. The newspaper was covering the name embroidered on his purple Quick Stop shirt, and Hannah had never been able to tell the twins apart.

"It is." Hannah set the bag on the counter. "I brought you a dozen Twin Chocolate Delights."

"Those are our favorites, and not just because of the name. I've been meaning to talk to you about your cookies. Do you think we could work out a deal to stock them out here?"

"Why not?" Hannah smiled at him. New business was always welcome.

"What'll it be? It's my treat."

"Just coffee, please. It smells wonderful."

"And for you?" He turned to Andrea.

"I'll have the same," Andrea answered, "With extra sugar and cream."

"And how about you, little lady?"

"I'd like a hot dog, please," Tracey spoke up, "but only if Mommy says it's okay."

"I guess we'd better ask her, then." Sean, or Don, slid off his stool and rose to his feet. Hannah caught a glimpse of the name on his shirt. This twin was Don. "Is it okay, Mommy?"

Andrea nodded. "She likes it with pickles and mustard, but go a little light on the mustard. And give her a package of chips, too. The plain kind, not flavored."

"Where's Sean today?" Hannah asked, following him to the glass-enclosed spit where the hotdogs seemed to turn eternally.

"I'm Sean."

"But . . ." Hannah began to frown. "Your shirt says you're Don."

"That's because it's Don's shirt. Mine haven't come back from the laundry yet." Sean glanced up at the clock that hung over the counter, then pressed a buzzer near the cash register. "Don's favorite program just ended. He'll be out here in a second."

When Don arrived, Andrea chatted with him while Sean prepared Tracey's hot dog. Once it had been decorated with mustard and chopped pickles, Sean wrapped it in a sheet of Quick Stop waxed paper and placed it in a cardboard carry-out box with a package of chips.

"Here you go." Sean handed the takeout box to Tracey and gestured toward an area near the front windows. "We have tables over there."

The tables had been painted an array of bright colors, and Andrea pointed to the bright orange one, the one farthest from the counter. "Why don't you eat your lunch at the orange table, honey? Your aunt Hannah and I need to talk to Sean and Don."

"Okay, Mommy," Tracey said with a resigned sigh. "I just knew you were going to talk about grownup stuff again."

When Tracey had left, Don turned to Andrea. "Grownup stuff?"

"She's talking about Connie Mac's murder. You heard about it, didn't you?"

Don frowned as he nodded. "The KCOW news team interrupted *Video Auction,* and I was all set to call in a bid on a coatrack with antlers instead of hooks. I thought we could use it by the front door."

"What about the murder?" Sean asked, getting back to Andrea's original question. "Do they know who did it yet?"

Hannah shook her head. "That's one of the reasons we wanted to talk to you. They're investigating anyone who might have had a reason to kill Connie Mac, and we found out that she fired her van driver that afternoon. Earl Flensburg said he dropped him off here yesterday afternoon to catch the bus home. His first name is Ray, he's in his early twenties, and he has short, dark hair."

"I remember him," Sean said. "Winnie Henderson was here buying new wiper blades and he offered to put them on for her. He sure seemed like a nice guy to me."

"That's what Earl said. We're just trying to find out if he has an alibi for the time of the murder. Did you see him get on the bus?"

"Yes. I was out front pumping gas and I saw him board."

"Where was he going?" Andrea asked.

Sean shrugged. "North. That's all I know. We're just a stop on the highway. The driver pulls up and honks his horn and the passengers go out to buy their tickets directly from him."

"He'll be back here around noon if you want to talk to him," Don added. "He's got a short run on Saturdays."

Andrea reached in her purse, pulled out two business cards, and handed one to each twin. "Could you have him call me on my cell phone when he gets in? It's really important."

"Okay," Sean promised, and then he turned to his brother. "You stand in front of the bus so he can't pull out, and I'll drag him in to the phone."

"No, *you* stand in front of the bus," Don objected.

Hannah grinned. The twins had a long history of arguing with each other. "Just work it out before noon. I don't care who does what as long as that driver calls Andrea before he puts his bus back in gear."

"Can I go see Grandma again?" Tracey asked, trudging through the snow to Hannah's cookie truck. "Please, Mommy?"

"Are you sure Grandma wants you to come back?"

"I'm positive. Grandma said she'd find a dress for me to wear, and I can help her show off her house. And Grandma Carrie said Uncle Norman would take my picture, too."

Hannah's eyebrows shot up. "*Grandma* Carrie?"

"That's what she told me to call her. And my real grandma said it was okay, because someone was bound to come to their senses eventually."

"Oh, brother!" Hannah muttered.

Tracey climbed into the back of the van and waited for her mother to get in. Once Andrea was settled in her seat, Tracey tapped her on the shoulder. "Why does Aunt Hannah look so funny? Does she have a headache?"

"I think she does."

"Then you should give her an aspirin, but we have to know exactly what kind of headache it is. It's very important."

"Why is that?" Hannah asked her.

"Because they have aspirin for different types of headaches. I learned all about it on TV. What type of headache is yours, Aunt Hannah?"

"It's the *mother* of all headaches," Hannah quipped, "and if they ever invent a special aspirin for that, I'll buy a whole case."

Hannah and Andrea waited in the back room of the Ezekiel Jordan House while Delores helped Tracey change into a costume in one of the two dressing rooms. Hannah opened the door to take a peek at the unoccupied cubicle and was surprised to see that her mother had decorated it to look like a man's dressing room. The wallpaper was gray with a silver stripe, and hunting prints hung on the walls. There was an oval mirror on a stand, a wooden rack with ball-and-claw feet that had been fashioned to hold items of clothing, and a high-backed chair sitting next to a table that sported a set of silver-backed brushes and combs.

"Oh, Hannah! Just look at this darling dress!"

Hannah shut the door and turned to look at her sister, who was examining the contents of a chifforobe that had been placed against the far wall. A variety of women's dresses hung inside, and Andrea removed a burgundy silk and held it up for her to see.

"I think I'll wear this for my picture. What do you think?"

"It's a nice color," Hannah said, frowning a bit at the tight waistline. From where she was standing, it looked ridiculously small. "Are you sure it's not too small for you?"

"I can get into it. It comes with a corset that pushes you up and nips you in at the waist. One of the maid's jobs was to lace you in."

"What if you didn't have a maid?"

"Then you looped the strings around a bedpost and used it to pull them tight. You've seen pictures from that period. That's why all the fashionable women had hour-glass figures."

"And misshapen ribs," Hannah added. "They also fainted a lot, probably because they couldn't breathe."

"It'll only be for a couple of minutes, just until Norman snaps the picture, and I want to look authentic. I think I should ask Bill to wear one of those tall silk hats."

Hannah glanced up at the rack that held the hats and began to chuckle. The only hat her brother-in-law liked was a baseball cap. "Do you think he'll do it?"

"Of course he will. Bill will do anything to make me happy. How about you? What are you going to wear?"

"I'm not having my picture taken."

"Yes, you are. Mother signed you up for a group picture with us. She wants to hang it on her wall."

Hannah groaned. The camera was her worst enemy. The darned thing always caught her with a crooked smile or one eye half-closed. To refuse to be in the portrait would mean an argument with Andrea *and* her mother, and she just didn't have the energy for that. "I'll do it, but I'll be the unfashionable aunt. At least I won't have to wear a corset that way."

"But it's going to hang on Mother's wall. You really should look your best. Just let me find something in here for you and . . ."

"Look at me, Mommy!" Tracey called out, emerging from the dressing room in a sky blue dress with a ruffled white pinafore. "Grandma says I look precious, and she even gave me this old teddy bear to carry around."

"*Antique* teddy bear," Delores corrected her. "It's a Steiff, and you have to be very careful with it. It belonged to Ezekiel Jordan's youngest daughter."

"I will, Grandma. I promise."

"Let's go, dear." Delores herded her toward the door that connected with the main part of the house. "You'll say your speech right after you enter the girls' room upstairs."

"I know, Grandma. 'This is my room. I sleep here with my sisters, Emily, Catherine, and Lucinda. My father and mother gave me this teddy bear for my fourth birthday. His name is Brownie and I love him very much.'"

"Wonderful!" Delores clapped her hands and then turned to them. "Tell Tracey how wonderful she was, girls."

"You were wonderful, honey," Andrea said with a smile.

"Yes, you were," Hannah seconded. "Do you have any more to say?"

"Just one more thing. When the guests are ready to leave, I stand by the front door and say, 'Thank you for coming to see the Ezekiel Jordan House that my Grandma Delores and my Grandma Carrie made.'"

The words *Grandma Carrie* set off warning bells in Hannah's mind. Every Lake Eden resident who took the tour would hear Tracey, and the phone lines would overload with rumors that she was about to marry Norman.

"We'd better run along, dear," Delores said, taking Tracey's hand. "Our audience is waiting."

Hannah walked over to grab her mother's arm. "Go ahead, Tracey. I need to talk to your grandma for a minute." She waited until Tracey was well out of earshot, and then she turned to her mother with fire in her eyes. "How could you, Mother! You know what people are going to think if Tracey calls . . ."

"Delores? I'm early." The back door opened and Luanne Hanks rushed in, cutting Hannah off in the middle of her planned tirade. She stopped short as she saw Andrea and Hannah, and then her face lit up in a smile. "Hi, Andrea. Hello, Hannah. How are you two? I haven't seen you in a while."

"We're fine," Hannah said, putting on a smile for Luanne's benefit.

Luanne caught the tension in the air and she glanced uneasily between Hannah and Delores. "Uh . . . if you're busy right now, I can come back later."

"No, dear." Delores shook her head. "I have to check on the tour group. Stay and visit with Andrea and Hannah until I get back."

Hannah sighed as her mother made good her escape. They would definitely have words later. Then she noticed that Luanne was carrying her Pretty Girl cosmetic case. "Are the portraits starting early?"

"No, I just came in to chat with your mother."

"You're not working at the café today?" Andrea asked her.

"I'm on vacation. Rose figured there wouldn't be much business, and she told me to take a week off."

"I hope it's a paid vacation." Hannah knew that Luanne needed every cent she could earn to support her mother and her two-year-old daughter, Susie.

"It is. Rose is paying me my regular salary and Norman's paying me, too. I'm making double the money for half the hours."

"That's great, Luanne!" Hannah was relieved.

"That's not the half of it. If the ladies who come in like Pretty Girl makeup, I might get some new customers."

"That reminds me," Andrea said. "I'm completely out of mascara and eyeliner. Do you have any with you?"

Hannah silently blessed her sister as Luanne opened her makeup kit and gathered up the items that Andrea had mentioned. She knew Andrea didn't use Pretty Girl makeup, but she bought it anyway to help Luanne. Hannah had done the same, and she had a guest bathroom medicine cabinet filled with unused makeup to prove it. Adding a few more things to the collection wouldn't break her budget, and Hannah walked over to the table where Luanne had set her makeup case. "I need another lipstick, Luanne."

"Where did the last one go?" Luanne asked, giving Hannah a suspicious look. "I've never seen you wear it."

Hannah knew that Luanne had a strong aversion to anything she regarded as charity, and she apologized to Moishe in absentia for what she was about to say. "My cat knocked it off my bathroom counter and it ended up in the toilet. I fished it out to save myself from a plumbing bill, but I didn't want to . . . well . . . you know."

"I'm really glad you didn't!" Luanne plucked a lipstick from her case. "I have your color right here, Hannah."

"Did you do Connie Mac's makeup yesterday?" Hannah asked, selecting two more items and handing Luanne the money for her purchases.

"No. I was all ready to come in, but Norman called and told me that she was having her personal beautician do it before she left the inn. I never even got to see her."

Hannah bit her tongue to keep from saying, *You didn't miss much.*

"Hannah?" Delores poked her head in the back room. "Could you come here for a minute?"

Hannah walked over, even though she felt like refusing. It wouldn't be polite to get into a knock-'em-down, drag-'em-out fight with her mother in front of Luanne. "What is it, Mother?"

"I thought you should know that I changed Tracey's last speech," Delores said in a hushed voice. "You were right. I overstepped."

Hannah's mouth fell open in shock. Her mother had never apologized to her before. She knew she should let sleeping dogs lie, but her curiosity got the better of her. "What made you decide to change it, Mother?"

"Carrie says Norman's going through a rebellious stage and she thought it might be pushing him too far. The last thing we want to do is upset the applecart."

Twin Chocolate Delights

Preheat oven to 350°F,
rack in the middle position

1 cup butter *(2 sticks—melted)*
2 ½ cups white sugar
½ cup cocoa *(unsweetened, for baking)*
2 teaspoons baking soda
1 teaspoon salt
2 teaspoons vanilla
4 beaten eggs *(just whip them up with a fork)*
3 cups flour *(no need to sift)*
1 cup chopped nuts *(optional—your choice of nut)*
2 cups chocolate chips

Melt butter in a large microwave-safe bowl. Add the sugar and mix. Then add the cocoa, soda, salt, and vanilla and stir until smooth. Add the beaten eggs and stir thoroughly. Mix in the flour, the chopped nuts *(if you want to use them)*, and then the chocolate chips.

Place rounded teaspoons of dough on a greased cookie sheet, 12 to a standard sheet. *(They'll flatten out as you bake them.)*

Bake at 350°F for 10 minutes. Cool on the cookie sheet for 2 minutes, then remove them to a wire rack to complete cooling.

Mother loves these cookies. If I bake them when she's mad at me, she sweetens right up.

Twin Chocolate Delights cookies should freeze well, but I can't swear to that—they never last long enough to try it.

Chapter
Fourteen

"Do you want to put your coat in a locker?" Andrea asked as they entered the Tri-County Mall.

"No, we won't be here that long." Hannah gazed around her at the throngs of people. "It's only ten-thirty. What are all these people doing out here so early?"

"The mall opens at nine and a lot of people make a day of it. What other place could you go to jog in the morning with the family, have lunch at a restaurant, watch a movie at the multiplex, mail your packages at the post office, buy a new book at the bookstore, and get your hair done while your kids play computer games? Malls are wonderful in the winter."

"I guess that's true," Hannah said.

"And in the summer they're just as nice. You can do all the same things in air-conditioned comfort, without ever having to swat at a single mosquito. If they'd put in a school for Tracey and let us sleep in a couple of the display bedrooms at the furniture store, I could live out here and be perfectly happy."

"Not me," Hannah said. "There's something about a controlled environment that makes me crazy. It's too much like being in jail."

Andrea turned to her in surprise. "Have you ever been there? In jail, I mean?"

"No, but that could change in a hurry if Mike finds out what we're doing."

Andrea agreed and dropped the subject, leading the way to the escalator. "Connie Mac's boutique is on the second level, where Greg Canfield's import store used to be."

The two sisters rode up to the second level in silence, and when they stepped off, Andrea sighed deeply. "If they haven't heard about Connie Mac's murder, you're going to tell them, not me. You stuck me with telling Alex and I don't want to do *that* again."

"Relax," Hannah reassured her. "Unless they're living in a plastic bubble out here, they've heard."

The kitchen boutique was in a prime location in the middle of the mall, only a few feet from the escalator. Giant banners in the window proclaimed, "Grand Opening Monday," and Andrea and Hannah walked closer to peer in the windows.

"There's a woman inside stocking the shelves," Andrea announced, trying the door and turning back to Hannah with a frown, "but the door's locked."

"Knock."

"But they're closed until their grand opening on Monday. It says so right on the sign."

"Knock anyway."

Andrea raised her hand and knocked softly on the glass door.

"She can't hear that. Knock louder."

Andrea gave a solid knock on the door, and the woman looked up from her work. Andrea knocked again and the woman walked toward the door, pointing up at the sign.

"Now what?" Andrea asked. "She's not going to let us in."

"Yes, she will." Hannah moved up to the door with a friendly smile on her face and motioned for the woman in the smart business suit to come forward. She looked like some sort of corporate executive. Under other circumstances, Hannah would have avoided her like the plague, but she needed information from someone who'd worked for Connie Mac, and this was her best shot.

"I'm sorry, we're closed," the woman said, raising her voice so that they could hear her. "Come back on Monday for our grand opening."

"I have a question about the china in the window," Hannah told her, moving right up to the glass.

"Just a moment," the woman answered, turning the lock on the door. She opened it and smiled what Hannah knew was her very best never-lose-a-customer smile.

"We need to buy a wedding present and we're looking for a complete dinner service for twelve. We'll need china, silver, glassware, linens . . . everything, really."

The woman's smile warmed considerably. "I really shouldn't do this since we're not officially open for business, but come in and take a look. I'm Rhea Robinson, and I manage the Connie Mac's Kitchen Boutique chain."

"This is really nice of you." Hannah matched Rhea's brilliant smile. "Our best friend's wedding is next Saturday and we have to find the perfect gift."

"I'm sure you'll find everything you need right here. We have a very extensive selection. I can't actually sell you anything today, but you could pre-choose and come back on Monday. We're giving a fifteen-percent discount to our customers on opening day."

"That's perfect," Hannah said, turning to Andrea. "What do you think of that china in the window?"

Andrea looked startled for a moment. Then she said, "I think she'd really love it."

"How about the glassware?"

"This is beautiful," Andrea said, heading over to a table with some cut-glass crystal goblets. "We should get two water pitchers, one for each end of the table."

"It's Baccarat and it's very expensive," Rhea warned them.

"Price is no object," Andrea told her. "We want to give her the best wedding present that money can buy. How about flatware? You'll have to advise me. I know next to nothing about silver."

Rhea's eyes began to sparkle, and Hannah knew that she was hooked. Now all Hannah had to do was figure out how to ask questions about Connie Mac.

"We have some exquisite gold-plated flatware. It was very popular in the forties and it's come back into fashion. It's the very top of our line, and to make it even more special, it's Connie Mac's original design."

This was just the opening she'd been hoping for, and Hannah did her best to look worried. "I just thought of something. We were listening to the radio on the way out here and we heard that Connie Mac was . . . er . . ."

"Deceased?" Rhea supplied the word.

"That's right. It's such a tragedy. And when you mentioned that the gold-plated silverware was her design, that made me worry."

"Worry?"

"Yes. What if our friend wants to buy more pieces, or replace something her staff might break? With Connie Mac dead, these stores could go out of business. We might be better off going to an older, more established place. I'm sure there are others out here at the mall."

"No, there aren't," Rhea said, stepping closer. "Connie Mac refused to sign a lease in any mall that had competing stores. She wanted to keep her image exclusive, and her boutiques are all one of a kind."

"I can understand that," Andrea agreed. "*She* was one of a kind. But now that she's gone, will her boutiques survive?"

"Of course. We have excellent financing, and our boutiques are very popular. And while it's true that Connie Mac did some product design, we plan to keep on producing unique products with her name. Perhaps I shouldn't say this, but other than the occasional personal appearance, Connie Mac was never actively involved with the boutiques. It's a separate division of Connie Mac Enterprises, and her husband has been in charge since the day we opened our first store."

"I'm so glad you explained that," Hannah said with a smile. "You'll see us back here on Monday, then."

After Rhea had escorted them out and locked the door behind them, Andrea turned to Hannah. "What did we learn?"

"I'm not sure, but I'll write it all down as soon as we get back out to the truck."

"Why don't you do it right now while it's still fresh in your mind?" Andrea pointed to a bench under a potted tree. "And while you're writing, I'll dash in and look for some shoes to go with the dress I bought last week. It shouldn't take more than five minutes."

"Good try, but no dice," Hannah said, grabbing her sister's arm and piloting her to the escalator. Andrea's five minutes would turn into an hour, and she wanted to get out to the dogsled race to tell Norman that he was a suspect.

"There's Norman," Andrea said, pointing toward the finish line, where three judges were gathered in a tight group.

"And he's got his camera." Hannah grinned as she spotted it hanging around his neck. "I guess he's hoping for a photo finish."

The two sisters crunched across the snowy clearing and made their way toward the finish line. They had to stop several times to exchange greetings with the bystanders they knew, and it was slow going. By the time they had navigated the crowd that surrounded the final quarter mile of the course, they'd learned that there were only five teams entered because Charlie Jessup had been disqualified for sled runners that were too wide, Eleanor Cox had hand-sewn leather booties for her husband's dogs, Jerry Larson had dropped out only a mile into the race when he'd upended and lost his earmuffs, and Sam Pietre's sled was sporting a schnapps-bottle holder that he'd designed in his metal shop last night.

"Go ahead," Andrea said, spotting Eleanor Cox in the crowd. "I want to ask Eleanor if she really made those booties. You'd better get a move on, though. I can hear the dogs."

Hannah could hear the barking in the distance, and she figured the two-legged contestants with their four-legged transportation were about a mile and a half away. "Okay. I'll pick you up on my way back."

The air was crisp and cold, and Hannah shivered slightly as she ducked under the rope at the side of the course and stepped knee-deep in a snowdrift. She'd have to change jeans, but that wouldn't be a problem. She always kept a change of clothes in the back of her cookie truck.

A wooden platform six feet high had been built at the side of the finish line. Two of the three judges had climbed to the top with binoculars, but Norman was underneath with his camera.

"Norman?" Hannah called out as she approached.

Norman turned and a smile spread over his face. Hannah couldn't see it under the ski mask that covered his face, but she could tell he was smiling by the way his eyes crinkled when he spotted her.

"Hi, Hannah. Did you come to see the race?"

"No, I came to see you."

"You did?"

Norman's eyes crinkled even more, and Hannah hated to disillusion him. On the other hand, he had to be told. "I came to warn you that you're a suspect in the murder case."

"What?"

Now Norman's eyes were big and startled, and Hannah mentally kicked herself. She'd given him the news with all the subtlety of a bulldozer. "Sorry, Norman. I should have said that better. Bill doesn't suspect you. It's just Mike."

"Oh," Norman said, and his eyes looked normal again. "I guess I shouldn't have lipped off to him this morning. Okay, Hannah. Thanks for coming all the way out here to tell me."

"Then you're not worried?"

"Not really. Once Mike cools off and thinks about it, he'll know I didn't do it."

"Maybe," Hannah said, trying not to sound too doubtful, "but I think you'd better come up with an alibi. Let's sit to-gether at the banquet tonight and talk about it."

"I'd like that, but I'm not going to the banquet. I have to develop the portraits I'm taking this afternoon and I won't have time. Could we get together later?"

"Sure. I should be home by ten. Why don't you come by my place and I'll buy you a cookie?"

"Sounds good. I'll be there."

Norman's eyes crinkled again and Hannah was glad. At least he wasn't too worried to smile.

"Are you going to stick around for the finish? They should be here soon."

"Sure. I'll make a dash for the sidelines."

"Stay with me and you can have a dog's-eye view. I'm going to be here under the platform. Get on my other side, just in case one of the mushers runs off course."

Hannah took up the position Norman indicated. It was probably crazy, but she felt a lot warmer under the platform, with the illusion of a roof over her head. The barking had grown steadily louder as they'd talked, and Hannah found herself wondering why the dogs ran and barked at the same time. Maybe it was just for the sheer joy of the exercise on such a crisp winter day.

"Here they come, and Otis is in the lead!" a voice yelled out from above.

Hannah wasn't surprised. Otis and Eleanor were dog lovers from way back. When they retired, they'd built a house on Old Bailey Road, just outside the town limits. There, the two-dogs-per-household rule didn't apply, and they'd taken in a host of strays over the past three years. The ones they couldn't find homes for, they kept, and Otis had trained all their huskies and malamutes as sled dogs.

As Hannah watched, the lead musher and his team came over the crest of the hill. It was Otis, and he was still in front.

"Look at his dogs." Norman slipped his free arm around Hannah's shoulder. "They're all smiling."

Hannah didn't point out that huskies and malamutes always appeared to be smiling because of the shape of their faces. It was simply too lovely a sentiment to dash. Actually, the dogs did seem to be having a huge amount of fun. Their tails were high and tightly curled, their tongues were wagging from side to side, and they were barking and yelping in excitement.

"Okay. Here we go!"

Norman dropped to one knee and focused his camera. A few seconds later, Otis and his dogs rushed by at lightning speed. Hannah laughed out loud in sheer pleasure as Otis slowed his dogs at the far end of the course and guided them through the break in the ropes where they would wait for the other contestants.

One by one, the other teams raced by and Norman took pictures of all of them. When he was through, Hannah told him she'd see him later and headed back for the sidelines to collect Andrea.

"Eleanor did make the booties," Andrea told Hannah on their way back to the truck, "and they're going up to the Iditarod next year."

Hannah was surprised. "Does Otis think he can win?"

"Oh, they're just going as tourists. Janice is going to stay at their place for two weeks and take care of their dogs."

Hannah unlocked the doors and they climbed into the cookie truck. It was still slightly warm inside, and it felt good after the bitter cold outside.

"Could you drop me off at the office?" Andrea asked as Hannah pulled out onto the highway. "I have to write up a listing."

"Sure. You got a listing at the race?"

"Eleanor's cousin, Roger, got a job offer in Wisconsin and it was too good to turn down. They were going to rent out their house, but I convinced them that renting was a headache they didn't need, so they're going to sell."

"But didn't they just buy it last year?"

"Seven months ago. I handled the sale."

"If they sell this soon, they'll lose money, won't they?"

"No. Roger converted the basement into two separate bedrooms and put in a full bathroom down there. Now I can relist it as a five-bedroom, three-bath, and that increases the asking price. Best of all, I think I've already got a buyer. I ran into Lelia Meiers at the cleaners yesterday and she's pregnant with twins. She asked me to keep my eye out for a bigger house, and this would be just perfect for them. I called her right away and she wants to see it tomorrow."

"You're amazing," Hannah said, and she meant it. Andrea was always looking for ways to list and sell real estate. It was an ideal job for her, because she could socialize and work at the same time.

"Call me later," Andrea said as Hannah pulled up in front of Lake Eden Realty. "I should be through here in about an hour."

"Okay. I'm going back to the inn to collect the cookies. I'll deliver them to the warm-up tents and then we'll figure out a place to meet."

As Hannah drove off, she glanced at her watch. It was eleven-thirty, and she'd be back at the inn before noon. If Lisa and Alex had finished the baking, she could have all the cookies delivered by one.

The truck seemed silent without Andrea, and Hannah switched on the radio. A moment later, she wished she hadn't, because the KCOW news team was covering the latest about Connie Mac's murder. Hannah winced as they mentioned that her body had been found at The Cookie Jar, and she hoped that the old adage was true. If any publicity was good publicity, it wouldn't hurt her cookie business.

As she turned off on the road that led around Eden Lake, Hannah noticed a plume of smoke coming from the one of the summer cabins that dotted its shores. She watched for a moment to make sure it wasn't a house fire, but the smoke was too confined for that. It was definitely coming from a chimney, and Hannah didn't think that any of the cabins on the far side of the lake had been converted into year-round dwellings. It must belong to one of the summer people who'd come back to Lake Eden for Winter Carnival and had decided to brave the discomfort of no central heat, frozen water pipes, and a lack of insulation to save on the price of a nice, snug motel.

Chapter Fifteen

Hannah pushed open the door to Sally's kitchen and stopped short as she saw the massive array of baked cookies on the counter. Lisa and Alex had finished the baking, and she immediately felt guilty for shirking her share of the work. Some of the cookies were already boxed for transport, and others were still cooling on the racks. Hannah walked over to take a closer look and smiled at what she saw. The Molasses Crackles were perfect rounds, the Chocolate Chip Crunch Cookies looked crisp and delicious, the golden-brown Peanut Butter Melts were crosshatched with perfect fork marks, and the Oatmeal Raisin Crisps tempted her with their spicy aroma. She was just reaching for one, to give it a taste test when Lisa and Alex came into the kitchen.

"Hi, Hannah," Lisa greeted her, lifting the box she was carrying up to the counter. "Where's Andrea?"

"She got a listing at the dogsled race and I dropped her off at Lake Eden Realty to write it up."

Alex lifted her box to the counter and smiled at Hannah. "Thanks for letting me help. I really enjoyed baking those cookies."

"You got that backwards," Hannah told her. "I should be

thanking *you*. Just let me mix up the Little Snowball dough and I'll show you how to make those."

Lisa shook her head. "It's too late. We baked them already. The instructions were right on the recipe and once we got going, we didn't want to stop." She stepped over to whisk back a towel that covered six of Sally's crystal ice buckets, and Hannah saw that each one was filled with small snow white balls. "They're absolutely delicious, Hannah. We just had to taste them."

"Of course you did," Hannah said, reaching out to take one. The Little Snowballs were so tender they practically melted in her mouth, and she started to smile. "Delicious."

"Are you sure?" Alex looked a bit worried. "I rolled them in powdered sugar twice, just like it said in the recipe. Once when they were hot, and once after they'd cooled. Do you think it's too much?"

"There's no such thing as too much powdered sugar. They're perfect, Alex, even better than I remembered. I'll help you two mix up the cookie dough for tomorrow morning and then I'll deliver the Little Snowballs to Edna."

"What cookies are we making tomorrow?" Lisa asked.

"It's basically the same lineup, except we'll substitute your White Chocolate Supremes for the Molasses Crackles. You can mix up the dough for those."

"I'll do the Oatmeal Raisin Crisps," Alex offered. "I read the recipe and I bet my boss would just love them."

"You mean Sally?"

"No, my regular boss."

"Who's that?" Hannah asked, trolling for a little information.

"I work for Remco. It's a big accounting firm based in Edina. My boss is the senior vice president. I'm on vacation right now. I had three weeks coming and I had to use it up before I lost it."

"Wait a second." Hannah turned to her with an amazed expression. "You took a temporary job with Sally on your *vacation?*"

Alex laughed. "I know this isn't exactly a vacation, but I wanted to see how a place like this was run. I inherited my parents' house last year, and I thought I might turn it into a bed-and-breakfast."

"Well, the inn is certainly a good example of what you can do with an old place," Hannah said, still watching Alex closely. She looked perfectly sincere, but she didn't quite meet Hannah's eyes. That made Hannah suspect that Alex wasn't telling her the whole truth and that she had a second reason for accepting Sally's job.

"I'll start in on these," Alex said, glancing down at the recipe. "I'll go get a fresh box of oatmeal."

When Alex had gone, Hannah turned to Lisa. "Did you find out anything more about her?"

"She's forty-five years old, she lives in Edina, she has two cats, she loves to dance, and she sews in her spare time. That's about it. You got more real information from her in two minutes than I did in two hours."

"You primed the pump," Hannah said, patting Lisa on the shoulder. "I just happened to be here when the water gushed out."

"Do you really think so?"

"Absolutely. Just keep working on her."

Alex came back in with a jumbo-sized box of oatmeal, and the three of them worked in silence for several minutes. It didn't take long to mix up the cookie dough with all three of them working, and that was all to the good. Sally's staff had begun to arrive to prepare the lunch buffet, and Hannah didn't want to get in the way.

"Don't worry," Alex said, noticing Hannah's concerned expression as more kitchen workers arrived. "Sally's serving soup and sandwiches for today's lunch buffet. She figured that most of the guests would be out at venues and she could keep it simple. All the kitchen staff has to do is lay cold cuts, cheeses, and breads on platters and carry it out. There's potato salad, but that's already made, and so is the coleslaw and the soup."

Another five minutes of work and they were finished. Hannah covered the bowls with plastic wrap, and Lisa and Alex stashed them in Sally's walk-in cooler.

"Why don't you go pull your truck around to the back entrance?" Lisa suggested. "We'll finish up here and then we'll help you load."

Hannah headed out to get her truck. As she walked through the halls to the lobby, she didn't meet another soul. Sally had been right. Almost everyone was out at the venues.

Her boots were on the rack by the front entrance, right where she'd left them when she'd come in, and Hannah sat down on the bench to pull them on. She was just putting on her parka, preparing to go out into the cold, when she noticed a small crowd of people out on the lakeshore. Two parka-clad men were unloading a wooden structure from a pickup truck that had been driven out on the ice, and Hannah realized that they were setting up for the ice-fishing contest. The actual contest would take place tomorrow, but the preparations had to be made in advance. By the time night fell, the surface of Eden Lake would be sprinkled with ice-fishing houses.

Hannah was about to step out the door when she noticed that the plume of smoke on the far side of the lake was still there. A die-hard Winter Carnival attendee would be out at the venues by now. He wouldn't be huddled in his summer cabin, feeding the fire in his fireplace. But this column of smoke showed no signs of diminishing. It was still just as thick as when she'd first spotted it.

Hannah turned on her heel and headed for the phone. If she remembered correctly, Janie's parents had owned a cabin on the far side of the lake. She had to find out if they'd sold it when they'd moved to Florida, and there was one person who could tell her that in a flash.

Two minutes later, Hannah had Andrea on the phone. But the moment she started to ask her question, Andrea interrupted her.

"Wait a second, Hannah. I've got big news. You can take Ray off your suspect list."

"The bus driver called you?"

"That's right. Ray rode all the way up to Duluth and his parents were there to meet him. The driver saw him get into their car. That was at eight last night, and the driver told me that the roads up north were a mess. He was an hour behind schedule, and there's no way Ray could have driven back to Lake Eden last night."

"Great. That'll make Earl happy. Now listen carefully, Andrea. I just got a wild idea. Didn't Janie's parents own a cabin on the far side of Eden Lake?"

"Yes, and they still own it. We rent it out for them every summer. They didn't want to sell, because they thought that someday Janie might want to . . ." Andrea stopped speaking and gasped. "Do you think she's there?"

"She could be, if the smoke I saw is coming from her parents' cabin."

"I know which one it is. I'll drive right out and check."

"No, you stay put," Hannah ordered. "There's an APB out on Janie, and if you find her, you'll have to tell Bill."

There was a long silence and then Andrea sighed. "You're right. I love Bill, but sometimes I wish I'd married a dermatologist. They never get called out on emergencies and you don't have to worry about what you tell them. You're going out there, aren't you?"

"I'm on the way."

"Are you going to turn Janie in?" Andrea asked, sounding very worried.

"Not until she tells me exactly what happened last night. And then I'll get her to turn *herself* in."

Hannah uttered a word that she would have swallowed if her niece had been a passenger in her truck. The road that ran around the lake was in poor repair, and this was the fourth time she'd hit the top of her head as she bounced over the ruts. She glanced in the rearview mirror and heaved a sigh of relief as she saw the cookie boxes, still exactly where they'd placed them. It would be a real pity to arrive at the venues with broken cookies.

Andrea had given her detailed directions, and Hannah turned left at the fork in the road by the green cabin with yellow trim. Every cabin she'd passed had been vacant. No one except a desperate person would sleep overnight in a summer cabin in this kind of weather. She turned off again, at the pink cabin, and took the winding road down to the lakeshore. Andrea had told her to look for the sky blue cabin, and she could see it through the pine trees.

As Hannah approached, she spotted a familiar car. It was Janie's. She breathed a sigh of relief. She parked next to a little snowdrift near the front door of the cabin and got out of her truck.

The padlock on the front door was open, and Hannah gave a polite knock on the door. Then she opened it and stepped in. It took a moment for her eyes to adjust to the dim interior of cabin after the brightness of the snow outside, but she could see a huddled shape in a sleeping bag by the fire.

"Janie?" Hannah stepped forward and the sleeping bag moved.

"Hannah?" Janie sounded very tentative as she poked her head out of the sleeping bag. Then she smiled as she recognized her. "Oh, Hannah! I'm so glad to see you! But how did you know I was here?"

"The smoke from your chimney, but that's not important. Are you okay?"

"I'm all right, but I really did it this time. And there's no way I'm going back, not even if she calls me to apologize. She's a horrible person and I'll find another job!"

Hannah didn't say anything, but her mind was working overtime. It was pretty obvious from what Janie had said that she didn't know Connie Mac was dead. "What are you doing here?"

"I didn't want to face all the rest of them this morning. I knew they'd be sympathetic, and I just couldn't stand it. That's why I'm here."

"But you went back to the inn to pack up your clothes. Didn't you see any of them then?"

Janie shook her head, and now that Hannah's eyes had adjusted to the lack of light, she could see tearstains on her cheeks. "I guess they were all busy, or in their rooms, or out somewhere else. That was a big relief. I was really upset and I didn't want to talk to anybody about it. She accused me of sleeping with her husband, Hannah. She said all sorts of awful things, and then she fired me!"

"Look, Janie . . ." Hannah winced slightly, but she had to ask. "Were you sleeping with Paul?"

"Of course not! I'm practically engaged, Hannah. Jim's saving his money and he's getting me a ring next month. I told her all that, but she just wouldn't listen to reason. She went ballastic and she . . . she started to throw things at me!"

"What did you do then?"

"I grabbed my purse and my coat and I ran out the back door. She's got a horrible temper, Hannah. It's practically legendary. I sure didn't want to be on the receiving end of it."

"Has she ever thrown things at people before?"

"Not me, but I've heard stories, and I know she fights with Paul all the time. I had the room next to them when we opened the boutique in Shakopee, and I heard her yelling at him and throwing things. The next morning he came down with a big bruise on the side of his head. He told everyone that he hit it on the side of a door, but I knew better."

"How about Connie Mac? Did she have bruises that morning?"

"You mean . . . from Paul?"

"Yes. I wouldn't blame him if he fought back."

"I wouldn't either, but he never did. And that wasn't the first time I heard them fight. She'd scream and throw things and he'd just try to calm her down. Paul's really nice, Hannah. I know he's never raised a hand to her."

"Let's get back to last night. Connie Mac was throwing things at you and you didn't just peg something back at her as you went out the door?"

Janie shook her head. "No. All I could think about was getting out of there. She wanted to fight and I just wanted to get away from her."

"Then Connie Mac was still alive when you left?"

Janie blinked and then she leaned forward to peer at Hannah intently. "Still alive? You mean she's . . . *dead*?"

"As a doornail," Hannah said, wishing she hadn't told Janie quite so abruptly. "What time did you leave The Cookie Jar?"

"I don't know. But I was back out at the inn by ten-fifteen. I looked at my alarm clock right before I stuck it in my suitcase."

Hannah did a little mental arithmetic. Janie must have left The Cookie Jar around nine forty-five. "Did you lock the back door when you ran out?"

"No, I just slammed it behind me. She was getting ready to throw your rolling pin and I didn't want to get hit with that."

"I don't blame you. That's a heavy rolling pin. Did you see anyone else around when you drove away?"

"No, but I was pretty upset. If someone was there, I might not have noticed. What happened to her, Hannah? Did she have a stroke or something?"

"Something," Hannah said, realizing that she had come to the point of no return. Janie had a right to know what had happened to her ex-boss, especially since she was a prime suspect. "She was murdered, Janie. Somebody bashed her head in."

Janie gasped sharply. Then she shivered and took a couple of deep breaths. "Tell me the truth, Hannah. Do they . . . do they think that I killed her?"

"It didn't look good when they couldn't find you. They need to talk to you, Janie."

"Of course. Will they put me in jail?"

"Over my dead body," Hannah said, and that comment earned her a small grin. "I'll take you out to the sheriff's station and we can get your car later. Just tell them everything

Connie Mac did and what you did, and everything will be all right."

"I'll right. I'm scared, but I know I have to do it."

"Good girl. They might say you have to stay in Lake Eden until they solve the case. If they do, you can bunk in with me. I've got a guest room at my condo."

"Thanks, Hannah. But are you sure? I mean, I don't want to go back to the inn, but what if I tell them everything and I'm still a suspect? You don't want to . . . to share your place with a murder suspect, do you?"

"Why not? Another one's coming over tonight. It's Norman Rhodes, and you can compare notes." The words popped out before Hannah could think about them and she sighed contritely. "I'm sorry, Janie. I shouldn't have said that."

"I'm glad you did," Janie said, and she ventured another smile. "I guess it can't be too bad if you're making jokes about it. On the other hand, you'd joke on your way to the guillotine."

"True. But just remember that you're only staying in my guest room. I'm actually dating the other prime murder suspect."

Little Snowballs

Preheat oven to 350°F,
with rack in the middle position

1 ½ cups melted butter *(3 sticks, ¾ pound)*
¾ cup powdered sugar *(that's confectioner's sugar)*
1 ½ teaspoons vanilla
½ teaspoon nutmeg *(freshly ground is best)*
½ teaspoon salt
3 ½ cups flour *(no need to sift)*
1 cup finely chopped nuts ***

Melt the butter. Mix in the powered sugar, vanilla, nutmeg, and salt. Add the flour and mix thoroughly. Stir in the nuts. *(If you work quickly, while the butter is still warm, the dough will be softer and easier to mix.)*

Form the dough into one-inch balls *(just pat them into shape with your fingers)*, and place them on an UNGREASED baking sheet, 12 to a standard sheet. Bake them at 350°F for 10 minutes, until they are set but not brown.

Let the cookies cool for 2 minutes and then roll them in powdered sugar. *(You must do this while they're still warm.)* Place them on a wire rack and let them cool thoroughly.

When the cookies are cool, roll them in powdered sugar a second time. Let them rest for several minutes on the rack, and then store them in a cookie jar or a covered bowl.

*** *Mother likes these with chopped walnuts. Andrea prefers pecans. I think they're best with hazelnuts. Tracey adores these when I substitute a cup of flaked coconut for the nuts and form the dough balls around a small piece of a milk chocolate bar or a couple of milk chocolate chips.*

Chapter
Sixteen

Hannah glanced at her watch as she pulled into the parking lot at the community center. Only an hour had passed since she'd driven Janie out to the sheriff's station and let Mike and Bill know, in no uncertain terms, that they'd better treat her with kid gloves. Once she'd made sure that Janie was all right, she'd driven into town and stopped at all the winter sports venues to drop off the cookies that Lisa and Alex had baked. Now the only thing she had left to do was to present Edna with the little snowballs for tonight's dessert.

The sky was leaden gray as Hannah walked across the parking lot and entered the lobby of the community center. The table where Connie Mac had planned to sign her books was deserted, and Hannah wondered what Marge Beeseman would do with two hundred copies of *Sweets For Your Sweetie*. A few people would buy them simply to support the library, but the huge crowd that Marge had expected wouldn't show up without a celebrity to sign them.

Hannah sighed as she trudged down the stairs to the banquet room, carrying her heavy box of cookies. She had to hold it to the side so that she could see the stairs. If she tripped and fell, Edna's dessert would go rolling down the green carpet like miniature cue balls on a pool table.

"Edna?" she called out as she entered the banquet room. She could tell that Edna had been busy, because all the tables were set and there was the tempting aroma of freshly baked bread in the air. "I'm here with the dessert."

Edna rushed out of the kitchen, wiping her hands on a dishtowel. Even though she was smiling, she looked tired and out of sorts, and Hannah suspected that baking all those crescent rolls had robbed her of a good night's sleep.

"You baked the cake?" Edna asked, motioning for Hannah to set the box down on an empty table.

"No, but I've got something just as good." Hannah opened the box and lifted out one of the crystal buckets filled with cookies. "These are called Little Snowballs and they're my Grandma Ingrid's recipe."

Edna's smile grew wider and she nodded so hard, her tightly curled gray hair bounced. "They're just perfect, Hannah. We can set one on each table and let everyone help themselves."

"You look tired," Hannah commented, noticing the dark circles under Edna's eyes. "Are you going to be all right?"

" 'Course I am, now that you're here. Baking all those rolls was a lot of work, and I don't know how I would've managed dessert. Maybe I shouldn't say this, but if I'd known that that woman would wind up dead, I never would have made all those changes to the menu."

Hannah grinned. "I take it you're not too upset about the Cooking Sweetheart's demise?"

"Some sweetheart!" Edna snorted. "Just look at these things her people delivered for the banquet."

Hannah glanced over at one of the tables and took in the array of bone china, lace tablecloths, and silver. "It's pretty."

"Pretty useless, if you ask me. We can't afford to have those lace tablecloths dry-cleaned, and if you try to wash 'em, they'll fall apart. The silver's got to be polished every time you use it, and that china can't go in the dishwasher. And if that's not enough, just look at these!"

At first Hannah couldn't see what was wrong with the dried flowers in ceramic baskets, but as she looked closely she realized that every basket had "Connie Mac's Kitchen Boutique" written on the side.

"They're just advertising for her new store," Edna sniffed, "and you can't clean those dried flowers when they get dusty. If she'd really wanted to give the community center a gift, she should have picked something we could really use."

Hannah knew. Edna had a point. The things that Connie Mac had chosen were impractical for a community kitchen.

"I was boiling mad when I unpacked those boxes," Edna declared, "especially since she built it all up as something wonderful. All I could think about was finding her and wringing her neck!"

Hannah's mind went into overdrive. Edna had a temper, and she'd been sorely tested by Connie Mac. First there was the generous gift that Connie Mac had promised that turned out to be more trouble than it was worth, and then there were the changes she'd made to Edna's menu. Was it possible that Edna's temper had gotten the best of her?

"Uh . . . Edna?" Hannah knew she was treading on eggshells, but she had to ask. "What time did you leave here last night?"

Edna gave a short laugh. "Before you start getting all suspicious, I've got an alibi. Right after she ordered me to bake all those rolls, I called my sister at the farm. Hattie drove in to help me and she stayed over at my place last night."

"I'm sorry, Edna." Hannah backed off. "I didn't mean to imply that I thought you killed her."

"That's okay. I might have, if she'd come waltzing in here while I was punching down that dough last night!"

Hannah glanced at her watch. "I've got a spare hour. Is there anything I can do to help you?"

"Nope. Everything's all done. The minute I heard that she was dead, I decided not to make that fancy molded appetizer she wanted to have. Not many people around here like liver anyway. I'm serving cheese and crackers, just like it says on my original menu."

"Hannah?" Marge Beeseman yoo-hooed her from the door of the library as she passed by. "Come in for a minute. You have to see what this wonderful young man brought me!"

Hannah stepped into the library and smiled at the young man who was standing next to Marge. He was blond, handsome, and about ten years too young for her.

"This is Kurt Howe," Marge said. "And Kurt? This is Hannah Swensen. She owns The Cookie Jar and she bakes the best cookies in the world."

"Glad to meet you." Hannah shook his hand when he extended it. She knew that Kurt Howe was the publisher's representative who'd had the fight with Connie Mac. "You must have done something special. Marge doesn't call just anyone wonderful."

Kurt shook his head. "All I did was bring her some signed copies of *Sweets For Your Sweetie*."

"Two hundred of them," Marge pointed at the cartons of books that were stacked near the door. "We're doing an exchange. I'm going to sell the ones that Connie Mac presigned."

Hannah turned to Kurt. "That was very nice of you."

"It was more than nice," Marge corrected her. "Now that Connie Mac is, uh . . . no longer with us, they'll be instant collector's items. I'm going to sit at that table in the lobby and sell them to the people who come in for the banquet. As a matter of fact, I've got to get started setting up. You'll excuse me, won't you?"

Hannah found herself on the horns of a moral dilemma once Marge had left. She was dying to ask Kurt about the fight, but she'd promised Mike not to question any of the Connie Mac people at the inn. Of course, she wasn't at the inn; she was in the library, and this opportunity was too good to pass up.

"I'm sorry about Connie Mac," Hannah said, easing her way into the subject. "I guess *Sweets For Your Sweetie* will be the last of her cookbooks."

Kurt shook his head. "Actually, no. Savory Press has at least three more in the works."

"You mean they're all written and ready to go?"

"Not exactly. It's like this, Miss Swensen . . . All the recipes in Mrs. MacIntyre's cookbooks come directly from her television shows. We just transcribe them from the tapes and put in some of the personal comments she makes."

"But her show is over now, isn't it?"

"Yes, but there's a large backlog of segments that haven't aired yet. And then there'll be reruns. There's plenty of material for at least three more cookbooks, maybe four."

"I see," Hannah said, filing that information away for future reference. Right now she had more important fish to fry. "Would you mind telling me where you were last night?"

Kurt's smile disappeared and his expression grew guarded. "I was in my room. Why do you want to know? Are you from the police?"

"No." Hannah decided she'd already jumped in with both feet and she might as well get thoroughly wet. "I'm asking for a friend who might be charged with Connie Mac's murder. I think she's your friend, too. Janie Burkholtz?"

"The police think *Janie* murdered Mrs. MacIntyre?" Kurt looked shocked.

"Yes, and unless Janie can clear herself, she's in big trouble. I just thought you might have seen her last night when she came back to the inn. I'm trying to establish an alibi for her."

Kurt's guarded expression disappeared. "I'd like to help Janie, but the last time I saw her was in the late afternoon. Our rooms are right next to each other, and I saw her leaving. Janie told me that Mrs. MacIntyre was having her portrait taken and she had to follow the limo to town."

"Your room is right next to Janie's?"

"That's right."

"And you were in your room last night?"

"That's what I said."

"Didn't you hear Janie when she came back to pack up her things?"

"No."

Hannah was puzzled. "But you must have heard *something*. Dresser drawers slamming, hangers rattling, suitcases bumping on the floor . . ."

"Uh . . ." Kurt began to look nervous. "Look, Miss Swensen. I was in my room last night, but I left around nine. I drove to Minneapolis to meet a friend, and I stayed overnight."

"Can your friend vouch for you?"

"Yes, but I don't want to bring my friend into it. If my boss finds out where I was last night, he'll fire me."

Hannah took one look at the stubborn set of Kurt's chin and decided it was time to play hardball. "The way I see it, you're in a lose-lose situation here. I know about the fight you had with Connie Mac and how she threatened to call your boss in the morning to have you fired. If I tell the police about that and I also tell them that you weren't in your room past nine last night, *you'll* be a murder suspect. How long do you think your job will last when you're suspected of killing Savory's biggest celebrity author?"

"I . . . I didn't think about that." Kurt's face turned pale.

"It doesn't have to be as bad as it sounds," Hannah told him. "I'm the only one who knows you weren't in your room last night, and I won't tell as long as you get your alibi to vouch for you. My lips are sealed if your story checks out."

"Okay." Kurt gave a resigned sigh. "I spent the night with Marcia, and her father owns Savory Press. She works there part-time, and he's death on intraoffice romance. He told Marcia that if she dated anyone on his staff, he'd fire the guy and send her off to finish college in Alaska."

Hannah whistled softly. "You *do* have a problem. Just get Marcia on the phone and let me talk to her. If she says that you were with her all night, I'll forget everything you told me."

Five minutes later, Hannah had all the information she

needed. After assuring Marcia that she wouldn't blow the whistle on them, she hung up Kurt's cell phone and handed it back to him. "You're in the clear. But just to satisfy my curiosity, why was Connie Mac so mad at you?"

"I guess it can't hurt to tell you." Kurt hesitated and Hannah noticed that he looked highly embarrassed. "I refused to sleep with her."

Hannah could feel her mouth drop open, and she closed it before she looked like the village idiot.

"The last guy who had my job warned me that Mrs. MacIntyre was sleeping around, but I thought that was just a rumor. And then she came on to me."

"What did you do?"

"What *could* I do? I love Marcia and there's no way I'd cheat on her, not even to keep my job. I tried to be diplomatic, but Mrs. MacIntyre didn't buy it. Right before she stomped off, she said she was going to call Marcia's father in the morning and have me fired."

"And that's why you drove to Minneapolis to see Marcia?"

"Marcia was wonderful about it. We decided that when the ax fell, we'd elope. She was willing to put college on hold so we could both work until I got established with another publishing firm."

"When did you find out that Connie Mac was dead?"

"Not until this morning. I drove back here early and got a couple hours of sleep. When I went down to breakfast, everybody was talking about it."

"Do you have any idea who killed her?"

Kurt shrugged. "Not really. Mrs. MacIntyre got to the top by climbing over a lot of other people. It could have been anybody she stepped on over the years."

Hannah thanked Kurt, assured him again that she wouldn't tell anyone about Marcia, and walked back out to her truck. It was only four-thirty in the afternoon, but night was falling and she switched on her headlights as she drove home to her condo. She'd eliminated some of her suspects without technically breaking her promise to Mike, but there were still a whole lot to go.

Chapter Seventeen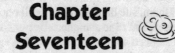

W hen Hannah inserted her key in her condo door, she heard an irate yowl from inside. She immediately went into defense mode, dropping her shoulder bag so she wouldn't be encumbered, and zipping her parka all the way up to her chin. Then she opened the door and held out her arms to receive the twenty-three-pound bundle of orange and white fur that hurtled itself at her chest.

"Hi, Moishe. Did you miss me?" Hannah cuddled him a moment before she dragged in her purse and shut the door. "What's the matter?"

Hannah figured that one of two things could have happened to upset her feline companion. Either his food bowl was empty again, or her mother had called. The moment Hannah set Moishe down, he led her directly into the kitchen, his tail flicking impatiently. There she discovered that it was two out of two. His food bowl was empty *and* the little red light on her answer phone was blinking.

"Okay, hold on a second." Hannah shrugged out of her parka and draped it over one of her kitchen chairs. She headed straight for the cupboard where she kept Moishe's food and unlocked it. When Moishe had first come to live with her, Hannah had been a big believer in what her vet called "free food." She'd made it her mission to keep the food bowl stocked so that Moishe wouldn't panic every time he saw a patch of white ceramic at the bottom. Her intentions had been good, but Moishe's table manners left a lot to be desired and he'd carried her "free food" program to the extreme when he'd learned how to open the cupboard door and help himself to the twenty-pound mother lode she kept in her broom closet. A few months ago, Hannah had decided that she'd swept up enough pilfered fish-shaped kitty crunchies to last her a lifetime, and she'd installed a hook and eye high up on her broom closet door.

"Here you go," Hannah said, scooping out the kitty crunchies and dumping them into his food bowl. "I suppose you want fresh water, too."

Moishe looked up at her and yowled. He had plenty of water in his bowl, but he liked it ice cold. Hannah turned on the faucet, let it run until it was cold, and filled his water bowl. Once she'd set it down on the Garfield mat next to his food bowl, she walked over to check her messages, wondering exactly when, in the course of their relationship, she'd become a slave to her pet.

The first message was from Andrea, who thanked her for finding Janie. She said she'd finished writing up her listing and she'd meet Hannah at the Winter Carnival banquet.

Hannah glanced over at Moishe. He hadn't been upset at hearing Andrea's voice, but when the next message came on, he bristled.

"Hannah? This is Mike. We just finished with Miss Burkholtz, and Bill's taking her out to get her car. She said she'd be staying with you. I know she's an old friend, but I can tell you right now, I don't like it. Just do me a favor and don't get involved, okay?"

"Right," Hannah muttered, bending down to give Moishe a pat. He hadn't liked the officious tone in Mike's voice, either.

"Hannah? This is your mother." The third and final message began to play, and Hannah stepped out of the way as

Moishe made a beeline to the answer phone to stare at it balefully. His ears were laid back, his tail was flicking, and he looked as if he'd like to tear it off the wall.

"Relax. She's not here. It's just a recording," Hannah said, but she knew it wouldn't do much good. Every time Moishe heard her mother's voice, it upset him.

"Carrie and I are passing on the banquet. We're going to buy Tracey a pizza at the mall and then we're going to see the new Disney film. Tracey was a big help this afternoon, and she deserves a treat."

Hannah grinned. Tracey had learned how to manipulate her grandmother, and it appeared that she'd had similar success with Carrie.

"Wear a nice dress to the banquet, dear. And please try to do *something* with your hair. I saw Babs Dubinski this afternoon and she said her son is here for the carnival."

"Oh, great," Hannah said and followed it with a long-suffering sigh. She'd met Babs Dubinski's son at her mother's urging, and his one and only topic of conversation was tax reform.

"He just got divorced," Delores went on, "and tax accountants make very good money. Babs told me that he pulled in over seven . . ."

Hannah hit the stop button, cutting off her mother in mid-quote. She knew that Delores would prefer Norman or even Mike, but any old son-in-law, even a boring one, would do in a pinch for the daughter she feared would remain a spinster.

"We don't have to listen to the rest, Moishe," Hannah said, smoothing down his ruffled fur. "Let's go to the bedroom and you can curl up on my pillow while I get dressed."

Ten minutes later, Hannah was in the shower, enjoying the heat from the steaming spray and trying out the new bottle of Pretty Girl shampoo she'd bought from Luanne that morning. It was scented with some kind of herbal mixture, as was her new bar of soap, another acquisition from Luanne.

When her hair was thoroughly rinsed and squeaky clean, Hannah cranked off the water, toweled herself off, and stepped out of the bathroom. She glanced at her bed, where Moishe had been waiting for her, but there was an empty indentation on her pillow and a few stray orange and white hairs. She could hear him meowing from the other end of the condo, and as Hannah listened, she began to smile. Janie had come in and she was in the kitchen, having a conversation with Moishe.

As Hannah dressed, she listened to the two-sided conversation. She couldn't make out the words, but the conversational dynamics were plain. Janie would say something, Moishe would answer her, and Janie would respond to that. This went on for several minutes as Hannah put on her best wool suit, slipped into her dress shoes, and brushed her hair. She pulled her frizzy red curls back into a barrette that she fastened at the nape of her neck, debated the wisdom of switching to a purse that would match her shoes, and decided that it would be more trouble than it was worth. Andrea would just have to tolerate the scarred leather shoulder bag she usually carried.

A spritz from the perfume bottle that her college roommate had given her, a touch of lipstick that Hannah immediately wiped off with a tissue, and she was ready. She gave one more glance in the mirror, concluded that she'd done the best that she could with what she had, and walked down the hall in heels that were bound to make her feel like a giant when she stood next to her petite sister.

"Hi, Hannah. You look nice." Janie greeted her when she entered the living room. She was sitting on the couch, and Moishe looked very content curled up in her lap. "I just love your cat. He's so friendly."

"Only to people he likes. Just ask Mother if you don't believe me. His name is Moishe."

"Hello, Moishe," Janie said, giving him a scratch behind his ears. "He's really smart, too. His food bowl was empty and he showed me where you keep his food."

"That figures. So how did it go at the sheriff's station?"

"Okay, I think. I did what you said and just told them

everything I could remember. When I asked them if I was a suspect, Bill said not to worry about it, but his partner told me to stay in town until they gave me permission to leave."

"That's Mike," Hannah told her, "and he's not exactly the reassuring type. Did you put all your things in the guest room?"

"Yes. I parked my car right next to your cookie truck. Is that all right?"

"That's perfect. This place comes with two parking spots. Why don't you change clothes and come to the banquet with me? I don't want you to sit here all alone."

"I'm not alone." Janie reached out to pet Moishe again. "Besides, I just want to take a shower and soak up the luxury of a real furnace. That cabin was cold!"

"Okay, if you're sure. There's plenty of food here. Just forage around if you get hungry."

"Thanks Hannah, but I'm not hungry." Janie gave a little sigh. "It's funny, in a way. Mrs. MacIntyre was always after me to lose weight, and now that she's dead, I probably will."

Andrea nudged Hannah to get her attention. They were sitting at one of the long tables in the banquet room and they'd just finished eating Edna's main course, a delicious pot roast with pan gravy. "That's the Connie Mac table over there. He's not here."

"Who?" Hannah asked, glancing over at the table of Connie Mac people.

"Paul MacIntyre."

"I didn't expect him to be here. Would you go to a banquet if you'd just found out that your spouse was dead?"

Andrea shivered. "I wish you hadn't said that. I worry about Bill all the time."

"I'm sorry," Hannah apologized. "I just meant that it wouldn't be in good taste for Paul to socialize tonight, under the circumstances."

"You're right. I was just hoping to talk to him, that's all.

Guess I'll have to settle for the second-best thing. I think that's Alan Carpenter sitting next to the woman in last season's Liz Claibourne."

"What makes you think that?"

"Because he's wearing an expensive suit with a silk tie, and he looks like a lawyer."

"Not that. How do you know the woman next to him is wearing *last* season's Liz Claibourne?"

"Because I keep up with the fashions. Living in a small town doesn't mean you have to be hopelessly out of style. I wish I knew somebody over there so we could walk over and say hello."

"I know someone," Hannah told her.

"Who?"

"Kurt Howe. He delivered some books to Marge this afternoon and she introduced me."

Andrea looked worried. "You didn't question him, did you?"

"Of course I did. I wasn't going to look a gift horse in the mouth. Kurt's alibi checked out and he's in the clear." Hannah pushed back her chair and stood up. "Come on, Andrea. Let's go over and say hello before Edna brings out my dessert."

By the time the buckets of Little Snowballs were brought out to the tables, Hannah and Andrea had met several people in Connie Mac's entourage. There were the two reporters who had been covering the Cooking Sweetheart's activities, the decorator who'd designed her kitchen boutiques, the writer who was working on her biography, and the man that Andrea had pegged as Alan Carpenter.

"It's a pleasure to meet you," Alan said, standing up to shake their hands. "Why don't you take our chairs? Kurt and I have to leave."

"Was it something I said?" Hannah quipped, and she was rewarded by a smile from both Kurt and Alan.

"Not at all," Alan told her, "but if we don't leave right now, we'll be late for the press conference I scheduled at my office."

"About Mrs. MacIntyre?" Hannah asked.

"Naturally. The media's in a feeding frenzy and they want to know the details. I'm the spokesman for the family and Kurt's going to handle any questions that concern Savory Press."

"This must be very difficult for you," Andrea commented, giving Alan a sympathetic smile.

"It's not easy, but I have a duty as the family counsel to spare Paul in any way I can. I'm sorry, ladies. I'd like to talk longer, but we really do have to leave now."

"Take some of these along with you for the trip," Hannah said, taking a half-dozen Little Snowballs from the crystal bucket that one of the serving girls had placed on the table, and wrapping them in a napkin. "There's plenty of sugar in these. They'll keep you going."

After Alan and Kurt had left, Hannah and Andrea returned to their own table. They visited with the other banquet guests for a few minutes, Hannah accepted compliments on the cookies, and they watched the coronation of the Prince and Princess of Winter. When the ceremony was over, they retrieved their coats and boots and walked up the stairs to the lobby.

"I wonder how many books Marge sold," Hannah mused as they sat down in chairs at the book-signing table to switch from their shoes to their boots.

"A hundred and sixty-three. I heard her talking to Bertie Straub about it. She's taking the rest to the warm-up tents, and Mrs. Baxter's girls are going to sell them for her."

"That's great," Hannah said, stashing her shoes in her purse and opening the door so that they could step out.

"It's snowing again!" Andrea complained, gazing up at the sky as they walked across the icy parking lot to their vehicles. "I signed us up for the family snowman contest, and Tracey's really looking forward to it."

"It's supposed to stop by tomorrow morning. I heard the KCOW weather report on the drive in."

"I hope they're right." Andrea arrived at her Volvo and unlocked the door to retrieve her long-handled brush and scraper. She brushed the snow from her windshield and tossed the essential piece of winter equipment into the back-seat. "I haven't built a snowman since I was a kid. Do you remember how to do it?"

"All you have to do is roll three balls of snow. You make a big one for the base, a medium-sized one for the torso, and a small one for the head. You stack them up, put on a face, and stick in some twigs for the arms. Then you decorate it with a hat or a scarf or whatever, and you're done. Anyone can build a snowman. It's easy."

"Since you know how, will you help us? Bill's going to be busy with the murder investigation, and it'd go a lot faster with three people. There's a time limit, you know."

Hannah sighed. She'd been had and she knew it. "Okay, I'll help. What time is the contest?"

"Two o'clock at the park. Thanks, Hannah." Andrea glanced at her watch in the glare from the dome light. "I've got to get a move on. Mother and Carrie are dropping Tracey off in twenty minutes. Do you want me to wait to see if your truck starts?"

"It'll start. And if it doesn't, someone will give me a jump."

Once Andrea had driven off, Hannah brushed the snow from her own windshield and started her truck. It fired up immediately and she cranked the heater up to high. As she waited for the engine to warm up, she took out her notebook and wrote down what they'd learned tonight, even though none of it seemed important.

By the time Hannah had slipped her notebook back into her purse, a whisper of tepid air was emerging from her heater vents. It was enough to chase away the frost from the inside of the windshield, but that was about it. Wishing that she'd opted for the auxiliary heater that Cyril Murphy had attempted to sell her when she'd bought her truck, she switched on her headlights and windshield wipers, and drove out of the parking lot.

Resisting the urge to drive past her shop to see if they'd taken the crime scene tape down, Hannah headed for the highway. Bill would have called if there'd been any change.

Hannah stepped on the gas, pulled in behind a rental truck with Michigan plates, and drove toward home. The only way she could get back into The Cookie Jar fast was to catch Connie Mac's killer, and that was turning out to be a lot harder than she'd hoped it would be.

Chapter Eighteen

"This is delicious, Hannah," Janie said as she bit into the sandwich Hannah had made for her. "I still remember the first time you made us a grilled cream cheese sandwich."

"So do I," Hannah replied, smiling at the memory. She'd decided to make grilled cheese sandwiches for Andrea and Janie one high school night when they'd stayed up late, cramming for a test. She'd buttered the bread, heated the frying pan, and only then discovered that someone had eaten the last piece of American cheese in the refrigerator. Since everything else had been ready, Hannah had sliced a block of chilled cream cheese and used that as a substitute. The resulting sandwich had been so delicious, she'd never made traditional grilled cheese sandwiches again.

"You should make cooking mistakes more often." Janie smiled at her. "You always end up with something fabulous."

"Not always. Remember the time I put tomato soup in my tuna hotdish? It was so awful, we couldn't eat it and we had to go out for pizza."

Janie made a face. "I wish you hadn't reminded me. But everyone's entitled to one flop, and you've more than made up for it."

"I need to ask you about something, Janie." Hannah turned

her mind back to the problem at hand. "I ran into Kurt Howe at the library today, and he told me that the television station has a lot of Connie Mac shows that haven't aired yet."

"Kurt's right. We taped the shows in June and Connie Mac did four shows a day, every other day."

"Four shows a day?" Hannah was surprised. "Isn't that an awful lot of work?"

"Yes, but not for her. The staff did all the setup work before she even got to the studio. All she had to do was assemble pre-measured ingredients while she talked to her guests, stick pans in the oven, and take out the ones we'd already baked."

"So she didn't actually cook the dinners?"

"No, we did it all in advance. That's why she worked every second day. We needed that extra day to get everything ready for her."

Hannah did a little mental arithmetic. "She did sixty shows in a month?"

"That's right. When we were all through, her producer picked out the best shows and the station put those on the schedule. They kept the rest as a backlog. I'm sure they have enough for at least a year, maybe two."

"Is that normal?" Hannah asked. "I mean . . . it's almost as if the television station expected Connie Mac to die and they prepared for it ahead of time."

"There's nothing unusual in what they did, Hannah. Taping ahead is standard business practice for any show that's so dependent on its star. They can't do it with shows that deal with current events, but cooking shows are timeless."

"Okay, if you say so." But Hannah decided she'd check it out anyway. "Was Connie Mac one of those *difficult* stars?"

"Only with her own staff, and she was never difficult when one of television executives was on the set. Then she was all sweetness and light."

Janie's eyes were drooping, and that prompted Hannah to glance at her watch. "It's almost eleven and Norman's late. I wonder what's keeping him."

"Maybe his car wouldn't start?" Janie suggested. "It's really cold out there tonight."

"That's possible, but I'm sure he would have called." The moment the words were out of Hannah's mouth, the phone rang. She grinned at Janie as she reached out to answer it. "I guess you were right. That's probably him now."

But the voice that greeted her wasn't Norman's, and Hannah felt a prickle of fear. "Luanne? Is there something wrong?"

"Yes. I called to tell you that I'm here at the hospital with Norman."

"The *hospital?*" The prickle of fear expanded into a knot in Hannah's stomach. "Are you all right?"

"I'm fine, but Norman's got a bad bump on his head. Doctor Knight says he could have a concussion."

"Was it a traffic accident?"

"No, Norman got mugged on the way out to his car."

For a moment, Hannah was speechless. As far as she knew, there'd never been a mugging in Lake Eden before. "Where did it happen?"

"In the parking lot outside the Ezekiel Jordan house. We had a late portrait sitting. When I left, Norman told me he was going to reload his cameras, and then he was going to drive out to your place. That's why I called you."

"Hold on a second." Hannah shook her head to clear it. "If you left, how did you find out that Norman was mugged?"

"I went back. Norman gave me a little stuffed giraffe for Susie and I left it in my makeup kit. I was all the way out to the highway when I remembered. I went back to get it and I found Norman facedown in the snow next to his car. It was really scary, Hannah."

"I'll bet it was. Did you see the mugger?"

"No, I didn't see anybody. Norman thinks I scared him off, because it happened right before I got there. I didn't want to leave Norman there and go call for an ambulance, so I helped him to my car and took him straight out to the emergency room."

"You did exactly the right thing, Luanne," Hannah assured her.

"Can you drive out here, Hannah? I have to get home and Norman doesn't have any way back to town."

"I'll be there in ten minutes," Hannah promised. "And thanks, Luanne. I'm really glad you forgot that giraffe."

"Me, too. 'Bye, Hannah."

Hannah hung up the phone and turned to Janie, who was staring at her curiously. "Norman got mugged. He's out at Lake Eden Memorial and I'm driving out there. Do you want to come along?"

"I'd rather stay here. Is there anything I can do for you while you're gone?"

"Yes. Check to make sure all the doors and windows are locked, and don't let anyone in."

"Why?" Janie looked worried. "Is there a problem?"

"I don't know, but Norman was a suspect in Connie Mac's murder, and so are you."

"Then you think Norman's mugging has something to do with Connie Mac's murder?"

"I won't know until I talk to him, but it's better to be safe than sorry."

"Okay, Hannah. I'll wait up for you. And I'll put on a pot of coffee so it'll be ready for you when you come home."

"Thanks, but the last thing I'm going to need when I get home is a load of caffeine. There's an extra gallon of wine in the broom closet, right next to Moishe's kitty crunchies. Shove it in the bottom of the refrigerator for me, will you? I have a feeling I'm going to need it tonight."

"Hannah!" Norman looked absolutely delighted to see her—as delighted as a man could look who was flat on his back on an emergency room cot with a blood-pressure cuff on his arm and a turban-style bandage wrapped around his head. "You came."

"Of course I came. Luanne tells me you've been testing out the theory that your head is harder than concrete."

"Wood," Norman told her, struggling up into a sitting position. "Doc Knight found a splinter in my ski cap, and he thinks it came from a baseball bat."

"Whatever. Are you supposed to sit up like that?"

"They didn't tell me *not* to sit up. I'm fine, Hannah. I've just got a little headache, that's all."

"Don't go all Mister Tough Guy on me," Hannah warned. "You have to be hurting. Where's Doc Knight? I want to talk to him."

"He's around here somewhere. Whatever you do, Hannah, don't call my mother. She'll be out here with chicken soup and a mustard plaster. And the soup will be straight out of a red-and-white can."

Hannah laughed. Delores had done the same thing when she was sick. "Okay, I won't call her. How about the sheriff's department? They should know what happened."

"They already know. Doc Knight called them the minute I came in, and they sent Rick Murphy out to take my statement. I couldn't tell him much. I never even saw who hit me."

"Okay, I'll be right back." Hannah walked over and touched Norman's arm. She had the urge to kiss him on the cheek, but she didn't. She just patted his arm, turned on her heel, and went out to find Doc Knight.

The first three emergency room cubicles Hannah passed were empty, but there was someone in the fourth. The curtains were drawn, but she could hear Doc Knight talking to someone about zinc powder and how often to apply it. Since there'd been a recent outbreak of athletes' foot at Jordan High, Hannah figured that the person behind the curtain was another shower-room casualty.

Doc Knight stepped out of the cubicle and he smiled when he saw Hannah. "Don't worry. He'll be fine. He can leave, but don't let him sleep for at least three hours. No alcohol and a liquid diet for the first twelve hours. Bring him right back out here if he shows any signs of concussion."

"Okay," Hannah said. "Norman told me you thought it was a baseball bat?"

"Either that or something similar. He took a hard blow and he's lucky it glanced off. A direct hit probably would have killed him."

Hannah winced. She didn't want to think about that. "Like Connie Mac?"

"I'd say so," Doc Knight looked wary, "but you didn't hear that from me. I took pictures, and I'll compare them when I get some breathing room. And I didn't tell you that, either."

"I understand. You're just a font of noninformation."

"And that's the way I want it. If the boys out at the sheriff's station find out I told you anything at all, they'll skin me alive. Now take him off my hands and give him some TLC. I've got a two-car accident coming in any minute and I need the beds."

"Aspirin?" Hannah asked.

"No. I gave him something for his headache, and he can have another pill in two hours. That should knock him out for the rest of the night."

"You got it. I'll take him straight home," Hannah promised.

"No, not home. Take him to your place. If you take him home, Carrie will kick up a fuss and he'll never get any rest. Let him relax for a couple of hours and then he can go home. And if Carrie starts weeping and wailing, give *her* one of Norman's pills."

"Well, there's one good thing," Norman said, accepting the mug of hot chocolate Hannah had made for him. "Until this bandage comes off, I won't have to wear a hat."

Janie laughed. "All you need is a jewel in the middle of that turban and you'll look like a sheik."

"I think it might take a little more than that," Norman said, taking a sip of his drink. "This is really good, Hannah."

"Doc Knight told me to keep you on liquids, and I figured a shot of liquid chocolate was better than low-fat chicken broth. How are you feeling, Norman?"

"Okay. I've still got a headache, but it's not as bad as it was before. Go ahead, Hannah."

"Go ahead and what?"

"Ask me those questions you've been dying to ask. If you hold them in much longer, you're going to pop."

Hannah gave a self-conscious laugh. Norman knew her very well. "Are you sure you're well enough to answer?"

"I'm sure. Ask me now, while everything's still fresh in my mind."

"Okay." Hannah flipped to a fresh page in her notebook. "I know you didn't actually see your attacker, but did you see or hear anything right before he hit you?"

"No."

"Did you feel anything? A leather glove? A fur jacket? Anything like that?"

"All I felt was the blow."

"Did you smell anything? A cigarette burning? A distinctive aftershave, or a scented soap?"

"No. I don't have a clue who hit me, Hannah."

"Okay," Hannah sighed, switching to another line of questions. "Who knew that you'd be taking portraits at the Ezekiel Jordan House tonight?"

"Beatrice and Ted Koester. They were my subjects. And Luanne knew because she did Beatrice's makeup. Our mothers knew because I told them. They were taking Tracey to a movie tonight and I figured they might drive past on their way home. I didn't want them to worry when they saw lights on inside."

Hannah groaned in tandem with Janie. Both of them knew that Delores was a virtual pipeline of information.

"There's one thing I know." Norman looked very serious. "I thought about it all the way back here. I wasn't mugged or carjacked. I was deliberately targeted for some reason."

Hannah stared at him in surprise. "What makes you think that?"

"If the guy wanted my car, he could have hot-wired it while I was inside loading my cameras. It took me a good fifteen minutes, and everyone else had already left. And I was carrying a waterproof gym bag with a couple of cameras and my wallet inside. I set it down on the top of the trunk while I brushed off my windshield. He could have just grabbed it and run. I think I was attacked by Connie Mac's killer."

"You're lucky he didn't kill you, Norman," Janie commented, and Hannah noticed that her face was very pale.

"I know. I think the only thing that saved me was that I dropped my car keys in the snow. He must have swung at me just as I bent down to pick them up."

"That would explain what Doc Knight told me," Hannah said. "He thought it was a glancing blow."

"Exactly. And I'm pretty sure he would have hit me a second time if Luanne hadn't driven up just then."

Hannah didn't want to think about what would have happened if Norman hadn't dropped his car keys. Instead, she concentrated on asking another question. "Let's say you *were* targeted by Connie Mac's killer. Why you?"

"I don't know. It's true that I was next door the night she was killed, but it's not like I could identify him or anything."

"No, but he might think you could." Hannah's mind raced through the possibilities, and one stood out. "Wait a second. Didn't you tell me that you were testing your fill lights that night?"

"Yes," Norman answered. "What does that have to do with it?"

"Did your lights flash when you were testing them?" Norman nodded, and Hannah began to smile. "Then I've got it."

"Got what?"

"The reason why Connie Mac's killer targeted you. What if he was hiding outside The Cookie Jar that night, waiting for a chance to get Connie Mac alone and kill her? He could have seen those flashes and thought that you were taking pictures of him."

"I just remembered something," Janie told them. "Connie Mac and I saw the flashes on the snow outside. She thought that some reporter was trying to take an unauthorized picture of her through the window, but I pointed out that it was coming from the Ezekiel Jordan House, and we decided that you must have been taking portraits over there."

Hannah leaned forward in excitement. "You have to develop that film, Norman. You could have a picture of Connie Mac's killer!"

"Impossible," Norman said, shaking his head. "My camera wasn't loaded. I didn't want to waste film when I was just testing the lights."

Hannah bit back a word that might have made Janie blush and groaned instead. "For a minute there, I thought we might have a shortcut to the killer."

All three of them were silent for a moment, and then Norman turned to Hannah. "Maybe we do have a shortcut."

"How? You said your camera wasn't loaded."

"It wasn't, but the killer doesn't know that. He still thinks I've got a picture of him. He'll have to try to kill me again, Hannah. I'm sure of that. And that means we can set a trap for him."

Hannah's mouth dropped open and she stared at Norman in shock. Then she shook her head furiously. "That knock on the head must have rattled your brains. If you had any sense left at all, you'd know there's no way I'd ever let you use yourself for bait!"

Grilled Cream Cheese Sandwiches

(Hannah Swensen's Very Best Mistake)

For each sandwich you will need:

2 slices of bread *(white, egg, wheat—take your pick)*
1 package of chilled block cream cheese *(not softened or whipped)*
Softened butter

Butter two slices of bread. Place one slice buttered side down on a piece of waxed paper. Cut slices of cream cheese approximately ½-inch thick to cover the surface of the bread. Put the other slice of bread on top, buttered side up.

Preheat a frying pan on the stove. Using a spatula, place your sandwich in the pan. Fry it uncovered until the bottom turns golden brown. *(You can test it by lifting it up just a bit with the spatula.)* Flip the sandwich over and fry the other side until it's golden brown. Remove the sandwich from the frying pan, cut it into four pieces with a sharp knife, arrange it on a plate, and serve it immediately.

This sandwich goes well with piping-hot mugs of tomato soup.

You can turn this into a dessert sandwich by using slices of banana or date-nut bread and sprinkling the sandwich with a little powered sugar. If you really want to go whole hog, top it with a scoop of ice cream. It's delicious that way.

Chapter Nineteen

Six o'clock came much too early and Hannah crawled out of the warm comfort of her bed reluctantly. It seemed as though just minutes had passed since she'd taken Norman to the scene of his assault to pick up his car and followed him home to make sure he got there safely. She'd idled outside the house for a few minutes, but no lights had gone on in Carrie's bedroom. When Hannah had been fairly certain that Norman wouldn't be required to deal with a hysterical mother in the middle of the night, she'd driven back to her condo and fallen into her bed for the hours of sleep that were left to her.

Hannah gazed around her, blinking in the glare from the lamp on her bed table. Moishe wasn't there. He'd probably crawled in with Janie in the wee hours of the morning. Even though she knew she was being silly, his defection disturbed her. Moishe was a male, and all the important males in her life had deserted her in one way or another. Mike had turned cool and coplike. It wasn't surprising, considering that he was in charge of a murder investigation, but she missed the good-natured banter they'd enjoyed in the past. And Norman was just as bad. He'd told her he wasn't jealous of the time she'd spent with Mike, and now he'd had the nerve to sug-

gest that he use himself as bait in a trap for the killer without
a second thought for her feelings. Then there was Moishe.
She'd taken him in, fed him the best cat food that money
could buy, and taken him to the vet for his shots. And how
did he repay her kind generosity? He'd left her bed in the
middle of the night and deserted her for a younger woman!

Her slippers were right where she'd left them, and Hannah pulled them on. She knew she was being ridiculous, but
she couldn't seem to help it. Moishe had been waiting for
her in her bed when she'd arrived home last night, and he'd
let her cuddle him for much longer than usual. He'd even
purred and licked her cheek with his raspy tongue. He loved
her; Hannah knew he did, and that was more than she could
say for either Norman or Mike. She was in a bad mood this
morning because she was tired, and she had to shake it off.

Once Hannah had showered, she felt much better. Ten
minutes under a steaming spray had loosened her cramped
muscles and erased some of the fog from her brain. She
dressed in a pair of jeans, pulled on the alternate Winter
Carnival sweatshirt she'd bought, and slipped her feet back
into the old pair of dorm slippers she wore around the house.
Then she padded down the hallway toward the kitchen. She
had a lot to do, and if she didn't get a move on, she'd fall behind schedule. Today would be a prime example of "hurry
up and get there so you can rush as fast as you can." That
was a smidgeon better on the frustration scale than "hurry
up and get there so you can wait," but not much. Somehow,
she had to get energized, and a strong cup of coffee was the
only cure for her case of drooping eyelids.

"Morning, Hannah," Janie greeted her. She was standing
at Hannah's stove, flipping something in a frying pan.
"Don't try to talk. Just sit down at the table and I'll bring you
a mug of coffee."

Hannah sank down in a chair. It was much more comfortable than she'd remembered, and she resisted the urge to put
her head down on her folded arms and snooze.

"Drink this," Janie ordered, plunking a mug of coffee
down in front of Hannah's nose. "It'll help."

Hannah inhaled the strong fragrance and took one huge gulp. The coffee was hot but not scalding, and she realized that Janie must have poured it when she'd heard her getting dressed. After she'd drained the cup and held it out for a refill, her eyes opened all the way and she smiled at Janie. "Thanks. I'm beginning to feel halfway human."

"Good. Now all we have to do is work on that other half. I take it Norman got home okay?"

"He should be fine. I stuck around for a few minutes to make sure his mother didn't wake up. What are you doing out here so early?"

"Moishe got me up. I think he was sorry he'd made such a mess."

"What mess?"

"He got into the cabinet where you keep the cat food. I swept it up and filled his bowl."

Hannah's gaze turned from Moishe, who was happily chowing down at his food bowl, to the broom closet door. It was locked up tight, and she knew she'd left it that way. "What happened?"

"He learned how to open the lock." Janie walked over to the door and pointed. "I think he jumped up on the top of the refrigerator and batted at the hook until it popped out."

"That figures," Hannah said, giving Moishe a baleful look. He stared back at her with wide yellow eyes, and he didn't look at all guilty. "What are you cooking?"

"French toast. Are you getting hungry yet?"

"You bet. It smells wonderful. Are you sure you don't want to move in permanently?"

"I'll think about it." Janie laughed and flipped the French toast out onto a plate. "I got the recipe from Helen, Connie Mac's cook."

"The Cooking Sweetheart had a *cook?*"

"Oh, yes. She got her best recipes from Helen. The Winter Carnival cake was Helen's recipe, and she made the original one."

Hannah remembered Connie Mac's conversation with Edna and how she'd claimed she stayed up most of the night to decorate the cake. It seemed that Connie Mac had been a fake as well as a nasty person. "How about the replacement you were baking?"

"I was supposed to bake all the layers. Mrs. MacIntyre thought that I could handle that. And when I was through, she was going to call Helen and have her drive to Lake Eden to decorate it."

Hannah took another gulp of her coffee. This could be very important, especially if Helen had hated Connie Mac as much as the other people who'd worked for her. "Do you know if Connie Mac called Helen?"

"She didn't. I told Bill and Mike about it and they checked." Janie carried the plate to Hannah, went back for butter and maple syrup, and sat down in the opposite chair. "I brought in the paper. Do you want the front section?"

"No, give me the comics. I can't handle hard news until I've had at least one pot of coffee. You read it and tell me if there's anything interesting."

The French toast was delicious, light and fluffy with a mouthwatering hint of cinnamon and nutmeg. Hannah finished it in record time and got up to get refills on their coffee. She was just pouring some for Janie when she heard her gasp.

"What is it?" Hannah set the coffee pot down on the table.

"Larry Kruger wrote another ghost story. He's speculating that Ezekiel Jordan's ghost is the one who bashed Norman on the head."

"You're kidding!" Hannah started to laugh. "I guess he doesn't know that Norman's family moved here from out of state. It's pretty unlikely that Norman could be related to anybody in F. E. Laughlin's poker game."

"Larry's got that base covered. He claims that Ezekiel's ghost was upset over the fact that Norman was taking pictures in your mother's re-creation of his house. It seems that Ezekiel Jordan was a spiritualist and he believed that a camera could steal a man's soul. He refused to pose for pictures or allow any member of his family to be photographed. According to Larry, that's why there aren't any pictures of him. Ezekiel wouldn't allow a camera anywhere inside his house."

"Larry's nothing if not enterprising," Hannah commented. "Does he think that Ezekiel's ghost hit Norman over the head to keep him from taking more portraits?"

"That's what he says. And a lot of people seem to be taking it seriously. Here's a story about another ghost sighting out at the inn last night."

"What time?" Hannah asked.

"At a quarter to ten."

"Then Ezekiel's ghost can be in two places at once. Norman told me that he was bashed on the head at nine forty-five."

Janie started to grin. "That must be an advantage a spirit has over ordinary mortals like us. Larry interviewed Sally Laughlin and she claims she saw something floating down the hall last night at a quarter to ten."

"*Sally* said that?" Hannah turned the article so that she could read it. Once she'd scanned it, she looked up with a frown. "That's an abrupt turn of face for Sally. When I talked to her yesterday, she told me she didn't believe in ghosts. I'm going to ask her about it when I get to the inn."

By the time Hannah got out to the inn, Lisa was already hard at work rolling dough balls for the Old-Fashioned Sugar Cookies. After apologizing for being late, Hannah pitched in to help. When the four ovens Sally had allotted for their use were filled and they'd rolled the rest of the dough balls, Lisa fetched them cups of coffee and they took a short break.

"Tell me what really happened to Norman last night," Lisa urged, sitting down on a stool next to Hannah. "I read Larry Kruger's story in the paper, but I didn't believe a word of it."

"Norman got bashed in the head on his way out to his car, Luanne Hanks pulled up just in time to scare his attacker away, and neither one of them saw who hit him. Norman figures it was Connie Mac's killer, and he asked me to set a trap and use him for bait."

Lisa's eyes widened. "Are you going to do it?"

"Of course not. It's much too dangerous. My big worry is that Norman's going to try to set up something himself."

"You could be right. A guy can be really foolish when he's trying to impress his girlfriend."

That comment stopped Hannah cold, and it took her a minute to recover. "You mean . . . me?"

"Yes, you. Norman adores you, Hannah. I've seen the way he looks at you."

"Have you been listening to *Doctor Love?*" Hannah asked the first question that popped into her mind.

"No, I hate that show. This is just common sense, Hannah. Norman loves you and he's trying to convince you that he's worthy of your love."

Hannah remembered having a remarkably similar conversation with Andrea. In Lisa's version, only the name of the man had changed. Was it possible that both Mike and Norman were in love with her? Life wasn't a B-movie, and she certainly wasn't the gorgeous ingenue who sashayed her way into a love triangle with two men.

"I'm right, Hannah. You've got to trust me on this."

Hannah still wasn't convinced. "Okay. What do you think I should do?"

"Think of some way to stop Norman before he gets himself into trouble."

"Right," Hannah said, wondering what that would entail. Putting Norman in a straitjacket would work, but she didn't happen to have one handy. Handcuffs were out, Norman could still walk around in those, and an enforced trip to a desert island was impractical. Instead of concentrating on a way to render Norman immobile, she had to think of a way to convince the killer that Norman hadn't taken his picture.

"The timer just rang. You sit here and think and I'll get the cookies out of the ovens. Be devious, Hannah. You're good at that."

Hannah wasn't sure if that was a compliment, but she sat

on her stool and thought as she gazed out the window that overlooked the dining room. A few people were beginning to arrive for the continental breakfast that Sally always provided on Sunday mornings, and Hannah noticed a man filling his cup from the urn of coffee on the bar.

As she watched the man carry his coffee and a sweet roll to a two-person table in the center of the dining room, Hannah's thoughts turned back to Norman. How could she save him from himself? If he was trying to impress her with his courage, it was having quite the opposite effect. She could just kill him for offering to bait a trap, but she might not have the chance if the murderer got to him first.

The man she'd been watching had eaten his sweet roll and now he was finishing his coffee. Hannah expected him to go back for a second cup, but he surprised her by pulling a small notebook from his pocket and beginning to write. He was probably a reporter, and that realization gave Hannah the perfect idea to take the wind out of Norman's macho sails.

"I got it!" she called out to Lisa. "Can you hold the fort for a couple of minutes? I have to find Sally and ask her who that reporter is."

"Which reporter?" Lisa asked, walking over to peer through the window.

"The one in the center of the room. He's wearing a blue Scandinavian sweater."

"That's Larry Kruger. Alex pointed him out to me yesterday. He's the one who's been writing those ghost stories."

"Bingo!" Hannah said and gave Lisa a hug. "I'll be back right after I plant the idea for his next installment."

Larry Kruger smiled at Hannah. "It sounds like you really enjoyed my story."

"Oh, yes, very much," Hannah said, resisting the urge to kick him in the shins for all the trouble he'd caused. "I'm a friend of Norman's, and he told me something about his attack that wasn't in the paper."

"Really?"

"Yes. Norman told me that he tried to take a picture of Ezekiel Jordan's ghost on the night that Connie Mac was murdered."

"No kidding!"

Hannah could practically see the wheels turning in Larry Kruger's brain. She had him hooked and she knew it. "Norman was right next door and he saw a very strange shape lurking around outside. He said it seemed to float. Of course he had no idea that the shape was a ghost. He just thought it was curious and he snapped a whole role of film."

"Did he . . . uh . . . develop the film?"

"Oh, yes. And absolutely *nothing* was on it. Of course, I wasn't surprised. I'm very interested in the occult, and I know that it's impossible to take a picture of a spirit. Their essence can't be captured by any mortal means."

"Uh . . . yes. I've heard that. Thanks for telling me about it."

"You're welcome. I really think people should know more facts about the spirit world. It's just fascinating. I've been toying with the idea of calling KCOW radio to tell them about Norman's experience, but I just hate to give them my name and . . ."

"You don't have to do that," Larry interrupted. "I'll be happy to call them for you. And I'll put it in the papers, too."

"And you won't use my name?"

"Not if you don't want me to," Larry promised. "I'll just say I got the information from a reliable source who knows Norman Rhodes. No one will ever connect you to my story."

Hannah put on her best grateful look. "Thank you, Larry. That'll be just fine with me."

Lisa was practically in hysterics by the time Hannah finished telling her what she'd done. "And he actually believed you?"

"Oh, yes. The story should be on KCOW radio by noon at

the latest. Now all I have to do is hope that the killer is listening."

"What are you going to tell Norman?"

Hannah winced. She hadn't thought of that. "I guess I'll just say that I knew how stubborn he could be and I wanted to save him from doing something idiotic."

"Don't say it like that!" Lisa looked appalled. "You have to be more tactful. Tell Norman that you care about him and you were worried about his safety. And admit that maybe you should have consulted him first, but you felt you had to do something."

"Okay, I can live with that. Now let's get going on these cookies. You mix up another batch of your White Chocolate Supremes and I'll start baking the Pecan Chews."

Lisa left for the pantry to gather up her supplies, and Hannah scooped out dough for the Pecan Chews. She'd just slipped the first two pans into the oven when Sally came into the kitchen.

"Pecan Chews?" Sally walked over to gaze at the dough in Hannah's bowl.

"Give the little lady a stuffed toy. Pull up a stool, Sally. I need to ask you something." Hannah waited until Sally was seated. None of the kitchen staff was close enough to hear, and it was the perfect opportunity to ask her about the ghost sightings. "I read the article in the paper this morning and it said you saw Ezekiel's ghost last night. I thought you didn't believe in ghosts."

"I don't, but your sister was right. Ghosts are good for business. The phone rang off the hook yesterday afternoon, and everyone that called in for reservations wanted to know if I'd actually seen the ghost. I happened to mention all the new business to Francine, and she thought we should actually have a ghost."

Hannah stared at Sally in amazement. "How do you actually *have* a ghost?"

"Francine offered to float down the hall like a ghost. She's going to put in appearances every couple of nights, just to keep the story going. I didn't want to do it at first. I mean, it's not exactly honest. But Francine pointed out that a lot of big theme hotels have events, and this was just another form of entertainment."

"That's as good a reason as any. How does Francine float down the hall?"

"She worked out a technique. You've got to see it to believe it. Do you want me to call you before she does her next appearance?"

"Absolutely," Hannah said, a plan beginning to hatch in her mind. If Sally gave her enough advance notice, she'd bring her mother and Carrie out to the inn for dinner and make sure they had front-row seats for the ghost sighting. If Francine was convincing enough, it might just scare the matchmaking schemes right out of their minds.

Lisa's White Chocolate Supremes

Preheat oven to 350°F,
rack in the middle position

1 cup melted butter *(2 sticks, one-half pound)*
¾ cup white sugar
¾ cup brown sugar
2 teaspoons vanilla
1 ½ teaspoons baking soda
½ teaspoon salt
2 beaten eggs
2 ¼ cups flour *(no need to sift)*
2 cups (½ pound) real white chocolate *(or white chocolate chips)*
1 ½ cups chopped macadamia nuts *(measure before chopping)*

Melt the butter. Mix in the white sugar and brown sugar. Then mix in the vanilla, baking soda, and salt. Add the eggs and stir again. Add the flour and mix thoroughly.

If you're using block white chocolate, chop it up into pieces roughly the size of chocolate chips. You can do this in a food processor by cutting the chocolate in chunks and processing it with the steel blade. If you're using white chocolate chips, just measure out

2 cups. *(You can use vanilla chips, but the cookies won't taste the same.)*

Measure out the whole macadamia nuts. Chop them into pieces roughly the size of peas with a knife, or use your food processor and the steel blade.

Add the white chocolate and nuts to your bowl and mix thoroughly.

Drop the dough by teaspoons onto an UNGREASED cookie sheet, 12 cookies to a standard-size sheet. Bake at 350°F for 10 to 12 minutes or until nicely browned.

Let the cookies cool for two minutes, then remove them from the baking sheet and transfer them to a wire rack to finish cooling.

Lisa developed this recipe, and it's just like they say in the potato chip commercials—you can't eat just one.

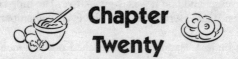

Chapter Twenty

"So what are your plans for the rest of the day?" Hannah asked Lisa when they'd finished loading the cookies into the back of her truck.

"I'm taking Dad on a tour of the Ezekiel Jordan House and we're making an appointment to have our pictures taken. Then we're going to the park to watch the family snowman contest."

"I'll see you there," Hannah told her. "Tracey's entered, and since Bill is working, I promised Andrea I'd help. Janie's coming along with me to watch."

"Tell Janie she can watch with us. I really like her, and I know Dad would like to see her again. I mentioned her name to him and he actually remembered her from years ago."

"He remembers quite a few things from the past, doesn't he?"

"That's one of the strange things about his memory. Dad can recall things from twenty or thirty years ago, but new things don't seem to register. Every time I take him to the senior center, he gets all excited because he thinks he's going there for the first time."

"At least he's never bored," Hannah said, attempting to put the brightest face on things. She knew Alzheimer's was a terrible disease, and that it was degenerative. The time could come when Jack Herman might not even remember his daughter.

"Don't be sad, Hannah." Lisa reached out to touch her arm. "I know Dad's prognosis, but at least he's happy now."

"He's very lucky he's got you," Hannah said, giving Lisa's hand a comforting pat. "And thanks for offering to entertain Janie while I'm off making a fool of myself."

Five minutes later, Hannah was zipping down the road toward her first venue. She was dropping off cookies at Jordan High, and the parking lot at the school ice rink was already dotted with cars. When she pulled in, she saw a familiar face, or at least part of one. It was Craig Kimball, and he was wearing a blaze orange ski mask.

"Hi, Miss Swensen!" Craig hailed her as she got out of her truck. "Do you need some help with your cookies?"

"Are you offering? I've got a bag of new cookies you can try if you are."

"You bet." Craig's eyes crinkled at the corners, and Hannah knew he was smiling behind all that orange yarn. "Just let me rope a couple of my friends into helping and we'll only have to make one trip."

Hannah opened the back of her truck while Craig jogged over to a group of Jordan High seniors. Before she had time to pick up the first box of cookies, she had six eager helpers. They carried the cookies over to the warm-up tent, and Hannah was amazed to see about a dozen spectators already in the bleachers that surrounded the rink. They were huddled in the front row in a tight little group, drinking steaming cups of coffee.

Once she'd paid off her volunteers, Hannah turned to Linda Nelson, who was running the counter. She was a senior, and Mrs. Baxter had told Hannah that she was the best homemaker in the class. "It looks like you've sold some coffee already."

"We sold one whole urn and we just made the second," Linda told her. "It's cold out there."

"What time does the speed-skating competition start?"

"At one o'clock. Some of the parents came early to see the warm-ups. You should come back to see it, Miss Swensen. Barry Withers is just incredible. If he can shave off a tenth of a second, he'll break the school record."

Hannah took one look at Linda's shining eyes and figured that a little romance might be brewing right along with that fresh urn of coffee. "I'll come back if I can. Right now I've got tons of cookies to deliver."

"Would you like a cup of coffee for the road?"

"I'd love it, thanks. And if you see Barry, tell him that I'm rooting for him."

Less than five minutes later, Hannah was back on the road, a fresh cup of coffee resting in the plastic carrier between her seats. The town baseball field was her next destination, and she was right on schedule.

As she pulled into the parking lot, Hannah saw that there was a flurry of activity out on the field. Two parka-clad teams of students were building snow forts at opposite ends of the field. In less than an hour, the "Great Snowball War" would begin, and the preparations were underway. Gil Surma, Jordan High's counselor and the assistant coach of the basketball team, was the general of the blue army stationed at first base. His team wore blue ski masks. The boys in the rival red army, which sported red ski masks, were engaged in building a fort by third base. They were commanded by their principal, Mr. Purvis. Both "generals" were out on the field, supervising the stockpiling of munitions to make sure that no foreign objects, such as rocks or chunks of ice, were rolled into the snowballs that were being stacked inside the forts.

Hannah parked as close to the warm-up tent as she could and got out to open the back of her truck. She stacked up as many boxes as she thought she could carry in one trip, picked them up with both arms, and headed for the entrance to the tent.

"Steady, Hannah." A familiar voice greeted her and strong arms reached out to take the top three boxes. "You were getting a little wobbly there."

Hannah smiled the moment the boxes were removed and she could see who her rescuer was. "Hi, Norman. How are you feeling?"

"Fine. My headache is gone and Doc Knight took off that bulky bandage. He says the stitches are already starting to heal."

"That's good. Did he say it was all right to judge the contest?"

Norman shook his head, and Hannah noticed that he winced slightly. No doubt his head was still sore. "I'm not judging. I came out here to take a couple of pictures for the school photography club."

"Doesn't the photography club take its own pictures?"

"Yes, but they asked me to come as backup. They want a shot of Mr. Purvis getting pelted for the yearbook."

"I guess things haven't changed that much." Hannah was grinning as they walked inside the warm-up tent with their sugary burden. "When I went to high school, we were always trying to get embarrassing pictures of our principal. You'd better not get too close to the action or you'll get a face full of snow."

"I know. That's why I'm using a telephoto lens," Norman explained, handing his boxes to one of Mrs. Baxter's students and following Hannah out to get more cookies.

After they'd carried in the last of the boxes that Mrs. Baxter had ordered, Hannah asked Norman to walk her back to her truck. When they arrived, she opened the passenger door. "Get in for a minute, Norman. I need to talk to you."

"Okay." Norman slid into the passenger seat and Hannah walked around to get in on the driver's side. Once she was settled, Norman turned to her. "What is it, Hannah?"

"I did something this morning that you might not like, but I had your best interests in mind," Hannah told him, and then she gave him the details of the story she'd planted with Larry Kruger.

"I wish you hadn't done that," Norman said when she was finished. "I rather fancied myself as bait. Is there any way you can retract that story?"

Hannah shook her head. "No way. I'm sorry if you don't like it, Norman, but I have enough to do without worrying about you."

"You were worried about me?"

"Of course I was. I was scared stiff that you'd go out and do something really stupid!"

The moment the words left Hannah's mouth, she wished that she could call them back. She'd completely forgotten about tact and what Lisa had advised her to say. She expected Norman to climb out of her truck and refuse to speak to her ever again, but all he did was grin.

"You're not mad?" Hannah asked him.

"I wish you'd asked me first, but I'm not mad. Actually, I'm quite the opposite." With that comment, Norman pulled her into his arms and hugged her hard. And then he tipped up her head and kissed her.

For a moment, Hannah was so startled, she almost resisted. Then nature took over and she found herself enjoying Norman's kiss thoroughly. Her instinct was to throw her arms around his neck and keep him right there in the front seat of her truck for a long, indefinite period, but before she could act on her impulse, Norman pulled back to smile at her.

"See? I'm not mad," he said, reaching out to tweak her nose. Then he opened the door and climbed out of her truck. "See you later, Hannah. I need to get some shots of Mr. Purvis inspecting those snowballs."

As Hannah drove off, she was smiling. She felt comforted, and warm, and more at peace than she'd been in days. But then her thoughts turned to Mike and she began to frown. She'd enjoyed Mike's kisses in the past, and she'd also enjoyed Norman's kiss. There was one big difference between the two. Mike's kisses made her feel sexy, on the verge of something slightly dangerous and very exciting. And Norman's kisses made her feel sexy, and natural, and good all over.

Hannah sighed. It was impossible to compare Mike and Norman. Mike was the man of her dreams, and Norman was

the man of her wide-awake hours. And every time she tried
to choose one over the other, she ended up wanting both of
them.

Lake Eden Park was a hubbub of activity when Hannah
arrived. Several shuttle sleighs were just arriving, and Hannah loaded herself up with boxes and carried them carefully
through the crowd.

"The cookies are here!" one of Mrs. Baxter's girls called
out as Hannah entered the warm-up tent. She rushed over to
take the boxes and motioned to two other girls. "Come on.
Let's go help Miss Swensen unload."

With four of them working, the unloading didn't take
long. On the trips back and forth to her truck, Hannah
learned that the girls had opened their concession thirty minutes early, they had already gone through three urns of coffee
and one of hot chocolate, and every one of their customers
had asked when the cookies would arrive.

"Here you go, Miss Swensen." One of the girls handed
Hannah a hot cup of coffee without asking. "Thanks for the
cookies."

Hannah left the tent intending to go straight back to her
truck, but she changed her mind halfway there. It wouldn't
hurt to check out the site to see which area they'd be using.

The family snowman contest would take place in the center of the park. As Hannah walked closer, she saw that the in-
dividual squares had been marked with brightly colored rope
tied to ski poles. Each area was tagged and Hannah found
theirs, number fifteen. It had a good-sized drift of snow in
the center, and Hannah figured they'd have more than enough
to make a man-sized snowman.

As she turned to leave, her eyes were drawn to a tall, familiar figure in a maroon sheriff's-issue parka. It was Mike,
and he was talking to a woman she didn't know, a gorgeous
platinum blond in a bright-red ski outfit. Under normal circumstances, Hannah would have walked over to say hello,

but these weren't normal circumstances. She was just turning to go in the opposite direction when Mike spotted her.

"Hi, Hannah!" A huge grin spread over Mike's face and he waved his arms.

Hannah grinned back. She didn't want to, but she couldn't help it. There was something about Mike's grin that was contagious.

"Come over here for a minute," he called out, motioning to her. "I've got someone I want you to meet."

"Of all the people in all this snow, I have to run into him!" Hannah muttered, borrowing heavily from *Casablanca*. If Mike meant the blond, and she was sure he did, Hannah didn't want to meet her. On the other hand, they knew she'd seen them, and to ignore them would be rude.

"Hannah Swensen, this is Kristi Hampton," Mike said. "Kristi was Mrs. MacIntyre's personal beautician."

"Glad to meet you," Hannah said without meaning it.

"Likewise," Kristi responded, but she didn't give Hannah more than a fleeting glance before she turned back to Mike. "Is it too late to enter the contest? I don't have family here, but I could recruit you."

"Sorry, I'm working."

Mike looked a bit embarrassed, and Hannah could see why. Kristi had her hand on his sleeve and was stroking it like the owner of a prized stallion.

"So, Hannah," Mike said, turning to her, "why are you here?"

Hannah smiled. It didn't hurt to be friendly, and Kristi had worked for Connie Mac. Perhaps she could learn something. "I just delivered cookies to the warm-up tent. I've got extras in my truck if you and Kristi haven't had breakfast."

"Thanks, but I never eat breakfast," Kristi said with a sultry gaze at Mike, "unless I've been up all night. And I already had my breakfast. Besides, I have to watch my carbs."

"I don't, and I could use a cookie," Mike said.

"Well, that's different." Kristi patted Mike's arm. "You men have to keep up your strength."

Mike smiled and removed her hand from his sleeve.

"Excuse me, Kristi. I'm going to walk Hannah to her truck. I have to talk to her about something private."

Hannah's eyebrows shot up as Mike grabbed her arm and they set off at a fast pace across the snow. She had all she could do to resist the urge to turn back and thumb her nose.

"I've got two pieces of news for you, Hannah." Mike's grip tightened on her arm. "Is Miss Burkholtz still staying with you?"

"Yes, she is. Is that against the law?"

"Of course not. It was nice of you to take her in. I just wanted to tell you that Bill and I worked late last night doing interviews with Mrs. MacIntyre's staff. I drew Kristi, and she was very cooperative."

I'll just bet she was, Hannah thought, but she didn't say it. She just waited for Mike to go on.

"I wanted you to know that Miss Burkholtz is in the clear."

Hannah almost forgave him for the sultry look that Kristi had given him. "That's great! Just wait until I tell her."

"One of the maids that Bill interviewed said she saw Miss Burkholtz leaving the hotel at ten minutes to twelve on the night that Mrs. MacIntyre was murdered. And Kristi told me that she saw her pull into the parking lot at the inn at ten."

"And since my shop is twenty-five minutes from the inn, Janie has an alibi?"

"That's right. Kristi was just leaving the parking lot, and Miss Burkholtz took the spot she vacated. I checked it out."

"How did you do that?" Hannah was curious.

"I took Kristi out to the bar at the mall last night, and a couple of the guys remembered that she walked in at ten-twenty. I'm not surprised they noticed her. Kristi's a very attractive woman."

Hannah bit her tongue so she wouldn't ask how long Mike's interview with Kristi had lasted and exactly where they'd gone after they'd left the bar. She told herself she should be grateful to Kristi for providing Janie's alibi, but that did nothing to reduce the sharp stab of jealousy she felt.

"You said you had two pieces of news for me. What's the second?"

"I cleared Norman Rhodes."

"How did you do that?"

"It was that attack he suffered last night. At first I thought it might be faked, but there's no way he could have bashed himself on the back of the head. I think the murderer hit Norman and only Luanne Hanks's arrival kept him from being killed. What I don't know is why Mrs. MacIntyre's murderer was after Norman."

"I do," Hannah said, unlocking the passenger door to her truck. "Climb in and have a cookie, and I'll tell you."

Mike went through four cookies in the time it told her to tell her story, and Hannah figured that it was a good investment. When she was finished, she leaned back in her seat with a sigh. "What do you think? Does it make sense?"

"It makes perfect sense. Good for you for figuring it out. Just between you and me, Hannah, I'm really glad that Norman's off my suspect list."

"Why?"

"Because suspecting Norman made me really uncomfortable. My gut instincts told me that he was innocent, but what if I'd been wrong? I had to warn you, Hannah."

"I understand."

"There's another thing, too. I was afraid you'd think I was jealous of your relationship with Norman, and that was the reason I put him on my suspect list."

"Really? I didn't even think of that!"

"You didn't?"

"It never crossed my mind," Hannah told him quite truthfully. It had crossed Andrea's mind, not hers. "You aren't, are you? Jealous, I mean?"

"No. To tell you the truth, I'm relieved. I'm just not ready to settle down yet, and I'd feel guilty if you just sat around like a lovesick teenager and waited for me to call."

Hannah bristled. "I don't think you have to worry about *that*."

"I know. I figure the time will come when I want that kind

of commitment again, but not right now. If I did want to get remarried, though . . ." Mike reached across the seat and pulled Hannah into his arms. He kissed her until both of them were breathless, and then he chuckled. "When I get to that point, you'll be the first to know."

Hannah sighed, still a little dazed from Mike's kiss. She had the urge to cuddle back up to him, but he'd been the one to break their embrace.

"I'll tell you one thing. Norman really impressed me."

"He did?"

"Absolutely. He left a message on my voice mail and I just retrieved it a couple of minutes ago. Do you know that he offered himself for bait so that we could set a trap for the killer?"

Hannah winced, wondering if she had messed up some sort of sting operation by planting the ghost story with Larry Kruger. "Are you going to take him up on it?"

"Of course not. We can't involve a civilian in something that dangerous. I called him right back to tell him that, but he wasn't home. I think we'll arrange a tail for him, though. He could be in real danger."

"I already took care of that," Hannah said. And then she told Mike what she'd done. "I was worried about him and I thought he might try to do something on his own."

Mike stopped in the act of taking another cookie and gave her a sharp look. "You were worried about Norman?"

"Of course I was. Norman's one of my very best friends."

Mike stared at her for a moment. "Yeah, he's a nice guy. Well . . . I've got to get back to work. Thanks for the cookies, Hannah."

Hannah waved at him as she pulled out of the parking lot and headed back to her condo to pick up Janie. As she zipped down the highway, she reached up to touch her lips with the tip of her finger. The thrill of Mike's kisses always lingered, and they made her hunger for more. But Norman's kiss had lingered, too. What kind of woman could be in love with two men? Or did it mean that she wasn't really in love with either of them?

Chapter Twenty-One

Hannah heard a door close as she climbed up the steps from the garage. The sound seemed to come from Mrs. Canfield's unit, and she bent down quickly to form a snowball and dropped it into the pocket of her parka. A moment later, Greg Canfield came around the corner of the building.

"Hi, Hannah. You're home from work early. Do you want to get a cup of coffee or something?"

"I'd love to, but I can't. I have to be back at the park in less than an hour. How's your day-trading going?"

"Just fine." Greg gave her a big grin. "Did you hear the latest news about Ezekiel's ghost?"

"I don't know. What's the latest?"

"KCOW radio says it attacked Dr. Rhodes last night because he tried to take its picture. They said that when Dr. Rhodes developed his film, it was blank, because you can't take a picture of a spirit. I figure that's about as believable as Paul Bunyan and his blue ox, Babe. How do they dream up stories like that?"

Hannah laughed. "I gave them that story. Thanks for telling me, Greg. I'm glad it's out there already."

Greg looked shocked. "Don't tell me that you actually believe in ghosts!"

208   *Joanne Fluke*

"Of course I don't."

"Then why did you tell a whopper like that?"

Hannah hesitated, but Greg was an old friend. She'd known him for years and she could trust him. "I'll let you in on it, but you need to keep it under your hat."

"My lips are sealed." Greg pantomimed zipping his lips, a childhood ritual they'd learned in second grade from Miss Gladke.

"Norman Rhodes is a good friend of mine, and I planted that story to keep him safe. We think Connie Mac's killer attacked him."

"But why?"

"Because he thinks that Norman took his picture."

"Did he?"

"No. Norman was next door the night that Connie Mac was killed and he was testing his lights. He didn't have film in his camera, and he wasn't even aiming it out the window. We think the killer saw the flashes when he was hanging around my shop, and he thought that Norman got a picture of him."

"Did Dr. Rhodes see the killer?"

Hannah shook her head. "Norman didn't see anybody. He didn't even know that Connie Mac was dead until the next morning."

"So he was just in the wrong place at the wrong time?"

"You got it," Hannah said with a sigh. "And he almost got killed for nothing."

"Wait a second." Greg looked confused. "I can see why you wanted to let the killer know that Dr. Rhodes didn't take his picture, but why didn't you just tell KCOW the truth?"

"The truth isn't news. I had to tie in the ghost so that KCOW and the papers would carry it."

"That's brilliant, Hannah." Greg looked impressed. "You always were the smartest one in our class. And that reminds me, Grandma said she heard that you helped to solve two murder cases already. Are you working on this one?"

Childhood friendships notwithstanding, Hannah decided that she'd gone far enough. She'd already been forced to tell several people that she was working to catch Connie Mac's killer, and it was past time to zip her own lips. "I offered to help, but they made it plain that they don't want me to get involved."

"That's a relief. I'd sure hate to see you mixed up in anything that dangerous."

Greg still looked worried, and Hannah reached out to pat him on the arm. "Don't worry about me, Greg. Two Winnetka County detectives have ordered me to stay out of it."

"But you never used to listen to orders. Remember what happened when our mothers ordered us to stop having those snowball fights?"

"Of course I do. We just escalated the battle, but I follow orders very well now." Hannah bit back a smug grin as she pulled the snowball from her pocket and let fly. It hit Greg squarely in the face and she hooted. "Except for times like this, of course."

"Janie?" Hannah called out as she opened her door. "Where are you?"

"I'm in here."

Janie's voice answered her from the rear of the condo. It came from the guest room, but it was strangely muffled. Hannah felt a surge of fear and she called out again. "Are you hurt?"

"No, but I need help."

Janie's answer added fuel to Hannah's feet as she hurried down the hall and barreled into the guest room. What she saw made her come dangerously close to exploding with suppressed laughter.

"Go ahead and laugh. I can just imagine how ridiculous I look. I'm afraid I'll crush something if I move, and I think Moishe is in here somewhere."

"Hold on, Janie. I'll help you," Hannah chuckled as she approached the walk-in closet. All she could see were Janie's feet. The rest of her body, including her head, was covered by mounds of old clothing that Hannah had been vowing to take to the Helping Hands Thrift Store for the past two years.

"Do you see Moishe?" Janie asked, her words almost swallowed by the old Navy peacoat Hannah had worn during her first year in college.

"Not yet." Hannah was ready to start extricating Janie from the clothing when she heard a meow. It came from above her, and when she looked up, she saw two round yellow eyes peeking out at her. "He's on the top shelf, hiding behind a box. I'll coax him down right after I get you out of the closet."

"I'm glad my mother didn't hear that!" Janie started to giggle.

Hannah stepped into the closet and grabbed an armful of clothing. She carried it out, tossed it into a corner of the bedroom, and went back for another load. It took several trips, but at last Janie could move.

"Oh, no," Janie groaned as she stood up and shook off the rest of the clothing.

"What's the matter? Are you hurt?"

"Only my pride. I'm sorry, Hannah. I crushed the velvet hat you wore to Andrea's wedding."

"That's okay. It looks awful on me and I haven't worn it since. What happened?"

"I don't know. Moishe was in the closet and I tried to get him out so I could shut the door. I was just bending down to pick him up when the closet pole gave way and everything crashed down on us."

"That pole was loose. I should have warned you. And Moishe does have a way of getting people into trouble," Hannah remarked, remembering the time she'd stepped out to retrieve the morning paper and Moishe had batted the door shut behind her. Of course it had been locked, and she'd had to run down to her neighbor's in her slippers and robe to call a locksmith.

At that moment, the subject of their conversation jumped down from the top shelf and walked over to them. He glared at them for a moment, as if the whole thing had been their fault, and then stalked off down the hallway.

"I'm just glad he didn't get hurt," Janie said. "He was after something in the closet, Hannah. Do you think it was a mouse?"

"It could have been. He's a good mouser. Sit down, Janie. I've got some great news for you."

Janie sat down on the edge of the bed. "What is it?"

"You're off the suspect list. Kristi Hampton saw you pull into the parking lot at the inn, and a maid spotted you when you left with your suitcases. That gives you an alibi, and Mike said to tell you that you're in the clear."

"That's wonderful!" Janie's face lit up in a smile. "Now I can go back out to the inn and see Paul. I didn't think I should talk to him while I was still a suspect, but I'd really like to offer my condolences and see if there's anything I can do to help."

"I've got some other good news, too. You're not the only suspect that Mike and Bill cleared."

"Norman?" When Hannah nodded, Janie's smile grew even wider. "I'm glad. I really like him, Hannah."

"I like him, too. We'd better get a move-on, Janie. Andrea will panic if I'm late for the contest."

"I'm ready. Or at least, I was. Just let me brush my hair again."

Hannah watched as Janie went over to the dresser and began to brush her hair. "Did you happen to think of anything special we could do with our snowman?"

"Yes. I forgot to tell you in all the excitement, but I think you should build a snow-woman."

"A snow-*woman?*"

"That's right. I thought it might catch the judge's eye if it was a snow-woman instead of a snowman."

Hannah turned to stare at the piles of clothing with a thoughtful look on her face. "Maybe we could straighten out that hat from Andrea's wedding and use it."

"Bad idea." Janie shook her head. "She'll think you didn't like it."

"I didn't."

"I know, but she chose those hats especially for us. You have others, don't you?"

"Oh, yes," Hannah said, thinking about the old adage, *Always a bridesmaid, never a bride.* "I've been in enough weddings to start a whole collection."

Armed with two shopping bags of snow-woman paraphernalia, Hannah and Janie arrived at Lake Eden Park. Hannah spotted Lisa and Jack Herman standing on the sidelines and she turned to Janie.

"I told Lisa that you were coming and she wanted you to watch with them."

"Great." Janie smiled. "Mr. Herman's an old family friend. He used to work with my Dad. It'll be good to see him again."

"Did Lisa tell you that he has Alzheimer's?"

"Yes. Don't worry, Hannah. I'll understand if he doesn't remember me."

When they arrived at the spot where Lisa and her father were standing, Janie greeted Lisa and then she turned to Jack Herman. "Hi, Mr. Herman. I'm . . ."

"Janie Burkholtz." Jack supplied the name, reaching out to take her hand. "I remember you from a long time ago. Your father and mother were good friends of mine, but I don't think I've seen them for a while."

"They moved to Florida a few years ago."

"Smart," Jack said, smiling. "Garland always said he wanted to get away from this . . . uh . . . white stuff on the ground."

Lisa smiled at her father. "The *snow* bothers a lot of people, especially when it's deep, like this year."

"Maybe Garland was smart. He always hated to shovel snow. Is there a lot of it in . . . where was it again?"

"Florida," Janie responded. "It's warm all year 'round down there. Mom likes it a lot. She practically lives in shorts."

"Isobel always did have pretty legs, but they couldn't

hold a candle to my wife's legs. I used to tell her she should insure them with Lloyd's of . . . whatchamacallit. That's what Betty Grable did, you know."

Janie laughed. "That's exactly what my Dad used to tell *my* mother!"

"Doesn't surprise me. Your father always stole my best lines. We all had fun back then. They lived right next door before they bought that place on Elm Street. We already had . . . our first baby."

"Tim," Lisa prompted.

"That's right. I think Timmy was about a year old, because he was already walking. Garland and Isobel just loved him. They used to try to get us to go out, just so they could babysit. I remember the day they got you, Janie. They were so happy to get a baby of their own."

"It's cold, Dad." Lisa noticed that her father was shivering, and she reached into his jacket pocket to pull out a pair of wool gloves. "You'd better put these on. How about a hot cup of coffee? I can go get you one."

"That sounds good, honey. How about the rest of you? It's my treat."

"Thanks, Mr. Herman. Coffee would be great," Hannah said.

"I'd like some, too." Janie turned to Lisa. "I'll come along and help you carry it, unless . . ."

Hannah knew exactly what Janie was thinking, and she reached out to take Jack's arm. "I'll stay with Mr. Herman to keep him company."

"I'm sorry, Miss . . ." Jack sighed, turning to Hannah after Janie and Lisa had left. "I forgot your name again. It starts with an 'H,' doesn't it?"

"That's right. I'm Hannah Swensen and I'm Lisa's partner at The Cookie Jar."

"Of course you are. I don't know why I can't remember your name. It just slips away from me sometimes."

"That's okay. Just ask me and I'll tell you." Hannah motioned to the gloves he was holding in his hand. "Better put those on before you get frostbite."

Jack laughed and slipped on his gloves. "You sound just like my daughter. When Garland and I were boys, we never wore gloves unless it was twenty below. It was some kind of crazy idea we had. We thought the girls would like us better if we proved how tough we were. I wonder if they still do things like that."

"I think they do," Hannah said, remembering that Craig Kimball and several of his friends had been gloveless when they'd helped her carry her cookies to the warm-up tent.

"It's good to see little Janie again," Jack smiled. "She's all grown up now, but I remember the day Garland and Isobel got her just like it was yesterday."

Something about Jack's word choice puzzled Hannah. This was the second time he'd referred to the day that Janie's parents *got* her. She'd noticed that Lisa often supplied the word that her father couldn't remember, and she decided she'd do the same. "I think it's nice that you remember the day that Janie was *born*."

"Oh, I don't remember that."

"You don't?" Now Hannah was thoroughly puzzled. "But you do remember the day they got her?"

"'Course I do. Garland got the call at work and he drove to that hospital in Minneapolis to pick up Isobel and the baby. But maybe I shouldn't have told you that. It's a big secret."

"What's a secret?" Hannah asked, even more confused.

"Janie's adopted, but her mother never wanted her to know. You won't tell her, will you?"

"I promise I won't," Hannah said, reaching out to take Jack's hand. "Will you tell me about it?"

Jack sighed. "Guess it can't hurt, now that I let the cat out of the bag. You see, Isobel had trouble having babies. She lost two in the first two years, and it just about killed both Garland and her. Then she got pregnant again and she had to stay in bed with her feet up. She was fine for months, but it happened anyway. Garland had to call for the ambulance one night and they took Isobel to the hospital."

"That's very sad," Hannah said, patting his hand.

"I know. Isobel lost the baby, and the doctors told her she couldn't get pregnant again. It upset her so much, she went into a . . . what do you call it when you can't eat or sleep, and you cry all the time?"

"Depression?"

"That's the word. Isobel went into a depression and they kept her there in the hospital. There was a girl in the next bed and she was in trouble, too. They got to be friends, Isobel and this girl, and the girl told her she wasn't married and she was going to give up her baby for adoption. And then she asked Isobel and Garland if they wanted to take it."

"And they did?"

"The girl didn't want any money or anything like that. She just wanted to make sure her baby had a good home. There was only one condition. She never wanted her baby to know about the adoption."

"And that's what happened?"

"Yes. The girl had her baby the next day and she signed Janie over to Garland and Isobel. Her name was Janie when they got her, you know. The girl named her after her grandmother, who'd just died. I know they kept in touch with the girl. Isobel sent her letters and pictures, and the girl sent back gifts for Janie. She asked them to say the gifts were from them, and they did."

Hannah's mind was spinning. It was a great story, but she couldn't help wondering if it was a figment of Jack's imagination. "How do you know all this?"

"Garland told me. He was so excited about being a father at last. He said he had to tell someone. And he knew he could trust me."

"And you never told anyone else?"

"Not even my wife. I figured it was nobody's business."

"Did Garland tell you the girl's name?"

"No, and I didn't ask."

"How about Janie's biological father?"

Jack shrugged. "I don't know his name, and I don't think Garland or Isobel do, either. The girl said that he got married before she found out that she was pregnant, and so she never told him. You're not going to tell Janie about this, are you?"

"No." Hannah shook her head. "It's your secret, and I promise I'll never tell her."

"That makes me feel a whole lot better. Say, Miss? Lisa said you were going to build a snowman. Aren't you a little old for that?"

Hannah laughed. "I'm much too old, but I'm helping my sister and my niece, Tracey."

"That name's familiar. Do I know her?"

"You met her yesterday morning and you showed her your animal collection. You even taught her about opposable thumbs."

"I did?" Jack smiled. "Well, good for me! She must have been that pretty little blond girl that asked me all those questions."

"That's Tracey."

"My daughter use to ask questions nonstop. I hope she didn't catch on that I made up the answers half the time."

"Here she comes now," Hannah said, gesturing toward Lisa and Janie, who were walking across the park toward them.

"I see her. They grow up fast, don't they? Who's that other girl with her?"

"Janie Burkholtz," Hannah said, waiting for some kind of reaction from Jack.

"Oh, yes. Did you know that her parents used to live right next door to me? They moved away from the . . . white stuff a couple of years ago. Somewhere in the south, I think she said."

"Florida."

"That's right. I remember now. Let's go meet them, miss. Looks like they're bringing hot coffee."

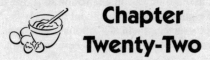

Chapter
Twenty-Two

Hannah walked over to meet Andrea and Tracey, who were just getting out of their car. Tracey was dressed appropriately in a bright-pink snowsuit with a matching ski cap and mittens, but Andrea had worn an outfit that was geared more toward a fashion magazine photo shoot. Her coat was made of powder blue suede. It was decorated with white fur around the collar and the hemline, and she wore matching gloves of thin powder blue leather. Her designer boots matched her gloves, and the only concession she'd made to the contest they were about to enter was a white fur hat that barely covered her ears.

"What's wrong?" Andrea asked, realizing that her sister was staring at her.

"Your outfit. There's a snowdrift in our spot and we're going to be up to our . . ." Hannah paused and glanced at Tracey, who was hanging on her every word. ". . . you-know-whats in it. Tell me you've got Bill's snowmobile suit and choppers in the trunk."

Andrea shook her head. "Don't you like my new coat? I made a special trip out to the mall this morning to pick it up."

"It's gorgeous, and it'd be just fine if you were trying out for the part of the winter fairy."

"I know it's not exactly practical," Andrea conceded. "I just thought there might be photographers here and I wanted to look my best."

"Well, don't blame me if you catch a cold while we're building our snow-woman."

"Snow-*woman?*" Tracey asked, tugging at Hannah's sleeve. "I thought it was a snow*man* contest, Aunt Hannah."

"It is, but *snowman* is generic. It's like when they said all men were created equal in the Declaration of Independence. They meant both men *and* women."

"Right," Andrea murmured to Hannah, taking Tracey's hand and starting out across the snow. "Tell that to Bill. I made more money than he did last month, and he still calls my career a *little hobby.*"

Once they'd said hello to Lisa and her father, and Andrea had given Janie a big welcoming hug, Hannah picked up the two shopping bags and they headed to their designated spot. They'd just figured out who should roll which ball when the whistle blew and the contest began.

"You're shivering," Hannah commented, lifting the snow-ball that Andrea had rolled for the torso and settling it on top of the one she'd rolled for the base.

"I know, but I look good," Andrea said with a grin, sticking out her tongue at Hannah.

"Careful," Hannah warned, picking up the ball Tracey had rolled for the head and plopping it down on top of the torso. "If you leave your tongue out for too long, it'll freeze and crack off."

"Are you fighting with Mommy?" Tracey asked, sounding a little worried.

"No," both Andrea and Hannah replied at once, and then they laughed.

"Aunt Hannah was just teasing," Andrea explained. "Sisters do that sometimes. It doesn't mean that we don't love each other."

Hannah reached out to tweak the pom-pom on the top of

Tracey's pink knitted cap. "Kids always squabble when they're growing up. You'll understand when you have a brother or a sister."

"Will you get the shopping bags, honey?" Andrea said to Tracey, and the minute that Tracey had gone to collect them, she turned to Hannah with a frown. "I wish you hadn't said that. Now she's going to be bugging me about having a baby brother or sister, and Bill and I want to wait for at least a year."

"Sorry," Hannah said, turning away to hide her grin. She was sure she knew something that Andrea didn't. Bill would be tickled pink and so would Andrea, once she'd gotten used to the idea.

"Let me see what's here." Andrea began to rummage through the bag that Tracey brought her. She plucked out a straw hat decorated with chiffon ribbons and silk flowers and held it up. "This looks like it came from a wedding."

"It did. I was a bridesmaid when my college roommate got married."

"It's almost a shame to use it. It's really rather nice." Andrea gave Hannah a sharp look. "I won't find the velvet hat from *my* wedding in here, will I?"

"Of course not," Hannah told her, silently thanking Janie for saving her from that particular blunder.

"Good. You really ought to wear it again, Hannah. It's still fashionable and it looks wonderful on you."

Hannah nodded and decided to change the subject, since the hat in question was as flat as a pancake. "If you don't mind, I thought I'd put one of my Cookie Jar aprons on our snow-woman."

"That's a good idea. It never hurts to advertise." Andrea turned to Tracey, who was digging through the second shopping bag. "Did you find anything you like, honey?"

Tracey held up a long rope of fake pearls. "I like these, Mommy. Now I'm looking for earrings to match."

"There aren't any," Hannah told her, walking over to glance at the contents of the bag. "But that's okay, because our snow-woman doesn't have ears. I think there's a pair of big sunglasses in the bottom. They're from a store display and they ought to fit her."

By the time the final whistle blew, their snow-woman was dressed and ready. The three of them walked over to the sidelines to chat with Janie, Lisa, and Jack Herman while the judges were deliberating.

"Do you think we'll win, Aunt Hannah?" Tracey asked her.

"I don't know, but we made a good snow-woman. I think she's just perfect."

"So do I." Tracey gave a little sigh. "I wish we could keep her, but I know we can't. She'll melt down into a puddle and go belly-up."

Andrea overheard her daughter's comment and her eyebrows shot up in surprise. "Belly-up?"

"That's what fish do when they die. We have guppies at school, and every time one goes belly-up, we tell Miss Cox and we get to have a fish funeral. Miss Cox says they go to the great fish tank in the sky, but they don't."

"They don't?"

"No. She just flushes them down the toilet after everybody leaves. I forgot my sweater once and when I went back to get it, I caught her."

Hannah felt an instant rush of sympathy for Janice Cox, who'd had to explain *that* to Tracey. "What did Miss Cox say?"

"She didn't know I saw. I just picked up my sweater and sneaked back out. And I didn't tell the other kids, either."

"Because you thought it might upset them?" Andrea asked.

"No. The fish funerals are fun and I want to keep on having them. We even sing a special song."

"I see," Hannah said, wondering what type of song they sang. A range of possibilities occurred to her. *Nearer My Cod To Thee*? *O Sole A Mio*? *If you knew Sushi like I know Sushi*?

"Why are you grinning, Aunt Hannah?"

"Oh . . . uh . . . I think the judges are finished." Hannah breathed a sigh of relief as the head judge walked up to the podium, where a microphone had been rigged. "Here we go, Tracey."

The judge announced the winner. It was Calvin Janowski and his family, and Hannah turned to her niece. She hoped that Tracey wouldn't be too disappointed.

"Don't be sad, Aunt Hannah," Tracey told her, before Hannah had decided which comforting phrase to use. "I wanted to win, but Calvin's snowman was really good."

"Okay," Hannah said, much relieved. Tracey had the right attitude.

A moment later the second place winner was announced, and Tracey let out an excited squeal. "We won, too!"

This was not the time to explain the difference between first place and second place, and Hannah just reached out to hug her. Then Andrea got into the act, and eventually all of them shared a group hug. Since Tracey was helping Delores with the tours again and spending the night with her grandma, Hannah made arrangements to meet her sister at the ice-fishing venue at Eden Lake, said her goodbyes to Lisa and her father, and set off with Janie for the trip back out to the inn.

"Aren't you coming in?" Janie asked as Hannah pulled up in front of the entrance to the inn.

Hannah shook her head. "Not right away. I have to drive down to the lake to take Mrs. Baxter some Short Stack Cookies."

"What are those?"

Hannah retrieved a small bag of cookies from the back of the truck and handed them to Janie. "Try them and see. These are seconds. They're a little lopsided."

"Thanks." Janie took out a cookie and sampled it. And then she turned to Hannah in amazement. "They taste just like pancakes with butter and maple syrup on the top! You really ought to write a cookbook, Hannah. You've got some wonderful recipes."

Once Janie had gone inside with her bag of cookies, Hannah drove down the circular driveway and took the access road to the lake. The snow at the shoreline had been plowed to create a temporary parking lot, and it was chock full of cars.

Hannah trolled the rows of cars for several minutes, but not a single parking spot was unoccupied. Since she had a four-wheel-drive vehicle, Hannah decided to make her own spot and she gunned the gas, mounted the icy bank of snow the plow had left, and parked at the back of the warm-up tent. Then she grabbed several boxes of cookies, hopped out of her truck, and hurried around the side of the tent to deliver the goods.

Mrs. Baxter was working at the end of the long counter in the warm-up tent, filling large foam cups with coffee and handing them to one of her students, a pretty brunette who was dressed in a fuzzy yellow sweater. The girl was clamping lids on the cups and setting them in a large, flat box.

"Hi, Mrs. Baxter." Hannah greeted her formally since there was a student present, and set her stack of boxes on the counter. "How's your cookie supply holding out?"

Pam Baxter turned to smile at Hannah. One of the younger members of Jordan High's faculty, and married to the shop teacher, she'd been nominated for best teacher two years running. "You got here just in time, Hannah. We're almost out."

"I've got more cookies in the truck. I'll go get them."

"You've done enough," Pam said, handing Hannah a cup of hot coffee and turning to her student. "Renee?"

The girl in the yellow sweater nodded. "We'll get them, Mrs. Baxter."

Once Renee had left with two of the other girls, Pam turned to Hannah. "I've got a problem. Mayor Bascomb said we could use his snowmobile to deliver coffee and cookies, but I don't know how to drive it. Keith Hauge said he'd do it, but he ran up to the inn to call Shelly Merkeson, and I don't think he'll be back in time."

"Do you want me to go up and get him for you?"

Pam shook her head. "I'm not sure I want him driving in his condition."

Hannah was surprised. As far as she knew, Keith was about as squeaky-clean as they came. "He's been drinking?"

"Heavens, no! It's just that he had a fight with Shelly last night and now he's apologizing to her. And from what Renee tells me, it's going to take a while before she lets him off the hook. Do you know anything about snowmobiles?"

"Sure. My father had one and we used to go out every weekend in the winter."

"Have you ever driven one?"

"A couple of times," Hannah said, remembering the rare occasions when her father had held her on his lap and let her steer.

"I'm really glad to hear that. Do you think that you could drive Mayor Bascomb's snowmobile for us?"

"I don't know why not." Hannah agreed with a smile. She'd be very careful starting out, until she got the hang of it. Once she got the mechanics down, it should be a snap.

"That's great!" Pam looked very relieved. "I'll have a couple of the girls load it up and you can get going."

"Okay. Where am I going?"

"Out to the ice-fishing houses. I promised to deliver hot coffee and cookies to all the contestants, and I'm already ten minutes behind schedule."

Hannah continued to smile, but she knew it was slipping. "You mean you want me to drive it out on the ice?"

"Yes. Can you do it?"

"Absolutely," Hannah promised, hoping she sounded more confident than she felt. She'd assumed she'd be delivering coffee and cookies to the crowd that lined the lakeshore.

"There's no black ice," Pam assured her. "Keith Hauge checked it out when he drove Mayor Bascomb's snowmobile back to shore."

Hannah's smile slipped even further. Anyone who'd grown up in Minnesota knew that black ice was thinner. But how could you spot black ice if it was covered with a blanket of snow?

"Are you sure you can do it, Hannah?"

"Positive," Hannah responded, setting her smile on straight. "Let's load it up and I'll get going."

Hannah watched as Mrs. Baxter's girls loaded the sled that was hitched behind the snowmobile. It was outfitted with an insulated box, and they packed it carefully with bags of cookies and containers of coffee. She was just settling down on the driver's seat, hoping she wouldn't make a fool of herself, when she spotted Andrea running toward her. Her sister had changed clothes since the snowman contest. Now Andrea was wearing a cherry red parka coat and a pair of matching moon boots.

Andrea arrived a bit breathless. "What are you doing on Mayor Bascomb's snowmobile?"

"I'm driving it out to deliver coffee and cookies to the contestants."

"That sounds like fun. I'm sorry I'm late. I stopped by the office to pick up my other coat. You were right. I was freezing."

Hannah gave her a smile of approval. "Good. I've got to get going. Why don't you wait in the warm-up tent until I get back?"

"No, I'll go with," Andrea said, climbing into the passenger seat. "I've never been inside an ice-fishing house before."

"That's not a good idea."

"Why not?"

Hannah glanced back at Mrs. Baxter's girls. They were within earshot, and she wasn't about to admit that she'd never driven a snowmobile before. "Because it could be a bumpy ride."

"You're crazy. The lake's as smooth as glass." Andrea grabbed the strap and buckled herself in. Then she leaned over and whispered, "I know you think I'm pregnant, but I'm not. And if you wait much longer, that coffee's going to get cold."

Hannah knew that she wasn't the only sister to inherit the

Swensen stubborn streak. Once Andrea had dug in her heels, that was that.

"Are we going, or what?"

"We're going," Hannah said with a sigh, driving forward onto the icy surface of Eden Lake.

Short Stack Cookies

DO NOT preheat oven—
dough must chill before baking

1 ½ cups melted butter *(3 sticks)*
2 cups sugar
2 large beaten eggs, any brand *(just whip them with a
    fork)*
½ cup maple syrup ***
4 teaspoons baking soda
1 teaspoon salt
1 teaspoon vanilla
4 cups flour *(not sifted)*
½ cup white sugar for coating the dough balls

*** To measure maple syrup, first spray the inside
of measuring cup with Pam so that the syrup won't
stick to sides of cup.

Melt the butter and mix in the sugar. Let it cool and
add the beaten eggs. Add maple syrup, soda, salt, and
vanilla. Mix it all up. Then add the flour and mix thoroughly.

Chill the dough for at least 1 hour *(overnight is fine,
too)*.

Roll the dough into walnut-sized balls with your

hands. Roll the balls in white sugar and place them on greased cookie sheets, 12 to a standard sheet. Flatten them with a spatula.

Put oven rack in the middle position. Bake at 350°F for 10 to 12 minutes or until nicely browned. Cool on the cookie sheets for no more than 1 minute, then remove the cookies to the rack to finish cooling. *(If you leave them on the cookie sheets for too long, they'll stick.)*

Edna Ferguson says these taste exactly like pancakes that are slathered with maple syrup and butter, and she wishes she could get away with serving them instead of real pancakes at the annual faculty breakfast.

Chapter
Twenty-Three

It was a great day to be out on the lake with a snowmobile. The ice was covered with a light blanket of snow that had fallen the previous evening, and it sparkled in the pale rays of a sun that had peeked out just in time for their deliveries. It was cold, but both Hannah and Andrea were dressed for the weather, and they zipped along from ice-fishing house to ice-fishing house, taking cookies and coffee to the contestants. Everyone was glad to see them. It was a break in a sport that could get rather boring if the fish weren't biting.

"I've never seen the inside of an ice-fishing house before, but they remind me of something familiar," Andrea said, buckling her seatbelt and waiting for Hannah to drive to their next stop.

Hannah looked over at her sister and grinned. "I know exactly what it is. Just think of the buildings on Grandma and Grandpa Swensen's farm, and that should jog your memory."

"What good will *that* do? Grandpa Swensen didn't go ice-fishing." Andrea thought for a moment. "You mean the corn crib?"

"No." Hannah pulled forward across the ice. "Guess again."

"The shed where he kept the tractor?" Andrea raised her

voice so that Hannah could hear her over the sound of the engine.

"Nope."

"Then what? Their farm was nowhere near the lake, and I know they didn't have an ice-fishing house."

"You're right. They didn't. But there's another thing they didn't have—indoor plumbing."

Andrea's mouth dropped open and then she started to laugh. "Really, Hannah!"

"Well, it's true. An ice-fishing house looks a lot like an outdoor privy. It's got four walls, a roof, and a bench. The only difference is, the hole is in the ice."

"It's true," Andrea admitted, still cracking up. "I wish you hadn't told me. Now I'm not going to be able to think of anything else."

Hannah grinned and headed across the lake at a good clip. They'd decided to start with the farthest ice-fishing houses and work their way back to shore. So far, they'd visited six, and they still had over a dozen to go.

"Don't tell me Pete's fishing from his car!" Andrea looked utterly amazed as they pulled up next to Pete Nunke's old Ford.

"Looks like it." Hannah left the snowmobile idling, and they got off to gather up Pete's cookies and his container of coffee. As they approached, Pete rolled down his window, and Hannah had all she could do not to burst into laughter. He was fishing from the passenger's bucket seat, which had been turned backward. Pete's car radio was tuned to KCOW, he had the engine idling and the heater going, and the backseat had been removed to make room for a hole in the floorboards that he'd lined up with the hole he'd chopped in the ice.

"Afternoon, Pete," Hannah greeted him. "We brought you coffee and cookies."

"Thanks, ladies." Pete reached out to take the bag and the coffee.

"Any luck?" Andrea asked.

"Not yet, but there's something down there." Pete pointed

to the small monitor that had been installed on the back window ledge. "See those blips on the screen?"

Andrea peered through the window. "You've got a fish locator. That's smart, Pete."

"Took it off my boat when I dry-docked it this fall. Want to climb in and warm up? You can share the driver's seat."

"Thanks, but we'd better get going," said Hannah, shaking her head. "We still have more cookies and coffee to deliver."

"Okay. I have to move on anyway. Looks like those fish are heading for the old sunken rowboat about twenty feet to the north. It's a natural habitat."

"Are you going to chop another hole in the ice when you get there?" Andrea asked.

"Already chopped it. I put in three holes yesterday and another three this morning. All I have to do is drive over and wait for the fish to get there."

Hannah and Andrea stood by and watched as Pete drove away in his mobile ice-fishing house. Then they headed back to the snowmobile and continued on their delivery route. After another twenty minutes of passing out coffee and cookies, they had only one ice-fishing house left, and it belonged to Mayor Bascomb.

"It certainly is big," Andrea commented as they pulled up in back of the mayor's structure. "I heard he really decked it out in style."

Hannah nodded. Mayor Bascomb always had the biggest and the best. As the son of Lake Eden's most successful land developer, he'd grown up with money, and he knew how to spend it.

"What's that?" Hannah asked, cutting the motor and listening. "It sounds like voices. Mayor Bascomb must have someone out here with him."

Andrea shook her head. "I don't think so. Bill was thinking about entering and I read the rules. It's a solo contest. You have to do it all by yourself."

Hannah grabbed the last bag of cookies and handed Andrea the last container of coffee, and they walked around to the front of the mayor's ice-fishing house. She spotted a generator sitting close to the wall, and there was an electrical cord that ran through a small hole to the inside. "He's got a generator. Maybe he's listening to the radio."

The door was shut, and Hannah knocked out of pure habit. It was a real door with a handle, and it even had little panes of glass at the top.

"Come in," the mayor called out, his voice muffled by the heavy door.

"I'm surprised he doesn't have a doorbell," Hannah muttered to her sister, opening the door. She took two steps forward and then stopped in awe as she saw what Lake Eden's mayor had done to decorate his ice-fishing house. Not only was it bigger than all the others, roughly the size of her guest bedroom at the condo; it was practically a second home.

Instead of the crossed two-by-fours that the other ice-fishing houses had in place of a floor to keep the structure rigid, Mayor Bascomb had a real floor covered with indoor-outdoor carpeting. This floor ended three feet short of one of the walls to expose a strip of ice with his ice-fishing hole in the middle. Against one of the carpeted walls was a television set in an entertainment center that also included a stereo and a VCR. The set was tuned to a golf tournament, and the ocean and palm trees on the screen indicated a tropical venue. Perhaps that would have kept some people warmer by pure suggestion, but Mayor Bascomb's ice-fishing house wasn't even close to freezing, thanks to two electrical space heaters that sat on stands. A leather loveseat sat against the opposite wall, and it was flanked by two tables that both contained lamps. A coffee pot on a shelf near the door gave off the delicious aroma of freshly brewed coffee, and a microwave sat next to it.

"Don't just stand there. Come in and shut the door," Mayor Bascomb ordered, swiveling slightly in the recliner he'd placed on a raised dais at the edge of the flooring. "I'm going to need some help here. I hooked a real lunker and I can't pull him in by myself."

"But isn't that against the rules?" Andrea asked, stepping in and shutting the door.

"Forget the contest. I'll disqualify myself. This is the biggest fish I've ever hooked and I want to bring him in."

"We're coming," Hannah told him, motioning for Andrea. "What do you want us to do?"

"You two steady the line and I'll operate the winch."

"You have a winch?" Hannah was amazed. She'd never heard of anyone who'd used a winch for ice-fishing before.

"It's bolted to the studs in the wall." The mayor pointed to the hand winch. "My wife bought it for me last Christmas."

"Your wife gave you a *winch* for Christmas?" Andrea asked, sounding amused.

"I know it's crazy, but somebody down at the hardware store convinced her that it was a good idea. I had to put it up, but I never thought I'd actually have a use for it."

"How about your line?" Hannah walked over to glance at the mayor's fishing pole. "Is it strong enough?"

"I hope so. I rigged it for one of those twenty-pound northerns and they can put up a fight. Whatever I've got here is a lot heavier than that. I just about popped a blood vessel getting him in this far. He's got to run twenty, maybe even thirty pounds."

With Andrea helping, Hannah let out enough extra line for Mayor Bascomb to tie it to the winch cable. When that was secured, they were ready to haul the fish up.

"Stay right there, one of you on either side of the hole." Mayor Bascomb looked more nervous than Hannah had ever seen him as he gave them instructions. "I'll crank him up slow, and you steady the line. Make sure it doesn't rub against the sides of the hole. This is going to be a trophy fish and I don't want to lose him."

"He's not fighting much," Andrea commented, glancing at the bobber that was just sitting on the surface of the water.

"I know. I figure he's trying to lull me into a false sense of security and he'll put up a real fight when he breaks the water. Shout out when he gets close. I want to wrestle him in myself."

The mayor cranked, and the line began to wind around the drum. It seemed to take forever, but at last Hannah could see something red rising toward the surface of the water. "He's red. I didn't know there were any red fish in this lake."

"Neither did I," Mayor Bascomb sounded puzzled. "What the heck is he?"

"Search me," Hannah said, watching as the patch of red came up another inch. Then she gasped and hollered out to the mayor. "That's enough! Stop cranking!"

Mayor Bascomb locked the winch. "Are you ready for me to bring him in?"

"Not yet." Hannah turned to Andrea. "Do you have your cell phone with you?"

"Of course. I never know when a client might need me."

"Go sit down over there." Hannah moved to block Andrea's view of the hole and gave her sister a nudge toward the loveseat. "I need you to make a call for me. It's important."

Andrea looked as if she might object, but one glance at Hannah's serious expression convinced her to head for the loveseat. When she got there, she pulled out her cell phone and sat down. "Who do you want me to call?"

"Bill. Tell him to get right out here with Mike."

"Okay, but why do we need *them*?" Andrea asked.

"Just do it, Andrea."

"All right, I'm doing it." Andrea punched in the number, and then the light dawned. Her eyes widened and the color blanched from her face. "You mean . . . it's not a fish?"

Hannah shook her head. "Not unless the well-dressed fish is wearing a gold watch this season."

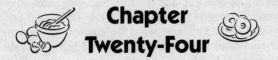

Chapter
Twenty-Four

Hannah paced along the strip of ice in front of the hole, waiting for Bill and Mike to arrive. She'd asked Mayor Bascomb to take Andrea back to the inn to warm up, and now she was alone with the mayor's "fish." Just when she thought her feet couldn't get any colder, Hannah heard a car pull up outside. A moment later, Bill and Mike came in the door.

"You found another body?" Mike asked, sounding incredulous.

"Yup."

"And the mayor hooked it with his fishing line?"

"Yup."

Bill began to frown. "Is that all you can say?"

"Yup," Hannah answered him. "My teeth are chattering too hard to talk."

"Go stand in front of the space heater," Mike ordered, pointing to the area in front of the loveseat. "Don't you know that heat leaves your body faster if you're standing on the ice?"

"I know. I just didn't want to leave him, or her, or whatever it is. I was afraid the line might break."

Mike grabbed her arm and helped her over to the loveseat. "What were you going to do if it *did* break?"

"I don't know. I was too cold to figure that out."

Mike turned to Bill. "I'll stay here. You drive Hannah to the inn and come right back."

"No." Hannah shook her head. "I want to stay."

"We're going to have to bring up that body, and it won't be pretty," Mike warned her.

"That's okay." Hannah's curiosity was stronger than the tide of revulsion that rippled through her stomach. "This won't be the first dead body I've seen."

Mike stared at her for a moment. "Okay. Let's get started, Bill."

With both Mike and Bill tugging, they managed to get the body out of the water. By the time they finished, the corpse was facedown on the ice, and both men were panting. Bill rolled him over and Hannah took a step closer so that she could see the dead man's face. "It's Alan Carpenter!"

"How do you know that?" Mike asked, giving her a hard look.

"I met him at the Winter Carnival banquet. He was just leaving for a press conference."

"Did you ask him any questions?"

"Of course not." Hannah assumed a look of righteous indignation. "You made me promise to stay away from the Connie Mac people while I was out at the inn."

Mike wasn't buying it. His eyes bored through her. "Hannah . . . ?"

"Well . . . maybe a few," Hannah admitted, "but I told you before. He was just leaving. I don't think I exchanged more than a dozen words with him, and Andrea was with me the entire time."

Mike turned to Bill. "Will you call Doc Knight and tell him we need him out here?"

"Sure. How about the forensics team?"

"Them, too. I don't think they'll get much, but you never know. This ice-fishing house was out here last night, wasn't it?"

"I saw the mayor hauling it out here yesterday," Bill said. "How about Sheriff Grant? Do you want me to give him a verbal report, or do you want to do it?"

"You can handle it. Just tell him what we know so far, and say that we'll keep him apprised of any new developments. Be politic. He's not going to be happy about this."

Hannah felt a rush of warmth for Mike. With each case they handled, he was giving Bill more responsibility.

"Anything else?"

"If you think of something I missed, take care of it. We're partners. You don't have to check everything out with me. And while you're doing that, I'll take Hannah's statement."

"What statement?" Hannah was puzzled as Mike joined her on the loveseat. "I've already told you everything I know."

"Not quite. Tell me about your conversation with Alan Carpenter. It could be important."

"Let me think," Hannah said, doing her best to recall every word of their conversation. "We were introduced and . . ."

"What time?" Mike interrupted her.

"Right before Edna's girls served dessert. It was around eight-thirty, I think."

"Go on."

"Alan said it was a pleasure to meet us. And then he said he had to leave with Kurt Howe and he offered us their chairs. I asked him if it was something I said, and he laughed. And then he said that if they didn't leave right away, they'd be late for the press conference he'd scheduled at his office."

"In Minneapolis?"

Hannah shrugged. "I guess so. When we gave Connie Mac the tour, she mentioned that her corporate offices were in Minneapolis."

"Did you ask him if the press conference was about Mrs. MacIntyre's death?"

"Of course I did. It was a natural question. He told us that that the media was in a feeding frenzy and they wanted the details."

"Okay." Mike jotted it all down. "What else?"

"He said he was the spokesman for the family and Kurt was going to handle any questions that concerned the firm that published Connie Mac's cookbooks."

"That'd be Savory Press. Did you say anything else to him?"

"I don't think so. I know Andrea said something about how difficult it must be for him, and he said he had a duty as the family counsel to spare Paul in any way he could. And then he left. With Kurt Howe."

"And that's all?"

"I think so. . . . No, wait. I gave them some cookies for the trip and I said that the sugar would keep them going."

"Okay." Mike closed his notebook and slid it back into his pocket. "It's obvious he drove back here after the press conference. We'll check to find out if anyone saw him when he got back to the inn."

"I could do that for you," Hannah offered without thinking, and then she winced as Mike started to frown. She wasn't supposed to interfere. She had to remember that. "Forget I said that. I'll just keep my nose out of it and leave everything up to you."

"Sure, you will."

Mike sounded a bit sarcastic, and Hannah decided the best thing to do was to change the subject. "I wonder what Alan was doing out here on the ice. It's not exactly a normal place for a walk before bedtime."

"He didn't walk."

"You mean . . . somebody dumped him?"

Mike looked sorry that he'd said anything. "That's what it looks like to me. Did you see that wound on the back of his head?"

"I saw it," Hannah confirmed, shivering slightly. "It looks exactly like Connie Mac's wound."

"That's what makes me think he was dumped. Somebody could have forced him to walk out here at gunpoint, but that doesn't make sense."

"Because then they would have shot him instead of bashing in his head?"

"That's right. We'll know more when Doc Knight gets here. He'll be able to tell us if Mr. Carpenter was dead when he entered the water."

"But how . . ." Hannah stopped in mid-question. She didn't really want to know how Doc Knight could tell something like that. "Never mind. I'd better go see how Andrea's doing."

"I'll take you back to the inn." Mike motioned to Bill. "Secure the crime scene and don't let anyone but Doc Knight and the forensics team in."

Hannah started to grin as she followed Mike out of the ice-fishing house. The moment the door was shut behind them, she grabbed his arm. "Are you going to rope off Mayor Bascomb's ice-fishing house?"

"I don't know. That all depends on what the forensics team finds. There could be trace evidence."

"DNA?"

"If that's where Mr. Carpenter went through the ice, I wouldn't be surprised."

"Then it'll be a crime scene, the mayor can't get back in?"

"Yes. What are you getting at, Hannah?"

"Mayor Bascomb's not going to happy about that, and neither is Sheriff Grant. I heard them talking about going up to Mille Lacs Lake next weekend. They do it every winter. Sheriff Grant reserves the spot and Mayor Bascomb brings his ice-fishing house."

Mike groaned. "I'll be taking plenty of flack about it, but there's nothing I can do. Rules are rules."

"So you're not going to bend those rules for the mayor and Sheriff Grant?"

"No." Mike turned to give her a puzzled look. "I wasn't just picking on you, Hannah. I had to secure your shop. And I may have to secure the mayor's ice-fishing house."

Hannah grinned up at him. "I'm probably crazy, but that makes me feel better. I still think you're pig-headed, but you're pig-headed with everybody."

"Thanks, I think." Mike grinned and held out his arms.

Hannah walked into them and they shared a hug. Then he opened the passenger door of the squad car and waited for her to get in.

"Are you sure you don't want me to ride in back?" she quipped.

"Don't be ridiculous. I don't have any reason to believe you're a suspect . . . do I?"

"When has that stopped you?" Hannah answered his question with a question of her own. "You suspected Norman, didn't you?"

"Not for long, and only because I had to. I told you before. I didn't really believe that Norman did it."

Hannah shut her mouth and climbed into the front seat of the squad car. Mike had certainly sounded serious when he first told her that Norman was a suspect, but this wasn't the time to remind him of that.

"Hannah?" Mike climbed in the driver's seat and reached out to touch her arm. "Uh . . . I've been thinking about that jealousy thing."

"What jealousy thing?"

"You know . . . that maybe I suspected Norman because I was jealous of the time you spend with him. That might not be so crazy, after all."

"Really?" Hannah said, and then she held her breath.

"What I told you this morning is true. I'm glad that you're not sitting home waiting for me to call you. But I do get kind of a wrench in my gut when I think about you with somebody else. I don't know if you can call that jealousy, but it's close."

"Okay," Hannah said, hiding a smile. "As long as we're being truthful, I got a little wrench when I saw Kristi Hampton dangling all over you. And I don't know if that's jealousy, either."

"Dangling all over me? Is that what you thought? She was just being friendly, that's all."

"Oh, I see." Hannah allowed her smile to come out. "In that case, maybe *we* should get a little friendlier."

"Maybe we should." Mike pulled her into his arms and

gave her a thorough kiss. It lasted for several minutes, until both of them were as warm as toast and breathing as if they'd just run a marathon.

"Friendly enough?" Mike asked as he started the squad car and drove forward across the frozen lake.

"Oh, yes," Hannah breathed, settling back for the ride.

When Mike got close to shore, he took the temporary road that had been plowed for the delivery of the ice-fishing houses. That led them to the parking lot and Hannah's truck. He stopped near her rear bumper and reached out to take Hannah's arm before she could open her door.

"What?" Hannah asked, wondering if he was going to make even more of a commitment.

"You're not going to snoop around, are you?"

Hannah gave an exasperated sigh. Leave it to Mike to spoil a perfect moment. "I promised you I wouldn't."

"I know, but that's never stopped you before. I tell you what. . . . Don't promise. Never make a promise you know you can't keep."

"Okay, I won't."

"So you are going to snoop around?"

Hannah winced, but she had to tell him the truth. "Probably."

"Okay. Just be very careful. That's all I ask. And call me right away if you need me."

Hannah reached out to touch his cheek. "I will," she said. "And that *is* a promise."

Chapter
Twenty-Five

When Hannah walked into the lobby of the inn, the first person she saw was Janie. Her temporary houseguest was standing by the desk talking with Sally, who was manning the phones.

"Hi, Janie," Hannah greeted her. "Did you get a chance to see Paul?"

"No, he's gone. Sally just told me that he's in Minneapolis at corporate headquarters."

"He left at noon yesterday," Sally explained, "right after he came back from his interview with Mike and Bill. He told me he'd be in meetings all afternoon and all day today. I'm saving his room for him. He'll be back in time for the grand opening of the boutique tomorrow."

"Did he leave someone in charge?" Hannah asked her.

"Alan Carpenter, but we can't find him, either. He's probably out at the mall making last-minute arrangements for the opening."

"I really need to find out if I still have a job, and Alan would know." Janie looked a little nervous. "If you have time, could you take me out there?"

Hannah felt the horns of a dilemma poke her squarely in the backside. She wasn't supposed to say anything about Alan's murder, but she had to let Janie know that a trip to the mall wasn't necessary. "Uh . . . forget the mall. Alan's not there."

"Are you sure?" Janie asked.

"Oh, yes." Hannah held her breath, waiting for Janie's next question.

"Where is he?"

"He's . . . um . . . out at the mayor's ice-fishing house." Sally's eyebrows shot up. "What's he doing out *there*?"

"Not much," Hannah said, and then she clamped her lips shut.

Sally stared at her for a moment and then began to frown. "You look like I do when I bounce a check and I don't want Dick to find out. Is there something you're not telling us?"

"You could say that," Hannah admitted, sending a silent apology to Mike for having to break another of his rules. "Alan's dead."

"I can't believe it!" Sally gasped after Hannah had told them. "Two of my guests . . . murdered!"

"Do they think it's the same killer?" Janie asked.

"Yes. I shouldn't have told you, but I couldn't see any way around it. Don't say anything to anybody until the sheriff's department officially releases the news."

"I won't," Sally promised.

"Me neither," Janie said. "Poor Alan. Sometimes he was a real pain, but he didn't deserve that."

Alex Matthews appeared at the doorway just then and waved to Janie. "Hi, Janie. I'm so glad you're back!"

"So am I," Janie said, and then she turned to Sally and Hannah. "I'll go talk to her for a minute. Don't worry. I won't say a word about Alan."

After Janie had left, Sally motioned for Hannah to come closer. "You're going to investigate, aren't you?" she asked.

"Of course I am."

"Is there anything I can do to help?"

"There may be," Hannah said. "The first thing I have to

do is find out exactly when Alan was killed. When is the last time you saw him?"

"Last night. I was bartending and he came in with Kurt Howe. It was right before the eleven o'clock news."

"Was there anything odd about him?" Sally looked puzzled and Hannah went on to explain. "Maybe he was more nervous than usual, or angry about something?"

"He was a little uptight, but he told me they'd just come from a press conference and they'd been fielding questions about Connie Mac's death. Alan said they needed to unwind or they'd never get to sleep, and he ordered Chivas neat for both of them."

"How long did they stay in the bar?"

"Until the news was over. Kurt left first. He said he was going up to bed. Alan stayed for another couple of minutes, and then he said he was going to take a walk before he turned in. Before he left, he said he was going to sleep in, and he asked me to save him a prune Danish from the breakfast buffet."

"Did you?"

"Of course I did. I wrapped it up and left it in the kitchen for him, but he never came to get it. I figured he'd gone out to the mall early and had breakfast out there, so I gave it to Earl Flensburg when he came out here for lunch."

"So, as far as you know, he took his walk and then he went up to bed?"

"That's right."

"How about his car? Is it still in the lot?"

"Your guess is as good as mine. I haven't been outside all day long. If you want to check, it's a silver Mercedes with tinted windows."

Hannah thanked Sally for the information and headed to the restaurant to see how Andrea was bearing up. She was still chilled and she wanted to warm up before she walked out to the parking lot to look for Alan's car.

The restaurant was only half full, and Hannah spotted Andrea sitting at a table for two. As she approached, her sister smiled a greeting. The color was back in Andrea's cheeks, and she looked as if she'd fully recovered from her shock.

"You look a lot better," Hannah commented, pulling out a chair and sitting down.

"I am." Andrea gestured toward the empty cup on the table. "You were right about the chocolate, Hannah. I had three cups of cocoa and I'm almost myself again."

"Where's Mayor Bascomb?" Hannah asked, noticing the second empty cup on the table.

"He went back out to the lake. Since he can't finish the ice-fishing contest, he's going to award the first-place trophy to the winner."

"He left you here alone?" Hannah was shocked. Mayor Bascomb was always polite to his constituents, and he carried courtesy and consideration to the extreme in an election year.

"I suggested it. All he could talk about was expanding the dump and building a new water filtration system. After fifteen minutes, I was bored to tears. And then, when he started discussing environmentally friendly uses for solid waste, I just had to think of a way to get rid of him."

One of the waitresses approached their table with a tray. Hannah watched as she set down a carafe, a clean cup and saucer, and two chocolate-covered doughnuts. When she'd left, Hannah turned to her sister. "What's this?"

"I figured you'd need a dose of your own medicine."

"Thanks," Hannah smiled. Andrea was right. A cup of hot chocolate was just what she needed.

Andrea took one of the doughnuts and ate it while Hannah drank her hot chocolate. "How about that other doughnut? Don't you want it?"

"Not really. I'm still full from breakfast. Janie made me French toast this morning."

"Can I have it? I'm still hungry and I don't know why. I've eaten like a horse today."

Hannah passed the plate to her sister. If there wasn't a baby in the making, she'd eat the velvet hat from Andrea's wedding, including the fashionable French lace around the brim.

* * *

"Here it is, Hannah," Andrea called out, pointing toward a car that was sandwiched in between a van and a midsize sedan with rental plates.

Hannah was amazed. All Andrea could see was the back end of the cars, and she'd spotted Alan's the moment they walked out to the parking lot. "Are you sure that's his?"

"Of course I am. I'm a real estate agent, and I know a Mercedes when I see one. Only serious buyers drive them."

"Because it means they have the money to buy a house?"

"Not necessarily, but they're expensive and you've got to have good credit to get one. Good credit's more important than money. Did you know that you can put the purchase price of a house on a credit card?"

Hannah shook her head. "You've got to be kidding! Does anybody really do that?"

"Yes. When the Ehrenbergs sold their summer cabin, the purchase price was thirty thousand. My buyers put the whole thing on their credit card."

"Why would they do that?" Hannah was confused. "I thought credit card interest rates were sky high."

"They are."

"Isn't the interest rate on a house loan much less?"

"Absolutely, but they had a really good reason for doing it."

"This I've got to hear," Hannah said, leading Andrea toward the car she thought was Alan's Mercedes.

"It's like this. They got a brand new credit card with a sweetheart rate: eight percent for the first six months. That's really good. And since their credit rating was excellent, they got a credit line of forty thousand."

Hannah whistled. "I've never heard of a credit line *that* high."

"It's pretty high, but between the two of them they made over a hundred thousand a year, and they always paid their bills on time. They just hadn't saved any money, that's all."

"Okay, I'm following you so far."

"The lowest interest rate they could get through a mortgage broker at the time was seven and a half."

"Hold on a second." Hannah stopped in her tracks. "If the mortgage rate was seven and a half and the credit card rate was eight, they were paying more interest by putting it on their credit card."

"No, they weren't. Not in the short run. His father's will was in probate and his inheritance was over forty thousand. The only problem was, he didn't have it yet. He told me the lawyer figured he'd get it in four months or less."

"So why didn't they take out a house loan and pay it off when he got his inheritance?"

"Because the first couple of years are almost all interest. You only pay a tiny bit off on the principal. Four months of mortgage payments added up to more than the four months of interest on the credit card. They made a financially sound decision."

"It still sounds crazy to me. What if something had happened to delay his inheritance?"

"It didn't. He got a check in four months. It was a calculated risk, Hannah. They took it and it paid off."

Hannah just shook her head. "You remind me of Greg Canfield. He's betting on the thing, too."

"I thought you told me he tripled his money on that stock he bought."

"He did, but he could just as easily have lost everything." They'd almost reached the car in question when Hannah had a dire thought. "Do you handle the finances, Andrea?"

"No. Bill takes care of all that, and he's very cautious. Sometimes it bugs me, but we've got a family to consider. Tracey already has a college fund. Bill started it the day we found out that I was pregnant."

"That's good," Hannah said, smiling slightly. Andrea didn't realize it, but Bill would be making another trip to the bank to open another account soon.

"So what did you learn?" Andrea asked, after they'd examined Alan's car and were walking back to the inn.

"Alan didn't drive anywhere this morning."

"How could you tell that?"

"There was snow on the windshield, and it stopped snowing about four this morning. I heard it on KCOW when I was driving out here."

"In that case, I learned something, too."

"Really? What?"

"Alan was killed before four this morning."

"You learned that by looking at his car?" Hannah turned to her sister in surprise.

"No, it was what you said."

Hannah was confused. "What did I say?"

"That it stopped snowing at four this morning. If somebody dragged Alan out there after four, there would have been tracks in the snow."

"That's true."

"Well, there weren't any. When we drove up, there was only one set of footprints leading up to the door."

"Good for you, Andrea. You're incredibly observant and you have a great memory for detail."

Andrea looked slightly uncomfortable. "Actually, no. The only reason I noticed was that I overheard Sara Thompson talking to Patsy Berringer in the café the other day. They were gossiping about the mayor's new girlfriend."

"I didn't know he had one," Hannah commented, feeling a wave of contempt for their town's illustrious leader. Mayor Bascomb had come within an eyelash of getting into big trouble for his last affair, and she'd hoped the close call had taught him a lesson.

"They didn't mention who his girlfriend was, and it might not be true. I usually don't put much stock in gossip, but I didn't want to interrupt him if he was . . . uh . . . you know. That's the only reason I noticed, Hannah. It was all because of the gossip I heard. But it helped, didn't it?"

Hannah's grin grew wider. "You bet! It narrows our time frame down to four hours and saves us a whole lot of trouble. This has got to be the first time in history that gossip actually turned out to be good for something."

Chapter Twenty-Six

"You concentrate on the Connie Mac people," Hannah told her sister after they'd reentered the inn and removed their coats and boots. "Most of them will be out at the mall, but you might find a few who stayed here. I'll talk to the maids and whoever was manning the front desk last night."

Andrea pulled her organizer out of her purse and flipped through it. "I've got my list of questions about Connie Mac. Do you want me to ask them anything about Alan?"

"Yes, but you can't say that he's dead."

"I know. I'll just tell them I'm looking for him and I can't seem to find him. I'll ask them if they saw him today."

"They didn't. You know that already."

"I know, but that'll lead me into my next question. They'll tell me about the last time they saw him and they won't even guess that that's what I was really after in the first place."

Hannah gazed at her sister in admiration. "You're really good at this, you know?"

"Do you really think so?"

"I wouldn't have said it if I didn't."

"That's true. You never say anything you don't mean. Sometimes I wish I had the luxury, but . . ."

"But you're a real estate agent." Hannah finished the sentence for her and they both laughed.

"Sometimes it bothers me a little," Andrea admitted, "but I'd lose a sale if I told a prospective buyer that the roof would probably leak within the first three years or the plumbing might need to be replaced."

"Caveat emptor?"

"I know what that means, Hannah. It's 'let the buyer beware.' I guess it's true to a certain extent, but I don't actually lie about anything. If they ask me straight out, I tell them. I just don't volunteer the negative things, that's all. And don't think you're so smart just because you know Latin. I picked up a few phrases in real estate school."

"Like what?" Hannah challenged.

"Like *Illegitami non carborundum*."

Hannah translated that in a flash. She wasn't certain that the syntax and word order were correct, but the meaning was clear and she stared at her sister in shock. "Do you know what that means?"

"Of course. It's 'Don't let the client grind you down.' Our instructor at school had it stamped on his briefcase and I asked him about it."

"I see," Hannah said hiding a grin. It was obvious that Andrea's teacher hadn't wanted to tell her the literal meaning of *illegitami*. "Let's get a move on, Andrea. Bill and Mike could be here any minute, and I don't want them to catch us asking questions."

The two sisters parted ways at the bottom of the staircase. Andrea went up, and Hannah headed for Sally's office. When she got there, Alex Matthews was just leaving.

"I'm glad I caught you, Hannah." Alex gave her a big smile. "I cleared it with Sally and if it's all right with you, I'm going to give Janie a ride to your condo and help her pack up her things."

Hannah was puzzled. "That's fine with me, but why?"

"Janie's moving back into her room out here. She spoke to Paul on the phone and he told her that he couldn't get along without her. He even gave her a raise to make up for all the trouble that horrible woman caused her."

"I'm glad to hear it, but I'm going to miss her."

"That's exactly what *she* said. You're one of her favorite friends, Hannah. Thank you so much for helping her."

"Hannah?" Sally hailed her from the open doorway. "Come in and shut the door. I've got some news for you."

Hannah walked in and took the chair in front of Sally's desk. "I've got news for you, too. We found Alan's car and it's been out there all night. We figure he was killed between midnight and four this morning, give or take half an hour."

"Well, that's one mystery solved. It explains why he never picked up his prune Danish," Sally said, and she sighed deeply.

"Don't think about that," Hannah advised, and then she started to frown. Whenever someone told her *not* to think about something, it had quite the opposite effect. Once she knew she shouldn't dwell on something, it took on even more importance in her mind. Rather than try to take back her advice, which was impossible anyway, she decided to enlist Sally's help on the one aspect of Alan's death that they could do something about. "I need your help, Sally. What was Alan wearing when you saw him in the bar last night?"

"A gray suit with a light-blue shirt. He was carrying a black overcoat when he came in and he put it down on an empty barstool. Was that what he was wearing when you found him?"

Hannah shook her head, deciding not to go into detail. Sally didn't need a mental picture of how Alan had looked when they'd pulled him from the icy water. "He must have gone up to his room to change clothes. You said you had news. What is it?"

"I checked with the maid who took care of Alan's room, and his bed hadn't been slept in. Do you think he was killed while he was out on his walk?"

"It's beginning to sound that way. I need a list of your night people, Sally. I have to find out if anyone saw Alan last night."

"They didn't. I already checked. And I talked to Chris.

He's the college kid I hired to man the front desk from ten to six. He said Alan walked out the door at a quarter past midnight, and he wasn't back when Chris left at six."

"Didn't he think that was odd?"

"No, he figured that Alan had driven out to the mall. Alan did that sometimes. There were a couple of nights when he left here at ten-thirty or eleven at night and went out to the boutique to work. He told Chris that there were too many distractions during the day and he got his best work done in the middle of the night."

"That makes sense to me," Hannah said. She'd pulled her share of all-nighters at The Cookie Jar with Lisa, especially in December when the parties were plentiful and they'd booked back-to-back catering events.

"I have a piece of good news," Sally said.

"Let's hear it. I could use some good news about now."

"Dick called me a couple of minutes ago and his mother came through the surgery just fine. They've already got her sitting up in bed."

"That's great," Hannah said, "and it must be a huge relief for Dick."

"Oh, it is. He's been worried sick. His mother's not young, you know. When he called, I knew everything was fine before he even told me."

"By the tone of his voice?" Hannah guessed.

"He sounded relaxed for the first time in almost a week. And that reminds me: he wanted to know everything that was happening here."

"You didn't tell him about Alan, did you?"

"Of course not. I could trust him not to say anything. That's not the problem. But he sounded so upbeat, I didn't want to say anything to change that. I told him about Greg Canfield, though. That was all right, wasn't it?"

Hannah shrugged. "Why not? Greg didn't tell me to keep it a secret."

"I mentioned that he made a real killing in the market, and Dick was really glad for him. But I must have gotten the name of the stock wrong. What was it again?"

"Redlines."

"That's what I told him, but Dick pulled Redlines up on his laptop while we were talking and he said it peaked about six months ago. Then the stock started dropping and the company went bankrupt at the end of last month."

Hannah frowned. That certainly didn't match what Greg had told her. "Is Dick sure?"

"Positive. He checked the history of the stock for me. About a week before Redlines hit rock bottom, there were rumors about a new infusion of foreign cash. Some investors bought in on the strength of the rumors, but it never happened and they all lost their shirts."

Hannah's frown grew deeper. She was positive that Greg had told her he'd invested in Redlines.

"You must have gotten the name wrong. Dick said there was no way anybody could have made any money on Redlines unless they bought when it first went public and sold at the peak six months ago."

Hannah thanked Sally for all she'd done and left her office thoroughly puzzled. Greg had told her he'd more than tripled his money on Redlines, and he'd lied to her. Was that because he was too embarrassed to admit that he'd made a bad investment?

There was a pay phone at the end of the hall, and instead of turning off at the entrance to the dining room, where she was supposed to meet Andrea, Hannah kept on walking and dug into the bottom of her purse for change. Sally had done all the legwork for her, and she still had forty-five minutes before she hooked up with her sister. There was no time like the present to talk to Greg about Redlines. She'd call him right now and ask him why he hadn't trusted her enough to tell her the truth.

One of Sally's waitresses headed for Hannah's table with the coffee carafe, but Hannah smiled and waved her away. She'd had four cups already and that was enough, even for her. She picked up a french fry and dipped it into the side of blue cheese dressing she'd ordered. French fries and blue cheese dressing was one of her favorite treats. Sally's french fries were perfect, golden brown and crisp on the outside and made from real, hand-peeled potatoes. Her blue cheese dressing was also made from scratch, with chunks of tasty Roquefort blended with heavy cream. Normally Hannah would have been in hog heaven, but today even the tastiest food had lost its appeal. There were too many questions buzzing in her mind, and her brain felt like a mixer that had gone into warp speed.

As she munched, Hannah tried to concentrate on the most important question. Who had murdered Connie Mac and Alan? She'd eliminated a lot of suspects, but she was no closer to solving the crimes than when she'd started.

The second question concerned Andrea's pregnancy. Was she putting her sister and unborn baby in jeopardy by agreeing to let Andrea help with the murder investigations? Andrea didn't know that she was pregnant, and she'd gotten a little hot under the collar the second time that Hannah had brought it up. That subject was obviously off limits, and other than driving to Lake Eden Neighborhood Pharmacy, buying a home pregnancy test, and forcing Andrea to use it, Hannah really couldn't confirm what she strongly suspected. She could always come up with an excuse to exclude Andrea from the sleuthing, but she'd be jeopardizing their friendship. And if it turned out that Andrea wasn't pregnant, her sister would never forgive her.

In addition to these problems, there were other questions of lesser importance. Some were minor. Did Mayor Bascomb really have a new girlfriend? How had Alex and Janie become such good friends on such short acquaintance? Was Francine going to get Sally and Dick in trouble by dressing up and pretending to be Ezekiel Jordan's ghost?

A final question, one that was very important, almost overshadowed Hannah's murder investigation. What was going on with Greg Canfield? Something was very wrong, and Hannah would be a lousy friend if she didn't even try to help him.

Greg hadn't been home when she'd called, but she'd spoken to his grandmother. The information that Mrs. Canfield had given her had caused Hannah to worry about Greg even more. Greg had claimed that he was trading stock on-line, but his computer had been broken for over two weeks. He'd said he'd tripled his money on Redlines, but the company had gone bankrupt. He'd also said that he'd paid off his creditors, but his former suppliers wouldn't be leaving urgent messages with his grandmother on a Sunday afternoon if that were true. As if all that weren't enough to handle, Mrs. Canfield was convinced that Annette had left Greg for good. She'd seen the packet of legal papers that had arrived for him last week from a family law firm in Denver.

Even though Greg's financial and personal world was crashing down around his ears, Hannah's immediate concern was for his safety. When he'd left the condo this afternoon, he'd told his grandmother that he was going to gas up his car and come right back. That had been almost three hours ago, and Hannah could understand why Mrs. Canfield was getting worried. There had been two murders in Lake Eden already and the killer was still out there. Hannah hoped that she was just borrowing trouble, but she was glad she'd told Mrs. Canfield to leave a message for her at the inn the moment that Greg walked in the door.

Chapter Twenty-Seven

Hannah was staring down at her french fries and wondering if she'd lost the knack of solving mysteries when Alex tapped her on the shoulder.

"Hannah?" Alex held out a key. "Janie asked me to find you and give this back. She's getting settled in upstairs."

"Thanks, Alex." Hannah dropped the key in her purse.

"Do you mind if I join you for a minute?"

"Not at all. Sit down." Hannah roused herself as Alex sat down in the opposite chair. If they chatted for a while, perhaps Alex would say something to solve one of the minor mysteries that had been plaguing her.

"I've only got a minute before I go back to work, but I wanted to tell you that I met your cat. He's a real darling."

Hannah smiled, feeling the way she imagined a proud mother would feel. She wouldn't have described Moishe as a *darling,* but he'd obviously been on his best behavior around Alex.

"He led me straight to the cupboard where you keep his food so that I could fill his bowl," Alex told her. "I think he's even smarter than Tarzan Five."

"Tarzan Five?"

"He was my grandmother's cat. She named all of her

male cats Tarzan. I know it's a little strange, but her name was Jane and she used to get a huge kick out of picking them up and saying, *You Tarzan, me Jane*."

Hannah laughed. "Sounds like your grandmother had a good sense of humor."

"She did. If I had the time, I could tell you stories that would make you roll on the floor. I was nineteen when she died. That was over twenty-five years ago, but I still miss her. And every time I adopt a male cat, I name him Tarzan. I have Tarzan Eight right now, and my tabby is Jane Three."

After Alex had left, Hannah went back to staring at her french fries. She hadn't learned anything helpful and she was at loose ends. Andrea was upstairs talking to the Connie Mac people, Bill and Mike were running their own investigation, Lisa was spending the rest of her day with her father, and Sally and Alex were working. She felt like a single woman at a couples party, with no one to talk to and nothing to do. All she could do was sit here and wait for the information to come to her, and Hannah had never been good at waiting.

Just to keep her mind sharp, she pulled out her notebook and paged through it. She found Alex's page and sighed as she retrieved one of the ballpoint pens from the bottom of her purse and wrote down what she'd learned. It wasn't much. Alex's cats were named Tarzan and Jane, her grandmother had started the tradition, and she'd died when Alex was nineteen. Nothing interesting there. Perhaps Alex was exactly as she appeared, an outgoing woman who made friends easily.

"Hannah?"

The sound of her name pulled Hannah out of her thoughts, and she looked up to see that Andrea had taken the opposite chair. "Sorry, Andrea. I didn't even see you come in. Are you through already?"

"Yes, and I've got something for you."

Hannah perked up immediately. "What is it?"

"I couldn't talk to the Connie Mac people. They're all out at the boutique, getting ready for the opening. But I talked to the writer who's doing Connie Mac's biography, and he told me that he saw Alan last night."

"Great," Hannah said, and she began to smile. "Good job, Andrea. What time?"

"Twelve-thirty. He didn't talk to Alan. He just saw him out the window, walking down to the lakeshore."

"He's sure it was Alan?"

"Oh, yes. He recognized him by his hat. Alan always wore one of those Russian fur hats when he went out for a walk."

"They're called *ushankas,* but other people wear them, too."

"I know, but . . ." Andrea stopped and stared at Hannah's plate of french fries. "Are you going to eat those?"

Hannah shook her head and pushed the plate to Andrea. "But what?"

"But Alan always wore it. . . . is there any ketchup?"

"Yes, here." Hannah picked up the squeeze bottle of ketchup and passed it over. "Alan always what?"

"He wore his Russian hat with the earflaps down. The writer said it looks really silly that way and most people just let their ears get cold, but Alan always pulled the flaps down and they looked like dog ears."

"Okay," Hannah said, picking up her pen to write down what Andrea had told her. She was about to flip to a new page when a name caught her eye. *Jane.* Alex's grandmother had been named Jane. "Hold on a second. I've got to check something."

With rising excitement Hannah found the section of notes she'd taken on the story that Jack Herman had told her. Janie's birth mother had named her in honor of her grandmother, who had died recently. Alex said her grandmother had died over twenty-five years ago. And Janie was twenty-five.

"What did you find?" Andrea asked, catching her sister's excitement.

"I'm not sure." Hannah pushed back her chair and stood up. "I'll be right back. I've got to talk to somebody and it can't wait."

"Do you need me?"

"Not this time. It'll only take a second or two and they might clear the table if both of us leave. Stay here and eat the french fries." Hannah picked up the side of blue cheese dressing and handed it to her sister. "Try dipping them in that. It's a lot better than ketchup."

"I . . . I don't know what you mean."

"I asked you a simple question," Hannah stated, giving Alex her fiercest stare. They were standing outside the service entrance to the kitchen, sheltered from the wind by two large metal Dumpsters. "Is Janie Burkholtz your daughter?"

Alex swallowed hard. And then tears came to her eyes. Hannah could see them well up, and she felt like a rat for harassing her. "Look, Alex. I really need to know. And I promise you, I won't tell anyone."

"But I . . . " Alex sighed and a single tear spilled over and rolled down her cheek. "I was so careful all these years. I never wanted Janie to know. Who told you?"

"That's not important."

"Yes, it is. I've never told anybody except Isobel and Garland. And I finally told Janie's biological father, but I know he wouldn't tell anyone."

Hannah reached out to take her arm. "It's okay, Alex. Nobody told me. I just guessed."

"But how?"

"I just wondered how you and Janie could be so close when you'd just met for the first time. That's all. Are you going to tell Janie that you're her mother?"

"No! I can't tell her, Hannah. It wouldn't be fair to Isobel and Garland. They're her *real* parents. They loved her, and they raised her, and they gave her a wonderful home. It might change the way she thinks of them, and that wouldn't be right. You won't tell her, will you?"

"I promise I won't," Hannah assured her. "Is that why you took the job as Sally's assistant, so that you could see her?"

"Yes. Isobel called to tell me that Janie would be here.

We've kept in touch over the years. She said she had a bad feeling about going away on the cruise. She was afraid that something might happen to Janie while they were away, and she wanted someone here to look after her. She also thought that I should meet Janie. I never have, you know. They've sent me pictures and videotapes, but that's not the same thing."

"No, it's not."

"And then, when I finally met Janie, it was . . . just wonderful. She's so bright and pretty and lovely. And she seemed to like me, too. It's been the best week of my life."

Hannah smiled. "We love Janie, too. How about her father? Was he angry that you hadn't told him before?"

"No. Of course he was shocked, but he's a very nice man and he said he understood why I did things the way I did. And since he's never had any other children, he promised that he'd look out for Janie anonymously and provide for her in his will. He also promised that he'd never tell her unless Isobel, Garland, and I all agreed that it was the right thing to do."

"Thank you for telling me," Hannah said, reaching in her pocket to pull out a tissue. She handed it to Alex and waited until the older woman had composed herself. "You don't have to worry, Alex. Your secret is safe with me. Now let's go back in. It's freezing out here."

When they reentered the kitchen, Alex went off to take inventory of the supplies that had been delivered that morning, and Hannah headed toward the swinging door to the restaurant. As she passed by the bank of deep fryers, where Sally was standing, a thought popped into her mind that chilled her more than the icy wind that had blown across the tops of the Dumpsters. Was it possible that Alex had caught a glimpse of Janie when she'd come back to the inn on Saturday night? If she'd noticed Janie's tears and the bruise on her arm, and if she'd suspected that Connie Mac had caused them, then Alex had possessed the perfect motive for driving to The Cookie Jar and killing Connie Mac.

"Hannah?" Sally pulled up one of the metal baskets filled

with golden french fries and hooked it in place to drain. "You look grim. What's the matter?"

Hannah glanced around her, but none of the kitchen workers were close enough to hear. "Where was Alex on Friday night?"

"In the bar with me. She served the hot appetizers and filled in for my waitresses when they took their breaks."

"She was there all night?"

"We closed at one and Alex didn't leave until one-thirty. I tried to get her to take a break around ten, but she said she was okay and she made me take one, instead." Sally paused and her eyes narrowed. "Don't tell me you suspect Alex!"

"Not really, but I wouldn't be doing my job if I didn't check everybody out."

"I guess that's true," Sally said, but she still looked puzzled. "I don't understand how Alex ended up on your suspect list. What possible reason could she have for killing Connie Mac?"

Hannah thought fast. She couldn't tell Sally the real reason, and she had to think of another. "She's mentioned several times that she didn't like Connie Mac."

"Who did? And before you ask, I have an alibi, too." Sally tipped the fryer basket and flipped the hot french fries out onto a plate. "You're going back to the restaurant, aren't you?"

"Yes. Andrea's waiting for me."

"Then take her these." Sally put the plate on a tray, added a dish of blue cheese dressing, and handed it to Hannah. "I made a double order so you could share."

Hannah stopped at the counter, sprinkled on salt, and balanced the tray in one hand as she went through the swinging door. The trip to their table only took a few seconds, but Hannah managed to snitch two fries on the way. When she set the tray down in front of her sister, Andrea was frowning.

"You took two of my french fries," Andrea accused her. "I saw you."

"No, I didn't. Sally made a double order so we could share."

"Are you sure?"

"That's what she said. I don't blame you for sending mine back. They're a lot better when they're hot."

"I didn't send them back. But you're right, they're better when they're hot. And they're delicious with this blue cheese dressing." Andrea took a french fry, dipped it in the dressing, and popped it into her mouth. "Get out your notebook and I'll tell you more about that writer."

Hannah pulled out her notebook and picked up her pen. "Are you trying to keep me busy so you can hog all the french fries?"

"Of course I am," Andrea admitted with a grin.

"That's what I thought. You always were a sneaky kid." Hannah grabbed a french fry with her left hand, dipped it, and popped it in her mouth. "See? It won't work. I can write and eat at the same time. Now, tell me what else that writer said."

"He said he saw someone follow Alan down to the shore."

"What?" Hannah stared at her sister in total amazement. "Why didn't you tell me that right away?"

"You didn't give me the chance."

"Yes, I did. You should have said that first, instead of telling me about the *ushankas* with the dog ears."

"Flaps that only look like dog ears," Andrea corrected her.

Hannah sighed. There were times when her sister could be just as exasperating as their mother. Andrea told stories in her own way, and it didn't work to rush her. "Go on. I'm listening."

"The person who followed Alan was dressed all in black and he skulked through the trees."

"The writer said *skulked?*"

"Of course he did. He's a writer and they use words like that. If you keep interrupting me, I'll never get to the end."

"All right. Go on."

"Every time Alan turned around, this person in black ducked behind a tree. The writer lost sight of them when they got down to the shore. He said there's a little hill and they disappeared behind it. He watched for another few minutes, but they didn't reappear, so he gave up and went to bed."

"That's great, Andrea." Hannah wrote it all down. "Did you ask if he could describe the man in more detail?"

"Yes, and he couldn't. He only saw him from the back."

"Anything else?"

"Yes. He had breakfast the next morning and he mentioned it to Larry Kruger. Larry told him he was going to count it as another ghost sighting and put it in his next story."

"That figures." Hannah wrote down the additional information, and then she looked up with a frown. "Eat up, Andrea. There's somebody we have to see."

"I did. I'm finished."

Hannah glanced at the plate of french fries. It was perfectly bare. Andrea had eaten every one. "You ate them all?"

"I was hungry." Andrea wiped her hands on a napkin and pushed back her chair. "I'm ready. Who are we going to see?"

"Ezekiel Jordan's ghost," Hannah told her, walking forward.

"But you don't believe in ghosts!" Andrea reached out to grab Hannah's arm. "What are you talking about?"

"You'll see. Follow me." Hannah was smiling as she led the way out of the restaurant. Even if her sister begged, she wasn't going to explain until they got all the way up to Francine's room. Andrea's curiosity might just kill her, but she deserved worse for snitching Hannah's share of the french fries.

"**I** know why you won't tell me where we're going," Andrea said, following Hannah up the stairs. "You're mad because I ate all the french fries. But it's not like I did it deliberately. Once I got started, I just couldn't stop eating."

Hannah glanced back at her sister. Andrea did look very contrite. "It's okay. I understand."

"That's good, because I sure don't!" Andrea replied with a frown. "I've never gone on food binges like this before. What's gotten into me, anyway?"

Several succinct answers occurred to Hannah, but she wisely let them pass. She just waited until they'd reached the top of the staircase, and then she pulled Andrea over to the side of the hall. "Let me tell you about the ghost."

As Andrea listened to the Hannah's story, she started to smile. By the time Hannah had finished, she was laughing.

"And it's all your fault," Hannah concluded.

"*My* fault? What did I do?"

"You told Sally that ghosts sell, and that's what gave Francine the idea. Come on. Let's go talk to Francine. I want to know if she's the one that writer saw last night."

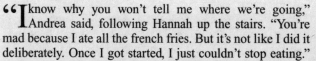

* * *

"It wasn't me," Francine insisted after Hannah had asked the question. "I never appear outside. His imagination must have been working overtime."

Hannah shot Andrea a warning glance. Both of them were convinced that the writer hadn't been imagining things. He'd seen someone following Alan, and that someone had been the killer.

"Do you want to see my ghost costume?" Francine smiled when they nodded and she walked over to pull the curtains. "It only works when the light's dim. Wait right here. I'll be right back."

In less time than they expected, Francine reappeared. She was wearing an old-fashioned black coat, black pants, and a black hat pulled down over her eyes. "It's a little too light in here. Try to imagine how I'd look at night and I'll demonstrate my ghost walk."

Hannah and Andrea watched as Francine demonstrated her special walk. She scooted along with her knees bent and bobbed up every few feet. By squinching her eyes half-shut, Hannah could get the full effect.

"That's wonderful!" Andrea clapped her hands. "It looks like you're floating."

"That's the general idea. I let people see me and then I duck down the back stairs. They're off limits for the guests because they don't meet the building code, but Sally gave me a key."

"How do you get back to your room?" Hannah asked.

"That's simple. I lock the stairwell door behind me and take off my ghost outfit on the landing. It's a couple of sizes too large and I wear it over my regular clothes. Then I stuff it in Danny's diaper bag, go down the back stairs, and come up the main staircase while everybody's still milling around. I'm always carrying the diaper bag anyway, so no one thinks it's suspicious."

"Is it working?" Andrea asked.

"Like a charm. People have been calling in from all over, and last night Sally told me she was all booked up until the end of March. You've just got to come see one of my appearances. I haven't had this much fun in ages."

"Just let us know when," Hannah said. "We'll come."

"And I'll scream," Andrea added. "My drama teacher at Jordan High said I had the best bloodcurdling scream he'd ever heard."

"What's next?" Andrea asked as they left Francine's room.

"I'm not sure," Hannah said, glancing at her watch as they walked toward the stairs. "We still have to talk to the rest of the Connie Mac people, but Sally said they never come back for dinner until eight."

"We could eat dinner. We probably won't have time later."

"You're hungry *again?*"

"Not really, but you have to eat. I'll just keep you company."

"Okay," Hannah agreed, starting down the stairs. "Since you ate all my fries, I get to pick the place."

"The Corner Tavern?" Andrea guessed, wrinkling her nose.

"You bet. I need brain food and I'm in the mood for a thick slab of steak."

"But fish is supposed to be brain food," Andrea objected. "At least that's what everybody says."

"I know, but I'm having a steak, blood rare, with an order of garlic bread. You can have a double order of fish. Then you'll be smart enough for both of us."

The Corner Tavern was crowded, but they managed to find a booth in the back. Hannah ordered the thickest porterhouse they had, and Andrea ordered the fish.

"You want your steak cooked the usual way?" the waitress asked Hannah.

"Slap it on the grill, give it thirty seconds on one side, and flip it over for another thirty seconds."

"I know, I know," the waitress said with a grin. "If it doesn't moo when you cut into it, it's overdone."

When their waitress had left, Hannah plopped her huge shoulder bag on the table and pulled out her steno pad. "We might as well be constructive while we're waiting. Let's go over the notes."

"Are you ever going to replace that?" Andrea asked her.

"Sure, when it gets full. I've got a whole bag full of new steno pads at home."

"Not that. I was talking about your purse. It's really a disgrace, Hannah. You've had it forever and it's completely out of style. Why don't you let me buy you a new purse for your birthday?"

"No way. I love this purse. It's just the right size for everything I need and it's perfect for me. That's why I've had it so long. This purse is like a friend. You don't ditch a friend because she gets old."

Andrea sighed. "If you won't give it up, maybe you should think about having it reconditioned. You could always have the leather dyed a darker color. Then the scratches won't show as much."

"Those scratches are like battle scars. They're badges of honor. This purse and I have gone through the wars together."

"And it looks like it," Andrea muttered, and then she started to grin. "We're doing it again, Hannah. We're squabbling like kids over your stupid purse."

"My purse isn't stupid," Hannah retorted, and then she laughed. "You'd better take that back or I'll tell Mother."

Several patrons at neighboring booths turned to stare at them as they both burst into laughter. One even asked them what was so funny, and that made them laugh even harder. When they finally sobered enough to speak, Andrea leaned closer. "Have you ever wondered why we call her 'Mother'?"

"Because she gave birth to us?"

"I'm serious, Hannah. We've always called her 'Mother' and never 'Mom.'"

"That's true," Hannah said, and she thought about it for a moment. "I think it's because she's always been so perfect."

"Perfect?" Andrea looked puzzled.

"I mean her appearance was perfect. She never slouched around in old clothes like the other moms, and she even had a special outfit she wore when she worked in the garden. I never saw her without her makeup, and her aprons always looked like they were brand-new. It was almost like she was starring as the mother in a television show."

"You're right," Andrea said, wincing slightly, "and I think I inherited it from her. I've got outfits for everything, too."

"Relax. That doesn't mean you're like Mother," Hannah reassured her.

"Are you sure?"

"I'm positive. Mother would never ride on a snowmobile with me. She knows better. Now stop worrying about it and get ready to eat. Here comes our food."

Hannah's steak was cooked perfectly, and she ate in silence for several minutes. When she glanced over at Andrea, she was only slightly surprised to see that her sister had eaten most of her fish and all of her green salad.

"What?" Andrea asked, noticing Hannah's interest in her plate.

"Nothing. I just thought you weren't hungry, that's all."

"I wasn't, but I like the way they do fish here. And that garlic bread smells so good."

"Here," Hannah said, shoving the basket closer to her sister.

"Thanks, but no thanks."

Hannah was puzzled. "But I thought you said it smelled good."

"It does, but I can't have it. Do you know that ingested garlic seeps out through your pores for hours after you've eaten it? It even makes the sheets on your bed smell like garlic."

"So?"

"That wouldn't be fair to Bill. It'd be different if he ate it, too. Then neither one of us would mind. But Bill's not here, and it wouldn't be fair for me to eat it without him. You don't have to worry about things like that because you live alone."

Hannah's lips twitched with amusement. Andrea had some strange ideas. "Just take a piece home to Bill and then there won't be a problem."

"That's a good idea," Andrea said, reaching for the basket. "Don't let me forget, okay?"

"I won't. Can you talk and eat at the same time?"

"Sure. I'm almost through anyway."

"Good. I want to go through my list of suspects again and make sure we didn't miss anybody." Hannah flipped through her notebook with her left hand and forked her salad with her right. "Here's Janie. We eliminated her. And here's Norman, but Mike decided that he couldn't have hit himself over the head. And here's Ray, Connie Mac's driver."

"I eliminated him," Andrea said proudly. "He was nowhere near Lake Eden at the time."

"Right. We eliminated Paul because he was with Alan, and Alan's eliminated because he didn't kill himself. And here's the man who got half."

"Huh?" Andrea looked thoroughly puzzled.

"The man Connie Mac and Alan were fighting about when Sally heard them in the bar. He got half of something and Connie Mac was really mad about it."

"I remember now. There were just too many suspects, Hannah. I had trouble keeping them all straight."

"Tell me about it." Hannah flipped the page. "Here's Kurt Howe, but I cleared him. And here's Alex, but I cleared her, too. Then there's Larry Kruger. We still have to question him."

"No, we don't. I ran into him in the hall and we talked for a couple of minutes. He said he was alone when Connie Mac and Alan were killed, but he had an alibi for the night that Norman was bashed on the head."

"What was it?"

Andrea started to grin. "He was interviewing Lake Eden's foremost authority on Ezekiel Jordan's life to get more information for his ghost stories. Can you guess who that is?"

Hannah sighed. Andrea was doing it again. She loved to tell stories her way, and now she wanted to play a guessing game. "It's got to be someone from the historical society. Am I right?"

"You're right. But who?"

"Someone who read the letters that Delores has. She said there was a lot of information in . . ." Hannah stopped speaking as the light dawned. "Larry Kruger was interviewing *Mother?*"

"That's what he said."

"She should be home by now. Call her to substantiate his alibi."

"I think you should call her. You're older."

"What does *older* have to do with it? Besides, you're the one with the phone."

The two sisters locked eyes; Andrea caved in first. "All right. I'll call her. But I'm not happy about it."

Hannah poured another cup of coffee from the carafe the waitress had brought and listened to the one-sided conversation as Andrea spoke to their mother. It was clear that Delores was confirming Larry Kruger's alibi. But then Andrea assumed a devilish expression, and that made Hannah go on full alert.

"She's right here, Mother," Andrea said with a grin. "We're having dinner together. Hold on a second and I'll hand her the phone."

Hannah shot her sister a look of betrayal as she took the phone, but she knew she might as well get it over with. "Hello, Mother."

"Is it true, Hannah?" Delores asked.

"What, Mother?"

"That you found another body?"

Hannah glanced at her sister. Andrea's shoulders were shaking with silent laughter and Hannah gave her a dirty look. "It's true, Mother. I did find another body. His name is Alan Carpenter and he was Connie Mac's lawyer."

"Oh, Hannah!" Delores sighed so loudly, Hannah came

close to holding the phone away from her ear. "I do wish you'd stop looking for trouble."

"I wasn't looking for trouble, Mother."

"Perhaps not, but you certainly seem to attract it. You've got to make an effort, dear."

Hannah glanced at Andrea again. Her sister was really enjoying this. "I will, Mother. I'll make a real effort to stop finding dead bodies, I promise."

"Well, I should hope so! You're destroying your reputation, you know."

"It'll be all right, Mother. I haven't noticed any small children cringing when they meet me on the street."

"Don't be sarcastic. It's not becoming. Tell me the truth, Hannah. Are you working with the sheriff's department again?"

"No, Mother."

"How about your sister? She has a child to think of, you know. You're not . . ."

"I'm not leading Andrea into any trouble, Mother," Hannah interrupted, hoping to nip that idea in the bud.

"I just feel it's my duty to warn you, dear. People are starting to talk. It won't be long before they start to avoid you. You'll be an outcast in Lake Eden."

"You're right, Mother." Hannah winked at Andrea. "I hate to cut this short, but I've got to go. People are starting to leave to avoid me, and I don't want to hurt the Corner Tavern's business. You have a nice evening, now."

Andrea took the phone and clicked it off. "Larry Kruger's in the clear. When Norman was attacked, he was eating coconut cake in Mother's kitchen. I'm sorry I handed the phone to you, but if I'd told Mother, she would have given *me* a lecture."

"That's okay. I forgive you," Hannah said good-naturedly. "Correct me if I'm wrong, but I think Mr. Fifty Percent is the only suspect we have left."

"You're right."

"We've got to find out who he is. Connie Mac knew, but

she's dead. And Alan knew, but he's not talking now, either. Paul would know, but he won't be back until tomorrow."

"Wait a second." Andrea looked thoughtful. "If we could get into Alan's files, we might be able to tell who Mr. Fifty Percent is without asking anybody. All we have to do is look for a contract that gives someone fifty percent."

"But his files would be in his office. And his office is in Minneapolis."

"That's his permanent office, but I'll bet he's got another office here."

"What makes you think that?"

"Because Alan lived in Minneapolis and the roads were really bad last night. If he had driven all the way there, he would have stayed over and come back this morning."

"You've got a point," Hannah said, grabbing her notebook and flipping through it. "Alan and Kurt left the banquet at eight forty-five. We saw them leave. But Sally told me they walked into the bar at the inn at eleven. There's no way they could have driven to Minneapolis, held a press conference, and gotten back here by eleven. You're right, Andrea. Alan must have a local office."

"So am I a genius, or what?" Andrea asked, preening a bit.

"Absolutely. It must have been the fish."

Chapter
Twenty-Nine

Hannah glanced at her watch in the dim light of the bar, and then she nudged Andrea. "Twenty minutes to show time. Where's Janie?"

"She's collecting the key from Sally and she's supposed to meet us in the lobby in five minutes. Let's leave now, Hannah. I'm getting nervous just sitting here."

"What do you have to be nervous about?"

"I'm out of practice. I haven't screamed in years."

Hannah almost laughed, assuming that her sister was joking, but Andrea did look very nervous. "Don't worry. Screaming is like riding a bicycle. Once you learn how, you never forget."

"Did you just make that up?"

"Yes," Hannah admitted, "but don't forget that you've got Janie to help you. You said she was the second-best screamer in your drama class."

Hannah left money to pay for their half-finished Cokes, and they left the bar for the lobby. She'd used Andrea's cell phone to make three calls on their way back to the inn. The first had been to Janie, who'd confirmed that Alan had used a small room in the back of the boutique as his office. He was the only one who'd had a key, but Janie was sure that his key ring was still in his room. Janie had worked with Alan long enough to learn his habits, and she knew he never took all of his keys when he went out on his walks. He just slipped his room key off the ring and carried it in his jacket pocket.

Hannah's second call had been to Sally to ask if she could go up to Alan's room to retrieve his keys. Sally had been willing, but she'd told Hannah that Bill and Mike had stationed Rick Murphy outside Alan's door and that no one was allowed inside. This had prompted Hannah's third call, to Sally's mother, Francine. They had to create a diversion to lure Rick away from his post so that Hannah could get in. Ezekiel's ghost would do the trick, and Francine had agreed to make a special appearance.

"I hope this works," Andrea said, entering the lobby and perching on the arm of an overstuffed chair.

"It will. If you and Janie scream loud enough, Rick will come running. You've got to keep him with you long enough for me to dash in Alan's room, find the keys, and get back out."

"If I have to, I'll faint," Andrea declared. "I used to be the best fake fainter in drama class, too."

"Whatever it takes. Janie thinks Alan's keys are in his top dresser drawer. She says that's where he usually kept them."

"How does she know that?"

"He sent her up to get them last week, when he forgot them. He told her they were in his top dresser drawer, under his handkerchiefs."

"I'm here," Janie called out, hurrying across the lobby and thrusting two keys into Hannah's hand. "The key with the tag is for Alan's room and the other one is for mine. My room is right next-door to his."

Hannah nodded, dropping the keys into her pocket. "I'd better get up there right now. Bring Andrea to your room when it's over. If I'm lucky, I'll be there with Alan's keys."

The waiting was tense, and Hannah paced the floor of Janie's room. It was now five minutes to showtime, and for someone who wasn't in the actual performance, she had a bad case of stage fright. The butterflies in her stomach felt as big as buzzards, and she hoped she wouldn't blow it. She was taking a big risk. If Mike found out that she'd gone into Alan's room after he'd declared it off limits, he'd lock her up for the rest of her natural life. Come to think about it, her natural lifespan might not be so natural if Mike got really mad at her.

Three minutes to show time. Hannah took a deep breath and let it out slowly. She wanted to be with Francine so that she could control what time the ghost appeared at the end of the hall. She also wanted to be with Andrea and Janie, to tell them when to scream and how loud. She wanted to be with Bill and Mike to keep them away from the second floor, and she wanted to be outside Alan's door with Rick, encouraging him to abandon his post and investigate the source of the commotion. Hannah wanted to be everywhere, but she was stuck here, where she also wanted to be, so that she could sneak into Alan's room and grab the keys. At times like this, she wished she could split like an amoeba and be everywhere at once.

One minute to show time. Hannah took out Alan's key and grasped it tightly, peering through the peephole in Janie's door. She counted down the seconds, as nervous as an astronaut on a first launch, and held her breath while she waited for the action. And then she heard the sweetest sound in the world.

Two bloodcurdling, high-pitched screams rent the air. A man yelled out, the screaming went on, and Hannah heard footsteps pounding down the hallway. It took a five full seconds, but then she saw Rick Murphy, the youngest deputy on the force, rushing past Janie's door on his way toward the source of the screaming.

Hannah opened the door and stepped out. There was a crowd milling around at the end of the hallway, and she could see someone down on the carpet. It was probably Andrea in a fake faint, but she didn't have time to confirm it. With fingers that shook slightly, Hannah sidled up to Alan's door and inserted the key in the lock. A second later, she was inside with the door closed securely behind her.

The clock was ticking. Rick could be back any second. She had to find Alan's key ring and get out. Hannah raced for the dresser and pulled out the top drawer, feeling frantically under the stack of clean handkerchiefs. No keys. Had Mike and Bill already taken them, or . . .

Hannah raced for the black coat that was draped over a chair. Sally had mentioned that Alan had been wearing a black coat when he'd come back from press conference. She thrust her hand into the pocket, drew out a clean hand-kerchief, one black leather glove . . . and the key ring!

The commotion in the hallway had decreased in volume as Hannah tossed Alan's coat back onto the chair. She sped for the door, opening it a crack to glance out. Rick was still at the end of the hallway, leaning over a woman's body. As Hannah slipped out and sidled back to Janie's room, she realized that there was a big hole in her master plan. If Mike and Bill ever realized that Alan's keys were missing, she'd need an alibi.

Her mind racing, Hannah considered the alternatives. Several people had seen her with Andrea earlier, and they might mention that she hadn't been at her sister's side. She had to convince everyone in the crowd surrounding Andrea that she'd been there when the ghost had appeared.

Hannah ran into Janie's room and filled a glass with water. Then she ran back out, shouting to the people at the end of the hall. "It's all right! I'm coming!"

Several people stepped back as she approached, and Hannah caught her first glimpse of Andrea. Her sister was stretched out on the floor, completely motionless. Not even her eyelids were quivering, and for one brief moment, Hannah wondered if Andrea truly had fainted. Then she remembered the time that her sister had played a comatose woman in a perfectly dreadful play written by Jordan High's drama teacher. Andrea was acting, and she was great at it.

"Stand back," Hannah ordered, holding her glass of water aloft. "I'll bring her out of it."

Andrea still didn't move a muscle, and Hannah figured that an Academy Award was in order. Of course, Andrea probably expected a cold washcloth on her brow, or a dose of pretend smelling salts. With a silent apology to her sister, Hannah upended the glass and doused Andrea's face with the water.

Andrea gasped and then started to sputter as she saw Hannah bending over her. Her eyes were blazing, and Hannah knew she had to say something before Andrea ruined her best performance. "I'm sorry, Andrea. It was the only way we could think of to bring you back to consciousness."

"I . . . I fainted?" Andrea asked, slipping right back into character like a trooper. "What happened? I don't remember a thing."

Janie leaned over her solicitously. "We saw the ghost and you screamed. And then you crumpled to the floor and passed out."

"And I ran to Janie's room for water." Hannah added her bit to the story.

"Just rest for a minute," Rick Murphy advised. "I'll go get a chair."

Andrea shook her head. "I think I'd rather lie down. I hate to trouble you, but could you help me to Janie's room?"

"Sure. No problem." Rick took her arm and helped her up. "Just lean on me."

Andrea smiled up at him and her lower lip quivered slightly. "Thanks, Rick. I'm so glad you were here and not another deputy. You won't tell Bill, will you? This is so embarrassing."

"Well . . ."

"Please? I really did think I saw the ghost. I swear there was something down there at the end of the hall, but it was probably just my imagination. You know how Bill is. If he finds out I thought I saw a ghost and fainted, he'll tease me about it for the rest of my life. Can't it be our secret?"

Rick grinned. "Okay, as long as you're sure you're not hurt. As far as I know, it's not a crime to think you saw a ghost."

* * *

The moment Janie's door had closed behind them, Andrea turned to glare at Hannah. "What got into you, Hannah? You didn't have to actually douse me with water!"

"Yes, I did. Rick was standing right there. He would have known something was fishy if I hadn't."

"Well . . . maybe, but you didn't have to enjoy it. And don't bother to deny it. I know you did. It's just like the water fights we used to have at the lake. I always got soaked, and half the time, you didn't have a drop—"

"Here, Andrea," Janie interrupted, tossing her a towel. "You'd better wipe your face. You can wear one of my sweaters. It'll be too big, but at least it'll be dry. And I've got a hair dryer you can use."

Andrea did not look in good humor, and Hannah knew it was time to mend fences. "You're an incredible actress, Andrea. I really thought you'd fainted."

"You did?" Andrea looked slightly appeased. "You're not just saying that?"

"No. And your screaming was perfect. I knew it was coming, but I jumped anyway. I really thought somebody was getting murdered out there."

Andrea gave a little smile. "I told you I'd do my part. Did you get the keys?"

"Yes, thanks to you." Hannah held them up for her sister's inspection. "They weren't in the drawer and I had to search for them. If you hadn't pretended to faint, Rick might have caught me."

"Well, all's well that ends well. Do I have time to dry my hair?"

"Absolutely. It's cold out there and I don't want you to go out with a wet head."

After Andrea had retreated to the bathroom, the phone rang. Janie answered it and then held it out to Hannah. "It's Sally, for you."

"Hello?" Hannah answered.

"Hi, Hannah," Sally sounded amused. "I heard it went really well. Did you get the keys?"

"Sure did."

"Great. I'm filling in on the switchboard, and your neighbor, Mrs. Canfield, is on the line for you. Do you want me to put her through?"

"Yes, please." Hannah crossed her fingers as she waited for Sally to put through the call. She'd told Mrs. Canfield to call her when Greg came home.

"Hannah?" Mrs. Canfield's voice was shaking slightly. "Greg still isn't home and I'm worried sick. Do you think I should call the sheriff?"

"I don't think that's necessary, Mrs. Canfield. I'm sure he'll be home soon."

"I hope so! I'm just so nervous and I . . . I wanted to talk to someone about it. Could you come down to see me when you get home?"

Hannah came very close to groaning out loud. She'd been looking forward to curling up with Moishe and watching some mindless television, but she couldn't let Mrs. Canfield down. "Sure, but I have to make a trip to the mall first. It might be pretty late."

"That's all right. I'm so worried about Greg, I won't be able to sleep a wink."

"Okay, Mrs. Canfield. The minute I get home, I'll come straight to your place."

"You're a darling, Hannah," Mrs. Canfield said, and she sounded relieved. "I'll see you later, then."

"What's up?" Janie asked when Hannah had hung up the phone.

"My neighbor's worried about her grandson. He's going through a rough time and she just wants to talk." Hannah picked up the key ring and handed it to Janie. "Do you know which one of these keys is for the boutique?"

One by one, Hannah and Janie examined the keys on Alan's key ring. Janie compared them with hers, and they marked the ones Hannah would need with a felt-tipped pen.

Janie had just finished sketching the layout of the boutique when Andrea emerged from the bathroom.

Hannah glanced up at her sister and her mouth dropped open in surprise. Janie's sweater was miles too big for Andrea, but she'd rolled up the sleeves and belted it in with the long scarf she'd been wearing around her neck. Her hair was pulled up in a loose knot at the top of her head and she looked fabulous.

"What?" Andrea asked, taking in Hannah's startled expression.

"How did you do that? You look gorgeous."

"No, I don't. You're just trying to make me feel better."

"I'm serious, Andrea. You look great."

"Well . . . I always make an effort. Aren't you going to comb your hair before we go?"

Hannah reached up to pat her hair. It felt all right to her. "Why should I?"

"Somebody might see you."

"Who? The mall's closed and all we're doing is breaking into Alan's office."

"But we could run into someone."

"I hope not," Hannah said. "And if we do, I don't think anybody at the sheriff's department is going to care if my hair isn't perfect for my mug shot."

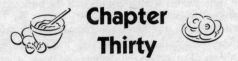

Chapter Thirty

As Hannah took the turnoff for the Tri-County Mall, she glanced over at her sister and noticed that she was shivering. "Maybe you should stay in the truck. I can do this alone."

"It'll take twice as long to go through the files if I don't help you."

"That's okay. I don't mind. Look, Andrea . . . what we're doing isn't exactly legal. I don't blame you for being scared."

Andrea shook her head. "I'm not scared."

"Then why are you shaking?"

"Because I'm cold. We should have taken my Volvo. It's got a better heater."

Hannah wasn't convinced by her sister's explanation. "Are you sure you're not shivering because you're scared?"

"I'm positive. I'm a little nervous, but I'm not scared. I'm going in, Hannah. At least it'll be warm in the mall."

"Okay," Hannah said, pulling around to the back of the mall and parking by the entrance the employees used. "Grab the flashlights and let's go."

A light snow began to fall as they got out of Hannah's truck and walked toward the door. Hannah glanced up at the huge flakes that were floating past the old-fashioned streetlights that were placed at intervals around the building. "It's snowing again."

"I know. Isn't it gorgeous? Nights like this remind me of Christmas Eve. Remember how Dad used to drive us down to see the official Christmas tree in Lake Eden Park, and we'd always just miss Santa Claus? You used to roll down the car window and say, 'There he is! Up there in the sky! I think he just came from our house.' And by the time I looked, he was gone."

"That was Dad's idea. Did you believe me?"

"I did for the first couple of years. After that, I pretended to believe because of Michelle. You were pretty convincing, Hannah. You even described the reindeer."

They arrived at the door and Hannah opened it with the key Janie had marked. She'd never used this entrance before, and she was a bit surprised at how dreary it was.

"It's not very pretty, is it?" Andrea echoed Hannah's sentiments as she surveyed the green-and-beige walls.

"I guess they figure they don't need to decorate just for the employees." Hannah reached out to take her sister's arm. "Come with me. Janie told me how to get up to the second floor."

"But we just take the escalator, don't we?"

"No, they shut them down at night. We have to use the stairs. If we run into anybody, let me do the talking."

"What are you going to say?"

"That Janie sent us out here to pick up some papers from the boutique."

"What if they don't believe you?"

"I'll just show them the keys. That should convince them we're supposed to be here."

"But what if they think you stole the keys?"

Hannah grinned as she started up the stairs. Andrea complained about Tracey asking question after question, and now she was doing the very same thing. "Relax. Janie promised to stay by the phone. I'll just give them her number and she'll confirm it."

The doorway to the second floor was locked, and Hannah

used the key to open it. When they stepped out into the deserted mall, Andrea shivered slightly. "It looks different at night," she whispered.

"I know," Hannah whispered back. "I'm glad they've got night-lights. At least we can see where we're going."

Hannah walked forward with Andrea at her heels. Even though she tried to walk quietly, her footsteps echoed in the huge, empty space. Without the sound of music on the speaker system and the crowds of shoppers talking and laughing, every sound was magnified. The heater vents whooshed like surfacing whales, there was a loud ticking sound that appeared to come from the clock that hung on the wall over the cash register in the Fanny Farmer Candy shop, and the hum from a flickering fluorescent tube in the display window of Sammy's Sportswear was deafening. The shadows loomed large, and Hannah couldn't dismiss the possibility that someone could be lurking behind one of the mirrored posts that held up the roof, or pressed flat against the little alcoves that surrounded the entrances to the stores. The setting reminded Hannah of every bad horror movie she'd seen, and it was unnerving.

Andrea glanced behind her more times than Hannah could count as they hurried toward Connie Mac's Kitchen Boutique. Hannah had a compelling urge to do the same, but she didn't. Two pairs of eyes facing in opposite directions were much safer. She wished they had four pairs of eyes so they could cover the area completely. *There's nobody out here except us,* she told herself. And she repeated it over and over like a mantra until they arrived at the entrance to the boutique.

Hannah's fingers were shaking slightly as she unlocked the glass door to Connie Mac's store, but once they'd stepped inside and relocked the door behind them, she felt much safer. Although the banks of tiny bulbs the store used for nighttime security didn't give much illumination, her eyes were adjusting to the low level of light. At least they wouldn't bump into a display stand and break something expensive.

"Can we turn on the lights?" Andrea asked, sounding hopeful.

"No. One of the security guards might see them."

"But there aren't any security guards at night."

Hannah turned to her sister in surprise. "How do you know that?"

"Bill told me. One of the guys at the department was looking for a second job right after Christmas. He came out here to apply for night security and the mall manager told him they didn't have night guards anymore."

"Well . . . that's good to know," Hannah said, not sure whether that revelation made her feel better or worse. A night guard could catch them going through Alan's files, but thinking that there was a guard in the building had made her feel a bit safer.

"So can we?"

It took a second for Hannah to remember her sister's initial question. "No, we can't turn on the lights. Somebody else could be here working late."

"But there were no other cars in the parking lot."

"That's true, but I don't want to take any chances. One of the other store owners could be pulling up outside right now. If he walks past here on the way to his store, he'll wonder why the lights are on. And if he calls the sheriff's department to report it, you could get busted by your own husband."

"Good point," Andrea said, giving up the argument.

The two sisters walked past counters and displays, heading for the back room. They were halfway there when Andrea pointed to a display of cast-iron pans. "Look, Hannah. Grandma Ingrid had pans like those."

"They're spiders," Hannah told her.

"Where?" Andrea jumped back. "I hate spiders!"

"I'm talking about the pans. They used to call them spiders."

Andrea gave a sigh of relief and stepped back up to the display table. "These prices are insane. Look at this little one. It's sixty-nine dollars and it won't hold more than one egg."

"Cast iron must be popular again. I've got a whole set of Grandma Ingrid's spiders, if you want one."

"You keep them. I don't cook anyway." Andrea moved forward, but she stopped at a display of cut-glass crystal. "This vase is just gorgeous. It's got to be Baccarat."

"Sleuth now, shop later," Hannah ordered, pushing her sister forward. "Come on, Andrea. It's almost ten-thirty and I don't want to be out here all night."

"Can we turn on the lights now?" Andrea asked, once they'd entered the back room and closed the door behind them.

"Not yet." Hannah pointed to the bank of windows on the outside wall. "Those windows overlook the front parking lot, and somebody might see the lights from the highway. Come with me. Alan's office is right over here."

When Hannah had opened Alan's office, Andrea gave a disappointed sigh. "He's got a window, too! Does that mean we have to go through his files with flashlights?"

"I'm afraid so," Hannah told her, moving to the file cabinet against the wall. "At least he's got two chairs in here. Sit down behind his desk and I'll bring you some files to go through."

Hannah took the files from the top drawer and gave her sister the contents of the bottom drawer. They positioned their flashlights to serve as lamps and worked in silence for about ten minutes, going through stacks of paperwork. Most of Alan's files contained routine papers relating to the management of Connie Mac's Kitchen Boutiques.

"I think I've got it, Hannah!" Andrea sounded excited as she pointed to a document she'd been reading. "It's Paul MacIntyre's will and it's dated the day before Connie Mac died. It's witnessed and notarized and it says that Paul leaves fifty percent of his estate to Connie Mac and fifty percent to . . . *Janie!*"

"Our Janie?"

"Yes. Jane Ellen Burkholtz. It says so right here. But why would Paul do something like that, unless . . ." Andrea stopped speaking and began to frown. "Do you think that Janie lied to you about having an affair with Paul?"

"I'm almost positive she didn't. There's got to be another explanation."

"But what? People don't just pick names out of a hat and leave them fifty percent of their money."

"No, of course not," Hannah said, and then the light dawned. Alex had told her that Janie's biological father was going to leave her something in his will.

"What is it, Hannah?" Andrea leaned forward to stare at her sister in the glow of the flashlight. "Do you know something I don't know?"

"I think I do."

"What is it?"

Hannah began to frown. She'd promised not to tell anyone that Janie was Alex's daughter, but she'd figured out the identity of Janie's biological father all by herself. "If I tell you, you've got to promise not to tell anybody else. Not even Bill."

"It's that serious?" Andrea gulped when Hannah nodded. "Okay, I promise. Tell me."

"I think Paul MacIntyre is Janie's biological father."

Andrea looked shocked for a moment, and then she shook her head vehemently. "You're wrong, Hannah. I used to go to Janie's house all the time when we were kids, and there's no way Isobel would have had an affair. She adored Garland. They did everything together and they went everywhere together, and . . ."

"Hold the phone," Hannah interrupted before her sister could protest any further. "I didn't mean to imply *that*. What I meant was, Janie is adopted."

"Adopted? But . . . are you sure?"

"I'm sure."

"If Paul's her real father, who's her real mother?" Andrea gulped and looked a little sick. "Connie Mac?"

"Not Connie Mac. I can't tell you who it is, but it's definitely not her."

"That's a relief!" Andrea said, letting out her breath in a giant whoosh. "Is it someone we know?"

"Yes, and that's all I'm going to say about it. Don't press me, Andrea. I promised I'd never tell and I won't."

Andrea sighed. "Not even one little hint?"

"Absolutely not."

"How about Janie? Does she know?"

"No. Isobel and Garland promised never to tell her. Her birth mother made it a condition of the adoption. She wanted Janie to have a real family with a loving mother and father, and that's exactly what Janie has. Her birth mother never wanted to take the chance of jeopardizing Janie's feelings for Isobel and Garland."

Andrea looked as if she might object, but she thought about it for a moment and then nodded. "Okay. I can understand that."

"Good. Now let's get back to Mr. Fifty Percent. That turned out to be Janie and we know that she didn't kill Connie Mac. The only other possibility is Paul, and he's in the clear, too."

"At least we know why Connie Mac was so mad the day she died. It must have been a real shock to find out that Janie got half of her husband's estate. Do you think she knew that Janie was Paul's daughter?"

Hannah shook her head. "I don't think Paul told anyone why he put Janie in his will—not even Alan. Alan might have told Connie Mac if he'd known, and Paul wouldn't have risked that. I think the only thing that Alan told Connie Mac was that he'd drawn up Paul's will and that Janie got fifty percent."

"And Connie Mac assumed that Janie was sleeping with Paul? And that's why she was in his will?"

"It makes sense. What would *you* think if Bill drew up a will and his lawyer told you that he'd left fifty percent to a woman at work?"

Andrea began to frown. "I see what you mean, and that almost makes me feel sorry for Connie Mac. But if Janie didn't kill her, and Paul didn't kill her, who did?"

"Search me. We're fresh out of suspects, Andrea."

"That's true," Andrea said, and she sounded very discouraged. "We followed all the leads and we did everything right, but we still flunked out. What are we going to do?"

"I don't have a clue. All I know is that I never want to go through another day like today. I'm still locked out of The Cookie Jar, I found another body, one of my oldest friends lied to me, and I struck out on a murder case for the first time. I'm on a losing streak, Andrea. We'd better put back these files and leave before we get busted for breaking and entering."

"Just sit here and rest. I'll do it." Andrea picked up a stack of files and returned them to the file cabinet. When she came back for a second armful, she looked puzzled. "You said a friend lied to you. Which friend?"

"Greg Canfield. He said he tripled his money day-trading, but he lied. I just found out that the company he said he invested in went bankrupt."

"I wonder why he lied about it." Andrea thought for a moment and then she snapped her fingers. "You used to date him, didn't you?"

"I didn't date anyone."

"Yes, you did. I know you had a date for the senior prom."

"That was a setup," Hannah answered truthfully, even though the memory still stung a bit. "Dad promised Cliff Shuman a summer job if he took me to the prom. You were the one with all the dates, even back then."

"But Greg used to come to the house all the time. I remember that."

"That's true, but we weren't dating. Greg and I were just really good friends."

"Do you think you would have dated him if his parents hadn't moved?"

You bet! Hannah wanted to say, but she thought better of it. She tried for a casual tone and said, "Maybe. I liked him and I think he liked me, too."

"Then that's probably why he lied to you. He didn't want to admit he failed, so he made up that story to impress you."

"Maybe. I called to ask him about it, but he wasn't home."

Hannah picked up another stack of files and handed them to her sister. "Mrs. Canfield's really upset. She thinks Greg's going through a personal crisis, and she's worried about him."

"What makes her think that?"

"Greg told her he'd be staying with her temporarily, just until Annette found a house in Colorado, but some legal papers came for him from a family law firm in Denver. Mrs. Canfield thinks that they were divorce papers."

"She's probably right. I met Annette and she didn't strike me as the type to stick around when the money got tight."

"I know. I guess Greg just wasn't successful enough for her."

"But he was," Andrea objected. "His store was making money. I know that for a fact."

"Then Greg didn't go broke?"

"No. His store had record sales in December. One of his clerks told me that they outsold all the other stores in the mall. That's why I don't understand why Greg lost his lease. It just doesn't make sense."

"Why not?"

"Because the mall charges rent, but they also take a small percentage of the profits from each store. Why would the mall refuse to renew Greg's lease if his store was making extra money for them?"

"I don't know," Hannah said and she began to frown. "That's like cutting off your nose to spite your face, unless . . ."

"Unless what?"

"Unless the mall manager had bigger fish to fry. Didn't Rhea Robinson tell us that Connie Mac wouldn't sign a lease in a mall with a competing store?"

"Yes, but Greg's store was an import business."

"Didn't you tell me that you bought a cookie jar at Greg's closeout sale?"

"I bought two. They were half price. And I bought a set of everyday dishes, too. They're really cute, Hannah. They've got blue cornflowers around the border."

"So Greg carried a lot of kitchen things?"

"Yes, he did. He had glassware, and flatware, and . . ." Andrea stopped speaking and she drew in her breath sharply. "I see where you're going and I think you're right. I'm going to look for the lease that Connie Mac signed."

It took a few moments, but Andrea found the right file folder. She handed it to Hannah and they flipped through it together.

"I'll take the lease," Andrea offered, pulling the legal document out of the file. "I'm more familiar with leases than you are. You look at the correspondence."

They worked in silence for several minutes. The only sound was the rustle of pages turning. Finally Andrea handed the lease back to Hannah. "There's nothing about competing stores in here. It's all standard boilerplate."

"But this isn't," Hannah said, holding up a sheaf of pages that were stapled together at the corner. "Here's a letter that Alan wrote to the mall manager. It says that Connie Mac agrees to open one of her kitchen boutiques at the mall, but there's a condition. She wants the mall manager to cancel Greg's lease when it comes up for renewal and give his space to her kitchen boutique."

"And the mall manager agreed?"

"Oh, yes. Alan drew up a four-page contract. The mall manager signed it, and so did Connie Mac and Alan."

"So Connie Mac and Alan put Greg out of business?"

"I'm no lawyer, but it sure looks that way to me."

Andrea thought about that for a moment, and then she reached for Hannah's notebook. "Do you want me to add Greg to our suspect list and write down what we've learned?"

"Definitely. People have killed for less. I don't believe Greg would murder anybody, but I have to check it out. I promised Mrs. Canfield that I'd come down for coffee when I got home and I'm going to take this letter with me. If Greg's there, I'll ask him about . . ."

Hannah stopped speaking abruptly and Andrea glanced up at her. "What?"

"I heard something. Douse your flashlight. Quick!"

Andrea clicked off her flashlight and so did Hannah. The room was plunged into near-darkness. The only illumination came from a distant streetlight that glowed faintly through the window.

"What did you hear?" Andrea asked.

"A car. I think it drove around the building and parked in back."

Both sisters listened intently. All was quiet for almost a minute, and then they heard the faint sound of a door clanging closed.

"The stairwell door," Hannah said, reaching in her pocket for the keys to her truck and dropping them into Andrea's purse. "I just put my keys in your purse. Take it and crawl under the desk."

"Why?"

"Because it could be someone from the sheriff's department. I'll stick with my original story about how Janie sent me out here to pick up something. Maybe I can convince them to call her to confirm it, but they might haul me in to the station for questioning, anyway. If that happens, just wait until they're gone and drive my truck back to the inn."

"But I can back up your story. It's probably someone I know, and they'll believe me."

Hannah grabbed her sister's arm. "No, Andrea. Get under the desk. Please!"

"But why?"

"Because maybe it's *not* a deputy."

"Oh," Andrea said, and she sounded a little sick. "Do you think it could be the . . . the killer?"

"If it is, there's no way he's going to get you. Get under there, Andrea. Now!"

"But with two of us, we'll have him outnumbered. I won't let you face him alone."

"Get under there now, and don't make a sound!" Hannah ordered, pulling her sister around the desk.

"But I can help you. Why should I hide under the desk like a coward?"

"Because I won't let you jeopardize the life of my new

niece or nephew," Hannah declared, shoving her sister under the desk and rolling the desk chair back into place.

"But I'm not . . ."

"Just shut up and do what I say!" Hannah hissed, interrupting her sister's denial. "Believe me, Andrea. If I say you're pregnant, you're pregnant!"

Chapter Thirty-One

Hannah's heart was racing as she slipped out of the back room. She moved quickly, hurrying down the center aisle toward the display windows at the front of the store. The lighting inside the boutique was dim, but someone passing by the windows could still glance in and spot her. Rather than take that risk, she ducked down behind a display of fine china.

The mall was so quiet, she could hear the faint sound of approaching footsteps. Hannah hoped that it was just another store owner, intending to restock his shelves before the doors opened on Monday, but she didn't hold out much hope. Since it was almost eleven on a Sunday night, that was about as unlikely as Moishe suddenly sprouting wings and zooming off into the wild blue yonder.

The sound of the footsteps was increasing in volume as the person approached, clunking against the decorative tiles that lined the floor of the mall. Hannah was convinced that they belonged to a man. The stride was positive and energetic, and no effort was taken to step softly. Perhaps she was doing women a disservice by even thinking it, but Hannah doubted that any woman alone, entering a deserted mall this late at night, would tread so boldly.

Her heart in her throat, Hannah willed the stranger to walk on by, but the sound ceased abruptly in front of the door. She risked a glance, peeking up over a platter that probably cost more than she earned in a week, and she gasped as she recognized the person standing in front of Connie Mac's Kitchen Boutique.

It was Greg Canfield.

Relief washed over Hannah in a giant wave. Greg was all right. All her dire thoughts had turned out to be baseless. She was just getting to her feet, preparing to call out and offer to let Greg in, when she had an unsettling thought. What was Greg doing out here on a Sunday night? And how had he gotten in?

Hannah ducked back down and thought about it for a second. Greg had kept his keys to the back door of the mall. That much was clear. And she'd told Mrs. Canfield that she was coming out to the mall. Perhaps Greg had driven out here wanting to talk to her about the losses he'd taken in the stock market and the fact that Annette was divorcing him. Hannah had almost convinced herself that this was the case when she heard a sound that shot holes in her newly formed theory.

That sound was a key in the lock, turning the tumblers. It was followed by a click, and then Hannah heard the heavy glass door opening. Greg must have kept the key to his store, and no one had bothered to change the locks when Connie Mac's Kitchen Boutique had taken over the space.

Hannah moved slightly and peeked out again, this time from behind a serving bowl. Greg was relocking the door behind him. But why would he do that? And why hadn't he called out to her if he'd guessed she was here?

Greg bent over to pick something up, and Hannah almost gasped out loud when she saw that it was a baseball bat. Had Greg come out to the boutique to vandalize the store that had put him out of business?

Like lightning, an image popped into Hannah's mind— one that made her shiver. It was Connie Mac's skull, crushed by an object that Doc Knight had thought was a baseball bat.

Alan Carpenter's skull had also been crushed in the very same way. And there had been a splinter from a baseball bat in Norman's ski cap.

As Hannah watched, Greg began to walk up the aisle, holding the bat like a club. He paused near the center of the store, and an awful smile crossed his face. It was the smile of someone who'd slipped off the edge into madness, a cross between a grin and a leer, which made Hannah's mouth go suddenly dry and her heart pound frantically in her chest. She'd never thought to see a smile like that on the face of one of her friends. But she had to stop thinking of Greg as a friend. He was the killer. He'd injured Norman and murdered Connie Mac and Alan.

The chilling smile seemed frozen on Greg's face as he started forward again. He was humming something under his breath, and as Hannah listened, he began to chant a phrase in a high-pitched, childish voice. "Come out, Hannah. Come out, come out, wherever you are."

There was a singsong lilt to Greg's voice that made Hannah's blood run cold. Greg was insane, dangerously insane.

"Red Rover, Red Rover, send Hannah over," Greg called out. And then he laughed, an eerie sort of giggle. "You're it, Hannah. I'm going to tag you. You can't get in free this time."

Hannah swallowed hard. All the games they'd played in the vacant lot at the end of the block were mixed up together in Greg's deranged mind. But this was no game. Greg had come out here with the intention of making her his next victim.

"I know where you're hiding. You can't fool me, Hannah Banana." Greg moved forward again, toward the back of the store. "You're in the office. I saw your flashlight and I'm going to get you."

Hannah gasped. Andrea was in the office. She couldn't let Greg go back there! With an inventiveness born of desperation, Hannah scuttled to the next display table, the one that held the heavy crystal vase that Andrea had admired. She grabbed it and pegged it toward the far wall as hard as she could.

The expensive vase shattered with a satisfying crash, and Greg whirled around toward the spot where the vase had landed. "So that's where you are, you naughty girl! Clumsy Hannah. Now see what you've done?"

Greg stalked past the display table where Hannah was hiding. She held her breath, preparing to run, but he didn't stop. He was wiggling the bat, the same way a power hitter might wiggle it before he hit a homerun, as he strode toward the place he thought she was hiding.

Hannah knew she had to warn her sister to stay hidden. Greg didn't know that Andrea was here, and if she stayed under the desk, she'd be safe. Hannah took a deep breath and called out at the top of her lungs. "You can't catch me, Greg Canfield!"

The moment the words had left her mouth, Hannah crouched low and scooted toward another display table. Greg whirled toward the place she'd been, but Hannah was already across the aisle, crouched low behind a table holding a silver service.

"Where are you, Hannah? Come out, come out!" Greg stalked forward, his bat at the ready.

"Why did you murder them, Greg?" Hannah asked.

Greg turned again toward the sound of her voice, but Hannah had moved behind another display table. She had to keep calling out and moving, leading Greg away from Andrea.

"They took everything!" Greg surprised Hannah by answering her. "Annette left me when she found out about Redlines, and it was all Connie Mac and Alan's fault!"

"Did they deserve to die?" Hannah asked, scooting to another position the moment the question had left her mouth.

"They did a bad thing. I had to punish them." Greg's voice had grown softer, and Hannah wasn't sure whether that made him more dangerous or less dangerous. "You understand, don't you, Hannah? They deserved the ultimate punishment."

"Do I deserve to die?" Hannah asked, moving crab-fashion to another counter.

"I'm sorry I have to kill you, Hannah, but I don't have a choice. The minute Grandma told me you'd gone to the mall, I knew you were going to find out. And I can't let you tell anyone what I did."

"They'll find out." Hannah moved again, crouching low.

"No, they won't. They'll think it's the ghost. They're so stupid, they believe in ghosts!" Greg laughed again as he moved in Hannah's direction. And then he started to chant, "Starlight, moonlight, hope to see the ghost tonight. Starlight, moonlight . . ." Greg stopped and gave another chilling laugh. "Remember that, Hannah? Remember the game we used to play? You were always the ghost. Now I'm the ghost and I get to scare you!"

Greg's back was turned and this was her chance. Hannah inched her way to the display of cast-iron skillets. She reached up and grabbed the biggest one, the same size Grandma Ingrid had used to fry chicken, and ducked back down again. And then she called out again to the madman who'd once been her friend. "I never thought you'd hurt me, Greg."

"I won't hurt you," Greg responded, moving toward the display of cast-iron cookware. "You deserve it for sticking your nose in where it didn't belong, but you won't feel a thing. Remember how good I am with a bat? I never miss the ball. I didn't hurt them, either. I made sure of that. I'm not a bad person."

As Greg lunged for the spot where he thought she was hiding, Hannah darted to the counter directly behind him and stood up. But before she could swing the heavy spider, Andrea popped up from the counter directly in front of Greg. She was holding a fire extinguisher in her hand, and as Hannah watched in total shock, her sister pulled the handle and foam spewed out, directly into Greg's face.

The next few seconds passed with what seemed like the speed of lightning. Greg hollered and dropped the bat, reaching up instinctively to cover his eyes. And while he was momentarily incapacitated, Hannah swung the frying pan, connecting solidly with his head. Greg didn't even whimper. He just crashed to the floor like a bale of hay that had been thrown down from the back of a truck. On his way down, he took out a Thanksgiving serving platter and several champagne glasses with silver rims, but Hannah didn't give a second thought to the damage. She just stepped over her former friend to hug her sister tightly.

"I did good, huh?" Andrea asked, looking a bit shocked at her own bravery.

"You were great," Hannah said, not about to spoil the moment by correcting her sister's grammar. "I think he's out cold, but I'll sit on him to make sure he doesn't try to get up again. You'd better call the sheriff's station."

"They're already on the way and they've got Greg's whole confession on tape. I held up my cell phone so the dispatcher could hear, and she patched the call through to Mike and Bill."

"Good for you!" Hannah declared, plunking herself down on Greg's back. She was careful to keep the frying pan at the ready, just in case. "Flip on the lights and see if you can find something we can use to tie him up."

After Andrea had raced off to the front counter, Hannah reached down and took Greg's wrist. His pulse felt steady, and now that the lights were on, she could see no sign of blood. She'd swung the frying pan as hard as she could, but she'd been a lot gentler on Greg that he'd been on Connie Mac and Alan.

Andrea came back at a run and handed Hannah a roll of red satin gift ribbon. The words "Connie Mac's Kitchen Boutique" were stamped along the length of the roll in gold. "How about this? It was all I could find."

"It'll do," Hannah told her, not missing the irony as she bound Greg's hands and feet with an unending reminder of the store that had replaced his. Then she stood up and stared down at Greg. She thought she'd known him, but she hadn't. People could change a lot in twenty years. And Greg hadn't known her, either. He'd assumed that once he called out for her, she'd simply present herself like a lamb to the slaughter.

"Are you okay?" Andrea asked, catching Hannah's pensive mood.

"Yes, thanks to you. Where did you get that fire extinguisher?"

"It was hanging on the wall in the back room, right next to the door."

"And you just spotted it hanging there?"

Andrea shook her head. "I knew where it was supposed to be. It's a legal requirement for every retail establishment in the county."

"And you knew that because you're a real estate agent?"

"That's right. Can I ask you a question, Hannah?"

"Sure."

"I thought you were going to take Greg's head off when you hit him with that frying pan. How did you learn to swing like that?"

"In Little League, I guess."

"But Dad took me to all your games, and you always struck out."

"That's true, but Greg's head is a lot bigger than a baseball. And I guess I just wasn't motivated enough back then."

Andrea nodded and then cocked her head to the side. "I hear sirens out on the highway."

"Me, too. It must be Mike and Bill."

"What are we going to tell them, Hannah?"

"As little as possible."

"You're right." Andrea looked thoughtful. "I'll take care of Bill. You take care of Mike."

The noise of the siren was louder now. It sounded as though more than one patrol car had responded, and that was good. Mike and Bill wouldn't ask too many questions if other officers were present. Hannah heard them pull into the parking lot, and she turned to her sister. "You go down and let them in. I'll stay here and watch Greg."

"They can get in. They've got a passkey."

"Is that something else you know because you're a real estate agent?"

"No, the dispatcher told me."

The sirens made a dying bleep and then the back door banged. Hannah could hear heavy footsteps on the stairs, and much sooner than she thought possible, the glass door banged open and a total of six deputies rushed in, Bill and Mike in the lead.

"We're okay!" Hannah shouted out. "We've got him tied up back here."

"You take Mike, I'll take Bill," Andrea reminded her, and then she rushed out to throw herself into her husband's arms.

After the four other deputies had carried Greg off, Hannah turned to Mike. He didn't look happy, and Hannah knew she had to say something. "I'm sorry, Mike. I know I shouldn't have come out here without telling you, but one thing led to another and . . . are you mad at me?"

"*Mad* isn't the word."

Hannah sighed. A hunk of granite was more yielding than Mike was being right now. "You've got to believe me, Mike. I didn't know that Greg was the killer. I'm as shocked as you are."

"Well . . . at least no one got hurt. Why did you come out here, anyway?"

"Andrea and I were looking for clues. I know we shouldn't have done it without telling you, but I figured that I could save you some time by doing some of the legwork. I was only trying to help you."

"Some help! You almost got yourself killed!"

"But I didn't know *that* was going to happen. Do you really think I would have brought Andrea out here with me if I'd thought it was dangerous?"

"No. I guess not."

Hannah stared up into his face. His frown lines had smoothed out, and she could tell that he was relenting somewhat. "We were going to come straight to you and Bill with anything we found."

"You're sure about that?"

"Oh, yes. Absolutely."

"All right. I believe you," Mike said and pulled her into his arms. "You don't leave me a whole lot of choice, Hannah. I've got to figure out some way to keep you safe."

Hannah looked up to study his expression. He didn't look angry, but there was no telling what was running through is mind. "You're not going to lock me up, are you?"

"No, I've got something else in mind."

"What is it?"

"We'll start by having dinner at the inn tomorrow night. Right after that, I'm going to show you what to do in a clinch."

Hannah wasn't sure what to say. Was Mike talking about self-defense classes again? Or did he have something else in mind? She was still trying to think of a response when Mike bent down and kissed her, and then she stopped thinking altogether.

Several minutes later, or perhaps it was longer, Mike released her. "I have to get back to work, Hannah."

"But why? You've got Greg's confession. The case is closed."

"There's still a ton of paperwork to do." Mike turned her around and marched her toward the door, where Andrea and Bill were waiting for them. "And I really ought to make you do it, since you seem to be angling for my job."

Chapter Thirty-Two

Hannah glanced at her reflection in the mirror that hung above the bar at the Lake Eden Inn. Mike had gone off to check on their reservations, and she was feeling very sophisticated tonight. She was wearing her new green silk dress, the one that Claire Rodgers had selected for this very special night. Hannah had dashed next door to Beau Monde Fashions on her prelunch break, and even though Claire had given her a discount, she'd still spent a small fortune on just the right outfit.

The dress really was beautiful, and Hannah knew it looked good on her. The deep green brought out the color of her eyes, and it made her hair look more auburn than red. Since she'd always believed that her hair could double as a beacon to warn sailors away from dangerous rocks, this was a minor miracle.

Even Moishe had seemed impressed with Hannah's new look. He'd curled up in the middle of her bed as she'd dressed, and when she was finished, he'd followed her down the hallway, purring and rubbing up against her expensive real-silk nylons.

How could nylons be silk? Hannah thought about that inconsistency for a moment before turning her mind to other, more pressing matters. Even though it had been late, she'd gone to see Mrs. Canfield the previous evening, to tell her that Greg was in jail for the murders of Connie Mac and Alan Carpenter. Fearing that she'd be forced to deal with hysteria, tears, or perhaps even worse, Hannah had been relieved to find that her elderly neighbor had taken it in stride. Mrs. Canfield would be all right. Minnesota women were tough.

Thinking about Greg had depressed Hannah, and after she had fed Moishe and crawled into bed, she'd turned her thoughts to the clinch that Mike had mentioned. By the time she'd dropped off to sleep, she'd managed to convince herself that Mike had simply chosen a unique way to tell her that he'd planned a romantic evening. Hannah wasn't averse to a bit more romance in her life. There was only one thing that bothered her about the evening that Mike had planned, and that was . . .

Norman. And there he was, in the doorway with Carrie and Delores. Hannah sighed and a wave of guilt washed over her. Why hadn't Norman taken their mothers to the Corner Tavern?

"Hi, Hannah. You look really pretty." Norman came over to take her hand. "I didn't know you'd be here tonight. How about joining us?"

"Uh . . . well, actually . . ."

"Hi, Norman." Mike chose that moment to return. "What are you doing out here?"

"I got roped into taking the mothers out to dinner. They're celebrating tonight, but they won't tell me why."

"Really?" Hannah's curiosity was aroused. "I spoke to Mother this morning, and she didn't mention anything about a celebration. It's not Carrie's birthday, is it?"

"No, that's in June. How about your mother?"

"Not until September fifteenth. I wonder what . . ."

"Hi, Mike. Are we late?" Bill interrupted Hannah's speculations as he rushed up with Andrea.

"You're fine. Sally's setting up for us right now," Mike answered, and then he turned to Hannah to explain. "Bill told me that he was taking Andrea out for dinner tonight, and I thought we'd make it a foursome. That's all right with you, isn't it?"

"Of course," Hannah said. What else could she say when Bill and Andrea were standing right next to her?

"Hey, Norman," Mike said, reaching out to pat him on the shoulder. "There's no reason why you should be stuck with the mothers alone. Do you think they'd like it if we all sat together?"

You've got to be kidding! Hannah thought with a sigh, her dreams of a romantic candlelight dinner with Mike vanishing into thin air.

"They'd love it, but are you sure we won't be intruding?" Norman looked a little worried.

"Not at all." Mike thumped Norman on the back again. "We're practically all family anyway."

"Okay. I'll go tell them. And I'll find Sally and say that we need a table for seven."

Hannah struggled to keep the pleasant smile on her face. At least Mike had said that he considered himself a part of her family. But he'd also implied that he considered Norman and Carrie a part of his family. Since Norman was supposed to be his rival, Mike was obviously unclear on the concept!

Once Norman had left, Bill and Mike began to chat about police business, and Andrea hoisted herself up on the stool next to Hannah. "How did you know?" she hissed.

"Know what?"

"That I was pregnant. I went to see Doc Knight this morning and he confirmed it."

Hannah shrugged. "I guess it was because you were eating so much, and you only do that when you're pregnant. Are you upset about it?"

"I was at first, but that's only because it was such a shock. You should have seen Bill's face when I told him. He was really happy and that's why we came out here for dinner."

"That's nice," Hannah said, but part of her wished that Bill had chosen another restaurant.

"I'm really sorry we horned in on your party. I know you wanted to be alone with Mike, but Bill didn't tell me until it was a done deal. I tried to call you to give you a heads-up, but you'd already left."

"That's okay."

"You look really nice, Hannah. I love that dress. Did you get it at . . . oh-oh! Here comes Mother!"

Hannah swiveled around and her eyes widened as she caught her first glimpse of Delores. Their mother was wearing a gold lamé pantsuit, and she looked like a brunette Barbie dressed for the Oscars. "She got her hair streaked again?"

"Bertie did it this morning. There's something a little unnatural about having a mother who looks younger than we do."

"Only in this light," Hannah pointed out. "But she does look good, and she really knows how to make an entrance. And that reminds me, do you know what Mother and Carrie are celebrating tonight?"

"No, I haven't heard anything about it."

"I have a feeling we'll find out," Hannah said, standing up with her sister to greet their mother and Carrie.

The dinner that night was festive, and to her surprise, Hannah found that she was enjoying herself. She was seated between Norman and Mike, and they seemed to be vying with each other to see that she had everything her heart desired. When dessert time rolled around, Hannah decided that it was time to make an announcement. "I contributed six pans of Multiple-Choice Bar Cookies to Sally's dessert buffet tonight. It's a new recipe and I need your opinion."

"Whatever they are, they can't be better than your blueberry muffins," Bill said with a grin. "They were the best I ever tasted."

Hannah turned to give him a long, level look. "How do you know? I thought the containers were being dusted for prints."

"They were, but they came out clean," Mike explained. "And since the muffins were two days old already, we . . . uh . . ."

"You shared them around at the station?" Hannah finished the sentence for him.

"That's right. We didn't think you'd want them back. You're not upset, are you?"

"Not really." Hannah did her best to be gracious. "I'm glad they didn't go to waste. Is there more coffee in that carafe?"

Both Mike and Norman made a grab for the carafe at the same moment, and Hannah almost laughed out loud. This was the first time in her whole life that two men were knocking themselves out to please her.

Mike got to the carafe first and filled Hannah's cup. Then he leaned forward to talk to Norman. "Are you all right after that knock on the head?"

"I'm fine, but if Lake Eden gets any more dangerous, I'm going to take karate classes."

"Karate won't do you much good unless your assailant is a two-by-four or a stack of cinder blocks. I'll tell you what, Norman. I promised to teach Hannah some self-defense moves, and I'll give you some tips, too."

"Thanks, Mike." Norman looked properly grateful. "Just let me know when, and I'll be there."

"How about tonight? I have to teach Hannah what to do in a clinch, and my apartment complex has a gym."

"That sounds great. I'll take the mothers home and then I'll drive out to your place. I really appreciate this, Mike. Ever since I met Hannah, I'm never sure when I'm going to run into trouble."

Hannah made a study of the coffee in her cup as her two Lotharios discussed precisely when and where to meet. This evening was definitely not turning out the way she'd hoped it would.

"Andrea, dear?" Delores reached across the table to tap Andrea's arm. "You didn't have any of the champagne I ordered."

As Hannah watched, Andrea's face turned a shade of pink that matched the dress she was wearing. "I'm sure it was delicious, Mother. I just didn't feel like drinking tonight."

"But why, dear? You're not driving, are you?"

Andrea's cheeks turned even pinker as she shook her head.

"Then why don't you have a glass?"

"No, Mother. Thank you, but I'm . . . I'm . . ."

"Pregnant." Hannah supplied the word that appeared to be frozen on her sister's lips.

"Really?" Delores looked stunned for a moment, and then she rushed around the table to hug Andrea. "That's wonderful, dear! When did you find out?"

"Today. But Hannah knew it yesterday."

Delores turned to give Hannah a sharp look. Hannah just shrugged. "Call me psychic."

For a few moments, everyone spoke at once, congratulating Andrea and Bill. Hannah sat back with a smile on her face and enjoyed her sister's time in the spotlight. Andrea looked happy, and that was what counted. And Bill seemed absolutely delighted.

"Hannah has some good news, too," Delores said when the commotion had died down a bit. "Tell them, dear."

"Tell them what?" Hannah asked, staring at her mother in total consternation.

"About the book. You're going to write it, aren't you?"

"Oh, *that* book." Hannah sighed deeply. Her mother had obviously spoken to Kurt Howe, who'd spilled the beans. Now she had to explain it to the rest of her extended family, and every one of them was staring at her curiously. "Kurt Howe came into the cookie shop this morning and asked me to write a cookbook. I told him I'd think about it."

"But you *have* to do it," Delores insisted.

"Only if I can work in some of our old family recipes and stories about Lake Eden," Hannah stipulated. "As Andrea would say, it's not a done deal yet."

Another round of congratulations followed Hannah's unplanned announcement, and then Delores clinked her spoon against the side of her champagne flute. When she was sure that all eyes were on her, she said, "Carrie and I have an announcement, too."

Hannah took a deep breath and held it. If Delores and Carrie had cooked up something together, it couldn't be good.

"I'm going into the antique business with Carrie," Delores declared. "Everyone who toured the Ezekiel Jordan House urged us to open an antique shop. And since Luanne Hanks has shown such an interest, we're hiring her to help us buy stock and run the store."

"That's great, Mother!" Andrea reached out to pat her mother's hand.

"It certainly is," Hannah added, giving a big sigh of relief. Opening an antique store would keep her mother busy and out of her hair.

"That's not all," Delores said, pausing for dramatic effect. "Carrie and I signed the lease this afternoon, and you'll never guess where we're locating."

Hannah was almost afraid to ask, but she did. "Where?"

"Right next to you, dear."

"You mean . . . on the same block?" Hannah asked, hoping that she'd misunderstood.

"Right *next* to you, dear. Carrie and I are turning the Ezekiel Jordan House into an antique shop. I've been feeling guilty because I don't spend enough time with you, and now I'll be able to zip over and have coffee with you every morning. Isn't that wonderful, dear?"

Somehow Hannah managed to keep the smile on her face. "Wonderful," she said.

Multiple-Choice Bar Cookies

Preheat oven to 350°F,
rack in the middle position

½ cup butter *(one stick)*
1 can sweetened condensed milk (14 oz.)

Column A
(1 ½ cups)
Graham cracker crumbs
Vanilla wafer crumbs
Chocolate wafer crumbs
Animal cracker crumbs

Sugar cookie crumbs

Column B
(2 cups)
Chocolate chips
Butterscotch chips
Peanut butter chips
Raisins *(regular or
   golden)*
M & M's *(without
   nuts)*

Column C
(2 cups)
Flaked coconut *(5 oz.)*
Rice Krispies
Miniature marshmallows
   (2 ½ cups)
Frosted cornflakes
   (crumbled)

Column D
(1 cup)
Chopped walnuts
Chopped pecans
Chopped peanuts
Chopped cashews

Melt the butter and pour it into a 9-by-13-inch cake
pan. Tip the pan to coat the bottom.

1. Evenly sprinkle one ingredient from Column A over the melted butter.

2. Drizzle sweetened condensed milk over the crumbs.

3. Evenly sprinkle one ingredient from Column B on top.

4. Evenly sprinkle one ingredient from Column C on top of that.

5. Evenly sprinkle one ingredient from Column D over the very top.

Press everything down with the palms of your hands. Bake at 350°F for 30 minutes. Cool thoroughly on a wire rack and cut into brownie-sized bars.

(Tracey loves to help me bake these—she gets to choose the ingredients.)

Index of Recipes

Please turn the page for an exciting sneak peek at
Joanne Fluke's

LEMON MERINGUE PIE MURDER

Now on sale wherever mysteries are sold!

"This is a nice location," Hannah commented, stopping her truck as close to the front door as she could get. "You can see the lake from here."

"You'll be able to see it even better when I prune the bottom branches on those pines." Norman hopped out of Hannah's truck and opened the door for Delores.

"It's a nice little house," Delores said taking Norman's arm and heading for the front door. "It's almost a pity to tear it down, but I suppose it's much too small for you with only two bedrooms. Once you make the smallest one into an office, there's no room at all for . . ."

"Houseguests," Hannah interjected quickly, shooting her mother a warning glance. Now was not the time to fish around for a proposal.

"Yes, guests." Delores looked slightly embarrassed. "Well, I'll go straight to work. I don't want to keep you two out here all afternoon."

Norman opened the front door. "I'd better turn on the lights so you can see better. The windows are small and it's fairly dark inside."

"The electricity's still on?" Hannah was surprised. She'd assumed that Rhonda had turned it off to save the expense.

"I told Rhonda to switch it over to my name. I'll have it turned off on Saturday morning before the demolition crew gets here."

When Hannah stepped inside the house, she was pleasantly surprised. She'd expected to be assailed by the clouds of must and dust that inevitably gathered when a house was unoccupied, but the only odor she could detect was lemon-scented furniture polish. "It's so clean in here!"

"I know. That's why I didn't bother to change clothes." Delores glanced down at the pale yellow dress she was wearing. "Andrea told me that Rhonda had a cleaning woman."

"What for? There hasn't been anyone living here since Mrs. Voelker died."

"I know, but the house wasn't selling and Andrea thought it might show better if it was cleaned. You know how some people are. They can't see past the dust and the cobwebs. Rhonda didn't feel like doing it herself, so she hired a cleaning lady. Come on, Hannah. We'll start in the living room and work our way through to the back."

The living room was cluttered with furniture and artwork, but with all three of them working, it didn't take long. Hannah put red tags on the furniture and artwork that Delores indicated and Norman packed the smaller items in boxes.

The guestroom didn't yield much for Granny's Attic, just a handmade patchwork quilt that Delores thought she could sell, but the master bedroom was a different story. Delores chose two Maxwell Parish prints and an old wooden rocking chair, and then she pointed to the quilt on the bed. "I'd like to take that."

"Why?" Hannah asked. She was almost sure that the quilt was machine made, the type that anyone could order from a mail order catalogue. "It's not an antique, is it?"

"No, but Reverend Strandberg can use it for the homeless shelter."

Hannah agreed and pulled the quilt from the bed. But instead of a bare mattress similar to the one they'd found in the guestroom, this bed was complete with sheets, pillowcases, and a blanket. "I wonder why Rhonda kept this bed made up? Do you suppose she stayed out here sometimes?"

"I doubt it, dear. Why would she want to stay way out here when she has an apartment of her own? The cleaning woman probably made it up by mistake."

"Do you want the rest of the bedding for Reverend Strandberg?" Norman asked, holding one end of the quilt while Hannah folded it.

"Yes. And if there's a linen closet, I'll take whatever's there. I think I'm through in here. Let's tackle the kitchen."

"Why don't you two go ahead," Norman suggested. "I'll load up the artwork and join you as soon as I'm through."

Hannah was the first to enter the large farm-style kitchen and what she saw made her stop cold. "That's one of my pie boxes on the table!"

"You're right. I wonder how long it's been here." Delores marched past her, lifted the lid on the distinctive box Hannah used for pies, and stepped back with a startled exclamation. "Yuck!"

"My pies are *yuck*?"

"They are when they're covered with ants."

Hannah walked closer, peered inside, and made a face. It was one of the lemon meringue pies she'd baked on Friday. Only one piece had been eaten and the rest was crawling with an endless line of small black ants that were industriously carting away the sweet pastry. "You're right, Mother. This pie is ant fodder. I'll dump it in the garbage."

"Here, Hannah." Delores walked over with a plastic garbage bag she'd found in a box under the sink. She held it open near the edge of the table and motioned to Hannah. "I'll hold the bag. You slide the box off the table, dump it inside, and carry it out."

"Yes, Mother," Hannah said obediently, resisting the urge to giggle. Delores was treating her like a backwards child, but the plan was a good one and to object would be petty. Once the box was safely transferred to the garbage bag, Hannah carried it to the back door and took it outside.

Two garbage cans sat on a cement slab next to the old

garage. Hannah peeked in the garage window, hoping to see an antique car up on blocks, but the interior was completely filled with fireplace wood. She'd have to remember to tell Norman about that. There was enough wood in Mrs. Voelker's garage to carry him through several winters. All he had to do was move it to another location before they tore down the garage.

Hannah held her bag at the ready and lifted the lid on the garbage can. She expected it to be empty and she was surprised to see several items in the bottom of the plastic liner. There were two Styrofoam boxes with seethrough plastic lids, the kind used for restaurant takeout dinners. One dinner was partially eaten and the other looked untouched. Both were Osso Buco, one of Hannah's favorite entrées. She recognized it by its distinctive marrowbone. Rhonda must have ordered takeout on the night she packed up the last of her great-aunt's effects and since there were two containers, it was obvious she'd expected someone to join her for dinner.

It was probably an invasion of privacy to go through someone else's garbage, but Hannah was curious about that uneaten dinner. She lifted the liner partway out of the can, and peered down at the other items in its depths. There was an empty Chianti bottle, and two plastic wineglasses. Rhonda had poured wine for someone, but that someone had left before dinner.

Hannah shrugged and added her garbage to the mix. She didn't understand why Rhonda hadn't taken the untouched entrée home. Even if she hadn't wanted it, she could have given it to one of her neighbors. For that matter, why had she left the pie? The same reasoning applied. One of Rhonda's neighbors would have loved it.

Just as she was about to close the lid, Hannah heard the rumble of a trash truck approaching on the road that ran past the house. Monday must be garbage day. Hannah lifted out the liner, tied it off, and rushed to the front to hand it to the driver.

"What took you so long?" Delores asked when Hannah came back into the kitchen.

"The garbage truck came so I carried out the bag," Hannah sniffed the air. "You must have found some ant spray."

"It was under the sink. Look at these dishes, Hannah. They're Carnival glass."

Hannah surveyed the rainbow of colored dishes Delores had stacked on the counter. "I thought Carnival glass was orange."

"That's the most common, but they made it in other colors, too. See this purple bowl? It's fairly rare and it'll bring a good price. Could you climb up and look in the top cupboards, dear? There may be more."

Hannah dragged a chair over to the counter and climbed up on the seat. She opened one of the cupboard doors and her eyes widened as she recognized a distinctive design. "Here's a big Desert Rose platter. You want that, don't you?"

"Yes. Hand it down to me."

Hannah handed the platter to her mother and reached for a stack of plates. "This looks like Blue Willowware, but it's green. I think there's a whole set of it."

"Let me see," Delores sounded excited as she reached up for a plate. She flipped it over and she gasped. "What a find! It's genuine Green Blue Willowware!"

Hannah coughed to cover a laugh. How could a plate be Green Blue Willowware? It sounded like a contradiction in terms. "Here's some pink. Do you want that, too?"

"Yes! Pink Blue Willowware is a collector's dream. Just hand me everything, Hannah. And be careful you don't drop any pieces. I'm just glad Rhonda didn't go through the cupboards. She missed some real treasures."

By the time Norman joined them in the kitchen, Delores had every flat surface stacked with dishes and glassware. "It looks like you found some things you want."

"Oh, my yes!" Delores turned to smile at him. "Are you sure you don't want a percentage? Mrs. Voelker had some valuable dishes and glassware."

Norman shook his head. "It's all yours and Mother's. I've been living with her rent-free and it's the least I can do."

"Well . . . that's very generous. Just wait until I tell Carrie and Luanne. They're going to be *in alt* over these fabulous dishes."

Hannah chuckled as she climbed down from the chair. *In alt?* It was obvious that her mother had attended a meeting of her Regency Romance group recently. Delores had explained that *alt* referred to altitude and the heroines in Regency novels often spoke of being *in alt* when something took them to the heights of pleasure.

When they'd packed up the glassware and dishes and Norman had carried the boxes out to the truck, Delores gave one last glance around. "I think that's all. I've looked in every room."

"How about the basement?" Norman asked. "I haven't been down there, but Rhonda said her great-uncle used to do some woodworking."

"Antique tools!" Delores's eyes began to gleam. "They're going for a premium right now. Do you have time for me to take a quick peek?"

"I've got time. How about you, Hannah?"

"It's fine with me." Hannah handed Delores the apron she'd discovered hanging over the back of a kitchen chair. "You'd better put this on, Mother. It might be dusty down there."

Delores tied on the apron and headed for the basement stairs. "Aren't you coming, dear?"

"I can if you need me," Hannah said, giving her mother an exaggerated wink.

"Of course I . . ." Delores caught the wink and interpreted it correctly. "Actually, I don't. I'm perfectly capable of exploring the basement by myself. Stay right here and keep Norman company. You're both so busy, you don't get much time to spend together and I know you'd like to discuss your plans for the house."

"Right," Hannah said, rolling her eyes at the ceiling. Her mother was about as subtle as a sledgehammer. "Holler if you need us and we'll come right down."

Norman waited until Delores had switched on the light

and gone down the stairs, and then he turned to Hannah. "What do you think about a picture window in the kitchen? Since it faces the woods, it would be a nice view."

"Yes, it would." Hannah could picture herself sitting at the kitchen table in the morning, sipping a freshly brewed cup of coffee and watching the deer emerge from the trees. That thought was dangerous to her preferred single state and she quickly asked another question. "How about the living room? That window will face the lake, won't it?"

"That's right, but the master bedroom will have the best view and that's where I'm building the balcony."

Hannah didn't want to think about the master bedroom with its wood-burning fireplace and incredible view. It was just too appealing. She changed the subject again, asking Norman about how he planned to furnish the house. That was interesting and it was only when she glanced up at the old kitchen clock on the wall that she realized almost fifteen minutes had passed and they hadn't heard a peep out of Delores.

"Maybe I'd better check on Mother. She's been down there a long time."

"I'll go with you." Norman led the way to the basement doorway. "Delores? Are you all right down there?"

Hannah stood behind Norman, waiting for her mother to respond. When there was no answer, she felt a jolt of fear. "Move over, Norman. I'm going down there."

"Not without me, you're not." Norman had gone down three steps when he stopped abruptly. "Here she comes, now. Back up to give her room."

Hannah backed up, but she gazed over Norman's shoulder to watch her mother climb the stairs. Delores didn't appear to be hurt, but her mouth was set in a tight line. Something had happened in the basement and judging by the way her mother was gripping the handrail, that something wasn't good.

"Water," Delores croaked as she reached the top of the stairs, and Norman rushed to get her a glass. She took one sip, handed the glass back to him, and shivered visibly.

"You look like you just saw a ghost," Hannah commented and immediately wished she hadn't when her mother's face turned even paler.

Delores gave a small smile, so small that it could only be classified as a grimace. "Not a ghost. I found . . . a body!"